DEAD OF LIGHT

DEAD OF LIGHT

Chaz Brenchley

Hodder & Stoughton

First published in Great Britain in 1995
by Hodder and Stoughton Ltd.
A division of Hodder Headline PLC

10 9 8 7 6 5 4 3 2 1

British Library Cataloguing in Publication Data

Brenchley, Chaz
Dead of Light
I.Title
823.914 [F]

ISBN 0-340-62807-3

Typeset by Avon Dataset Ltd, Bidford-on-Avon, B50 4JH

Printed and bound in Great Britain by
Mackays of Chatham PLC, Chatham, Kent

Hodder and Stoughton
A division of Hodder Headline PLC
338 Euston Road
London NW1 3BH

This book of bad blood
is for Quin, by definition:
too late, too bloody soon.

ONE

GOOD NIGHT MARTY

It was a good night, the night my cousin Marty died.

Not a great night, by definition: a great night would see me in bed with Laura, sated and sleepless and sublime. I didn't have great nights. By definition.

A good night, though. That, for sure.

Good night, bad bad morning.

Actually we'd been on a rage that evening, pre-arranged: Rick and Angie, Dermot and Vanessa, Colin, Laura dark and lovely and me. Two medics, two linguists, one lit-freak, one agric and one fine artist, not necessarily in that order. Not necessarily in any order, rarely the same order from one term's end to the next. Always something of a group, though, always coming back together at the last, however often or however violently we might fall apart betweentimes.

Just then we were a peaceable kingdom, two steady couples and three singletons and not a quarrel among us, not a bone to be picked, seemingly no tensions: only my own long hunger that I'd long since learned to hide. To tell truth I was never sure if any of them even remembered, these good close friends of mine.

It was Laura who'd phoned that day – or at least had phoned

the upstairs neighbour, who'd come down to fetch me and then unashamedly listened in, her perk for the service – Laura who'd set this particular ball to roll. "Coming out to play, Ben?" she'd said; and not a question, that, it was a command. Not allowed, to say no to that particular invitation. Impossible, in any case, to say no to her.

So I only asked when, and where. Where was Albuquerque, a glossy, glitzy video bar, far too pricey for every day but Laura didn't, wouldn't talk to me every day and this was a rage anyway, we wouldn't be there long; when was six o'clock, cocktail hour. "If you're going to mix your drinks," she said, "which we are," she said, "you might as well start with a mixture. Don't be late."

"Would I?" I asked.

"No," she said, "you wouldn't. Not you," and for a moment she sounded wistful, almost, and I thought that maybe one at least of my good friends did remember. She ought to, she of all of them, she had most cause. She *was* the cause, damn it (but never *damn her*, never that; all unwitting, it was none of it her fault), she was the be-all and end-all, she ought at least to remember that.

I was early and she was late, and that might have been deliberate but probably wasn't. We spent enough time on our own together, *no need to get paranoid about this, Macallan.* Except that love is paranoid, it has to be, that's how it works. *She doesn't want to be alone with me,* my sweetly treacherous mind was telling me, *she's hanging back to be sure the others are here.* And maybe she was, but there could be other reasons. She always liked to make an entrance, Laura.

And she certainly did it that night, she swept in like a star, a constellation of one. Dark star, all in black tonight and radiant, pulsing, dangerously electric. Touched us all where we stood at the bar, a pat on the bottom or a squeeze of the shoulder; I got a fist in the ribs, when I passed her the drink that stood waiting.

"Don't get clever, Macallan," she said, growling, scowling, sipping.

"I know what you drink," I said, *and what you like best to eat, and to wear, and to dance to; I know your shoe size and your bra size and the size of your slim, slim waist.* "What's your problem?"

Which was tempting fate, perhaps, she just might be in the mood to answer that; but no, she let me off easy. She only said, "Don't take me for granted, right?" as if I ever would or could or had the grounds to, and clinked her glass privately against mine before she drank again.

Too many messages in that, too complex to work out in company; or else there was nothing at all, just a brief light-hearted interchange between two friends in a bar at the start of a long light-headed evening. I smiled, toasted her silently, more with my eyes than my glass, and turned to talk to Angie; and if Laura didn't know how hard that was for me, to turn those few inches from one friend to another – well, it was only one more small entry in the very comprehensive list of things that Laura didn't know about my sad life, the long sad years before I met her and every sad and solitary hour since.

If she didn't know.

It's a short step from Albuquerque to Milan. Or in this case *il Milano*, which is the best Italian in town, and therefore the one that knows us best. We got our regular table and our regular waiter, young Gino with the big eyes and the cherubic smile, the party soul and just as well his mother's in Treviso, she wouldn't want to see what we've made of her cute son or what he does for fun these days. She really, really wouldn't want to see it.

Two litres of the house red to get us started, orders for *gamberoni* – "shells *on*, for Christ's sake, Gino, I shouldn't need to tell you that, where've you been, sodding Treviso?" – and *antipasti* and sardines; and the cigarettes came out while we were waiting, and already the lights were starting to shine a little brighter, we were sharp and witty and laughing loud, we loved ourselves and each other and too bad if the rest of the world didn't love us, what the hell did they know?

No need to hurry: no pressure from the staff, and we weren't going anywhere that wouldn't wait for us. So we ate through the menu, and idled over espressos and liqueurs, amaretto or *sambucca alla mocca*, pale blue flames and three coffee-beans floating, "like drowned flies," Vanessa said, because she always did say that, it was the ritual.

And then it was out into the street and into the first pub we came to, one quick pint and on to the next; and now we were hurrying suddenly, last orders like a whip to sting us on. Not a problem, last orders, this was a rage and we weren't going to *stop*, we weren't going home at eleven o'clock, like good little children ought. It was a challenge, that was all, something to be defied, to be stared down and defeated.

After the pubs, the clubs. We wanted to dance, we *needed* to dance; with such a load aboard, on such a night, we needed to move and sweat in a hard light, we needed each other's hot bodies as a counter to our own.

Rites of Passage is a queer club, by and large; *Gay Rites* they call it, as they would. But they're a tolerant crowd, they give us rights of passage, in and out as we choose most nights and welcome on Thursdays. This was a Thursday; a good rage doesn't happen by chance, it just has to feel as if it did.

So we pulsed and thundered, music in our bones and every cell awoken. Between dances we drank Red Stripe viciously cold and straight from the cans and then hauled each other back to the dance floor again. And yes, I danced with Laura, how not? Been

4

doing it for years. Warm body, fine bones, skin oiled with her own sweat and mine and five hundred others', the air was sodden with it. And oh, it was cruel to hold her, separated by so little and so much; and oh, what the hell, it was just my life, that was all. And so much better than the other thing, not to dance with her, not to see or speak, not to touch or hold or sweat with her at all.

After the sauna, the ritual plunge into ice water; after being so hot, crucial to be cool for an hour. We left *Rites* before it closed, waited for Colin to be sick in the gutter – just another part of the ritual, he always was; not the booze, he said, it was the dancing and the heat and then the sudden change, air and silence did him in – and straggled arm-in-arm up a quiet alley that was only a little noisier for our arrival. Cooling already, we were, running close to empty.

We hammered discreetly on a discreet little door, no lights showing, no noise. And known here too we were let in, we were found a table and a bottle of bad German wine; and we sat still like good children and listened to the jamming. Blues and easy jazz, nothing frenetic this time of night, just souls in harmony doing what comes right.

About four o'clock they threw us out. Nothing aggressive, just, "Don't you kids want to go home?" and *take the hint, if you want to be taken back.*

We did that, we always did. A night at Delilah's was a privilege and we valued it, wouldn't abuse it. Wouldn't take risks, so we took the hint instead, said goodnight and left them. Stumbled over our feet a little on the way out perhaps, but it was dark in there and the tables were too close, and the aisles filled with bags and instrument-cases and people's big feet; and swayed all across the road as we headed for home, perhaps, but there wasn't any traffic and we were just reclaiming the highway for pedestrians, and what was wrong with that?

Split up when we had to, going this way and that. Said goodnight slowly, slurringly, fumbling over arrangements to meet again, some of us one place and some in another; and said goodnight again, and some had hugs for everyone and some had kisses for a few. And I got hugged and kissed, no different; but not as I should have been in a world with no wicked sense of humour, not as I yearned to be. She kissed me, sure, but only on the cheek and fleetingly; and her hand squeezed my arm, and what did that mean?

"Night then, Ben," she said; and *Yeah, right,* I thought, supplying the elision for her, getting at least one message I could read tonight. *Good night, chalk it up as that, that's good enough.*

And I smiled, brushed a hand meaninglessly across her shoulder, jerked it at the others like a last brief wave and went walking off up the hill alone.

Again.

Naturally.

Home to a dark flat, and the Yale achingly hard to get into the lock, scratching and scratching; and then at last inside, grabbing the door to stop it crashing too loud against the wall, not to wake Jacko. Closing it so, so softly; and going through to the kitchen almost on tiptoe, opening a fresh pint of milk and swallowing it straight from the carton, chug-a-lug; and dribbling toothpaste onto my treasured silk shirt when I cleaned my teeth, and standing for a minute over the toilet wondering if I was going to puke, and thinking maybe I should take a bowl to bed with me just in case, and *no, that'll only make it more likely, forget it, you're not going to puke, not you, boy, not tonight . . .*

And keeping a hand on the furniture or the wall all the way through to my bedroom, and stripping off in about ten seconds and dropping onto the bed because I couldn't stand upright any longer, feeling my way under the duvet almost comatose already and the last thing I heard was Jacko coming in, being desperately quiet, not to wake me . . .

And that was the night, that good good night; and then there was the morning.

Which began with a hammering, more than in my head, dragging me halfway up from sodden dreams; and then light and action, more than movement, a tremendous shaking; and I opened claggy eyes on the morning and my hangover and Jacko.

He was bending over the bed rolling me to and fro with hands of long experience, almost a year my flatmate and this the only way to wake me. Surprising that even this worked, after a good rage; and we'd never had the chance to find out before, no one had ever *wanted* to wake me after a good rage, and why the hell was he doing it now . . . ?

I grunted, shoved him away, glared at him as best I could with no focus yet to my bleary sight. I could see his wild hair, an afro wrecked by sleeping, and I could see his weak beard, too thin to hide the weak chin behind it; I could see his bathrobe hanging open, showing his scant red body-hair and his bones beneath; I still couldn't see what he was here for.

Couldn't ask either, I was in no fit state to shape an English sentence. Sour saliva pooled behind my teeth; if I tried to use my mouth too cleverly I could yet throw up, and with a witness now. So I ran a hand down over my face, rubbed at a night's rough stubble, grunted again, the best he was going to get. It was enough, apparently.

"Your sister's here," he said.

Which was instant chill, a dose of wide-awake potion and my mouth suddenly desert-dry, no question of chucking up.

"I haven't," I croaked, "haven't got a sister." *Send her away, get rid of her, get her out of here . . .*

"Well, she says she's your sister. And I wouldn't want to argue, the mood she's in. Very stressed-out, this girl is."

I disinvested, I divorced her, I disowned them all and denied them thrice before cock-crow; I've got a decree absolute, no family, none of mine . . .

But yes, that sounded like my sister; and if she was here, she wasn't going away. Not fair, to send Jacko back with unforthcoming messages. She'd just shred him, and then come through to find me.

"Give me a minute," I said.

"Sure. Make her a coffee, shall I . . . ?"

"No." That surprised him; the question was pure rhetoric, of course he'd make her a cup of coffee. But, "No," I said again, and meant it. *Not in my flat. No welcome, no refreshment, no returns.* "Go back to bed," I said, "I'll deal with Hazel."

And not in my bathrobe, either. That was a lesson early learned, not to put myself at any disadvantage. I pulled on yesterday's jeans and a sweatshirt, slouched through to the bathroom for a pee and a quick wash, no distractions and no hostages to fortune. I pulled a comb through my hair, checked myself in the mirror, even thought about shaving; but no, no need to go overboard. If I was going to play student for my sister, I had to look the part. So I rumpled my hair again, *I'm hung over, right? And it's Friday morning and I'm cutting lectures, and for God's sake give the girl what she expects to see,* and unbolted the door at last.

We never bolted the bathroom door, Jacko and me; but Hazel was in the flat and I hadn't even stopped to think about it. All my life I'd been snatching refuges from Hazel, bolting doors against her.

And now I walked down the passage damp and fresh and afraid, head numb and stomach twisting for more than all last night's alcohol; and I hesitated by the closed living-room door, and my hand was trembling where I lifted it to the handle.

And I walked in and yes, there was Hazel.

In her leathers, stood by the window, watching the bike perhaps in this neighbourhood, as if anyone in this neighbourhood would be stupid enough to steal Hazel Macallan's bike.

Her helmet was on the table, her hair was cropped to keep it neat under the helmet, her eyes were hard and sisterly. I looked away, trying to be angry with her for coming, *why don't you, why didn't you ever, ever listen to me? Go away, we're through, it's over, no more family* . . . But all I could manage was contempt, and that was all for myself, *too scared to meet her eye to eye, eh, Ben old buddy? Your sister, your twin, and you can't even look her in the eye* . . .

My twin, yes, half an hour older and she'd exploited that all our lives; but I'd let it happen. Along with everything else I'd let happen, just because that was easier than the other thing, easier far than standing up to her or Laura or anyone. I wasn't good at standing up, and especially not this morning; already I wanted to drop onto the sofa, pull a cushion down over my face, give myself away completely.

Didn't do that, still had just a hint of pride left – *family pride*, something whispered, *Macallan pride*, and maybe it wasn't so easy after all, you couldn't just walk away from blood – so I gestured vaguely, said, "Sit down, Hazel," the first words I'd spoken to my sister in three years, near enough.

And she jerked her head in an abrupt negative, and already I felt foolish and ineffectual; and then my rough and heavy-handed sister did what she'd come to do, used what she had, no compromise and no allowances allowed.

"Marty died last night," she said.

And then I did sit down, or drop down rather, straight down

and lucky the sofa was there or I'd have gone all the way to the floor; and after a second of staring I brought both hands up to cover my aching eyes, to give myself a moment's rest from this world of family and never mind what Hazel thought, she knew it all already.

My cousin Marty. Three years older, three stone heavier than me: at least that and likely more by now, so long since I'd seen him and *never more and isn't this what you wanted, aren't you supposed not to care?*

Of course I was supposed not to care. I'd divorced them all, Marty included; and if not one of the reasons, Marty was at least a symptom of why I'd done it. He was a bully and a bruiser, shaven head and tattoos and scar tissue in unexpected places, that he delighted in showing off; and he was an enforcer, that was his talent and that was how my family used him. To lean on people, to encourage them to be convenient – and to punish if they were obdurate, if they made a nuisance of themselves. Marty used to enjoy the punishments.

But it was Marty who taught me how to swim as a kid, even if his idea of lessons did include a lot of duckings in deep water; and it was Marty who really taught me how to drink, for all that I like to tell that story differently, back when I was fourteen and even the family face wouldn't see me served in any pub in town. And the year after that he got me laid for the first time, he devoted half an hour of his own birthday party to that generous cause; and I hated his life but I loved him regardless, and he was my cousin, and he was dead.

And that didn't happen, not to family. Not at twenty-five.

"How?" I demanded when I could talk again, when I could face a world with Marty gone and Hazel right there, back in my life again.

"You'll hear," she said like the good soldier she was, always had been. Under orders, clearly. "They've called a meeting. Everyone's coming."

And *everyone* manifestly included me, except that I was no good soldier. I'd handed back my shilling and decamped.

"Not me," I said. "Remember?"

"Don't be stupid, I haven't got time. Get some shoes on, and a jacket. I'm leaving in two minutes."

"You're leaving alone, Hazel." Marty or no Marty – and *no Marty*, that was the thing, *never any more Marty* – I wasn't putting myself back in the cage again. Escaping once was major, twice would be impossible.

"No," she said. "Hurry up. Or do I have to do it for you?"

She would, she'd do that; I knew from past experience. A few years back now, when I was seventeen and only starting to rebel; she'd crammed my feet into Docs and my arms into sleeves and dragged me out by main force, and she'd do just the same again if she chose to. And I might be older now, I might have a body significantly larger than hers, but I still wouldn't use it against her. Couldn't possibly.

So I stared at her, starting to sulk, feeling my grip sliding to nothing; and said, "I don't have a helmet."

"It's my bike," she snorted. "We won't be pulled over."

"Not the point. People have accidents, on bikes. That's what the law's for. I won't ride a bike without a helmet, I've got too much respect for my head."

So she picked her helmet off the table and chucked it over, and I didn't have an excuse any more; and I went to the family meeting because that was what Hazel wanted me to do, and it had been inevitable ever since the decision was made in her hard and efficient head, same size as mine but so much stronger.

We passed a patrol car on the way, not even on the dual carriageway yet and Hazel was doing upwards of eighty with no helmet on; and the car just went on quietly trawling the kerb, the one glance to spot who we were and they didn't so much as look our way again, the brief time they could see us.

No sensible policeman was going to stop a Macallan in a hurry. One of the laws of nature, that; along with *I always do what Hazel wants*. Or you could substitute any other member of my family, more or less, in either position there. Most people did what Hazel wanted, relatives no exception; and me, I could never come face to face with any of them without kowtowing in the end. Among other notable absences in my make-up, I seemed to be missing a spine. Even my escape, my renunciation was only on sufferance; they let me go because they had no need of me. If that should change, they'd whistle me back soon enough.

As now. I couldn't believe that they needed me, I thought that they were whistling only as a matter of form: *this is a family crisis, the whole family should be here and that includes Benedict; Hazel, will you fetch him, please?* And of course she'd be only too pleased to renew her influence over her renegade, her spineless twin.

Influence? Dominion, more like. And she'd always enjoyed that, Hazel. She might have left me alone, but she had never let go of the leash.

And so we came to my uncle's house that fine and sunny Friday, and my head was snug in my sister's helmet and hammering louder than the engine of my sister's BMW as she raced it down the valley, down and down, all downhill from here. And I sat with my arms around her, but it was she who held me, as she always had; and I watched the swift road unwind in a hurry beneath my booted feet, and I thought it was dappled with death.

TWO

MY FAMILY, AND OTHER CRUELTIES OF GOD

Actually the roads were blocked by death, near enough. There were cars parked down the private lane, all the way back to the junction; and the lane is narrow, for all that the civic authorities very kindly keep it well maintained. On four wheels, we'd never have got through to the house. Such a crush, such a gathering: even if I hadn't known already, there would have to have been a death. Nothing else could have brought them all together in this way.

Jags and Micras, old Ford Escorts and new Volvo estates: I was seeing symbols in everything, and this long line of cars said that there was nothing united about my family, nothing shared beyond the blood. Blood was enough, though. It fetched them in.

Besides, there was the family business too: what paid for the cars and kept bread on the table, the wolf from the door. Everyone had a share in that.

Everyone except me. Some weeks I ate pride more than bread, and the wolf scratched deep runnels in the paintwork. But *in extremis*, friends would see me through; and I'd take my friends any day, over the people who'd bred me and fed me and held me within the shelter of their strong, strong arms all the years of my childhood.

My sister's strong arms steered her mean, lean black machine past the cars and through the high stone gateway into my uncle's grounds. Gravel spat around us, onto lawns and flower-beds; I didn't look back to see but the way Hazel drove, the way Hazel did everything, hard and fast and heedless, we'd be digging ditches in the drive. Not to worry, though. My uncle employed people to rake and tidy. That was how he lived, he walked a road constantly made smooth before his feet.

That was how he tried to live, at least. Might not find it so easy now. Hard to smooth away the death of a son so many years too soon, so very much out of proper order.

There were maybe a dozen people in sight as we approached the house. In twos and threes they stood about, darkly dressed, all with something of black about them. The men wore suits, even the cousins of our own generation, Martin's cohorts, as comfortable in collar and tie as they would have been in stilettos and lace. A family in mourning, though, doing the thing properly, as my family did everything properly. Even my sister's leathers were unadorned black; and I might be wearing Hazel's helmet but I was wearing my own clothes: padded ski jacket in electric pink, maroon jeans with purple pockets and turn-ups, scarlet boots.

Ah, well. Maybe they'd think it was a message, maybe they'd read it right. *I don't belong here, I don't belong with you.*

They were reading something from me, at any rate: staring and glaring, treating me like an open book with dodgy illustrations. Maybe I should wave, say, "Hi, guys," something like that. Family, after all. Cousins and aunts. Nobody would want to kiss these particular cousins, but maybe I should offer to kiss the aunts . . .

Maybe not. I kept Hazel's helmet on, dark visor down. Let my clothes say what they liked, that was all the information I was giving out for free. The rest was silence. A young man's entitled to some privacy, even from his family.

Especially from his family.

Hands in cool nylon pockets, trying to look oh so casual and not at all like a man with a Daniel complex, *hi, cats, remember me? Nice den you got here.* I followed my sister's eloquent, contemptuous back through that gauntlet of gazes and on into the house.

Uncle James met us in the hallway, fat and fifty-odd, pale in his dark suit; and just for a moment, just briefly he wasn't family at all, he was only a man whose son was dead, and I could feel for him.

But then a girl came to my elbow, to take my jacket and my sister's helmet. She was fifteen, sixteen maybe, and it was a struggle, because I wouldn't have seen her since she was twelve; but I felt the spark in her, my skin tingled when our fingers touched, and eventually I placed her as a second cousin some little distance removed. And my perspective shifted again. Of course Uncle James would be using cousins for his maids today, aunts no doubt for his cooks. He wouldn't want unrelated staff in the house, people not bound by blood; this was family business, and a stranger is by definition a spy.

And that was too much access to his mind, it was all too familiar. Sympathy shrivelled, in the light of such logic. I gave up the shadowing helmet and the proclaiming jacket both, faced him as I was: nephew and rebel, in the family but not of the family, never that.

Held my hand out to shake his like a stranger, like a spy; and he took it briefly, coldly, none of the warmth due to family. No hug, no kiss of greeting for the boy who'd done half his growing up in this house, who'd been practically an adopted son sometimes when things were a little too hot at home.

"Benedict. Welcome," each syllable hard and detached, pebbles dropped individually into silence, hard to imagine anything less welcoming. Hard to hear that from my uncle's fleshy lips, and to see how quickly he pulled his hand back from mine.

Harder still not to do the same thing, in response or in revenge. Harder to be civilised, to say what was right and due and proper, what I owed both to the living and the dead despite all divorces.

"Uncle James. I can't, I can't believe that Marty's gone. He was such a friend to me when we were younger, it'll never be the same world without him . . ."

You ought to be glad of that, his eyes accused me, *the things you've said of the family, of men like Marty and me.* And I agreed with him, or some part of me agreed; but that was all he was seeing, my rejection and my walking out. Where I stood there was a wider picture, and it had a great gaping hole torn in it, edges fraying in a bad wind.

"You'll want to view the body," he said, and now I couldn't agree with him at all, no part of me wanted to view the body. But, "You're the last," he said, "I'll take you up myself." And he was already turning towards the stairs, and spineless Benedict Macallan asserted himself exactly as much as he usually did, and followed quietly in his uncle's wide wake.

There would be a wake, I realised suddenly, a wake for Marty from now until the dawn. I hadn't been invited, though, not for that. This was a blood meeting upcoming and I was blood, I had a duty to attend; but the mourning party after would be for true mourners only, not for the likes of me.

Not that there were any others like me. I was renegade, I was outcast, I was alone.

By my own choice, and apparently forever; and *oh Laura, Laura, not fair to send me into this alone, where's your compassion?*

Up the stairs to the first landing, and I turned automatically to the next flight, thinking of Marty's old room in the attic, thinking they would have put him there. But Uncle James was going the other way, along the corridor where I almost was a stranger, where children had never been welcomed when I had the run of this house, when I was a child. That made it easier, a little. I didn't want to see Marty still and dead in the room where I'd seen him so often death's opposite, so full of life, laughing or wrestling or hustling me out with hard hands and hard words and a girl mysteriously half-seen in the shadows behind him, perfume in the air.

And if they'd changed the room, or he had – if there were no posters on the walls now, no sports teams or women posed half-naked and provocative; no broken childhood toys gathering dust in cupboards; no adolescent trophies, this girl's bra and that girl's knickers; no clothes kicked in corners, no reek of sweat and after-shave, no Marty – I didn't want to see that either, like an underlining that there was no Marty in the world.

I followed Uncle James, hustling a little to catch up; and he took me past half a dozen doors firmly closed, and brought me to the one that stood a little open.

He pushed it wider, gestured with his head; and I hardly hesitated, hardly paused for one last breath and momentary eye-contact, *I don't want to do this*, before I went obediently in to Marty.

It was dim in there, heavy lace curtains over the windows and no lights on. My stupid hand was already reaching for the switch before I caught it and dragged it down again, feeling Uncle James' eyes still watching me.

This must have been a guest-room ordinarily, there was nothing personal in it. Pale blue wallpaper, a couple of prints, heavy furniture with china doodahs on lace doilies, an ashtray on the

window-sill. Only a single spray of flowers, white lilies and or-
chids on a low table by the bed.

Queen-size, the bed, and in the middle of the room; and on the
bed, of course, my cousin Marty.

Naked to the waist, he was; or naked all the way, rather, but
there was a sheet drawn neatly up for decency, only its weight to
shadow the shape of him from the chest down.

I was surprised, I'd thought to find him in his best clothes like
the rest of them, suit and tie and a flower in his buttonhole; and
what surprised me more, someone had spilt ink on his shoulder.

No, couldn't be ink. *Get real, Macallan.* But something there
was, a black stain on his skin; and I was leaning closer, trying to
make it out in this uncertain light – better to look at a little part of
him than the whole, better a small puzzle than the big one, who
and how and why – when someone did flick that switch on the
wall behind me.

Then the light was certain, the light was definite and unam-
biguous and I didn't want anything to do with it. I turned quickly,
half to see and half to protest; but seeing was enough, the protest
died somewhere between tongue and teeth.

It was Marty's brother stood there in the doorway. Marty's kid
brother, young Jamie. My age, my playmate; often my shield and
defender against Hazel, and for a long time my very best-loved
friend.

No friend now, we had the whole family between us; and after
today I thought we'd have Marty too, the way Jamie looked,
the way he was looking at me. Once we used to unite against
Marty, two allies under constant threat of war. Now he was going
to lie between us, cold and dead and irrecoverable, like so much
else.

"Go on," James said, soft and chilling, lean and tense in his
tight suit, hard-trained and utterly out of any control but his own.
"Have a closer look, you were going to anyway. That's what

you're here for, that's why you've come . . ."

That's why I was brought, I thought; and, *That's why he's got no clothes on,* I thought that too, suddenly seeing clearly, bright as the light around me now.

And I turned away from Jamie, more for escape than to satisfy my curiosity, because he looked too dangerous to bear. But the one led to the other, not looking at Jamie meant looking at Marty, no other choices in that room that morning; and again I looked at the shoulder more than the face, thought about the skin sooner than think about what that skin contained, cooling bones and heavy flesh already part putrescent.

It wasn't only his shoulder, I saw that now, although his shoulder was worst affected. There were black marks on his arms too, in little patches; and on his knuckles, where his hands lay folded atop the white sheet. I thought of ink again, understanding the pattern of them suddenly.

Marty had made his first tattoo at school, done it himself with a needle set in a wine-cork and Art Department inks. He was maybe fifteen then but already a big lad, already a bruiser, loving his own reputation; when he'd picked the scabs off there was a crude face on his forearm, with a black eye and missing teeth, and *THE OTHER GUY* in wobbly capitals around it. I was staying in the house just then, so I got to witness the row, and the week of cold silences after; and neither of us ever let on that Marty had used my idea and my original sketch to work from.

That early amateur effort had been removed inside the month, and was never mentioned again. But Marty left school the following year and left home temporarily, to establish at least a little independence; and that was when he started paying for his tattoos.

Last time I'd seen him he'd had *LOVE* and *HATE* across his fingers, like any self-respecting thug; and he'd had any number of designs up his arms, flags and football teams, impossible women;

but his pride and joy, his new acquisition, what he'd taken his shirt off to show me was a dragon.

No ordinary dragon, this. Brazen and bejewelled, it had clung to his back with all four legs and its wings outstretched, claws dug in and beads of blood dribbling down. Its tail wrapped around his buttock and arrowed into his groin, he said, though he didn't show me that; its head peered over his left shoulder, and its eyes were laughing.

That's how it was, that's what he wore under his clothes last time we met. He carried a dragon on his back, between his skin and him.

No longer. What he carried now – except that he carried nothing, would never carry anything again – what marked his body was a puffy, crusted black blister where the dragon's head had been, and lesser scabs to cover all his other tattoos.

I thought they were burns, perhaps. I thought Uncle James had come after him with a blowtorch, flames to scrub him clean of filthy pictures. Or I didn't, I only wanted to; from first understanding, I knew that this was something entirely other, something entirely worse.

"Don't piss about," Jamie said behind me, coldly vicious. "Have a proper look, why don't you?"

And his hand reached past me, gripped his brother's chilly shoulder and heaved.

Awkwardly, ungainly in death as he never had been in life even with all the weight he had on him, Marty shifted; Marty stirred under his brother's ungentle hand, fell back and stirred again, finally rolled over with that fine white sheet only a tangle now between his legs.

Not good, this. Not a kind thing to do to a cousin, an old friend, an adoptive brother. But that was the crux, of course, because I wasn't any more. That's why he was so angry, so set against me;

whatever the summons of blood, I was the closest he could find right now to someone from the other world, outside the family. And someone outside family had done this, and I represented them all . . .

First glance, Marty's back looked like a Mandelbrot in bad colours, black with livid purple edges. It wasn't, of course, the shape was wrong; but it still looked fractal, it had that regularity and the sense of depth, the feeling that however close you got you still wouldn't reach the bottom of it.

Second glance and it just looked foul, it looked like a dreadful way to die.

The hard smooth crust of black scab had fractured under his weight, shattered almost, into a craquelure that showed harsh red in the cracks. Maybe it wasn't his weight that had done that after all, maybe it was his writhing and bucking as he died; because he surely must have done that, he would never have gone easy and this must have hurt.

Whatever this was, that much I was ready to bet on, that it must have hurt. My cousin Marty, whose major ambition in life was to learn how to eat beer-glasses for fun and profit, who'd hold his finger in a lighter-flame and laugh as the blister came up after; I was ready to bet that he *screamed* as these blisters came up.

"Jamie?"

"What?"

"How did they, how did they ever *do* this?"

"Don't know," he said, softening a little suddenly, standing beside me; allowing the question, allowing me to be *us* instead of *them*. "Nobody knows. Allan's on his way, though. He'll find out."

Yes. Allan was the eldest of the brothers, Allan and then James and then my father Charles. Allan was the intellectual, the sophisticate, the man who had known how to erase Marty's first primitive tattoo that time. He'd sniff out whatever had been done

21

last night, he'd understand. Whether he'd point the finger after, whether *how* would give us *who* – that was another question, and nothing we could do but hope.

And I did find myself hoping, unexpectedly. Standing over Marty's body, I felt a part of this family as I hadn't for years. Beside me, Jamie seemed to have burned his anger out; now his hand was slack on his brother's head and I could hear his breathing catch and harden, carrying too much memory in a room where memory could only equal pain.

"Come on," I said quietly, "let's get him tidy again, yeah? Before someone comes?"

Jamie nodded mutely, and between us we turned Marty over and straightened him out. It was impossible not to touch those repugnant scabs, though I avoided them as much as I could, and I could see Jamie doing the same, trying to fit his fingers around them. They felt hard and dry, colder somehow than Marty's body was. That had to be illusion or imagination, surely, but I thought Jamie was sharing it. Evil always feels cold. Christ, I should know. I'd shivered enough under my uncles' eyes, some of my cousins', my father's sometimes.

We pulled the sheet up from either side of the bed and folded it tidily, well above his groin to hide the black scar where the dragon's tail had pointed into his pubic hair, *treasure lies here*. I didn't know how many girls had gone looking, but he'd had more than his fair share, had Marty. Taken the best part of my share too, I thought sometimes; but only statistically, and not at all by his intent. It had been my choice earlier, another way to defy family traditions, to frustrate their expectations and mark myself out as different, even more than I was marked already.

And then there was Laura and nothing else applied, no other girl need bother. *Sorry, no vacancies.*

We did that last duty for Marty, we laid him out nicely, and I

22

couldn't remember the last time I felt so brotherly to both of them, so close. Then we left him, pulling the door to behind us but not quite closing it, leaving a little gap for him to hear the party downstairs if he was listening. He wouldn't have wanted to miss a party.

And then we walked down together, side by side; and for the length of that corridor and the staircase I lost my perspective again, lost it utterly. Jamie was only my close relative and my oldest friend, his brother my cousin had died and he was grieving, we were both grieving and that was all.

But Uncle James waited at the foot of the stairs, vengeful and malign, and there it went again. Not possible to keep good hold on such a view, too much evidence stacked against it.

"In the big room," he said. "Now," he said, "we won't wait for Allan."

"Where is Uncle Allan, anyway?" I murmured, following Jamie down the corridor. It felt right, it felt essential to keep my voice low; the house was too tense for normal conversation, it had to be whispers or screams. And I wasn't sure how people would react, if they thought I was asking too many questions.

Jamie showed me then how right I was, giving me a glance that was all family, our brief alliance already broken; but he did at least answer. "Shetland," he said. "He's been sent for, he's coming."

That made sense, to find Uncle Allan so far north. The only one of us who ranged far outside the town, he'd always trumpeted our Celtic lineage, louder than necessary and too often to be interesting. I'd never felt it applied, in any case. There were other Macallans, to be sure, and they were profoundly Scottish; but they weren't us. We were border people, in any sense you cared for.

The big room must presumably have been called something else at some time, something more formal. But the big room we kids had christened it when Uncle James bought the house fifteen years back, give or take; and the big room it had remained.

There would never have been an easy label, in any case. Too broad for a gallery, too much to one side to be a hall, far too grand for any more domestic title, it would always have demanded a name to itself: the long room, perhaps, or the sun room after all its south-facing windows. But it rained just as often as the sun shone, and for some obscure childhood reason even our illicit games of indoor cricket had been played width-wise, we'd never used the length of it. All we ever called it was the big room, and the adults caught the habit from us as adults will.

And now we were adults also, and one of us was dead, and the big room was barely big enough to hold all us men in comfort. I'd not seen a family gathering, a clan moot on such a scale: not since my grandfather died, at any rate. My family tended not to assemble in such numbers, it wasn't entirely safe. Not even for us.

Shivers slicked my tingling skin as soon as I walked into that room; every hair on my body was suddenly alert, and the air cracked dangerously in my lungs. I eased my way past relatives on sofas and relatives in chairs, all of them male; I set my feet carefully in the spaces between younger relatives sitting on the floor, lads all except my sister; I hurried quietly across to an open window, where I could breathe something other than concentrated Macallan.

And yes, I might be blood and my blood might allow me to survive in here where surely a stranger would be sick and maybe dying already; and yes, I might have shared memories with these people, shared affections grievously bruised today; but no, I was no part of this. I didn't belong and I didn't want to belong.

So I leant against the wall breathing what breeze there was that would venture into this house, with my head turned to the grass and the hills and the river. Couldn't turn my ears away, though, couldn't turn them off. I heard my uncle make his way to the far front of the room, and then I heard his speech.

"My son," he said, *my eldest son, my pretty son, my pride*, "my son is dead, you have all seen him now. What was done to him, you have seen. If any of you understands it, I would be glad to hear from you now."

Not a murmur, not the hiss of a pensive breath. My family does silence very well.

My family does everything well.

"Well, then. Allan will find it out, when he arrives."

To be sure, Allan would find it out. And there would be no other autopsy for Marty: no police, no cold knives and his body opened under a harsh light and the harsher eyes of strangers, no inquest beyond our own.

"But how the thing was done is secondary now. That it was done, that my son was *killed*, by whatever agency – that is a matter not for Allan, but for us all."

And I felt the agreement swell around me, I felt the tight-leashed anger build and build, my skin burned with it and there was a stabbing pain in my head; and how could it be otherwise, at a gathering of such a family at such a time?

But even so, my uncle was too certain, too confident of blood. Not for the first time, he was discounting me; or counting me in, rather, counting me an insignificant addition to the pack when in truth I was far outside it.

I had loved Marty and he was dead, strangely and horribly dead; but if that was a matter for my family, then by definition it was no matter for me.

THREE

NO LUNCH FOR THE WICKED

The meeting ran on, as any meeting will; but there was no point to it, everything that mattered had already been said. And was implicit anyway, hadn't needed even that much saying. One of the family was dead, and this was vendetta.

When the last person who wanted to speak had spoken, Uncle James allowed just a minute of that good Macallan silence; then he dismissed us with a spread of the hands like a release, like a blessing, *go out into the world and find these fuckers, and bring them back to me.*

Not that anyone was going anywhere yet, except for me. There was still that wake to come, and none of my family was much for missing a good party.

Trying to filter through the crowd as it spilled out into the hall to join the women, trying to be invisible, hoping to catch my sister quickly without anyone else catching me, I failed utterly. And no surprise there, it was just something else that marked me out from the rest of them. They succeeded, and I failed. That was a given.

Specifically, in trying to escape everyone's attention I came face to face with my parents.

Dad gripped my arm and said my name, heavy with last night's beer and this morning's sentiment. His belly had grown to overhang his belt now, and he had jowls where he used to have a jaw. That made it easier, a little. Easier to stand off, to hold yourself apart from a man when you only see him in time-lapse and his body is melting.

My mother wasn't melting, she was fading gently as her black funeral dress was fading into grey. Her hair was on its way from blonde to white, caught in that uncertain ground between; the fine creases of impending age had softened the lines of her face, so that it too seemed to be losing definition. She was a classic Macallan wife, my mother. Quietly pretty and well domesticated, subservient and content, she might have been made for the role, unless she'd been remade to fit it. We were a male line, almost without exception; wives were necessary adjuncts, for the breeding of more men. Daughters likewise, and daughters were expected to marry cousins. Never mind genetics, inbreeding was a boon to us. What we had, we kept to ourselves.

Or they kept, rather, what they had. Not I. I had none of it, and blessed be. It was a birthright impossible to sell, and loathsome to me.

"Benedict, lad," my father rasped, punching me lightly. "How's the rebel, eh? How's the rebel?" Meaning, *you came, of course you came,* and *so much for your rebellion*, and *welcome back, my son.*

My mother had always had the greater share of whatever brains there were between them. She looked at me and shook her head, said, "I expect your sister brought you, didn't she?"

"Oh." Even Dad could follow that. "Oh, did she?"

"Yes, Dad. Of course she did." *You think I'd have come here else? Even for Marty?*

"He's your cousin, Ben." No part of his true talent, but sometimes my father could read minds. Read mine, at least. We'd often had these conversations, where he replied to what I hadn't said.

"He was," I agreed. "Not any more." And let them read that whichever way they chose, whether the relationship ended with my leaving or with Marty's death. It didn't matter. They'd still misunderstand me, either way. That was one of the facts of my life, that my parents truly didn't understand.

And then my sister joined us, with the smell of soap on her hands.

"We've been dressing him," she said. "For the wake." And her eyes glancing at me said what I'd already deduced, that I wasn't invited for the wake. *Time to go, bro*, her eyes were telling me.

"You taking me home, then, or what?"

"Get a bus, Ben," she said wearily, tired of me now; and that was what I did. Of course it was. I always did what Hazel said.

I looked around for Jamie on my way out, but didn't spot him and wasn't going to search. I was as keen to go as Hazel was to see me gone; and a friendly goodbye from my closest coz would have been good, maybe, but I couldn't depend on it. And didn't need it, either. *Divorced, disinvested, disowned*, right?

Right.

So I positively sauntered out of the house under the eyes of those of my relatives who could be bothered to watch, who betrayed that much interest in me: hands in pockets and head high, all the treacherous insolence of youth and none of the respect due either to death or to family. *Get you gone and good riddance*, I wanted them saying, *don't come back.*

I walked out on my gathered family for the second time in my life, and had no intention of going back.

The bus stop was up on the main road, ten minutes' steep climb from the house; and buses were one an hour or used to be, and unless they'd changed the timetable radically I'd just missed one.

No hassle, that was utterly cool. I'd been climbing this hill and

29

missing those buses half my life, I wasn't going to get uptight about it now. Nor was I going to resent Hazel's cavalier dismissal, nothing so foolish. *She brought me here, she could at least take me back* – but such a thought would be stupidly inappropriate, and I wasn't going to think it. This was Hazel, after all. Hazel was as Hazel did, and this was exactly the sort of thing that Hazel did. I'd had a lifetime of it, or at least a childhood and adolescence; and three years'-worth of other living wasn't anywhere near enough to break an acceptance so deeply in-grained.

I walked slowly up the lane, past all the cars and past little groups of people coming down. Non-family, these: guests invited for the wake or some part of it, the public part. Important people, councillors and bankers, the movers and shakers of the city all coming when my family whistled, and doing this last stretch on foot because they couldn't get their cars anywhere near and not even grumbling because you didn't do that, you didn't grumble at any inconvenience the Macallans might put you to.

What I wanted to do, what I really wanted to do was stroll up that lane with a coin or a key in my hand, digging deep into the cars' paintwork, leaving a multicoloured scratch behind me all the way from the house to the road. And of course I didn't, I would never have dared; but not from fear of the witnesses, all those movers and shakers.

I was a Macallan, my inheritance too clearly marked on my face, unmistakable; and they wouldn't have said a word, those important people.

But I didn't mark the cars, I only dreamed about it; and when I reached the road I only sat politely in the bus shelter, stone-still, bone-still, still as Marty's bones. No chucking pebbles at the traffic as I used to do with Jamie, points for contact and bonuses for breakage; no solo games of chicken; no games at all. I was too old now – older than yesterday – and too much alone, and we'd learned all those from Marty.

And having no one to talk to now about girls, as Jamie and I used to do sitting right here waiting for buses to take us to them, to carry us to the girls of our dreams, all I did was sit and think about girls, about one girl, waiting for a bus to take me at least closer to her, to the girl of my dreams, *oh Laura*.

When the bus came, I didn't know the driver from Adam; but he knew me. Or the set of my features, at least, he knew that. He'd have to, driving this route.

And he drew back a little in his chair, waved my proffered money away with a mutter I couldn't make out, didn't bother to give me a ticket.

It happened, even in the centre of town it happened, and I was almost ready for it today, with so much out of kilter and my new life all but lost in this sudden surge of past tides. I nodded politely, trying to look accustomed, and made my way to the back where I could sprawl with my feet up and look, aye, every inch a Macallan.

It was an old wreck of a bus, vinyl seats slashed and torn and leaking foam rubber, smoking very sensibly forbidden but the reek of stale smoke in the air regardless, stubs on the floor. I didn't like the feel of those seats, cool smoothness and sudden cracks, recalling Marty's blisters to my fingers' ends; so I shoved my hands back in my pockets again, *feel nothing, nothing to feel*, and turned my eyes to track the route outside: familiar, resurgent, and I'd thought it all so thoroughly suppressed.

Back in the city, telling myself *back home*, I didn't go back to the flat. Jacko would be full of questions, just when I was emptied out of answering; and besides, it was no safe refuge any more. Hazel had been there once, and forever after I'd be falling silent at the sound of an engine slowing in the street, wondering *is that a bike, is that her, if it's a car it could be one of the others come to get me again* . . .

No easy life, being the family traitor. If the family started to show an interest, it would be, I would be paranoid and impossible.

What I wanted, I wanted to run to Laura, my only true refuge, my inherent safety. But lessons learned hard bite the deepest, and I'd never, never put her in that position again. She couldn't cope, bless her, she couldn't handle being so elevated out of the common pool of my friends; she needed not to be different just when I needed to announce her difference, and neither her logic nor mine could handle the discrepancy. The one time I tried to force the issue the whole system crashed, and took months to rebuild. We were on safer foundations now, with those limits clearly, brutally defined. She'd be a friend in need, of course she would, that lay well within her parameters of friendship; but she'd never be the friend I needed.

So no, I didn't run to her, didn't strand myself on her doorstep and both of us on a desperate shore. Best I could do, best I could hope for was to persuade fate into a chance meeting, let her find me in trouble, let her think I hadn't come to her. Not good, not what I needed; but as with so much – as with everything that touched Laura, everything that Laura touched – it would at least be a long way better than nothing.

Fate and chance are flexible concepts, and I manipulated them as much as I dared. Walked past her flat twice before I even looked up at the windows, saw that the curtains were pulled and loitered instead for ten or fifteen minutes at the corner, hoping she'd come palely out for a paracetamol or else robustly in search of bacon and sausages for a serious breakfast. Some people eat and eat after a rage, some simply repine. It epitomised my life and the waste of it, that I didn't know which school Laura followed.

Never had the chance to observe, and I didn't ask questions, not about the ordinary things. There was too much I didn't know; once get started and the questions would never stop. I'd want it all and that was the trap again, the temptation to do the forbidden, to raise her out of the ordinary.

She didn't come, nor any flatmates I could interrogate; so I thought maybe she had hero blood in her veins, maybe she'd gone in to college. I bought a couple of cheese pasties to munch on the way – I'm an eater and I hadn't had the chance yet, my body was howling empty – and hustled down to the campus. I had Laura's timetable fixed firm in my head, knew it better than my own; if she was there, if she wasn't just sleeping and sleeping because there are a few lucky souls who can do that too, who don't need to be conscious until all the damage is fixed, she'd be scalpel in hand among the cold cadavers, learning what made the human body cease to tick.

No question of interrupting her there. There are ways to suicide and ways not; and sauntering into the dissection labs with a smile for Professor Duncan and a glance around, "Hi, is Laura here, sorry but I need her, she's the only thing that counts" – no. That numbered not. He would have peeled me in that palace of peeled flesh, she would have dismembered my joints.

Eventually, he'd have to let them go, though, *class dismissed and don't forget your homework*. It was coming up lunchtime, and even medics have to eat. And let them scatter where they would, left and right, upstairs and down, to the med school cafeteria or the union bars; let them flock and chatter, I knew what Laura would do. This once, at least, I could get ahead of her.

It was Friday; and Friday lunch was ritual, Friday lunch was sacred. If she was in school – *if* she was, if she wasn't sleeping and sleeping – her sweet size nines (Bigfoot the other girls called her, if they were talking shoes) had a predestined path to follow.

It was Friday; and Friday was kosher day, *last chance before Shabbat* and not to be missed. Five minutes from campus, in an alley off a side street, area steps led down to a plain cream-and-green eatery, bench seats and communal formica-topped tables and ugly white counter, no food in sight and no style at all. One sign on the wall outside, *Morry's Deli*, otherwise you might have thought yourself in Orwell territory, 1984 a decade on.

And oh, how wrong you would have been.

Morry Green and his family – and it was, it was all family again, another family business: from the accountant to the washer-uppers, everyone was blood – they served their God and their community, devout hearts and a strong sense of duty. Just so happened they also served the best classic Jewish food north of Primrose Hill.

They didn't give a toss for the décor, and quite right too. Mostly they catered for us, the student body in its separate hungry cells; we'd squash up happily, six to the bench and tuck your elbows in, for good cheap food and plenty of it. Keeping the place ugly kept the prices down and it kept the business community out, which suited Morry and it suited us.

Four days a week, Morry's was open early till late. But they closed at three on a Friday, to be at home and bathed and properly ready by sunset; and of course they didn't open again until Monday, so everything had to be used up or thrown away, and they really didn't like throwing anything away.

Fridays in town, we wouldn't have lunch anywhere else.

It was Friday, and it was early yet, good children were still in school. If Laura was being good today, a medic she and no sweetly slumbrous girl, I had maybe an hour to kill.

Not a problem. I'd wasted more, far more time than that in places where I was far less likely to find Laura.

So I went inside. The place was near enough empty, just a few scattered skivers like myself sipping coffee and waiting to be hungry, no one serving. I swung the door to and fro a few times before I closed it, making the bell jangle, letting them know there was another customer in. Old Morry appreciated it.

I claimed a table and a bench, settled myself nice and comfy against the wall and closed my eyes, hoping not to open them again till a mocking chuckle and a light-fingered touch told me that Laura had arrived.

Not a chuckle, though, next thing I heard; and not a dreamgirl's hand, next thing to touch me.

Actually what I heard was a rattle, as of cup in saucer in earth-quake, or at any rate in palsy-stricken hand. Behind that I could hear someone breathing, hard and fast and frightened.

That was all so unlikely that I opened my eyes regardless. The service at Morry's might be rough, might even be slapdash if you were a friend and they were busy, but it didn't generate those sorts of noises.

So I looked, and saw Warren. And on one level that was ex-actly right, exactly what I expected to see this time of day, what I'd been banking on; and on another level it was all very peculiar indeed, because he looked pale and his hands were trembling, and he wasn't at all pleased to see me.

Warren was a fixture, or possibly a fitting: at any rate he be-longed there, as much as Morry himself belonged. He was family, naturally, some species of cousin, though no one seemed to know how close. Or more likely they did know, they surely must have known, it was only that they didn't want to say. *Shame on them*, we all thought, where maybe we should have been ap-plauding the fact that they acknowledged him at all, let alone gave him a job out front where he could brandish the relationship as he brandished so much else.

He must have been late forties when we knew him, lean of

build with greying, thinning hair close-cropped and a nose to make Corporal Klinger blush; and he was cheerfully and screamingly camp, was Warren. He'd have been a burden to any decent family, let alone a religious one. It needed a liberal despot like Morry to make a place for him; a weaker *paterfamilias* or a more bigoted would have allowed the slow tides of contempt and disgust and what-will-the-rabbi-think? to force Warren out, to drive him into an exile that he would never have chosen, that he didn't have the strength to survive.

I knew all about exile, and survival. I knew what it took, and I had a pretty good idea of what Warren had, and that wasn't enough.

We all knew Warren. He loved us students, loved his job because the customer base was ninety per cent student and he could be a happy man all day, running around at our beck and call and doing more than any man should to please us.

Sometimes, maybe often, a student would make him a happy man all night also. I wasn't sure how many times I'd met him on a Sunday morning (but never on a Saturday, never on *Shabbat*, he owed that to his family) in someone's flat or someone else's house, making breakfast in a borrowed bathrobe: still willing, still serving, totally content. These were only ever one-night stands or brief affairs, nothing serious, nothing for long. The boys used to say they did it for his experience, for his openness, for the laugh: "Well, come on, give us a break, Ben, it's not going to be for his mind, is it? I mean, is it? We're not talking intellectual giant here. We're not talking anything giant, it's just a laugh, that's all."

How much of a laugh it really was for Warren, I was never certain. But he went on smiling, went on serving, was always happy to see us and the more the merrier.

But not today. Today he wasn't happy at all, and he certainly wasn't happy to see me.

* * *

His hand shook, and the saucer shook in his hand, the cup rattled in the saucer and the coffee slopped. Warren loved to anticipate; he always brought us coffee first thing, we didn't need to order it. Today was no different, except that it looked like the last thing he wanted to be doing. I'd never seen a man that frightened, never dreamt of seeing anyone that frightened of me.

"Warren? What's up?"

Actually, it was perfectly clear what was up: I was here, and he was having to serve me coffee, and he was trembling with terror as he did it. The true question was *Why?*, but I couldn't ask that directly. *Warren, why are you scared of me suddenly, what have I done?* – no, I couldn't do that. Not fair to either one of us. He just might be scared enough to answer me.

He got the cup and saucer down finally, dropping rather than putting it on the table and an awkward stretch away from me, with more coffee in the saucer than the cup.

"Not to worry," I said, trying a smile to see if it helped. "I can slurp it."

Didn't help at all, that smile. He seemed to read a threat in it, where there was truly nothing but a promise, *don't panic, Warren, I won't bite, honest.* He scurried back, all but ran through into the kitchen and out of my sight.

I sighed, shrugged for any curious observers – *just Warren, that's all, nothing to get worked up about* – and went over to the counter for a wad of serviettes, not to drip coffee down my shirtfront.

Too early still to hope for Laura, but I did that anyway, watching the door and listening for footsteps; and was still doing it when spitting fury came at me from the other direction, came from the kitchen, scorching down Warren's wake.

Not Laura's hand that touched me, and not light-fingered as

Laura was: this was a man's grip on my shoulder, digging deep, digging to the bones and hurting.

I startled, gasped, tried to pull away and couldn't.

Looked round, and there was Morry. Short and heavy in his whites, shadow on his jowls and dark wiry hair curling even on the backs of his fingers, where they were clamped on me.

Absolute rage in him, making him also tremble even as he held me, this always-courteous man, this friend of mine.

"Out," he said, lifting me one-handed from the bench, finding that so much easier than talking, his usual fluency down to mono-syllables now and those making no sense to me. "You," he said thickly, "out. Now."

And pushed me towards the door, force enough to send me staggering into it, hard enough to bruise.

"Morry, what the hell . . . ?" Angry in my turn, I twisted round to face him and never mind the audience now and never mind the dangers of too much truth, this was too much to let by. "What's going on here, what have I done?"

He reached for me again, and that was all his answer; but I lifted a hand to resist him, and saw how he flinched back sud-denly, this great squat bull of a man. That was all the answer that I needed.

A family affair, this was: my family and his, and I'd walked into the middle of something, where I clearly wasn't welcome.

Oh, my priceless, Christless family. They could screw my life up without thinking, without realising, even; though if they real-ised they'd do it all the same. Probably do it with a little more relish, knowing what they did.

Understanding at last, I had nothing to offer Morry, no restitu-tion in my gift. And I was still angry at him for manhandling me in front of witnesses: too angry to explain, even if he'd been calm enough to listen.

So I nodded abruptly, to let him know I had at least caught up with the action here; and then I opened the door and walked out, and thought, *That's another pleasure, another freedom gone. Terrific privilege, being a Macallan . . .*

And I climbed the steps and stood irresolute on the pavement, bewildered and bereft; and that's where Laura found me when she came, when she finally did come. Still there, still dithering, going a little this way and a little that and utterly unmindful of her.

FOUR

BELLA, HORRIDA BELLA

"Uh-huh," she said, standing too far off and only her eyes touching me, not enough. "What's with this, then?"

"What?"

"This tribal war-dance, this soft-shoe shuffle, whatever you want to call it. This jigging around on the pavement."

"It's Friday," I said helplessly.

"It's Friday, right. I *know* it's Friday." A long-suffering smile, a patient pace forward to pat me on the shoulder, and, "*Think* about it, Ben. Think about bagels, think about smoked salmon and fresh cream cheese. Think about *latkes*, think about *blinis* and fake caviar and sour cream. Lashings and lashings of sour cream, think about that. Then tell me why you're jigging about on the pavement; but tell me *inside*," taking my arm and steering me, positively pushing me towards the steps when she found me recalcitrant, "don't ask me to jig along with you, right? Morry doesn't serve out here. What was it, were you waiting for me, is that it? Or somebody else, Vanessa and that crowd, anyone?"

"I can't," I said.

"Can't wait? Me neither."

"Can't come in. I've been thrown out, Laura. Morry threw me out."

41

"Christ on a bicycle." She gazed at me, horrified, giving due respect to the gravity of the situation. "What on earth did you do? Stupid?"

"I didn't *do* anything. It's who I am, is enough. And don't ask why, I don't know. Just the Macallans up to something, and he won't have me in the place."

"Oh, Jesus." All teasing fled now, she held my arm in both of hers, what comfort she could give; and said, "I'll find out, shall I? If he'll talk to me?"

"Please. I'd like to know."

Laura nodded and ran light-footed down the steps, left me with nothing but a touch-memory of where her hands had been. Better than nothing, I supposed. I reminded myself.

And I waited, I did my solo dance on the pavement as before, and was hailed by Dermot and Vanessa coming for lunch, for friendship and conversation and not at all for this. I explained again, I had to; and they waited with me, of course, and wanted to talk, to wonder, to guess; and all I wanted was to wait, to jig, to change my name and my bad, bad blood.

When Laura came back she came slowly, dragging a heavy weight with her up those steep steps. Barely a nod of greeting she had for our friends, and only a whisper of voice for me.

"You got a, a cousin Marty, Ben?"

"Yeah, sure." And then remembering, *I had a cousin Marty*, "Why, what's he got to do with this?" Coming out sharper than I meant, perhaps, because even Laura flinched; but the true question, what I wanted answered actually went the other way, *What's this got to do with him?*

"They said, they said you were kin to him. And he's done them so much damage . . ."

There'd been damage done, that much was certain. I'd seen it, scabbed black on Marty's skin. I might have forgotten it tempo-

42

rarily, I might have tried to scratch myself out of that picture altogether, *family business, no business of mine*, but that probably wouldn't have worked in any case; and here were people, my friends, drawing me firmly back in again. So okay, they wanted me there, I'd be there. Consequences would be on their heads, not on mine.

"What," I said, and my voice sounded harsh even to myself, was surely harsher far than Laura had ever heard it, "are you talking about, for God's sake? Damage, what damage?"

"I think you'd better come and see," she said. "It'll be all right, Morry said so . . ."

"Oh, he did, did he? What did he say? Exactly?"

"Exactly?" She didn't like this, from me; she was getting nasty herself now. "He said, *exactly*, 'You can tell that little bastard I won't hurt him. He's not really a part of it, I know that. He hasn't got the guts.' Okay?"

Yeah, fine. Pretty good judge of character, our Morry. Only the one thing he had wrong: it wasn't lack of guts that kept me from participating in the family business. I did lack guts, that was sure, that was evident every time I met my sister; but there were other chickenhearts among us, and they found a role for themselves. What had always sidelined me wasn't my cowardice, it wasn't even my deep disgust. That was subsequent, maybe consequent. No, what had put me and kept me on the other side of the fence was my total lack of talent.

The family couldn't use me: which was the only reason they had let me go even so far out of their orbit.

But if I couldn't work as my kin did, all open and upfront, maybe I could spy for them on my own account. Never mind that they frightened and disgusted me. Marty had had some kind of face-off with Morry Green, and now Marty was dead; and that was important, that mattered. Whoever it was took Marty's life had taken some part of my own also, and I was feeling the loss of it badly.

43

And Laura didn't know. Remembering that, I took some kind of grip on my turbulent soul. I'd been wrenched too far to manage my usual neutral, the masque I kept for Laura; but I nodded slowly, found half a smile from somewhere, and said, "Come down with me?"

She stiffened. "I don't want to do that," she said, and it had nothing to do with me. That much was clear.

"Please?"

"We'll come," from Dermot, behind me.

"Laura?" I said. "*Please?*"

She hesitated, then nodded in her turn. "All right. Just the two of us, though," over my shoulder, "this isn't a circus turn. You guys wait here, okay? I don't, I don't think we'll be long . . ."

We'll go somewhere else for lunch, she was saying. *If any of us want to eat.*

We wouldn't want to stay, she was saying, *even if we were wanted, and we won't be.*

And she took my hand and held it all the way down the steps, which was meant for comfort but only underlined how all things were turned perverse: that what I had dreamed about so often should come to me with such very bad timing, Laura's hand in mine when my head was all with Marty and with Morry, all questions, hungry for explanation and wanting nothing from, having nothing to offer to her.

Went back down, down and down, it had never felt so far; down and in, to where Morry waited behind the counter.

Not exactly welcoming, Morry. He stood there staring, and his broad hands twitched on the white melamine like they wanted to twitch on my flesh again, to close and grind and pulp, get themselves coated with my dirty Macallan blood.

But, "I want you to see this," he said. "I want you to see what your filthy family has done to us. Come with me."

And he swung back the hatch in the counter-top and let it bang flat, to make a passage through for us. Difficult to hold hands, going single file through that narrow gap; but Laura managed it somehow, she kept a precarious hold on my fingers.

Through the kitchens: bright lights and white walls, smells of frying. Warren watching uneasily from the sink, rubber gloves on his hands and *I'm not serving, I'm not going out there again* on his face, and who could blame him? He might meet more Macallans.

Through a door and then through another, and into a different world: from tiles and lino to wallpapers and carpets, pictures on the walls and the dust-smell of recent Hoovering, a staircase going up.

Up we went too, following Morry's broad back. *Not too close*, his shoulders said, *don't get too close to me.* And I was being careful, I was alert and obedient to unspoken messages; I was getting them from Laura too, feeling the reluctance in her, how heavy her body had become and how weak her legs, *help me, Ben. I'm only here to help you.*

I slipped an arm round her waist on the landing, and there wasn't a thought in my head except to help her, to hold her against the threat of what was coming. She knew what it was, I didn't; she was welcome to lean on my ignorance.

One more door and we were in a bedroom, and now I could understand, and I didn't want to be here any more than Laura.

Second time today, this had happened to me: a bedroom not my own, something I didn't want to see, a big man saying *Look.*

"Look," Morry said. "See? This is what your stinking cousin Marty has done to us, to our family, to our life . . ."

Yes, but what have you done to Marty in return? That was the last aggressive, the last responsive thought I had for a while.

Feeling Morry's strength, feeling his anger, thinking that if not he, then someone in his community might have the knowledge.

Then I crossed the threshold; then – obedient again – I looked, and I saw.

Smelt, too. Not only the deli, this whole building was a place for smells, seemingly; and here without eyes I would never have thought *bedroom*, only *sickroom*. Flowers and herbs I could smell, not strong enough to overcome the stinging astringency of disinfectant; and that in its turn not able to do its proper job, not able to mask what underlay it all, the slow and heavy smell of old corrupted meat.

A woman's bedroom, this. Lace at the windows, lace around the bed, lace at the neckline of her nightie. Shadows of lace on her skin, too, it seemed, overlying her twisted face and the backs of her hands where they lay on the flowery duvet.

But not shadows, no. I looked again and saw lines, a network of creases deep-drawn in the soft flesh of her cheeks, as though a fine mesh were hidden in the folds.

A mesh, or a web: and nothing natural.

Nothing to do with Marty, either.

Almost the worst of this was that I knew the woman in the bed. Everyone knew Aunt Bella. Again, you'd need to be an expert to understand her position in the family tree. Even Morry called her Aunt, but she couldn't conceivably be an aunt to all of them. Just a courtesy title, then, at least from some; but why anyone would choose to be courteous to such a wickedly sharp-tongued old harridan, I never had been able to work out.

She had her place, did Bella: down in the deli, on the customer side, just where the counter met the wall. She'd stand there, leaning on one elbow dunking pieces of doughnut into a bowl of coffee and talking, talking. She'd be the first thing you'd see, coming in, and the only thing about Morry's that could ever make your heart sink. Not enough to keep you away, of course – after all, she wasn't always there; and she was a character, a part of the ambience almost, well worth putting up with for the sake of the food and the company and the Friday prices – but enough to take the gloss off if you weren't in the mood for excoriation.

Old motormouth, Rick called her once; but that was only half of it. It wasn't just the engine that drove her tongue, it was the landscape she drove through, and the mud she so liberally spattered on everyone in hearing. You walked in and she looked at you, up and down in one jerk of her head, like a bird getting your measure; and then it began.

"Tcha, look at that, now. Warren, would you *look* at that? Does he call those decent clothes for going out in, to show himself in the streets, to come and eat lunch in a nice establishment? Does he call himself *dressed?* That shirt's not clean, I can see the tide-mark from here. Look at those cuffs. Doesn't he know how to launder a shirt? Of course he doesn't; and his mother's not here to do it for him, so does he bother? He does not. He just walks around in filthy clothes. Unshaven, too. And not enough beard to boast about, such a fuzz, he should hide his embarrassment, not flaunt it . . ."

And like that, and she really didn't stop. No one was safe; the only protection was to come in groups and talk louder than she did, sit with your backs to the monologue and override it. Worked well enough, though it didn't work well.

Ah, she was bad, was Bella.

Had been bad.

Would be bad no longer. That sharp and savage tongue hung from slack lips now, one all-seeing eye drooped and had a milky glaze across it, her neck couldn't lift the weight of her head to seek a target, she had to have it propped up on a pillow; and God alone knew what was going on in her skull, we

47

didn't have access to that any more.

She'd have looked like a stroke victim, more or less, if it wasn't for the web.

This was no stroke, though. Just another deathbed scene, this, and my second of the morning; there'd be no clawing-back from here, no territory reclaimed. Gone this far, she was gone for good, only that her corpse still breathed. If she were thinking still – *look at that, call this fit company for a woman passed away, what do they think they're doing. Morry coming up here straight from his stoves and the reek of the fat still on him, does he have no respect for the dead* – then she might as well quit now. No more use to her than if she were in her coffin already, thinking away six feet under.

I'd seen those webs before, I knew what they did. I'd even felt them, more than a time or two when I was younger.

At first, the feeling like a plastic bag had been pulled tight over your head; a moment's blind panic before you realised that you could still breathe, even still see a little through the blurring shock of it, and the pain that rode in after.

Then came the slow panic of understanding, and actually that was worse.

This was a binding, like in a dream when you have to move and you can't move: only that there was never any question of this being a dream.

And then it pulled a little tighter, came in under your skin and then there was nothing to see or hear, no world outside and nothing but overarching pain within, your body just a bag of hurting flesh around the bones that shaped it and you just the register of hurt.

And that was a child playing games, no more; and no, it was nothing to do with Marty.

Bella didn't look to be hurting any more, that was something. Though it wasn't really possible to tell. Maybe pain was a kernel, a core of volcanic fire somewhere deep inside: invisible from here, buried too deep but burning, burning.

"What happened, Morry?" I asked, the wrong question again. I knew what, and I knew who. What I wanted was why. Might get that, might not. Morry might not even know.

"Your bastard family *happened*," he said, and his voice was all bile and bitterness; and I wondered how many hundreds, how many thousands of people in this city could only ever speak of the Macallans like that, with that level of hatred and despair.

"Yes, but specifically, I mean . . . ?' *If you can bear to tell me . . .*

"You want specifics? I'll give you specifics. *Specifically*, your shithead cousin Marty came here three times last week, dunning me for cash. I've always been sensible, I've always paid you off and there's never been trouble. But now he wants more, suddenly he's demanding a lot more, and I haven't got it. And I wouldn't give it anyway, such a sum, it would ruin my business to pay such sums; and so I told him. Yesterday he came the third time, and I told him out there," a jerk of his head, "in the street, I wouldn't have him in the shop. And he went away with threats, promising trouble; and that was only yesterday, and last night this."

"This wasn't Marty," I said instantly, unthinkingly, only wanting the record to be straight.

"Oh, what, this just happened, did it, a healthy woman is struck down and it's coincidence, it's nothing to do with you, is that it?"

That's it, it's nothing to do with me. I disinvested. But, "I didn't say that," I said. "It wasn't Marty, that's all." If Marty had been leaning on them, things would have got broken. Bricks, bones, like that. This was altogether too light a touch for Marty, not his fingerprints at all. Not his style, and not his gift. Webbing was unique, even in our family.

"Oh, not Marty, is that right? So who, then, tell me who?"

"There was a girl, right?" *There must have been a girl.*

Morry paused, frowned; said, "Yes, there was a girl." And he'd clearly given her no thought at all, he'd passed her over as unimportant. Listened to Marty's shouting, and no more. *Big mistake, Morry.* "The last time, there was a girl. But she was inside the shop already, I didn't realise at first that she was with him. Bella did, though, Bella put a flea in her ear . . ."

And his bull voice drained of strength then, realising what I was telling him. We both turned involuntarily, to glance again at what had been done to Bella. Hoarsely, almost whispering, he said, "They'd come on a motorcycle, and she was driving. That surprised me, I remember . . ."

I nodded, utterly unsurprised. "Her name's Hazel," I said, figuring that I owed him this much, on my family's behalf. "She's my sister."

And this was her work, no question. Webbing was her talent. And a poor thin moonlight talent it was, just a surface scratching next to the deep-mined riches that others in the family enjoyed; and so much in contradiction to what she was herself, loud and confident, assertive and demanding.

It was enough, though. Put her one-on-one with an ordinary human being and set a moon in the sky, and it would be enough. As it had been. Too much for Bella. My sister had the family pride in full measure, or perhaps a little more than measured, in compensation for the weakness of her gift; she expected herself and all Macallans to be treated with respect, and she didn't know Aunt Bella.

This didn't have anything to do with Morry's not paying up. He could have handed over every penny Marty demanded, it would have made no difference. Hazel had lost face; through her the whole family had been demeaned, at least in Hazel's eyes. And hence this. Punishment or revenge, it didn't matter what you called it. They're interchangeable concepts in any case, it's all a matter of perspective.

"I'm sorry," I said.

"Is there anything . . . ?" Suddenly he was pleading, shaming himself, pride losing out in the face of need: not a concept that would ever have occurred to Hazel. "If you spoke to her, I mean, she could undo it, what she's done . . . ?"

"I don't think so," I said slowly, drawing back as his hand reached out to touch me, for added persuasion. "I don't think she can. She goes this far, it's a one-way street. I'm sorry," again.

"But I sent the money," he said, tears in his eyes now. "First thing this morning, I sent Marty a cheque for the money . . ."

Then you sent it to a dead man. But I didn't say that. Maybe he was conning me here, maybe this was all cover: *Of course I didn't know Marty was dead, how could I? Look, I even sent him a cheque this morning, you can check the postmark, look . . .* Maybe his tears were only remorse, he was surely a sentimental man and if he'd taken a hard revenge on the wrong person, he'd enjoy the chance to regret it. But I didn't believe that. Looking at him, looking at what had happened here, I didn't think he'd had anything to do with Marty's death. His anger was too helpless. He was a strong man on his knees, and he knew it, and that was why he raged.

And he raged only against me, the one Macallan he could be certain wouldn't bite back. To the rest of the family, he sent a cheque. I very much believed in his cheque.

One last time, "I'm sorry," I said. Wasn't the first time I'd apologised for my sister, though I couldn't remember having to do it in worse circumstances, or for a greater offence.

He nodded slowly, acknowledging my weakness in this, as in everything; and ran a meaty hand down over his face, and brought it away damp with sweat or tears, both; and said, "What will, what will happen to her now?"

Webbed like a fly, trapped and taken: what did he think would happen? "She won't die," I said, and tried to make that sound like a positive outcome. *She'll be a living, breathing torment to you, she'll need constant care and she'll snag like wire at your mind, you'll never be free of question: is she conscious, is she suffering, does she understand? And you'll never have any answers, because there's no way of finding out.* Hazel used to web us – usually me – in a temper, or for a joke, or just because she felt like it; but only ever lightly and only briefly, she never let go of the web. She didn't take risks with family.

Animals, though – animals were a different matter. We'd taken a sheep from the moors once when we were twelve, when we were curious and uncaring; got Cousin Ronnie to fetch it down to Uncle James' back paddock in his van, and Hazel had webbed it hard and left it twenty-four hours, moonlight to moonlight. When she'd tried to take the web off, she couldn't. Made sense, we'd thought. It really was like a web, like a net: keep tight hold when you threw it, you could draw it back again. Let go, and it was gone.

We'd dragged the sheep into a muddy dip where no one was going to notice, and charted its progress over the next several days. It had got thinner and dryer, and eventually it had died; but not of the web, we thought. Only thirst and hunger, maybe shock. Maybe pain. We'd tried to find out, we'd experimented as best we could, but we never could be sure if the pain went on, after Hazel let go of a web.

One certain thing, there was no way of asking Aunt Bella, nor would there be. Wherever she'd gone, she wasn't coming back.

Another certain thing. I wasn't coming back to Morry's. If Hazel were concerning herself with his business, I was out of there. Out and gone, I didn't need Morry or anyone to push me. I wouldn't willingly cross paths with my sister, let alone swords.

FIVE

FAMILY FEELING

"I'll come with you," Laura had said, doing her friend-in-need bit and doing it well. Doing it very well, considering. "Of course I will," she'd said. "If you're sure you want to go."

I wasn't sure I wanted to go, no. I wasn't even sure I'd be let through the gates if I did go. But I had all that history pressing at my back, cold and heavy, positively glacial in its resistibility; and I had a conscience of sorts, or at least some kind of moral aesthetic saying that it would be a right deed and a good deed and very possibly a beautiful deed if I did go. And then I had that extra little promise, Laura beside me when I went; and that was the decider that shifted "maybe" into "yes".

And so I went, we went to Marty's funeral.

I wasn't particularly pleased with myself, for taking Laura. She'd seen the Macallans at work now, or at least their aftermath. In the flesh, rather than simply by report. Took her a long time to stop shaking after, and this didn't feel good, bringing her back into their ambit. Good for me, no doubt, good for my craven soul and aesthetically a delight as ever; more than delightful to have her face catch at the corner of my eye when I wasn't even looking for her. Morally, though, not clever. Not right action.

Still, she was here now, I couldn't send her back. And *know thyself* was always a good principle, something to cling to. I knew myself for a coward; and this was appropriate action for a coward, surely, taking his beloved into danger where a brave man would walk alone. More than a confession, then, an honest declaration: I could hold my head high, stepping off the bus and seeing the cemetery railings and reaching instantly for her hand. No shame in it, only fit and proper behaviour for the thing I was . . .

And so on, all the games you play in your head to convince yourself of something patently untrue, to make yourself look a little better in the mirror of your mind. I was playing them all that day, and losing badly. But facts remained, and she *was* there, dressed in black denim and even her lustrous hair looked raven-black today, as if it had darkened a couple of shades as a sign of respect for the departed. Ah, my changeable love, reconfiguring herself for strangers when she wouldn't do it for me, she wouldn't change the simplest thing about her, the one perversity in her, that she didn't love me . . .

Off the bus, along the pavement and here were all those cars again, parked both sides of the street with their wheels up on the kerb and never mind the double yellow lines, no one was going to be handing out tickets to that lot. Macallans and civics, both had immunity in this town.

In the gates and yes, as expected, there were a couple of heavies on guard. Cousins both, so no riff-raff could fool them, no journalist could claim a spurious relationship or any other right to be there. *Know thy cousins* was a family rule, though it was pretty much unnecessary. Most of us carried the family features, stamped heavily on face and body. Big noses and broad flat hands marked out nineteen Macallans in twenty.

Just now two of those noses were pointed directly at us, and the hands that came with them were reaching already. Briefly I thought we really were going to get bumped straight out of there, arse-first if we didn't run now.

But I didn't run, and those hands didn't in the end do any damage. Steve shook my hand, with about as much genuine feeling as he would have accorded the dignitaries who'd arrived before us. He at least seemed to have taken me at my own estimation, rubbed me out of the family bible and barely remembered my name.

Meanwhile Lamartine was scowling, hard fingers right at my throat as he pulled my tie straight.

"Show some respect, for Christ's sake, Ben."

"Uh, sorry, Mar— I mean, Lamartine . . ." He'd been Little Marty all my life, standing just half an inch down from his namesake; but that namesake had sole possession of the name today, and maybe from here on in. Would keep tight hold in his box, maybe, not let it out for common use again.

Lamartine nodded, accepting his full name without violent protest for the first time in my memory. Steve gestured us on down the hill, past another line of cars. Larger, these, more expensive. Distantly, they turned black and enormous. That would be the cortège proper, the hearse and the limousines for family only with the Mayor and his cohorts tagging along behind, chauffeured and official, trying to pretend that they counted for something here.

Tough luck, guys and gals. Lord and knights and ladies. They wouldn't, couldn't fool anyone but themselves and each other. In a gathering like this, only blood counted. The civics were here on sufferance; they could posture as much as they liked, but there were no cameras here to see them. They'd get their hands shaken, no doubt, they might even get their egos stroked a little, a few words from a clan major; but it would mean nothing. If they were honest, they'd know that. Physically rubbing shoulders with Uncle James didn't mean they stood close to the centre of power, or anywhere near it.

But then, of course, if they were honest they wouldn't be civics. Not in this town.

Down the hill, past all the shiny cars; and for the second time in a week I was hand-in-hand with Laura, and for the second time in a week I couldn't give that its rightful priority, I couldn't make it up as a red-letter moment in my private, all-too-slender volume of such moments. Her hand in mind had too little to do with us, too much to do with the crowd of Macallans down there where this line of cars ended, the family standing all together around an open darkness while the civics clustered at their backs.

Traditional people as ever, my family was all in black, as I was; and the only white stood out whiter in consequence. I suppose it's always like that at funerals, I suppose it's meant to be; but even surrounded by a mass of Macallans, any one of whom would act like a magnet on the eye if they were alone, it was the priest who held the power here. The stark surplice helped, limning him in light; that he had the only speaking part, that helped too; and that he had the voice to carry it, a booming baritone we could hear already, carrying to us clear and easy.

What helped most, though, was his simply being himself, the man inside the cassock that was under the surplice, Father Hamish MacDowd.

Our family priest, was Hamish. He baptised us, married us, buried us when need arose. It had never occurred to me that anyone else might stand at Marty's grave-head. No one else had the qualifications. Greed and corruption, those were crucial and Hamish had them in generous measures; but along with them he had a burning faith and a sense of showmanship that had kept us all gobsmacked when we were children, and kept us quiet still. And whatever it was that he did to work that rare magic, it worked as well on the older generations. He had a vampire soul, he could suck the aura from any number of Macallans and appropriate it to himself in an instant charisma-transplant. I never suffered myself, having nothing to lose; but I'd seen cousins and uncles stranded and temporarily baffled, feeling their charm being stolen from them. Those moments were among my happiest adolescent memories, quiet unfading pleasures. Nothing like it when you're ultimately weak and unregarded, to see the strong laid low.

Laura's eloquent hand stilled me at the back of the packed mourners, among the civics. Suited me. I wasn't proud, couldn't afford to be; and no more than she did I fancy squeezing through to the place my blood might entitle me to, right upfront with family at both elbows and at my back, Marty's new home dead ahead. I'd settle for this, hanging around at the fringes and seeing little, only glimpses through the crowd. It all felt woefully familiar. I'd lived most of my life at the fringes, acknowledged and tolerated, but always too weak to be truly welcomed even before I turned traitor and fled.

Besides, it was safer for Laura. Hamish could take it, Hamish could stand in a tight circle of Macallans and feel nothing, seemingly; but I wouldn't chance Laura's more tender flesh among the strange currents and contrary fields that would be warring around that grave now. Mortal girl wasn't made to keep that kind of company. I'd once seen four cousins pack around a punter in a pub, just for the joke of it; he'd done them no harm, only a man trying to get served at the bar. Marty's idea, and no surprise there: "Let's show Ben," he'd said. "Come on, all of us, make it better that way."

The others had grinned, and gone with him. They'd crowded the poor guy without even touching him, just making a wall of their bodies around him. Briefly, I lost sight of him; but then there he was, thrusting them heedlessly apart and reeling towards the door like a man long gone in drink when he'd only just come in, he hadn't had one yet. I saw his face good and close, saw the sweat standing out on his pale skin, saw the tremble under his skin. And then his mouth opened and a thin vomit gushed out, and he doubled up around his voiding stomach; and they hadn't even *touched* him, he'd only stood for a few seconds too close to too many Macallans.

Some of these civics weren't looking too good even now, even with fresh air at their backs and my family's eyes and minds turned altogether the other way. Those who'd gone to the wake, I thought, would have had a dreadful time of it; and no, I wasn't exposing Laura to the least risk of that. Shouldn't have brought her in the first place, in all honesty. Here despite that, I had a duty to keep her safe, as well as an overmastering wish. I'd keep her physically as far as possible from any congregation of my family, and hurry her away at the slightest sign of distress.

I couldn't see the grave now, for the mass of people between it and us; but Hamish's rich voice came rolling out to us quite undiminished. Solemn and heartfelt, it talked of sure and certain hope. The only thing that I was sure and certain of was that Marty was dead and gone, far beyond hope, but still I couldn't call Hamish a liar even in the most private recesses of my mind. Hamish *believed*; you had to give credence to that, whatever else you knew about the guy.

The old traditional service, sonorous and potent; prayers and hymns and my sister's acid voice cutting through the mumbles all around me, high and clear and doing properly whatever was there to be done, be it singing the soprano line or simply saying "Amen".

The surprise was Laura at my side, warmly contralto and equally loud. Perhaps I shouldn't have been surprised; I knew she could sing, from sessions at the Irish Centre and kitchen ceilidhs and walks home from the pub. And I knew too that she had as little patience as Hazel with tasks skimped. Of course she would sing out, now that I thought about it, too late. Perhaps I could only legitimately be surprised that she knew the words; but then, a country doctor's daughter, she'd probably been hauled along to church every Sunday, as I had.

I loved her voice, as I loved everything about her, but just that day I could have lived without it. Most people go to funerals to be seen by the living, by the relatives, to have their sorrow duly observed and registered; but not I, not that day. Arrive late and leave early, straight after the last "Amen", that was the plan. Be there for Marty, but not at all for any other of my blood. What I wanted was to come and go entirely unnoticed, except for the cousins on the gate.

With Laura's rich voice laying umbrous sweetness on the day, there was little chance of that.

Our civic neighbours glanced at us, awkwardly askance, *who is this girl? Doesn't she know what's right, what's fitting at a funeral?*

I wasn't worried about them, though. What bothered me was the heads turning from further forward, the attention we were surely attracting from the graveside and the grim and certainly untearful mourners grouped there.

Might just as well push my way through to join them, *hi Mum, Dad, Uncle James. Hullo, Hamish.*

Hullo, Hazel.

Close my eyes and I could *feel* Laura's singing, pulsing through her fingers into mine, beating into the very bones of me.

So I did that for the last hymn, closed my eyes and felt, felt closer almost than ever before; but as soon as Hamish had pronounced the blessing I shifted my hand in hers, from a linkage to a firm grip. Tug and turn, and *let's get out of here* . . .

I tugged and we turned, and it was too late already.

With my eyes closed, of course, I hadn't been watching our neighbours; hadn't seen someone else shuffling sideways, shuffling silently between the civics, drawn like any predator to the sound of innocence, the sound of Laura's voice.

Jamie smiled at me, from barely two feet away.

Pale in his black suit, inevitably shaken at his brother's funeral, it wasn't too striking a smile, but it did the job. It held me, for the time it took to think *no*, to think *no, can't just nod and push by, not here, not today. He's burying his brother, how can I not give him what he wants?*

So I stood still, drew Laura a little closer, did my best to smile back.

"Ben," he said. "I'm glad you came."

"How could I not?"

"Yeah," he said. "Right." And then his eyes shifted, me to Laura and back to me. His face quirked a question, teasing even here as if to show me how far he'd come, how much better he was than he had been, how much more himself: *who's the girlfriend, Ben boy?*

"Uh, Laura, this is Jamie," I said reluctantly. "My cousin, James Macallan. Junior," because I could tease too, even in this situation, even doing the one thing I'd always sworn to avoid, introducing Laura to my family. "Jamie, Laura."

"Hi, Laura," Jamie said, seeming not even to register how little I'd given him there, barely a name and nothing more.

"Hullo." And she slipped her hand free of mine, to shake his; and she didn't need to do that, he wasn't offering. I saw the tingle hit her, saw her eyes stretch briefly in surprise. She recovered quickly, though, didn't even pull her hand back till he released it. Then, remembering her manners like the nicely-brought-up girl she was, "I'm sorry about, um," and she glanced at me for help and didn't get it fast enough, because I was off on another track altogether, remembering girls at parties, girls at discos. Marty and Jamie deliberately touching them up just for the shock value, just to see how they reacted. In comparison, Laura had come out pretty well. Naturally.

Meanwhile, she was having to busk. "Your cousin?"

"My brother," Jamie said; which doubled the reproach in the glance Laura shot at me, *you could have told me that.*

"Oh, that's terrible. I'm so sorry; but I don't suppose that helps, does it?"

He shrugged, wordlessly agreeing: yes, it was terrible and no, the sympathy of a stranger didn't noticeably help. Then he turned to me again, said, "You should go and say hullo. Let them know you're here, at least."

No. "Why?"

"They'll find out anyway."

And he was right, of course they would. The cousins on the gate knew already; they'd tell someone, even if Jamie didn't. Even if I hadn't been spotted already, if Laura's voice hadn't attracted more than one cousin's curiosity.

Benedict came, they'd be saying to each other over the sandwiches after. *Didn't you know? No, I didn't see him, no one did. Not to talk to. Came late, slipped away early. Like a coward*, they'd be saying, no doubt, *like a thief.* Which was more or less what I was, in their eyes: frightened of my rightful place in the world order, and consequently thief of the family honour.

Ordinarily, I could live with that. But Laura was with me today and I didn't want to score so poorly under her gaze, too scared to talk to my own relatives at a cousin's funeral.

Still, there wasn't an option, actually. Which was how I liked it, cowardice made compulsory.

"I'm not taking Laura into that," I said, jerking my head towards a tight circle, Macallans all in orbit around Uncle James and his anger, his dead son.

They'd both understand that, I thought, though they would understand different things by it. She'd think I meant only the raw emotional aura of a family in turmoil and distress; he'd know how much more I actually meant, how frightened I'd be for her in that company.

"No," he said. "It's all right, I'll look after Laura. Go on, shouldn't take you a minute." *They're not going to want to talk.*

Laura nodded. "Go. We'll be fine," looking at Jamie with puzzlement and interest, mixed with sympathy. Her fingers would still be tingling, I guessed.

And now there truly wasn't an option. I nodded, turned away and left her; walked alone into the dangerous circle of my family, as dangerous to me, perhaps, as it would have been to her; found my sister there, of course, and my parents, and Uncle James swollen up by grief and anger, where most self-important men would have been reduced.

And, important to us all, I found Uncle Allan there also.

Allan Macallan, head of the clan, didn't seem so much at first sight. Line up the three brothers, my grandfather's sons, and the eldest looked far the least of them. He was the shortest by some inches, and easily the lightest; where Uncle James was heavy with purpose and good living, where my father Charles was heavy with beer and inaction, Uncle Allan was lean as a whip. The family features, the nose and the hands looked utterly misplaced on such a small man. He resembled a steeplechase jockey more than a godfather.

But the nightfire burned in his eyes even in daylight, when they were none of them strong. It wasn't only birthright that held the family obedient under him, that gave such weight to his will. He might carry it modestly, but Uncle Allan had more talent to give away than Uncle James would ever possess. Talent was power; we Macallans always listened to talent, and the town listened to us, from long experience of the consequences of not listening. Which gave Uncle Allan more power locally than he wanted or knew what to do with.

Luckily he was wise as well as talented. I remembered Marty grumbling often when we were kids, grumbling in his father's voice, saying that Allan used his power far more against his own family than in their support; and privately I always thought that was how it should be. Intellectual and constantly questioning, it was the theory of talent that fascinated him far more than its practice. The only time I'd ever seen him in his true light was once when he had to come down hard to contain one of his brother's cruder schemes – a beacon Allan had been in his anger, his skin blazing; trees had died that night simply for his standing beside them – and thank God for someone who could do that, who could give the town at least a little protection. With no curbs at all, Uncle James' greed backed by the strength and simple unconcern of my younger cousins could have built a tyrannical hell out of what was in any case an oligarchy of blood.

Shuffling my way through the pack of my relatives, nodding back recognition where it was nodded at me, shaking what few hands were offered me and pausing politely to listen if anyone deigned actually to speak, I thought that this was easy after all, that I could simply slither my way through like grass through a Canada goose and be out and free again, just a little shit hurrying back to Laura.

But I had to be polite to Uncle James; and of course Uncle Allan was standing right next to him. Such an occasion, where else would he be?

Allan had always been special to me. Special to all of us, I think; but to me he was the father-figure my father never was, the god of my childhood and the consolation of my hard adolescence.

And I hadn't seen him for three years, he had necessarily been disowned along with the others, guilty by definition; and there was no question of my passing him by with a nod or a handshake or a false polite smile.

No question of that, even if he'd been willing to allow it. In fact it was he who detained me, hand on my arm and, "Benedict. Good to see you," and no question of that either, he meant it truly. "Can we talk?"

I glanced sideways, but Uncle James had already turned away, after a cold word of greeting and a fleeting handshake.

"Of course we can talk, uncle. Please, I'd like to." *I need to.*

He nodded, receptive as ever, and guided me away, still keeping that grip on my arm. He'd always been one for touching; but he had a purpose over and above the implicit messages. *You're family*, his fingers said on my skin. *Whatever happens, you belong. We belong together, you and I.* All that was there and hard to argue with, because only fingers said it and no way was I pulling free; but more than that, his fingers asked a question and found an answer in my flesh.

He asked the same question aloud, though, as soon as we were alone, in the shadow of a high mausoleum. Never one to hide his thoughts, he stroked my shaven cheek and said, "Still nothing, then, my poor Ben?"

"Not a glimmer," I said, trying to sound ebullient. "Believe it, uncle." *Believe what your fingers tell you, there's no thrill in my blood, no potent tingling.* "Whatever talent there was my father passed down, my sister got it. Came first, and grabbed it all."

"Mm. Well, it's not strong in your father, of course. And he did marry out." Briefly, Uncle Allan sounded like nothing so much as a disappointed scientist, seeing a breeding experiment gone wrong. "Too much dilution, I suppose . . ."

Ever the theorist, he'd been fascinated by me since I reached puberty, and my lack of talent became increasingly evident.

There was no history of twins in our family; that came from my mother's side, where for once a Macallan hadn't married a cousin. No one had known what to expect of Hazel and me, so of course they'd expected what was normal between brother and sister, that I would develop a talent and Hazel none. That it had come out entirely the other way around had been a source of profound embarrassment to my father, the cause of many a battle for me until I'd simply stopped fighting, and a matter of endless detached interest to Uncle Allan.

"Uncle?"

"Mm?"

"What, what *happened*?"

"To Marty? I can't say. Yet," with just the glimmer of a promise in the word, *I'll find out*. "I'm not clairvoyant, Ben, as you know; and I wasn't even in town at the time. But – well, one conclusion seems unavoidable, doesn't it?"

"Does it?" To him, perhaps. Not to me.

"Come on, Ben. Concentrate. You've never been stupid. And you saw Marty's body, I'm told."

"Yes." Everyone had seen the body. But it was no surprise if Uncle Allan had asked specifically about me. I thought he'd been keeping a particular eye on me, even through my exile-of-choice.

"Well, then? What were your own conclusions?"

That Marty had died in pain, largely; that he'd been attacked by something his bull strength and his rough-riding spirit couldn't begin to fight. I'd not thought about it beyond that, too busy with my own reactions to look for ultimate causes. But as Allan said, one dispassionate glance and it was obvious, it was inescapable.

"Talent," I said. "Whoever did that to him had talent." Unusual talent, to be sure, and more refined than anything I'd seen before, but talent none the less.

"Yes. And you know what that means, Benedict Macallan?"

"Yeah." I was a good boy, me, or I had been once. I knew my catechism. "It means we've been wrong all these years. It means we're not alone after all, we're not the only ones . . ."

And more than that, it meant whoever else was out there had come looking for us; and they weren't friendly, and we didn't have the first idea who they were . . .

SIX

DRIVING TO DESPAIR

It was them and us, as ever; only that *them* had suddenly become *us* again, or seemed so. Particularly when I got back to Laura, and found Jamie chatting up my girl.

Felt like coming home, that did. Felt like I'd never been away. All the fruits to the victor and the sweets to the strong, that was in the family catechism also, always had been; and I'd never been strong, rarely victorious.

Already wasn't either, with Laura. Folly even to think of her in those terms, as *my girl*, the one thing she indisputably was not. And it seemed nothing but normal to discover Jamie standing too close to her, concentrating too much, giving her more attention than he ought on such a day, in such a place as this. Likewise nothing but normal to see how she allowed it to happen, where with any other near-stranger she'd be backing off, powering down fast, shutting him altogether out.

"Ben." It was Jamie who noticed me first. He smiled and took an easy pace away from her, making room for me; but that was nothing to do with ceding territory, or acknowledging a prior claim. It was an expression of power and utterly Macallan, a message to Laura only: *Look*, he was saying, *I'm interested, but not that interested. I write the definitions here, I set the parameters.*

Your choice, to accept that or reject it; but either way, it's the last and only decision to fall to you.

And there was a twitch of disappointment to her face as he took that step back, as he gave her space to breathe in; and I'd seen this so often before, and I knew what happened after, and I couldn't bear it. Not for her, not for Laura . . .

"You can't go," I said, on the bus going home. "Not with him, not a Macallan. For God's sake, Laura," trying to set some parameters myself, trying to exercise a little power on my own behalf and hers, "you couldn't be so stupid. You mustn't. I've told you what they're like, I've told you and told you . . ."

"I'm curious," she said, "that's all. What's wrong with that? You've been talking about them all this time, of course I'm curious to see them for myself. Who wouldn't be?"

Almost anyone else in this town wouldn't be, I thought, *they've all got more sense, they're all scared shitless. Seeing Macallans for themselves, in the flesh, is the very last thing they're curious to do, and quite right too.* But I couldn't say that aloud, she'd only look on it as a challenge.

"I don't talk about them," I protested weakly. "Except to warn people, I mean. I *never* talk about them . . ."

"You just think you don't. You're obsessed, Ben. You're on about it all the time, how they run this town, how they're behind everything that happens. Even when you're not saying anything, I can see you thinking about them. And you do things just because they wouldn't, or because they wouldn't approve. Your whole life's still mediated by being a Macallan. It's just that these days you're trying to be a bad Macallan, because you know you'll never make a good one. Striving for the opposite only confirms the potency of the original state."

Oh my dear, darling Laura. She talked like that sometimes, when her psychology textbooks got the better of her. When she

68

forgot about the sympathy thing, when she was irritated enough to go for honesty and just say what she saw.

Oh my dear, darling, clear-sighted Laura . . .

"And that being so," she added, a little more gently and a lot too late, "I'm entitled to be curious, aren't I? About my friend's obsessions?"

"That's not," I said thickly, "that's not why. Is it? That's just camouflage. You're only trying to make me feel better."

"All right, yes. I'm trying to make you feel better. That's allowed, isn't it? That's legitimate? It's not as if I have to do it, I'm not obliged. You don't have any lien over my activities. Try being grateful, why don't you? Just for once?"

"*Grateful?* Christ . . ."

"Or if you can't do that," and she was pulling herself back now, reining in the sharpening anger and making one last effort to keep things peaceable between us, "at least try being sensible. It's not like he asked me for a date or anything," with just a hint of wistfulness in her voice, as though her curiosity stretched further than she were willing to admit even to herself. "I only said I'd go, *we'd* go," touching my hand where it gripped the seat in front, "I said we'd go out for a drink with him, for his birthday. What's wrong with that, for God's sake? It's you he wants anyway, not me. I was just a tool, to make sure you said yes. Because you wouldn't have, would you? If he hadn't asked me first?"

I wasn't sure. A week ago, no, definitely not; but things had changed, were changing. Old loyalties were resurgent, old feelings coming to life again. I might have said yes, I thought. Or I might not, couldn't be certain.

But Laura had said yes, with no equivocation. "Yes," she'd said, "I'd like to. Very much," she'd said; and after that again I didn't have the option. Call it jealousy, call it chivalry, call it what you will: no way was Laura going out with Jamie without me there to sit between them. I could act as a blanket, at least, even if she thought me a wet one. I could use the advantages of my blood as a weapon against the advantages of his, to keep between her and the tingle of his touch. To keep curiosity from turning to fatal fascination. For her own good, I could act as insulation.

"He said you were like brothers," she told me, "when you were kids. And it was almost like losing a brother, when you walked out. He said that. He said, when Marty died, he said it was almost like the second time around. He wants you back, Ben, that's all. What's wrong with that?"

There was plenty wrong with that, and she should have known it without asking. Hard to believe that she could be so naïve.

If it were true, if Jamie did want me back, he wasn't the only one. Allan would welcome this straying sheep's return, that was clear. Jamie might simply be his missionary, his message-bearer . . .

I sat there on the bus, silent for the rest of the journey, thinking about the implications; but when Laura nudged me, "Wake up, guy. I want to get off, if you don't," I still hadn't come to any resolutions.

Specifically, I still hadn't worked out which scared me more: that Jamie had been telling the truth, that he simply wanted me back and was using Laura as a means to that end; or that it worked the other way, that he wanted Laura and was using me to get her.

Either one was possible; and either one, I thought, spelled disaster. For me, or else for her and me together. Laura's disasters were my disasters, that was foreordained. Whatever happened here, I couldn't escape it; and it couldn't, couldn't possibly be to the good.

Off the bus and into school like good children, she to her lectures and I to mine. That was likely to be my last sight of her for a few days, and I didn't like leaving her like this. I should never have

70

taken her with me, that was obvious; if I were honest, it had been obvious all along, only that I hadn't been seeing clearly or hadn't chosen to. One selfish or wrong decision, and suddenly she was dangerously exposed, and wouldn't let me protect her.

I'd been anxious earlier about their effect on her, and I'd let bad sense override my judgement. What I hadn't had the wit even to wonder about was her effect on them. Perhaps I'd been too long away, perhaps I had genuinely forgotten a dozen, two dozen minor humiliations during the long agony of my adolescence. I remembered them well enough now, too late, when they should have been hot in my mind before. I should have known, no way could I turn up at any family gathering with a girl in tow, and not have one of the cousins see that as a challenge. It had always been one of their games, *let's take his new toy away from Benedict.* They could do it, they always had been able to do it; and because they could, they did.

And now it was happening again, and that it was Jamie making the moves and Laura the target only added to my grief.

I did no good work that day. I barely listened in the lectures, made no notes and no contribution to that afternoon's seminar. I should have gone to the library as soon as we were out, to sweat for an hour over an essay already overdue; instead I drifted off into the park, watched little kids hurl bread and gravel at the ducks, and let my feet slowly take me back to the flat.

Walking in, I heard music. Through to the kitchen and it got loud, fiddle and whistle riding a relentless rhythm: Jacko and his posse, playing jigs and reels in the back yard. I glanced out of the window to see Jacko himself perched on the wall eight feet up, hammering his bodhrán with vigour.

Jacko was a drama student, but – unusually for that crowd – he seemed to have no strong vocation as an actor. Too much realism in his make-up, probably. You need more than talent to make it in any career so dependent on the public's approval; and while I couldn't speak for his ability, I'd never seen him act, I knew Jacko's body too well ever to imagine his name in lights. Frail and pale, chicken-skin stretched over a frame of animated wires and topped with a face too crudely made: he didn't stand a chance.

And I thought perhaps he knew it, perhaps that was why he didn't spend all his time talking or dreaming or studying theatre as so many of his cohorts did, what hours they weren't rehearsing or performing. Jacko performed, just as much or more; but his passion was folk, pure Irish for preference but anything trad in a pinch. He was currently gigging with three separate bands, both student and semi-pro, and he'd travel miles for a casual session in a pub any night he happened to be free.

He could play almost anything with strings, or so it seemed to me, who couldn't find three chords on a guitar; but he'd put down the fiddle or the mandolin anytime, to pick up his bodhrán. He had an actor's love of drums, there at least his training showed: inherent drama, speaking directly to the blood. He'd said to me once, "You don't need melody at all, it's rhythm that makes music work. Rhythm makes the bones. Like everything. Rhythm makes the world work. It's all just a matter of timing."

"Nah," I said, coldly certain. "Light," I said. "Light makes the world work."

"That's what I said," he said. "Light *is* rhythm, didn't you know? Go back to first principles. *Everything* is rhythm."

He was the one with the physics "A" level, not me. I hadn't argued any further. I knew what I knew, and I didn't really want to persuade anyone else that I was right. Too, too depressing, for me and them both.

I checked the time, then stepped through the open door into the yard to count heads.

Jacko up on the wall, Colin leaning casually against it with his fiddle tucked into his elbow rather than under his chin; he always played like that, maddening the purists – Jacko included – and producing a sweet, swift sound they couldn't criticise, that only maddened them more. Joe the guitarist, sitting on an upturned dustbin; Carol all but swamped by her giant squeezebox, while her eight-year-old Nicky strummed a washboard beside her, frowning with concentration, not to lose time; and Lynn on penny whistle made six in the band this afternoon.

I filled the kettle and set it to boil in anticipation; tea-breaks were a regular feature of band practice. Then I filled the pressure-cooker, also with water, and set that also to boil. The seal was broken, so it didn't actually work under pressure, but it was the largest pot we had.

Outside the music thinned, just fiddle and penny whistle playing a measure together and playing it again, Colin teaching Lynn on the monkey-see monkey-do principle. The door opened and Carol came in, with Nicky at her heels.

"Nick wants a drink," she said. "Got any juice?"

"Sure." One certainty in this flat, there was always juice. We could be vicious with each other, waking up dry and desperate to find the fridge empty. There was a corner shop twenty yards down the street, but that was no use to us; juice needed to be shockingly cold, warm just didn't do it.

"Orange or grapefruit, Nicky? Or, what's this, apple juice, how's about apple for a change?"

Change wasn't on the menu, apparently; Nicky wanted orange. I waited for Carol to see to it, then said, "What about the rest of you, then? Cup of tea?"

"Love one. I'll fetch the mugs in, shall I?"

"No, me," Nicky said. "I'll do it."

He skipped off out, came back more cautiously with six mugs clutched in his two small hands. I emptied a mound of wet teabags out of our giant brown teapot, put in another handful from the box; Carol rinsed the mugs under the tap, and fetched milk from the fridge.

Waiting for the kettle to boil, I got back to working out the rice. Carol watched, asked, "What's that for?"

"Tea," I said. "You lot get started, you're not going home to eat. I mean, are you?"

"Well, no. We don't get many chances, all of us together like this; shame to waste them when they come. But isn't it a bit early?" Checking her watch with one eyebrow already raised to underline what she knew she'd see, big hand on the three and little hand just past the four, not even Nicky's tea-time yet.

"Yeah, but I'm driving tonight. Have to be there at six. It's silly for both of us to cook, and Jacko won't want to stop anyway; so I'll leave him a mound of rice and other stuff all ready, and when you're hungry he can just chuck it in the wok and that's that."

"Time and motion," she said, nodding. "Neat."

"Yeah."

"So what are you driving? Van, taxi? Choo-choo train?"

That brought me up short, briefly: just a quick reminder that not everyone I counted as a friend was familiar with the intimate details of my life. I only knew Carol through Jacko, through casual encounters like this; and I really only knew Jacko through his music. We shared a flat amiably enough, but we didn't talk much. I tended to forget, family history doesn't pass itself around by osmosis, even though it seems that way sometimes. People have to be interested enough to gossip.

I shook my head. "Dangerous doctors."

"I'm sorry?"

"The Doctors' Deputising Service. DDS. Dangerous Doctors for short," only the joke was too tired, sometimes too accurate even to smile at now. "Basically, if GPs are too lazy to do their own night calls, they pay the service to provide a locum. The service pays the company I work for to provide a car, a radio, and a driver; and that's me. I do a couple of shifts a week, sometimes a double shift at weekends."

Carol nodded. She lived a student life, even though she was ten years past being a student; she was used to seeing her friends take any short-term, part-time work they could to eke out an uncertain income. "What's the money like?"

"Not brilliant." Essential, though. It was more or less all I had now. No State benefits for students, and no grant for Benedict Macallan. Uncle James had seen to that, with my father nodding support somewhere in the background. I'd had life easy up to then, I'd been told flatly; if I wanted to go through with this ridiculous rebellion thing, then I could have it the other way. No middle course, ever, with Uncle James. If I wasn't with them then I was utterly and irrevocably against them, and he'd see that I suffered for it.

At the time, that had suited me perfectly. I'd wanted to make a martyr of myself. I had too much guilt and muddle on my back; poverty was a relief, an atonement almost.

Now it was just a bore. I'd taken all the loans I was entitled to, and as much more as I could screw from my bank manager before Uncle James got to him too; but some weeks I could barely feed myself, and the rent was a major crisis every month.

Garlic, onion, courgette and tomato, and a little red pepper for a treat; fry 'em all up in the wok, add the rice, break an egg in and there you go. Eat with chopsticks and chilli sauce, to make it taste of something.

Vegetarian by necessity, sometimes I longed for meat. I wanted to set up self-help groups for people with the same desperate cravings: "Hullo, my name's Ben, I'm a carnivore." Like any self-confessed addict, I didn't dare allow myself the slightest taste of what I so desired; like many, I found in symbolism what bare strength I needed. It wasn't just the cost that kept me a meat-free zone. Walking away from my family, I'd walked away too from the habits and traditions that bound us together, at least as far as I was able; and diet was one of the easiest to change. All my life I'd lived with bacon for breakfast and a roast at dinner, plenty of cold meat in the fridge for sandwiches between, and the constant impression that a meal wasn't a meal unless some animal had died to provide it. It had been no hardship at first, to reject that along with other, more significant family values.

Now though – ah, now I hungered for the taste of blood in my mouth sometimes, and wouldn't take it even when it was offered. Perverse or essential, it was one of the rules I'd lived by ever since I'd started writing my own rule-book, and not subject to change even if I'd had the means to change it.

Which at the moment I most emphatically did not; and I'd better hurry, if I wanted to cling on to the most basic means to live. They had a waiting-list of willing drivers for Medicall, despite the antisocial hours, so they could afford to be unpleasant if you turned up late.

A run for the bus at one end, a run from the stop at the other: I made it with three minutes to spare, before my six o'clock shift. Cutting it so fine brought its own punishments. No choice of cars, for a start. We drove white Fiestas with no markings, not to draw attention to the highly-marketable drugs we were carrying around in the boot; unfortunately, a fair few policemen also drove anonymous white Fiestas with whip aerials just like ours. The local lads used to hot around the area in their stolen Sierras looking for cops to ram, and once a month or so they'd ram one of us by mistake. It didn't do the cars too much good. They got serviced, of course, they got patched up as well as the garage could manage, but there were always one or two rogues in the pool, with erratic problems no one had sorted out yet.

There were rogue doctors too, inevitably: that "dangerous" tag wasn't too off-target, in some cases. Others were terrific, working Medicall shifts on top of a day-job for the very best of reasons, but drivers couldn't pick and choose. Turn up early and you might strike lucky, as I did on good days, having a favourite doctor ask for me specially. Turn up in the very nick of time, like tonight, and luck just wasn't a feature.

I was last in, and there was just the one doctor waiting for me, in a bad mood already with a hefty list of calls to make down the dodgy end of town. I'd driven this guy before, and spending six hours cooped up with him in the closest of quarters was some considerable distance from my definition of a good time. I sighed inwardly, as I collected keys from the desk controller. It was going to be a long night.

His name was Devereux, *Doctor* Devereux to me and my kind, we common drivers; and if we existed on a lower social level than his own sweet self, then his patients for the night were so far beneath him he could barely be bothered to feel contempt for them.

"Scum of the earth," he said, as we headed downhill towards the first of the night's calls. "You can chart it, demographically. The closer you come to the river, the more inbred they are. And the more stupid, the more ugly, the more vicious . . ."

I nodded vaguely, concentrated on driving. I'd heard it all before. And besides, I had my own experience of inbreeding, and of stupidity and ugliness and viciousness. There wasn't much he could tell me about it, but neither was I on any safe ground to start an argument.

We'd been four hours on the road, we'd worked our way through that first list we'd started out with – the good doctor spending an average of three minutes and fifty-five seconds in each house, I was passing the time by counting – and we'd had as many calls again come in on the radio. Normally I brought sandwiches and a can of Coke to tide me over, but I'd been too much rushed tonight; and while some doctors were amenable to refreshment breaks – one even bullying me back to his house a couple of times for a chicken curry if we were on top of the work – I wasn't going to broach the subject with Devereux.

Instead, I decided that the car was going to break down. Not badly, just enough that I'd need to pull into a garage and fiddle under the bonnet, and buy myself a pint of milk and a stottie while I fiddled.

Not yet, though. I'd wait a little longer, and hope that things quietened down a bit.

On the way from one call to the next, trying to find one small cul-de-sac in a dead-end estate that was all dirty concrete and no street-lights, every other window boarded up and not a street-name to be seen, I heard something that was neither the radio nor Devereux's endless, grumbling voice.

Instantly, automatically, I had the car stopped and my door open, to hear better.

"What?" Devereux demanded. "What is it, why've you stopped? This isn't what we're looking for . . ."

No more it was; but suddenly here it came again, somewhere close, a man's voice screaming in high agony.

That time Devereux heard it too, and was still for a moment; then, "Not our responsibility," he said, as I should have expected. "Leave it alone, for God's sake, we're not the police."

Ignoring him, I got out of the car – and then I could see, as well as hear. Then I knew. Not my responsibility, no, I'd disinvested; but not well enough, seemingly. At any rate, there was no question of my leaving it alone.

Through an archway under a run of flats, through a short square tunnel came that wailing scream again, and a light that failed as the scream failed: a cold, pale, flickering light, the nightfire that marked all my family but me.

Somewhere through that archway there was a Macallan in desperate trouble, his strength no succour now; and me, I was already moving.

SEVEN

TOTAL MELTDOWN

Through the tunnel at a run, heedless and stupid, and what was that Devereux had been saying about inbreeding? "Vicious" I might have argued with, back then at least, but the rest was plain to be seen.

Through the tunnel and into a mugger's paradise, one of those Sixties housing experiments that went so dreadfully wrong. It was an enclosed court, with blocks of flats three or four storeys high and no grass, only paving underfoot. Just the one way in and out for cars, but several more of those tunnel passageways; and balconies and stairwells all around, any route you fancied to go under or over or through, and hardly a light to see it by except for the car burning like a torch, like a lantern, like a sign.

No noise, no heat. Nightfire's no true flame, unless it's the opposite of that: unless it's the truest expression of flame and mortal fire is only a clumsy imitation.

Nightfire doesn't feed on what it burns. Destruction isn't incidental. Where it touches, damage is cold and slow; the light it throws is blue and thin and telling. Seen once, there's no mistaking it.

Here was a car burning that way, the metal of it writhing as I watched; and someone of my kin had set it to burn there. That was a given, didn't need debating.

No one in sight, though, no one at all. There should at least have been faces lining the balconies, peering down. Not all those flats were empty. A fire, and a man's screams: they should have been irresistible.

But maybe these riverine families weren't so stupid after all, however inbred they might be. I guessed that the people who lived around here would know nightfire as well as I did and were being as wise as they knew how, keeping behind closed doors and shuttered blinds. If a Macallan was screaming, they truly didn't want to know.

That's what it was, no question: the man who set that fire to burn was the same man who'd been tearing the night apart with his howls. This was Jacko's universal rhythm in action, and inarguable. The light had flared with the scream, searingly bright, striking out through that passageway to find me; and now in the scream's silence it flickered and guttered, bright enough in here where no light was, but no beacon now.

I might have no fire of my own but at least I wasn't vulnerable here, my blood was worth that much to me. I could walk up to the flaming car, and did; I could and did walk around it, looking to see inside, seeing nothing but fire and distortion; being that close I could and did stumble over the body lying dark on dark paving, lying where no one would see him because they'd all be looking into the light.

It was only logic now, told me that this was a Macallan. All his skin was moving.

I knelt beside him when kneeling was the last thing I wanted to do, or close to the last. Kissing him would have been bottom, maybe, but any form of getting closer was bad. Kneeling was quite bad enough. It took me near enough to see and to smell what was happening to him, without doing what it was meant for. My eyes searched him desperately, clothes and skin, looking for any giveaway, any clue as to who this was; but seemingly I didn't know my family well enough. Take their faces away, and I couldn't tell one cousin from another.

This one, this cousin wasn't dead yet, and neither was his body dead, though I thought perhaps the two of them were independent now. I thought his body might go on containing life for a while, only that it wouldn't be his own. I thought giant maggots infested his flesh, because I could see them writhing.

Even in that cold light he looked hot, and when I touched him his skin was baking dry, baking from the inside out and scurvy with salt, where all his moisture was leaving him. Touching him, I felt something buck and swell beneath my fingers, hardening like an egg in a hurry as it grew, as I saw it distend on his arm.

I snatched my hand away, too late ever to forget how that had felt.

Watching, surely doing no more than wait for an inevitable death in the family, it never occurred to me to call for the doctor somewhere in the night behind me. Even if I'd liked the man, if I'd wanted to let him anywhere near any cousin of mine, there was no work for him here. This was talent at work, and way beyond any talent there might be in the medical profession. We might inhabit the same world, but Jacko would say that even the molecules in our bodies marched to a different beat.

I had a body in my arms now, I was hugging a cousin I couldn't name, although I loathed to touch him. I only watched his face, but there I saw things swell like muscles clenching and move like internal leeches through his veins.

His eyes were open, watching me; but he was long past screaming now. All the whites of his eyes were black, and God only knew what he was seeing. I didn't believe it, try though I might, though I did; but still I hoped, I *hoped* he saw a cousin, he saw family come to hold him at the last.

I couldn't help it, we're a sentimental breed. Rod McKuen poetry and big-eyed little kittens, and all that candyfloss crap. It worked, somehow; even for me, even then, it still worked. Went with the territory, I guess. When home is the definition of comfort and family is the only definition of home, emotions need to be as artificial and dishonest as the environment, and they need to feel as real.

And you could see through it, as I had; and you could try to walk away, as I did; and you still wound up taking it all with you. "Seasons in the Sun" could still make me sniffle. And yes, if a man had to die, I still thought he should die with his family around him.

Christ, sometimes I still thought that was what I wanted for myself. Morbidity went with the territory too, especially the territory that I occupied then, that I'd hacked out for myself; I thought about dying all the time. And when I thought about doing it slowly and in a bed, it was family I imagined being there with me. Faces in the gloom, Jamie and Uncle Allan. They were the ones I wanted. Not my parents, so much; they could be there if they chose, but I wouldn't send for them. Favourite uncle and favourite cousin had always been my choice, and still was.

And Laura, of course. Family, right? Favourite uncle, favourite cousin, wife. That was how I dreamt it, when I allowed myself to dream.

Dreaming's shit, sometimes.

Dreaming's shit, but dying's worse; and watching someone die, that comes somewhere between the two I guess. It ain't good, but it's got to be better than the other thing, better than doing it yourself. Hasn't it?

*   *   *

Couldn't hold his gaze, not with pale blue irises bulging at me, all
but engulfed in sick black; but I didn't take my eyes from his
changing face. I owed him that much, at least, whoever he was;
and slowly, slowly I worked it out. All the flesh on him was in
motion, heaving and subsiding like mud in a geyser-hole, a little
too thick to burst; but his bones were holding their shape, I could
see how long his jaw was. And his brown hair chopped short and
thinning a little on top, but still thick as a hedge round the sides;
and those eyes the clincher, pale blue and unusual. Only one slender side-branch of the family tree had run to eyes like that in this
generation, from another tramontane wife. I hadn't seen Tommy
for years, hadn't spotted him at the funeral or anything; and had
surely never thought to see him like this, grotesquely dying by his
own thin light.

Tommy was a leg-man, none too bright a flame in my bright
family. He was a hod-carrier, taking messages and driving trucks,
doing the bog-standard everyday stuff that none the less they
wouldn't trust to anyone not Macallan. He must have had talent
of some sort, but I'd no idea what; and one thing for sure, it
hadn't been enough to save his life. The best he could do was set
a nightfire burning on a car, to mark where he was and how needful.

Just his bad luck, that the only Macallan who came to check it
out was Benedict the renegade, the talentless, the wimp.

"Take it easy, you, Tommy," I said, only to let him know that I'd
got him placed, at least, that he wasn't going utterly unremem-
bered.

Not leeches under his skin, no. It wasn't that. His face bubbled
and bubbled, and finally some few of those bubbles did burst.
There was a filthy spray across my clean-white-for-driving, let's-
look-smarter-than-the-doctor shirt; and then the real stink of it

85

rising, released now to choke me. All I'd had before was a sniff of putrescence, contained within his skin; now I had it all over me, all his blood turned black and boiling out of him, smelling like something long rotten.

He was surely dead now, though I hadn't felt his going. That was the only blessing, that he was gone from this rampant decay, though his body was still dreadfully working. He was erupting, inside his clothes; his joints jerked, and I instinctively clung on tighter, not to let his bones dance away from me. But what I held, what I hugged was slimy and stinking, slithering and dead; my virtuous, thrifty dinner came up and spewed all across it, before I could turn my head away. His bad blood on me, my sour vomit on him; fair enough, I suppose. Look at it whichever way you like, I had the better of it. I was the one still breathing, though what I was breathing wasn't air by any reasonable definition.

After the vomit, hot tears and snot, my own body doing its best to replicate what had spilled from his. I think, at least I hope that some of that was for Tommy, not just for myself: not only a biological response to the bite of bile in my mouth or an early touch of self-pity for the state of me, vilely saturated and my future dreaming well supplied with nightmare stuff to weave from.

The nightfire flickered out, no one now to sustain its burning; and still no one came, no other cousin, none more useful than myself.

I'd have to tell the family by telephone. There'd be the police also, I supposed, at least some token enquiry before the dead weight of my uncles' displeasure stifled any questions; but the police I could cope with, they wouldn't trouble me. Telling the family, though, would be something else, something entirely other. They'd have questions, they'd pick my bones with questioning . . .

Still sniffing, barely holding it one step down from sobbing, I pushed myself finally to my feet, and let the corruption that had been Tommy fall away from me, wetly onto concrete. I wasn't any too steady on my feet, but I made it across the court to the nearest flat not boarded up, and hammered on the door until I got a response.

They didn't open it, nothing so foolish. I only heard a hoarse, strained male voice shouting out, "Who is it?"

"Benedict Macallan," I yelled back, truly thankful for once for all the associations that name carried.

It got me inside, on the instant and no questions asked. Two people there, a man and a woman and both of them bigger than me; but there was terror on their faces as they looked at me, terror mingling with the disgust.

"I need to use your phone," I said, as mild as I could manage. "And if you could let me have a shower and a change of clothes, that'd be brilliant . . ."

No chance of better than that, no chance of getting to go home.

Behind me, I heard a querulous voice call, "Driver!" I almost smiled for a moment, kicking the door shut without looking back. Stupid, no doubt: I couldn't afford to lose this job. But what the hell, this was an emergency. If he made a fuss with the desk controller, I'd see to it that he came out smelling a lot worse than I did. Worse than I did right now, which was really saying something. He was the Christless doctor, after all, and he'd done nothing.

Besides, these good people wouldn't want him in their flat, while I cleaned up. It was for their sakes I was shutting him out as much as for my own. We inbreeds had to stick together . . .

Taking their mute shrugs for an invitation, I found my way through to their bathroom first, needing to feel clean at least on the outside before I talked to my family. No proper shower, but they did have a length of plastic hose that fitted over the mixer tap at one end and had a shower-head at the other.

I stripped off, dumping my soaked and stinking clothes in the washbasin; then I stood in the bath and rinsed myself off with the water as hot as I could bear it, which was just about as hot as it would come.

Not enough. I poured half a bottle of cheap shampoo over my head and worked it into a vigorous lather to cover every inch of skin, sluiced that away and did it all again with the other half.

The walls here were apparently made of some flimsy cardboard-substitute; even above the noises of the plumbing and the rushing water, I was conscious of tight, murmuring voices in the room next door, then of someone moving around the flat.

Content at last, if not exactly happy – I wouldn't be happy till I'd soaked for an hour in a better bath than the paddling-pool we had back at the flat, and doused myself with some more powerful eau-de-cologne than I'd ever use from choice, to get the clinging stink of Tommy's putrefaction out of my nostrils – I dried myself quickly, tied the towel around my waist and opened the bathroom door.

And found a rough pile of clothes on the floor there, waiting for me. Jeans, sweatshirt, jockey shorts and socks. I called my thanks through the closed living-room door, and went back into the bathroom to dress. No surprise that nothing fitted; the man I'd seen wasn't my shape in any direction. But I could make shift with these, at least until I got home. Better than a towel, and infinitely better than what I'd been wearing before.

A sudden thought took me over to the basin: my wallet was still in the pocket of my trousers. Picking with fastidious fingers, touching the sticky fabric as little as possible, I managed to manoeuvre it out. Checked inside, found a couple of fivers. Not much, but it would have to do. There were coins loose in the pocket also, but I wasn't fishing for those.

I left the cold tap running into the basin with the plug out, so that a constant flow of water could carry at least the worst of the slime away, and hopefully the worst of the smell with it. Then I picked up my shoes, which had escaped pollution by virtue of the fact that they'd been beneath me as I knelt, and went through to find my reluctant hosts.

They were sitting close together on the fake-leather sofa, very upright, very uptight. I tried a smile, which did no good at all; then I thanked them politely for the use of their facilities and the lend of their clothes, and asked where the phone was.

The man showed me, with a stiff jerk of his head. I went over to the window-sill, found it hiding behind a curtain – saved on the bills, I suppose: what you don't see, you're not so tempted to use – and phoned Allan.

Found the number coming automatically to my fingers, though I hadn't used it or thought about using it for years.

His wife answered, her voice neutral before I gave my name and neutral again afterwards, though I thought I could hear the effort she made to keep it so.

"Aunt Jess, can I speak to Uncle Allan, please? It's really important . . ."

"I'm sorry, Benedict, he's not here just now."

"Oh, Christ . . ." Too late, I remembered that it wasn't a good idea to swear in front of Jess; it used to cost a lecture every time when we were kids, and once it had even cost me my birthday present. This time, though, there was an advantage to it.

"What is it, Benedict? What's happened?" Her voice had crisped up with distaste, but behind that she was responding to what she was hearing from me, a genuine need backed up with resurgent shivers as the heat of the shower started to wear off. Being rid of the foul residues of Tommy's death had freed me to remember the fact of it, the awfulness, how much he'd suffered. This wasn't just a duty call I was making, I realised suddenly, a fraction later than my aunt; it was a cry for help.

"There's been a, another accident," I said, a long way from

telling the truth but close enough, I hoped, to prod her towards it. "Like Marty," I added reluctantly, in case not. "And I, I'm on my own here, Aunt Jess, and I don't know what to do . . ."

"Who was it?" she asked sharply, her voice high with anxiety. No children of her own, but that wouldn't make a difference. Anyone's death would diminish Aunt Jess; she was the hub the family turned around.

"Tommy," I said, and heard her sorrow in the quietest of sighs down the line. But there was more to say, and I couldn't spare her. "It's horrible, Auntie. Not an accident," telling truth now that she knew it already, no more harm to be done. "What do I do, do I call the police or what? I wanted Uncle Allan," I wanted to dump it all on his strong shoulders, "but if he's not there, then . . ."

"Where are you?" Jess demanded, interrupting as I started to babble.

I told her, gave her the best directions I could; and, "Wait there," she said. "And no, don't call the police. We'll do what needs to be done." Of course, don't call the police; of course, the family would deal with it. I should have known that, her voice said. I did know that, I wanted to reply, I was only babbling.

Too late, she'd gone. Hung up on me without a goodbye, but no blame for that, in the circumstances. Nothing for me to do now but wait; but I couldn't do it here, under the gazes of this family I'd barged in on, hostile and afraid.

I offered them one last smile, which they duly ignored. So I said thanks instead. "Thanks," I said. "I, um, I'll see that you get these back," plucking at the ill-fitting clothes I wore.

"Don't you bother," the man said, each word a problem, seemingly clinging to his mouth, needing to be spat out hard. I gathered that if the clothes did come back, they'd go straight in the rubbish, if not straight onto a fire. They'd touched a Macallan's body, after all, and were by definition contaminated now. How could they tell what evil might not cling to the fibres, though they were washed and washed again?

I would have liked to disillusion them, I would have liked just once for people not to assume that I and my family were one; but I couldn't have it both ways. I'd already traded on the illusion, on the family name to get what I wanted from them. Too late now to deny a power I'd already exercised.

So I nodded, found my wallet, took out what money I had and set it on a sideboard where they could pick it up or leave it lying, as they chose. "There's cash in the trousers, too," I said, again leaving it up to them what to do about it.

One last nod, and I was out of there and closing the door behind me, just to forestall their slamming it after my departing back.

The cold car's wreck still sat in the court, dark now and utterly unattended; Tommy's body lay beside it still, equally alone. I didn't like that, it didn't feel right. I thought of going back to stay with him, till someone came. No need to kneel in the muck again, I could just stand around there, safe clean concrete under my shoes . . .

But those shoes didn't take a step towards him, my feet couldn't lift their weight in that direction. It was understandable, I thought, and not such a great mutiny.

Hearing voices I looked around, looked up, saw some heads peering over one of the higher balconies. Teenagers, indulging a stupid, a dangerous bravado; but they ducked out of sight again, as soon as they saw me looking. A minute later, a door snicked quietly shut up there. I grinned, frankly enjoying myself for a moment; then I turned and ventured that tunnel again, to see if the Medicall car was still there, with the doctor *in situ*.

It wasn't, and neither was he. Buggered off back to base, most likely, to put heavy black marks against my name and my future prospects. Well, let him. I was still confident that I could talk my way out of any bullshit he stirred up, and with any luck talk him straight back into it. There was always the threat of public exposure to fall back on, if I needed it. It'd look great in the local paper: *Doctor Deserts Dying Man, Leaves Driver to Cope Alone.* And I could always threaten to add a *Medicall* to the front of that headline, if the desk controller sided with Devereux.

I could get it on the front page, no question. Regardless of the inherent news interest. Just mention my name, and hey presto.

I didn't want to do that, it made me no better than what I'd made such a loud point of rejecting; but if it was necessary, yes, I'd do it. I'd done it already once tonight. Do it for Tommy, I could surely do it for myself.

I waited in the dark there, quite unafraid in this most dangerous of estates, and even there I was trading on my family's reputation, exploiting it shamelessly. I waited for perhaps half an hour; and then there were lights out on the road and the sound of a heavy engine slowing. The lights poked like fingers into the court, the car behind them followed, and I walked slowly over.

Black Mercedes limousine with darkened windows: I'd not seen this before, but it had to be Uncle James in there. Cars say more about a man than clothes ever can.

Not my uncle driving, though. That was something else he'd always enjoyed, being driven. A power statement, I supposed it was; and the sort of statement he'd need to be making tonight, with another Macallan dead and the family's grip on power looking just a little vulnerable.

One of the rear doors opened, and yep, there was Uncle James in all his solidity and his sombre suit. He straightened up, glanced at me with the briefest of nods, glanced over to the wrecked car, and Tommy's remains; then he pulled open the passenger door and said, "Come on, then. What are you waiting for?"

Jamie stepped out: but not Jamie as he ought to have been,

dressed dark and dangerous, a young man shocked and vengeful. Dangerous he was, no question of that, but he didn't look it. All he looked was drunk. Young man out for a good time, hitting the clubs in his dancing clothes.

He wasn't bubbling, maybe, the news had suppressed him that much; but he wasn't ready, either. No way was he ready for this.

Curious, I looked into the limo through the open door, to see who was driving.

Laura looked back at me, pale and silent.

EIGHT

FRIENDS AND RELATIONS

She looked frightened, as she surely should have done; but not of her own folly or the company she was keeping, not of what she was getting into or what she'd come driving to find.

Briefly, she looked frightened of me.

Then, coming on hard, coming on aggressive when aggression was the last thing I needed from anyone and let alone her, she said, "Don't be difficult about this, Ben. Just don't do it, right?"

I shook my head, but only in response to the dizzying world, not in response to her. And dropped into the passenger seat, soft smooth hide still warm from Jamie; and looked at her, saw the bright clothes and the sweat-spiked hair, his-and-hers dark glasses on the dash. Watched the beat of her pulse under the line of her jaw and the flush of heat rising on her face while she stared straight ahead, and caught the echo of another beat, other heat still in her. Thought again about soft, smooth hide still warm from Jamie.

And said, "You do my head in. You really do." My head and my heart and my hopes, but one was enough for now.

"Look," she said fiercely, but still not looking herself, or not in my direction. Uncle James was out there, and Jamie was with him, and her head was turned that way; whether she saw them, I couldn't say. "This isn't a good time, but let's get one thing straight, can we? You don't own me, however much you'd like to. You certainly don't make my choices for me."

"I don't want to . . ."

"Which? Think about it."

I shook my head again, avoiding the challenge. "My family owns everything in this town, everything that matters. Nearly everything. I just, I just don't want them owning you too . . ."

"They don't," she said, in defiance of the evidence. "They won't."

"You're here, aren't you?" Already chauffeuse to Uncle James at need, and God knew what to Jamie.

I still couldn't understand how it had happened, and I wasn't going to ask; but she told me anyway. Seizing the moment, perhaps, finding this just a fraction easier than asking me what exactly lay on the ground out there, what my uncle and my cousin were bending over, looking closely at.

"Look, listen," she said. "Going for a drink with Jamie, the three of us – well, it wasn't such a good idea, right? Not for me, at any rate. Not if I want to get to know the guy. You know what you'd be like: squeezing between us, squaring up to him all the time, getting all possessive where you've no right to be, biting my head off if you didn't like the way I was behaving . . ."

She was right, of course, I'd be exactly like that. Exactly what she needed, though she wouldn't thank me for it. Though she'd taken steps, clearly, to avoid it . . .

"He knew, too," she went on, "or he guessed, from the way you were at the funeral. So he phoned me, invited me out on the quiet tonight. Sort of a pre-emptive strike, I suppose you'd call it."

"Where did he get your number?"

"I don't know. Not from me. I didn't ask."

From the college, then, most likely. Against the rules, but

easy. Walk in, smile at the secretary, tell her what you want; and yes sir, Mr Macallan, straight away, sir, here it is . . .

"Where did you go, then, where did he take you?"

"The boat," she said, where she might have said *mind your own business*, and I almost wished she had. The boat made one of our rages look like a sophisticated night out.

More properly known as the *Queen Casilia*, the boat was an ex-cruise ship permanently moored on the river, converted into a night-club and casino. It was brash, it was gaudy, and the other thing we called it was the knocking ship. It was where you took a girl you wanted to get off with, an outright statement of intent.

"Laura . . ."

"We had a good time," she said defensively. "All right? I like Jamie. And it's interesting, getting another angle on you."

"What was he saying about me?" I demanded.

"Quite a lot, actually. But in confidence, I'm not passing it on."

I would have pressed her pointlessly; she'd never buckled under the weight of my demands, and never would. But her eyes strayed outside again, to where Jamie was again bent over. Not looking at Tommy now. He was doing the other thing, doing what I'd done, reacting to Tommy: doubled up and retching while Uncle James watched him with fastidious distaste, utterly untouched except in his *amour-propre*, his sense of family pride.

Laura made a soft noise in her throat and reached to open the door, to go to Jamie. Unfamiliarity held her up, as her fingers couldn't find the catch in the dark; and that was just long enough for me to grip her arm and hold her, to say, "Wait. Just one thing, how come you're driving for them?" How did she get from the boat to the Merc, that's what I wanted to know – and what were the stages in between?

"We took a taxi," she said, "out to his place." Which meant Uncle James' place, because as far as I knew Jamie still hadn't set up home on his own; and that meant yes, Laura meant to sleep with him tonight. No one would go that far in a taxi and still pretend they just wanted to have a coffee and look at some etchings and then go home like a good girl. "But when we got there," she said, "Mr Macallan was on the phone, sounding really upset. So of course Jamie asked what was up, and he told us about, about that," with a gesture through the windscreen, "and Jamie wanted to come too. But he couldn't drive, he'd had way too much to drink; so he asked me."

"Did he know I was here?" I asked dully.

"I don't know. I think so. Yes, Mr Macallan said. What does it matter? Look, I've got to, I can't just sit here and . . ."

And with that she was gone and I let her go, no protest. I sat numbly in Jamie's seat, absorbing all the messages that Jamie had meant me to receive, that Laura had no idea she was passing on.

Being drunk had never stopped him driving, any more than any policeman in this borough was going to stop him for being drunk and driving. This was a statement, it was a power play again, *I've got her, Benedict boy, see me?*

And that she wasn't drunk, that she reckoned herself sober enough to drive, that was another message he wanted me to pick up. *I had her in between the sheets, all but. Her choice, boy, and nothing slurring her decision. How far did you ever get her?*

Which if they'd talked about me at all, he knew the answer to already, and this was gloating, nothing more.

We'd been brothers, near enough; but brothers are competitive by definition. That had been a part of our definition, at least, until I'd dropped out of the game, as puberty got left further and further behind and still hadn't brought me anything but humiliation.

Competition is a habit, and he hadn't lost it, seemingly. Was exulting in it, even if the victory was a walk-over that brought glory to no one, even on a night when something other than alcohol was bringing him to his knees and bringing up his dinner.

And Laura, Laura was on her knees beside him, arm around his shoulders and hand stroking back his hair, all comfort and concern. A prize loudly and publicly claimed, whatever she might assert. She didn't have a voice in this. It was a game, and no one had explained the rules to her. She wasn't a participant, not a competitor, no . . .

Sitting in Jamie's seat the same night he stepped into my dreamed-of shoes: it all carried too many overtones, too much difficult baggage to be comfortable, despite the softness of the leather and my own bitter exhaustion. Not long after Laura was I up and out of there, walking over to where he was getting palely to his feet, Laura's strong hands on his arm to help him up.

Been there, done that at least: thrown up in public places, chucked my cookies and been mopped up by Laura. Except that she'd only ever played doctor-and-friend for me, cool and sympathetic and passing me a tissue. For Jamie she was playing some other role entirely, tucking herself under his arm in something more than support, wiping his face and his mouth for him, murmuring privately in soft concern.

When he saw me he tightened his hold on her, just enough to be sure that I'd seen; then he smiled thinly, abruptly much closer to sober that he'd been before. "Hi, bro. How're you doing?"

Not so well as you, bro. But oh, I was short on brothers and he was what I'd missed most, these three dead years. And someone out there was attacking the family, we'd both seen the results tonight and both reacted the same, the same sourness on our breath and in our heads. I nodded and touched his arm – his other arm, not to be thought to be touching Laura, or disputing his claim – and said, "Okay, I guess. Not brilliant, but okay. You?"

A shrug one-shouldered, and, "Yeah. Pretty much the same. Christ, I used, I used to go *fishing* with that guy, Ben, he gave us my first rod. Still got it, somewhere . . ."

"Yeah." I remembered Jamie fishing, though not with Tommy. With me, occasionally. I'd never seen the attraction of sitting around for hours getting bored, but Jamie's attraction had been fierce.

"So what happened? You were here . . ."

Someone left him on too long, and his blood all boiled over. I shook my head, with an involuntary glance at Laura. Family unity or misplaced chivalry, I wasn't certain; either way, I didn't want to tell him in front of her.

Either way, he understood. A fractional nod for me, *thanks* as much as *I get you, right*, and he touched her cheek lightly, the one that wasn't already pressed against his collarbone. "Don't you look, love. It's nasty . . ."

She showed no signs of looking, she was only looking at him, her eyes dark and enormous; but she twitched impatiently at that, said, "For Christ's sake, Jamie. I'm a medic, remember? I cut people up in class. Whatever it's like back there, I've seen worse."

"No, you haven't," positively from both of us at once.

She glanced between us and her lips twitched, giggles not too far away.

"Hark at the double-act," she whispered. And then, startling me at least and perhaps both of us together, "Are we still on for Friday, then?"

"Friday, what's Friday?"

"Jamie's birthday. Drinks, remember?"

"Can't afford it," I said quickly, seizing a true excuse.

"Don't be boring, Ben."

"We'll pay," from Jamie. "I will," sensing a movement in Laura, a quiet *I can't afford it either.*

So instead of that handy excuse, "I thought you didn't want me," I said, moved to cruelty.

"I never said that," she flashed back.

And true enough, thinking back, she hadn't. Quite. I made a gesture of acquiescence, and she nodded, taking it for an apology.

"All right, then. We'll do it. You two," she said, "need to talk."

And she was right, we did, we both knew it. We needed to talk about her.

More than that, though – if there could be anything more than that – we needed to talk about what was happening to the family, what was happening to us. And couldn't do it that night, because Uncle James stultified any meaningful discussion simply by being there. He was more outraged than grieving, more insulted than concerned; the sheer weight of his offended *gravitas* crushed us into silence when he came back to the car.

He used his mobile phone to summon reinforcements, the muscle that would remove Tommy's remains; but we didn't wait to see that. No one was going to touch Tommy in the meantime. He gestured to Laura and she put the car silently in gear and drove away, *your obedient servant, Mr Macallan*. But then, he would have expected nothing less.

No talking on the drive, not even about what mattered. I'd anticipated an interrogation, and didn't get it. The rat Jamie had snaffled the front seat before I could claim it; displaced again, I sat in the back with Uncle James and he addressed not a word to me until Laura surprised him, I think, by turning off the main road west and bringing me to the door of my flat.

I suppose he'd expected her to take us all back to his place. She was dead right, though, I didn't want to go. I'd held my cousin's death in my arms, I'd seen my girl in Jamie's; it was enough, for one night. Enough of family, enough of grief and horror. I wanted the familiar darkness of my own bed and the dark familiarity of my own mind's dreaming, and never mind if nightmares came.

Uncle James looked at me and nodded, as if he could read all that on my face. He couldn't, not he; but whatever it was he thought he saw, it persuaded him.

"Tomorrow, then," he said, and it was my turn to nod. I'd have to answer their questions sometime. Might as well be tomorrow. One thing for sure, I wasn't going into college.

Letting myself into the flat, I remembered there was half a bottle of Famous Grouse in the cupboard, that Jacko had brought home from some gig or other and we hadn't got around to drinking yet. Now might just be the right time to do that . . .

Except that it would be more bravado than need, *look how grown-up I am. I drink whisky when I want to go to sleep.* And it would take a while, maybe most of that half-bottle before I could be sure of its sliding me off into unconsciousness; and I couldn't think of anything else to do while I was drinking, and the last thing I wanted was to sit around staring at walls, painting pictures in my head. Reliving and reliving this night, both terrible sides of it, the one cousin with his life stolen from him, the other too busy stealing mine . . .

So I left the whisky where it was, thanked God that Jacko was in bed – if not exactly sleeping yet: there was an extra bike in the hall, the murmur of voices, an occasional squeal of knackered bedsprings from his room – and made myself a secretive mug of cocoa to go to bed with, another inescapable legacy from my childhood, still and always a guaranteed sleeping-potion in times of crisis.

I slept long and late, too shaken perhaps to want to come back to the world. When I did there was a boy, not Jacko, in our kitchen: wearing Jacko's decrepit bathrobe, crunching toast one-handed while he drifted round making coffee with the other.

He grinned at me, his lips freckled with crumbs, his eyes still flecked with sleep.

"Morning. You're Benedict, right?" And then, when I hesitated, "Jonathan. Jonathan Hayes."

"Jonathan. Right. Hi . . ." But had we met before, was that a reminder, or was it an introduction? I wasn't certain, couldn't figure out a polite way to discover. It was a problem I'd faced before, though, distinguishing Jacko's boyfriends, and in the long run it never seemed to matter. They none of them actually got that long a run. Bed could never triumph over music; and as far as I could remember, for whatever private reason of his own, he'd never brought a musician home.

We shared an amicable breakfast. At first I thought Jonathan's constant easy chatter was going to drive me up the wall, but far from it. Whether it was driven by sensitivity on his part, or else by shyness, or simply his habit in the mornings, I didn't know and didn't care. Left alone I'd have been sullen and moody, I might very possibly have worked myself up to being scared; a steady wash of talk that kept a light finger-hold on my attention turned out to be just what I needed.

I didn't contribute much myself, but I did ask where Jacko was, whether he was still sleeping. Jonathan shook his head.

"He's a good boy," around a mouthful, "he's gone to lectures."

"Not you, though?"

"I'm not a student. I'm not anything really," but he was easy with it, grinning again, quite unembarrassed. "I windle a bit, do odd jobs for people: bit of gardening, bit of decorating, stuff like that. And sign on between."

"Windle?"

"Window-cleaning. My dad's got a business. I help out, but only sometimes. There's not enough work, really."

"Right."

"Tim said I didn't have to hurry off . . ."

Took me a second, but Tim was Jacko. "No, sure, that's fine. Stick around till he gets back, if you like. Doesn't bother me." To tell truth, I'd be glad of his company in the flat. Not to talk to, nor even to listen to, particularly: just the consciousness of someone else being around while I waited for my uncle, someone to keep me centred, to remind me that there was still another world and I had a place in it.

"I said I'd meet him tonight, at the Duke. There's a session there. But, well, you know, I live down the river, and there's nothing to do at home anyway . . ."

"So stick around," I said. "Not much to do here either, mind."

"I'll think of something."

When my uncle finally came, it wasn't James, but Allan.

And Hazel came too, they arrived together.

Good news, bad news, all in one interesting package.

Squeezing past the bikes they followed me through into the living-room, Uncle Allan staring about him with fascination, learning how I lived now. I saw him politely suppress a shudder at the carpets, so I politely suppressed my amused grin also.

"Have a seat," I suggested, waving a hospitable arm. "That one's the most comfortable, Uncle, but it's also the hardest to get out of, after . . ."

He smiled, "I'll risk it, thank you, Benedict," and lowered himself cautiously into my favourite chair. Hazel shook her head in a single denying jerk, and went to stand fidgeting by the window, glancing out as often as she glanced at us. Bodyguard duties, I diagnosed; self-appointed, for sure. Uncle Allan needed no protection. Certainly none that she was capable of giving, unless perhaps her unrestful presence could serve as a reminder that even Macallans were apparently vulnerable now, and he should keep alert for danger.

Not a position he was used to, certainly. He was probably as uncomfortable with that as he was in the chair, perched awkwardly forward where the only proper attitude was to sprawl. But with two cousins dead, I honestly didn't think he'd need reminding. Hazel had just forced herself on him, at a guess, bullying him as successfully as she bullied everyone else. *No one should be going round alone*, she would have said, *not even you, Uncle Allan. Especially not you, we can't afford to lose you. I'll come with you, watch your back . . .*

Fat lot of help she'd be to him in a crisis, fat lot he'd need her; but it did her good, I could see that. Which was maybe why he'd allowed it, in the last analysis. Times like this, a family could fragment; but the welfare of each contributed to the whole, and Allan always had the family's welfare most at heart.

Anyway, she was there, and he was. He declined my offer of a coffee, wise old uncle that he was – a Blue Mountain man at heart, he'd have had trouble swallowing Best Value instant, an anonymous brown powder that came in kilo tubs – and said, "Tell me about last night, Benedict. Everything you remember."

"There's not much. Truly. I was too late, that's all," and that's what would haunt me for a long time to come, if not forever. Never mind that I'd have been useless anyway, however promptly I came to the rescue. I had no rescue in me, I didn't have the equipment; but that wasn't the point. Not to have been there at Tommy's most need: it was everybody's failure, but mine most of all simply because I'd been closest.

"Well. Tell me anyway."

So I did. I explained about the driving, though he knew already; and then I explained about the screaming, though I really hadn't wanted to do that and he hadn't wanted to hear it either by the look of him, the way he tightened up around the mouth.

"I didn't know who it was," I said, "till I saw the nightfire. But then it had to be one of us . . ." And even after I'd found him it had taken me a while to work out who it was, but I wasn't telling Allan that. Some things he was entitled not to know.

"Describe what you saw," he said. "Exactly."

I described the courtyard and the flats, and how the car had been burning, with Tommy lying in its guttering shadow. And then, at his prompting, I described everything I'd done, everything I'd seen and heard all the time I was there, until Uncle James' car arrived. I told him about the filth of Tommy's death because he'd know about that already, he would have seen the corpse; I told him about the shower and the clean clothes and phoning Aunt Jess, though that of course he knew about also. I told him about the teenagers spying from the balcony when it was quiet, when it seemed safe; and that nearly raised a grin in him as it had in me.

All this time Hazel was restlessly doing her bodyguard bit at the window; but then she stopped, and went to the door. Gestured impatiently to me, to be quiet; and hissed, "There's someone else in the flat. Who's here?"

Took me a moment to remember, but then I heard what she'd heard, the chink of dishes in the kitchen.

"Oh, that's Jonathan. Friend of Jacko's. Relax, will you?"

She jerked her head in a hard denial. Relaxing, it seemed, was not on the agenda today. Nor could I blame her for that, in all honesty. Not if she'd seen the body; and she would have done. Even in my family, no one had ever managed to keep Hazel out of anywhere she wanted to get into.

"Who is he, then? Friend, what sort of friend?"

"Just a boy, that's all. Eighteen, nineteen, something like that. Jacko likes boys."

Hazel made a grimace of distaste. If my sister had a sex-life at all, it would be strictly hetero, strictly conformist, except that she would insist on dominating in bed as she did out of it. But if she did have a sex-life, I'd never heard of it.

Like sister, like brother, I thought wryly. I'd had one once, but no more.

She wasn't finished with Jonathan yet. "Has he been listening?"

"I shouldn't think so. Why would he? Don't get paranoid. He's just a boy."

"Someone is *killing* our *people*, Benedict. They're not supposed to be able to *do* that. It's not paranoid to be suspicious, it's just common sense. It could be any of them," and her gesture contained the whole town and the world beyond, "we just don't know; so we can't trust anyone. Right?"

I shrugged. "If you say so."

"And you shouldn't be so bloody blasé about it, either. You're not labouring under the illusion that you're *safe*, are you? Think about it, for God's sake. Marty, Tommy – they were neither of them heavyweights, when it came to talent. Whoever's doing this is picking off the weakest, one by one. Who's the weakest, Benedict?"

I hadn't thought of that. Hadn't seen it that way at all. And damn it all, I'd disinvested . . .

But I took a breath, gave her a smile as unconcerned as I could make it, and said, "You and me, pet."

"You, Benedict. *You*," fiercely. "Don't think they won't remember you. You can't hide from us, and you can't hide from them either."

She had a point, though I wasn't going to admit it.

"I'm not hiding," I said. "I'd be in the phone-book, if we could only afford a phone. And who's 'them', anyway? Don't postulate ahead of your facts, it's a recipe for trouble."

She just glared at me. "We've got two cousins *dead*, Benedict. Those are facts. What the hell more do you want?"

Allan made pacific gestures with his hands, as he always had: with some success when we were children, less later on, none at all now.

But he was looking at me a little anxiously, a little unworldly, something troubling him outside our spatting or the family's major trauma.

"Benedict," he said, patting his pockets, feeling for something and then finding it, drawing out a chequebook, "do you need money?"

God, for a brilliant man, he was bloody slow sometimes.

"*No*," I said venomously. "Not yours, anyway. Put it away."

Later – after they'd gone, unsatisfied but finally accepting that I had nothing more to give them, no information worth the having – Jonathan put his head around the door.

"Haven't got a bucket, have you?"

"Somewhere, yeah. Why?"

"I saw that ladder in the yard there, thought maybe I'd go around and windle a bit. Get some cash together, for tonight."

The ladder was the landlord's, left over from the last time he tried to save money by fixing the roof himself. Afterwards the rain had still leaked into our upstairs neighbours' flat, and from theirs on down into ours; so we'd clubbed together, paid to have the job done properly, and deducted it from the next month's rent. He'd not been happy, but he still hadn't come back for his ladder.

I laughed, and went to find the bucket.

"What about you," he said, "you coming down the Duke?"

"No money." Absolutely no money, I'd left all I had with my unwilling hosts last night.

"Well, me neither. That's why . . ."

And we looked at each other with a wild surmise; and so I spent all afternoon up and down ladders, begging buckets of hot water from cynical housewives and scraping long-dried birdshit off window glass for a handful of coins.

NINE

NEVER GENTLE ON MY MIND

In the evening we went to the Duke.

The Duke of Northumberland – colloquially known as Percy's Piss-Pot, but only to those who had personally met the current Duke, we had a *strict* rule about that – was a pub down at the river's edge, once surrounded by factories and housing both, thriving on the trade. Now it was surrounded by nothing, just a rubble wasteland, 'scheduled for redevelopment' as soon as they could locate some investors stupid enough to put themselves willingly into my family's capacious pocket.

The Duke throve no longer. At least, not on its former clientèle. The brewery that had owned it sold up, the company that had taken it over went bust, a new landlord had bought it on a bank-loan with nothing left over for refurbishment. Bare boards and tobacco-stained walls, no juke and no video, no local trade: what he'd needed more than anything was a new customer base, and he'd found it at the university. Getting some real ales in and selling the Duke as an authentic, unreconstructed pub –making a feature, making a virtue of necessity – he'd made the place as popular with us as any drinking-hole in town, five nights a week.

Thursdays and Sundays were different. Thursday and Sundays, the folkies took over in the back room. Musicians lined the walls and filled the tables, handing instruments around, singing and smoking and playing, playing, endlessly playing. Those few who had no gift for music and were there only to listen squeezed in where they could, rarely finding a seat and often giving it up unasked to a musician. The hierarchy was absolute.

This particular Thursday, anything that could move me faster or further from the night before was welcome; riding on jigs and alcohol fitted the bill quite neatly.

Jonathan and I arrived at about nine, the best of buddies, bonded by hard work equally shared. Our bellies were heavy with fish and chips, my classic veggie compromise, and our pockets were heavy with cash.

The back room didn't have a bar, only a hatch in the wall. Jonathan squeezed into the queue, after a quick consultation; I scanned the room, checking out who was there.

Jacko, of course, ensconced in a corner he'd probably established as his own way back at opening time. And Colin was with him, his elbow-cradling fiddle technique showing to advantage in these crowded quarters, where very likely it had been developed. Carol was there too but the other side of the room, on Squeezebox Bench with another piano-accordionist, an older woman with wicked fingers. True Irish, she was, and a fixture here.

For once, Carol didn't have Nicky in tow. I had seen him at a session here a couple of times, but I thought perhaps the landlord had had a quiet word. Babies were welcome, babies and dogs; teenagers were tolerated, so long as they sat quiet and at least made a pretence at drinking Coke until they were legal; but an eight-year-old was neither one thing nor the other, and certain trouble if authority poked its suspicious head around the door.

There were a dozen other familiar faces, but I started running out of names quite fast. I waved, smiled, nodded around, then found a narrow section of wall to lean against and thought I'd better decide that this was comfortable, because chances were I'd be there till closing. As usual there were too many people, not enough chairs.

Jonathan edged through the crush with two pints carefully held, handed one to me and squashed up at my side, turning his feet out sideways not to obstruct the narrow passage through to the hatch; but his eyes were already turning towards Jacko, shifting guiltily back to me and turning again.

I grinned. "For Christ's sake, you don't have to talk to the one you came in with. It's not an obligation."

"Sorry?"

"Go and see Jacko, will you? He's what you came for."

"Well, but . . . You'll be on your own . . ."

"Never alone with a good pint," and Conciliation is a fine bloody pint. "Besides, I'm used to it. Go on, I'll see you later."

That was all the encouragement he needed. I watched him slide between tables and knees, greet Jacko just with a touch on the shoulder and then settle to the floor at his feet; and I felt the usual pang, *it should have been me. It should have been me and Laura* . . . But Laura was I knew not where and doing I knew not what, I could only hope not with Jamie; and I was here, on my own and used to that, boasting about it. No time for pangs. *Get your head straight, Macallan.*

Straight wasn't really an available option, though, that evening. Not thinking about Laura meant thinking about Marty, thinking about Tommy, thinking about someone out there with the power and the will to kill. That had its own magnetic flux that could warp any head out of true, let alone a Macallan head. Here was something we really weren't used to. My father wouldn't be a factor, he only ever did what he was told and very much preferred not to have to think at all; but I wondered how the uncles were handling it. How they were keeping the family calm, while Uncle Allan presumably played Holmes, while Uncle James played the Godfather. That's how I'd cast it, anyway; but maybe I'd ask Jamie on Friday, if I went. If I could bear to go . . .

But there was Laura again, turning thoughts sharply away from straight; and the only other choice tonight was not to think at all, or not at all clearly.

Conciliation deserves more respect than chug-a-lug, untasted down the throat; but that's all that happened to the first pint. First flesh it touched was my tonsils.

Then I headed for the hatch, with just a glance down the tables to confirm that Jonathan wasn't ready for another yet, nowhere near. Got a couple anyway, while I was there, and a double Jameson's for added bite. Fingered the change in my pocket, thinking that at this rate it might not last the evening; and shrugged, and went to reclaim my piece of wall, lining the drinks up along the mantelpiece beside.

Drinking alone, you drink faster. It's a universal law.

Whether you get drunk faster, that's more open to debate. I think company gets you drunk, as much as alcohol. Certainly that night I was going for it hard but not getting anywhere much, so far as I could tell.

Then Carol swam up beside me, and all right, maybe I wasn't so sober after all. Talking was the acid test, and I hadn't been doing any of that hitherto. My teeth felt strange in my jaw as I smiled, and they were a little hard to work when I said hullo.

"Hi." Maybe she was getting somewhere herself, the way she tucked her arm through mine, more contact than I was used to. "Are you all right?"

"Sure, fine. Why not?"

"Stuck here on your own. I was worried about you."

"No, really. I came with Jonathan, but . . ."

A twitch of my head, all I needed to point out where Jonathan sat, still on the floor, hugging Jacko's knee now while Jacko's long fingers played with his hair, those brief periods between tunes.

Carol nodded. "I saw you come in. It's not fair, him abandoning you like this."

"I told him to," I said. "I don't feel abandoned." Only isolated by blood and temperament and habit, all three.

"Well, come and join us. What are you drinking?" as Mike the landlord bellowed loudly, "Last orders now, please!" from the hatch, while someone in the other bar jangled a hand-bell hard.

"No, it's okay . . ."

"No, it's *not* okay, Ben. What are you *drinking?*"

"Um, Conciliation, then . . ."

"Right. Since when has buying a man a drink been such hard work? Wait here," and she was gone, pushing into the pack, short and aggressively blonde and always a pleasure.

In fact I didn't wait where she told me, I followed her towards the hatch, and took the drinks she passed back to me one by one; then, obedient again, I let her tug me through to Squeezebox Bench and stood quiescent while she bullied the others into crushing up a little tighter, to make room for me on the end.

"That's better," nodding with more than a hint of triumph to her voice. "Now you won't be standing over us like a, like a hawk over a flock of rabbits."

"Do rabbits flock?"

"God knows. Ask Nicky, he'd know. He knows everything."

"Where is he tonight?"

Crushing the spirit out of some poor baby-sitter, if his mother were any guide; but, "With his father," she said. "We swap him around, on a mutual-convenience basis. He handles it pretty well, we think. He's not noticeably psychotic, at any rate. Probably helps that we still get on, Richard and I . . ."

"I'm sure." Family breakdowns were a mystery to me; they didn't happen to Macallans. Except of course for the big breakdown, the big failure, the one they still talked about; the boy who turned his back on the whole business, who would have changed the very blood in his veins if it had been medically achievable.

But then I was a mystery to me too, as I was a mystery to everyone, inside the family or out.

A mystery to Carol too, seemingly; she was looking at me askance, obviously working up to one of the big questions.

"Go on, then," I said, barely even on a sigh. "Ask us. If you don't ask, I'll never tell you."

"Does that mean that if I do, you will?"

I shrugged. "No promises. But I usually do." That was one of the important things in being free, supposedly: the chance to be honest, to tell the truth without fear or favour. Particularly, in this case, without fear.

"Well, then. You've done this brilliant thing, right, you've walked out on something that revolted you, which couldn't have been easy; you've done the hard part, so why are you mucking it all up now? Why aren't you *happy*, Ben?"

For a second I just stared at her, knocked right out of kilter. Then, "I'm happy enough," I muttered, into my glass.

"No, you're not. Don't bullshit me. I've watched you, and I've talked to Jacko."

Jacko was in trouble, then. I glared at his unseeing head, promising retribution; then shrugged, said, "So what's happy?"

"Happy is measuring your life against the options," she said decidedly, "and not wanting to change it. It's getting the best of a series of bargains, bad or otherwise. And you've worked for that, so what's spoiling it?"

"Christ." Not sober enough to resist, I ran her criteria through my mind; and shook my head hard at the results, couldn't tell her that. "Aren't you supposed to be playing a tune, or something?"

They were playing a tune all around us; but her turn to shake her head now, as she said, "Right now, I'm supposed to be getting your head sorted out. Self-appointed duty, and I never let myself down if I can help it. Come on, give."

Someone's killing off my family. And never mind that I despise everything they stand for, they're still my family and I can't break free after all. And not being free, I couldn't tell her that either; Macallan business was private business, always. So in the end, when her hard stare still offered no compromise, I copped out and told her the other thing, that should have been just as private.

"The girl I love is going out with my cousin," *whom I love, whose values I despise*, "is that enough for you?"

She only snorted. "Love how? How long for?"

"More than two years now," and barely one-eleventh of my life; but all of it that counted, sometimes.

"Uh-huh. And what, you split up, is that it?"

"No." Never got that far, Laura and I.

"Ben, man, for God's sake," as she caught on, or started to. "Have you ever slept with this girl?"

"No."

"Ever been out with her?"

"No." Well, yes, often; but even those times we were alone it was never a date in the way that Carol meant, only ever as friends on the piss or a cultural jag or whatever; and I wasn't up to dishonesty tonight.

"For crying out loud, and you call that love? Ben, how old are you?"

"Twenty-three."

"Twenty-three, right, and you sound like a fucking sixteen-year-old . . ."

I shook my head mutely. I'd been a lot more sussed than this, when I was sixteen. It was having to start again that was the killer, and not knowing what was babies and what was bathwater.

I liked the feel of that in my head, so I said it aloud; and she said, "Explain." So I tried to tell her how it felt, to reject not only everyone you'd grown up with but also everything they'd ever taught you was true: to lose all your value systems at a stroke, and end up floundering. And she said that just sounded like classic teenage rebellion, and I said no, I thought it was more than that; but even if she was right, I said, a lot of teenagers got well fucked up in the course of the rebelling, didn't they? And that certainly had happened to me, and to some extent I was floundering still. But I'd found or built myself a couple of rocks to cling to, and Laura was one of those, I said . . .

And somewhere in the midst of this confessional, Mike the land-lord came round for our glasses. "See your drinks off now, please, it's half eleven . . ."

Which was already later than the law allowed, but even Mike didn't have any great urgency in his voice, and nobody noticeably moved. Looking around, I saw that a lot of people had pints hardly touched in front of them, and didn't seem concerned about it. Largely, they just went on playing.

I shrugged, took a sip rather than a gulp, and went on talking.

A bit later, needing the loo, I left off talking and went through to the other bar.

On the way, I noticed that the door out was closed and barred and bolted.

When I came back, a girl I didn't know was standing on a table, giggling and swaying and conducting a chorus of 'Happy Birthday' to herself. Carol had her squeezebox in motion again, which limited my room to sit down; when she saw me hovering, she laid off the chords long enough to reach in her pocket and find a fiver.

"Get us a couple of pints, will you?"

"What? No, hang on, it's my turn . . ." And I already had little enough money left, and maybe I'd better just leave now, if I could find anyone to let me out.

"Don't be stupid. Take it."

Jacko really had been talking to her, clearly; and punishment would most surely follow. My financial problems were my own affair, certainly not that of a casually-known accordionist.

Back at the hatch they were serving again, and Jonathan was there, waiting in the queue. He grinned at me, a little ruefully. "Sorry, didn't know it was going to turn into a lock-in . . ."

"Don't worry, I'm fine." I had someone to talk to, however much I might resent some of what she knew or wanted to know; and getting plastered, getting totally out of my box might prove the answer to several questions, including the little matter of getting to sleep tonight. There's a limit to how much cocoa I can drink.

The birthday girl was called Jo, and she wanted a song from everyone. Didn't get one from me, sing I don't. But Carol sang, an old yiddishe number, to break the relentless Irishness; and someone else sang country, and a couple sang a ridiculously silly duet, and this wasn't a lock-in any more, it was a party.

So no surprise that when Jo invited people to move back to her flat, "more comfy and I've got some grass," she included everyone in that invitation; and no surprise that along with almost everyone, I said yes. Said yes, please. Getting stoned would add one more layer of detachment, another degree of separation. And the more the merrier, it seemed to me just then.

Carol came too and I did the gentlemanly thing, I carried her accordion for her, though she laughed at me for doing it. And on the march up I manoeuvred us next to Jacko and Jonathan, and did a little promissory work with my elbow in Jacko's ribs, murmuring about the trouble he would find himself in, all my old pride unexpectedly rising, *you don't gossip about me, right?* He just grinned, shook his head mockingly, *don't talk stupid, everyone gossips about you*, and said Carol was just what I needed.

Wrong. What I needed was all that I couldn't have, and I didn't come anywhere near Carol's definition of happy.

But even Carol's value-system recognised that happiness is relative: it's only ever a matter of what you measure it against, how you define your standards.

Chemical interference can do a lot, to make the scales weigh things differently. Happiness is an attitude of mind; thought is an electrical activity taking place in a chemical stew; ergo and therefore, stir a few more chemicals into the pot, and you can come up like a beamish lunatic and *mean* it.

Alcohol's a chemical; so's tetrahydrocannabinol.

Alcohol I had already, sloshing around in my bladder and my brain, and some still circulating in my bloodstream, waiting its turn. By any reasonable definition, I'd had enough; but that is not to say that there was no room for more. Moderation, I guess, is another sign of contentment, and so – by definition – inappropriate. I lived from feast to famine, famine to feast; and tonight, the table was loaded.

Literally, the table was loaded. Not me, but a dozen of us had brought carry-outs from the Duke; those were stacked up on the living-room table as we trooped in, next to the tray of cans that Jo had in already, and the couple of wine-boxes and the bowls of crisps and Shanghai nuts and olives.

At the back of the table, teasingly lurking, was a bottle of cheap whisky with a ribbon round its neck and a label attached.

I didn't read the label, didn't need to. Probably it was in code, probably it said *Happy Birthday, Jo* or something similar, something equally appropriate for a bottle of altered states; but actually it was an instruction. Whatever it said, it said *Drink Me.*

And no one else was doing that. I waited, I watched for five minutes, and they were all drinking beer or lager or wine. So I found myself a glass and filled it, settled my butt on a windowsill and sipped quietly.

One of the bedrooms in Jo's flat opened directly off the living-room. Half the musicians camped themselves in there, spreading out across bed and carpet and leaving the door open, unpacking instruments and tuning up and laying down a base of sound, firm footing that the party could spring from.

Or, in my case, a mattress of music I could topple back into, any time my mind slipped free of the talking.

Carol had let up on me, at least for the moment; I could hear her squeezebox underlying everything, through in the other room. I was talked out, in any case. All I wanted to do was to listen, and drink, and not be alone. Not be at home and in bed and thinking about Tommy, or alternatively thinking about Laura.

The whisky was rough, coldly burning like nightfire in my throat and threatening later dismay to my stomach; but it was right for now, and now was all that mattered. Sufficient unto the day, unto the hour was the evil thereof: Father Hamish had taught me that, at confirmation class.

Matter of fact, Father Hamish had also taught me to drink. Also at confirmation class. At least that's the way I used to tell it when Marty was around to challenge me, to take offence, to growl "No he didn't, you little bugger," and remind me with hard knuckles of the lessons I'd had from him. It was a ritual, it was a game we played together; and if it ended up every time with me bruised and yelping through my giggles, so what?

But in all honesty, Hamish had got in first. *This is the blood of Christ*, he'd said, offering a sip of Communion wine to my thir-teen-year-old and curious tongue, *and this is the fermented juice of the grape*, sloshing a tumbler full of Liebfraumilch and pushing it across the desk. *You'll despise that stuff later, when you've learned discrimination*, he'd said, and sure enough he'd had a different bottle for himself, and wouldn't give me so much as a taste of it; *but it'll suit your palate well enough for now. And all you need to know for now is how to discriminate between the one and the other, the sacrament and the indulgence.*

Under his tutelage and my cousins', I'd learned discrimination in wine and other things; but again, babies and bathwater were too confused in my mind to be distinguished now. I still drank Liebfraumilch, when it was offered. Drank it like a statement, indeed, like mute defiance hurled in the sweet teeth of my childhood truths.

But now I was drinking rotgut whisky, in defiance of memory and incipient dream; and circling the room – like the smoke and the conversation circled, in better order than my mind was circling – here came the last temptation, the ultimate persuader. What I was here for, in all honesty. Company was good tonight, and music was good, and drink was maybe better than either; but tetrahydrocannabinol, some nights that could just win out over anything. THC and alcolhol mixed, no contest.

Three or four people were building joints with varying degrees of concentration and urgency, and the first couple were already on their way. Travelling in contrary directions around the room, and luck had landed me right where their meandering paths were doomed to cross. I'd barely taken hold of the first, barely started to suck in the heavy, soursweet smoke, before the second reached me; smoke leaked between my lips as I nodded a grinning thanks and kept right on inhaling.

Three hits off a joint is about right, I reckon, each time it comes around. Any less and you're a dilettante, you're not taking it seriously; any more and we're into bogart territory, greed winning out over manners. And it's enough, for me at least. Three tokes at a time will get me going nicely.

But that night I was charting territories of excess, and being gifted the opportunity. Two joints in my hands, and more on the way: no one would be going short, so I took four times from each cardboard roach before passing them along.

Smoke's bite and whisky's bite on the cables of an over-stretched mind, and already it wasn't likely that I'd just perch still and quiet on my windowsill and listen to the party rolling on. I could yet tilt either way, alcohol dragging me down into melancholy and fear or dope bubbling me up into euphoria; but one way or the other, balance simply wasn't on the cards.

Something had to give, and something did; but not at all what I'd expected. Not my equanimity, not my mood unleashed but something far stronger and far more vicious, something I didn't even know that I held housed within me.

Eyes closed and head back against the bunched curtain, weight of glass in my hand unsupervised and my body relaxing in defiance of my dizzy mind, I breathed deeply and wondered what would come, what was on the rise tonight – and was overtaken, more than clutched at: gripped and seized and wrenched by monstrous need, appalling desperation.

My body arched, that much I knew, every muscle suddenly going into spasm; and I fell, of course, into the tangled protests of the party.

Fell and rolled, arched and bucked across the floor, across a mess of legs and crisps and spilling drinks and yelling. And my eyes were open, they say, but I was seeing nothing there; nor feeling any of the damage I did, with my sight spun inward, searching for the horror shouting in my mind.

All my life my sister had leaned on me, literally and emotionally and in my dreams also. Not for support, only to keep me down: only because she could, I often thought, because it was a talent she'd had before anyone was looking for signs of talent in either one of us.

Often and often I'd be dreaming and she'd be right there in my dream, uninvited, leaning. Putting her small strong hands against me, choosing her spot and pressing with her fingers, *see what I can do? And you can't stop me. Weakling . . .* And I'd wake up, dragged painfully out of the dream, and I'd have a dead leg or my arm would have gone to sleep, wherever she'd been leaning; and I'd look across the room to where she slept and see her, wide awake and smiling in the dark.

Not for years now, never since we'd reached puberty: since she'd developed her small talent, in other words, and I none at all. Or since I'd left, perhaps that was the significant moment, since I'd revealed myself as beneath even her rich contempt.

But now I wasn't dreaming, Christ, and she wasn't leaning either.

She was screaming. They say that I was screaming too, they say I rolled and screamed and threshed around like a mad thing on the carpet, running with saliva at the mouth; but all I knew was my sister, back in my head again and screaming this time, screaming for me.

TEN

ALL FLESH IS GLASS

Later, thinking back, I could never remember a time when it had happened like that. The opposite, yes, often: myself screaming for Hazel to come and help, to rescue me. Sometimes she'd do that, sometimes not. Sometimes she'd only come to laugh. But never this, never my strong sister screaming for me.

Maybe that's why I reacted so badly, so urgently. One reason. Maybe.

More likely it was only that she was being herself, *in extremis* as in everything. Bullying, demanding, taking possession: this time of all my mind, so that I lost my body with it.

Not even my sister could scream forever, not even inside my head where she didn't need breath to do it. When she stopped, she didn't go away; there was still a mute and dreadful hunger, *I need you*, dragging like gravity, sucking like the earth sucks, not to be resisted.

But at least I could breathe now and feel myself do it, at least I could choose to move and have my body understand me. My eyes saw carpet, and my fingers felt the same. Tremblingly I pushed myself up onto hands and knees and tried to crawl to the door, only that I didn't know where it was.

I had to lift my head, to look; and saw people's legs in a circle around me, every direction barred. Looked higher and saw their faces, dimly through the stinging water running from my eyes like my sister's tears, acid and disorientating. Heard their voices then, vaguely, though I couldn't make out any words through my sister's sobbing call; then felt an arm around my shoulders, strong and insistent.

Turned my head and saw Carol crouched beside me. Felt her hand in my hair, more rough than tender, tugging for my attention; and her voice to follow, "Ben, listen. *Listen* to me, Ben. Are you listening? Can you hear me? It's all right, do you understand? It's okay. Whatever's happening to you, you're with friends here. We'll look after you, but you have to tell us what's going on or we don't know what you need . . ."

And so on, insistent, inescapable, oddly comforting: the voice of a woman who's talked more than one person down from a bad trip.

But this was no trip, and wasn't going to go away by talking. I shook my head against her fingers' grip and surged upwards, snatching for balance; fought free of the hands that clutched uncertainly at my clothes, and plunged towards the door.

Frantic, struggling with complexities – *the Yale won't turn, I can't open the door, why won't the Yale turn? Because it's on the snib already. Just pull it, Benedict, just pull the door* – while my mind sang like a wire with the simplicity of Hazel's despair, I made it at last into the air.

Outside, things were better. Only marginally, but we're a marginal people and I was operating right on the margins here. I took a breath and stood in the quiet of the street, turning and turning, feeling for her.

"Ben?" Carol's voice, in the doorway behind me. I shushed her with a dizzy anger, too shaken yet to speak; and went on turning, though my head was twisting still in some other direction and my stomach churned in sympathy with neither.

Don't give up on me, sister. Keep yelling . . .

Mathematically, I couldn't prove it; there was no sense of a signal increasing or tuning in more precisely. But even when we were very little, "Ben, where's Hazel?" would produce a finger pointing, unerringly accurate over short distances and fairly reliable over miles. Not a trick I'd thought about for years, but now she was trying, now she needed me, and I was certain.

That way, then; and not close, not a quick sprint and Benedict to the rescue, a black sheep redeemed by valour, the ugly duckling made beautiful at last.

Don't give up on me, sister – though probably she would, I thought. I'd never been reliable before, why should she depend on me now?

Because there's no one else, an easy answer to one of tonight's questions. It was in the blood more than the mind, I thought, but I shadowed her, I still echoed when she shouted. There was no one else she could reach this way, so of course it had to be me.

And of course I had to go; and was going already, was running at a stagger down the road.

Carol caught up with me before I'd reached the corner. She grabbed my arm with a fierce strength, and dragged me to a halt against all my pulling.

"Ben, what *is* it? What's wrong?"

My mind was still yearning towards Hazel, giddy and hurting with it; it was hard to find space in my head to make the words. "My sister," I said effortfully, thinking that I owed Carol that much, at least. "My twin. She's in trouble . . ."

She nodded briefly, didn't ask how I knew. It was already a night for faerie and Celtic myth, for the mysteries of blood; and besides, I was a Macallan.

"Where is she?" Carol asked; and oh, the echoes were strong tonight. How many years since anyone had asked me?

"That way," pointing, as I used to point as a child.

"How far?"

"I don't know. Miles, I guess . . ."

"Well, you can't run it, boy. You're in no state." She looked at me consideringly, and I could see the pattern of her thoughts, better than I'd ever seen my sister's. *He should phone someone else*, she was thinking, *one of his cousins; but he won't*, and she was reading me right also, *he thinks he's got to go himself. His sister, his twin* . . .

"Come on back inside," she said briskly, the decision made. "We'll find someone to drive us."

Going back with my eyes less blinded, I saw something at least of the damage I'd done: bowls spilled and broken, nuts and tortilla chips crushed into the carpet, broken glass and wet patches. The greater damage, though, was in the near-silence I walked into, the unsure glances and the nervous shiftings back. Friends and strangers, they were all visibly remembering that I was a Macallan, and that strange things happened around people like me. When I was gone, I knew, they wouldn't talk about me, or not for long. Safer that way. My family had a regiment of spies, and traditionally didn't like to be gossiped about.

Carol found a man prepared to drive me where I wanted to go, but he wasn't exactly a volunteer. More a reluctant conscript. Fear of that unspoken family name helped, I guess; more persuasive perhaps was the equally unspoken pressure from everyone else at the party, *get him out of here, before something worse happens*, or else it was Carol's relentless urging, the way she gripped the man's arm and pleaded for me until he took the easy way out, and said yes.

Carol came too, sitting in the back with me, holding me close with one arm while the other hand squeezed mine: holding me to the world, I thought deliriously, as my head still spun with my sister's singing terror. Others had offered to come, Jacko and Jon together; but one was enough, and Carol was better than either. More genuinely concerned, maybe, and certainly less frightened.

Finding Hazel was easier than any of us was expecting. We drove north because it felt right, Carol translating my mumbling and my sharp little cries into directions for the driver, and not often misunderstanding. After a couple of miles, thinking perhaps a little more clearly – unless it was just that the options narrowed as we left the city, as we drove into less familiar territory – I remembered one of our childhood haunts, a sudden valley with a bizarre garden hidden and abandoned behind high walls.

Taking a gamble, or else responding more deeply that I knew I could to Hazel's summoning, I hauled up old memories that told me which way to go. Wrong turns in the darkness fazed me, but not for long; soon we were pulling into a drive of weeds and broken tarmac, that led to locked wooden gates topped with rusty wire.

And there, ticking gently in the cool night, was Hazel's bike.

For a moment I only sat looking at it, trying to send a message of my own, *I'm here, sis. I've made it this far, at least.* And not too late, seemingly, because I could still feel her in my head, less strongly now but no less urgent.

My hand fumbled at the car's door, getting nowhere. Carol leaned across me and worked the catch for me; I almost fell out onto the gravel as the door swung open.

Standing was difficult, the ground seeming to buck beneath my feet. Stoned and drunk and desperate, I staggered to the gates and briefly had no idea how to get past them. There was no strength in me, to jump and scramble over. But memory rescued me again, surfacing slowly through the chaotic stew inside my skull; I left the gates and blundered along the wall, hands pressed against gritty stone while my feet ploughed through nettles and dock and stumbled over branches fallen from the overhanging trees.

Soon I was in a ditch, dry at this time of year, choked with growth. Brambles caught at my jeans like wire, tangling my legs, making all but impossible what was hard enough already; but it couldn't be far now. Guided by my hands' fumbling more than my eyes in starlight, I groped my way onward while Carol tracked me along the road, above and behind. I was conscious of her as a voice calling my name, puzzled and anxious; but I paid no attention. Hazel was calling me the other way, calling me on, and hers was the only voice that counted.

Stones and lichen and old, crumbling mortar against the palms of my hands – and here at last, here the stones shifted under pressure. And here was greater darkness, a wide gap in the wall where a tree's slow-time pushing had tumbled it into rubble. Here I could clamber up and over even in the dark, and drop down the other side into the blindness of the wood.

Soft beneath my feet, the ground sloped steeply down. Foolhardy, I let it draw me into running from tree to tree, catching my weight against each trunk as I came to it and sighting ahead for the next. This was memory again, the memory of muscle and bone; we always ran here as children, usually tripped and fell sprawling into the mast and loam. And got up straight away and ran on, ignoring bumps and scratches. Too tough to cry herself, Hazel never let me cry either. If withering contempt wouldn't keep me quiet, then a hard hand over my mouth and a fist grinding into my side, whispered threats of major retribution later always would. Nothing was allowed to spoil Hazel's fun, particularly not a dirty and grizzling brother.

Tonight I didn't trip, though I slipped and skidded and should have fallen half a dozen times. Saved by trees and shrubs and simple luck, anything I could grab, I plunged recklessly all the way down to the water.

Too small for a river, though that's what we'd always called it, too wide and full-flowing to be a stream: it came down through farmland rough and unready, then dressed itself smart and civilised for its passage through the garden before vanishing into a culvert under the road and not showing again on the other side.

At night with no moon up it was black and alive, flat and wriggling with the stars like flying sparks reflected in its flanks. My hectic descent had brought me down at an angle I hadn't intended, careering almost into the hedge that divided the wood from the farmer's fields. The water rushed and gurgled through a mess of brick and ironwork, half choked by banked-up rubbish; then it ran on free and clear, and I ran beside it to where low walls and a high arched gateway marked the limits of someone's forgotten garden.

There was no house. So far as I knew, there never had been a house. We'd never found any sign of it. Only the garden, private and secluded, hidden and wonderful.

The gate under the arch was long gone, though its hinges still rusted in the bricks. I went through, sobering abruptly as I felt my sister sliding from my mind.

I called her name nervously, "Hazel?" into the darkness. Nothing came back to me.

This side of the wall, the water was broad and hushed between stone edgings, running into pools where fish flourished despite our childish efforts with bamboo and bent pins. There were bridges and a roofed verandah, slate benches and plinths where statues must once have stood. We'd loved this place once, Hazel and the cousins and I; now suddenly I hated it, as I'd always hated anything that scared me.

"Hazel?"

Still nothing. Only the water moved and all the shapes were strange, stark shadows against the sky.

Slowly now, all my urgency displaced by a creeping terror, I made my way along the water's bank to the first of the bridges, where we'd carved our names once with Marty's knife in the rail; and that's where I found Hazel.

She was lying slumped and still on the mouldering planks, and even she looked alien for a moment, her head rounded and swollen and black, faceless and shining with stars.

I shuddered, too breathless to scream; I stood over her remembering Marty, remembering Tommy and frightened to touch.

But it wasn't her head, of course, it was only her helmet. Once I'd understood that – though it took a while, before I could bear to look close enough to see – I was all brother again, dropping to my knees and reaching for her, fumbling under her chin to undo the strap and lift the helmet off.

And then for the second time and far too soon after the first, I knelt in the dark with someone in my arms I couldn't recognise.

Hazel it was, it had to be. The short-cropped hair was Hazel's, and the helmet, and the leathers. But oh, the face was not hers; for one mad second in the starlight I thought it was Aunt Bella still in Hazel's web, and in her clothes now also.

Nothing identical about us, Hazel and me; no one had ever confused the one for the other even when we were babies in nappies and there was nothing for guidance, which was which. But still our faces had had the stamp of one womb on them, easy to tell that we were twins.

Looking at her now, I didn't know her.

A harsher web than Hazel could ever lay claim to had seized my sister. All the skin I could see was painted over with lines, in a bizarre geometry; but those lines danced with nightfire, and stung where my fingers touched.

I snatched my hand back, and I think cried out in shock or grief or some more complex feeling, more appropriately family. Even that, though, even my voice so close couldn't move Hazel now. Her open eyes were looking not at me, they ravaged the sky. Searching for a moon, I thought, even at the last; and cursing an ill-made pattern of stars and circumstance that had left her moonless tonight when she most needed what strength she could borrow. Had left her with nothing but me to shout for, and me too certain to come too late, and helpless . . .

As I watched, the nightfire glimmered and died.

After a little, my tingling fingers reached for her face again.

Those lines were cracks, black cracks seared in her skin, pathways for the fire to run. Between the lines, my hard sister was harder now than ever, nothing soft or human remaining to her. Crazed glass more than skin, brittle and sharp-edged, shattered into a craquelure of fragments.

Nothing of herself in that cracked and broken face, which meant nothing of me either. Losing sight of her, I lost also sight of myself. A more valued edition of what I saw in the mirror, all our lives her features had defined mine. With those now gone, I felt myself blurring, losing definition. If I looked now into the water, if there were light enough to see by, I was weirdly uncertain what I'd see.

I cradled her dead the way I never could when she was alive, the way I'd never wanted to; but it was her own true self I mourned, not some fictional dream-sister, sweet and amenable and loving. I knew too well what the world, what the family and what I had lost here. She'd taken a half-share of my life, or more than half, and I could never disinvest from Hazel; how could I help but mourn her?

* * *

I cradled her, I rocked her and my face was wet with tears; and I thought myself totally alone and free to howl and curse, until I heard feet crashing down the hill behind me.

Standing, it was oddly easy to lift Hazel in my arms, not to let her go yet. Turning, I didn't care who came. It wasn't the cavalry, it wasn't rescue for my spiky sister. That was my task, at which I'd roundly failed; and that being so, what did it matter who came now, later even than I was late?

I could hear breathing, rough and gasping from the fear and effort of that downhill run in the dark. Then a slow hiss of indrawn air at the first sight of the garden, the first touch of wonder; and then a darker shadow in the shadow of the arch, a figure moving in my tracks.

I stood still on the bridge, I held my dead sister in my arms and wasn't worried. Let come what would, the night's work was done already.

And then a voice calling, soft and nervous in the night. "Ben?" she said, and it was nothing, it was no one, it was only Carol come down from the road.

"Ben, you've been so long, and I heard, I thought I heard . . ."

"I thought you would have left," I said; and though she knew I was there, though her eyes had half-found me even, still she jumped at the sound of my voice. "I thought you'd be gone by now."

"Mick left," she said. "But I couldn't, how could I leave you here? He wouldn't wait this long, not knowing what you were doing, whether you were coming back; but I said I'd stay, I'd see you back home one way or another."

I shook my head, although she wouldn't see it. No business of hers, but I didn't think I'd be going home this night.

Closer now, her hands stretched half in front of her as though it were darker even than it was, as though she really didn't want to see, she saw despite that; and was too honest to deny it, to herself or to me.

"Is that," she said, "is that your sister?" And then, not needing me to speak with the answer so transparent, "How is she?"

"She's dead," I said, the words as light on my tongue as Hazel's body was light in my arms, and as facile.

"Oh God, my love, I'm so sorry. What is it, what happened to her, can you tell?"

I shook my head, part in answer and part denial as she stepped forward. *Don't come any nearer.* She wasn't family, she had no right to see.

She nodded and stayed where she was, just a little shy of the bridge. Water murmured a short fall beneath my feet, reminding me that I stood on no good ground here.

But stand I did, and nothing more. I could think of no move to make, nowhere to go. And Carol stood, for no better reason than that I wasn't moving; and we might have stood there all night, both of us stilled by the stillness that was Hazel in my arms, if there hadn't been other footsteps unexpectedly on the path, coming light and unhurried through the archway.

I turned just my head to look, thinking, *This time, maybe?* And still not scared, not concerned, barely curious.

And not this time either, as it happened.

This time it was Uncle Allan, appearing impossibly out of the night, a cavalry on his own and riding at last and too late.

ELEVEN

HERE COMES THE SUN

"Benedict," he said softly. "I heard her calling you . . ."

"Did you?" I said dully. "That was clever." It had always been a private trick, strictly between us – strictly from her to me – or so we'd always assumed. None of the cousins could emulate it, at any rate. But Allan was ever the smartest, ever the most brightly talented and the most technically interested in talent. No surprise if he'd cracked this as he'd cracked so much else, so many questions. Sometimes he found answers to things we hadn't even thought were questions.

He looked at Carol then; and I think because I was there, and because of what had happened, he said please. He wouldn't have otherwise. I saw him read her and dismiss her, *only cattle, and hence of no account*, and then he did it aloud; but for my sake, at least he was polite about it. Even *in extremis*, you didn't hurt family feelings. Not if you were Uncle Allan.

"Would you leave us?" he said, glancing at her briefly, moving nothing more than his eyes. "Please?"

If she'd so much as hesitated, I think he'd have moved her himself, despite me. I'd seen him do that before, to an irritating punter. We'd laughed then, at the man's expression as his legs carried him away under another's will, in jerking marionette steps; but we'd been younger, I'd been too young to see that it wasn't funny. Too young to know, then, that I would never be one with my cousins, playing like that with the punters.

But Carol was sensitive to the night and the threat and the vicious edge of emotion, or else she was just nicely brought up. Either way, she nodded briefly, bluntly; and said, "I'll be, I'll be up on the road, Ben. If you want me."

I sketched a wave of acknowledgement, and let her fade from my mind as the sound of her footsteps faded.

"Uncle . . ."

"Hush, lad. Let me see."

He took my sister from me, and laid her out again on the dank boards of the bridge. Then he lifted his eyes, only his eyes, and set nightfire to burn all along the rails on both sides. Probably he just wanted to see better what had been done to her, but to me it seemed like a tribute, like a candle to a saint.

My sister was no saint, but nightfire is no candle either, nothing so holy.

His seeing meant that I saw too, at least until I turned my head away; but that was detail only, and detail meant nothing. In the cold light I could see that even the whites of her eyes were crazed like windscreen-glass. So? Her life was all run out, through wider cracks than that. Who cared for the whites of her unkind eyes?

I thought that, but still I turned my head away. She never liked to be touched, my touchy sister, and Uncle Allan's hands were all over her. Gentle and respectful, but still touching, still questioning. I resented it for her, didn't want to watch.

When I heard the sounds of her zips, when I knew that he was touching where – so far as I knew – no man had ever touched Hazel, not looking wasn't enough any more. I took myself off into the wood.

I walked among trees, only shadows of themselves in the thin, guttering nightlight that threw my own shadow in amongst them. They felt real enough to my fingers; but then so did I, and I felt myself only a shadow now. Shadow without substance, as I always had been. Only now the substance that had defined me was gone, the loud noise faded to which I'd only ever been an echo. I thought that I'd fade too, that my little worth would diminish to nothing without my womb-sister's rough strength to back it.

Uncle Allan understood, I think. When he called me, when his voice softly named me in the night and I turned back, Hazel was dressed again, as decent as she could be in her cruel death. Even her helmet was on her head again, its blank visor hiding what I couldn't bear to see again. *Thanks, Uncle . . .*

"Will you carry her?" he asked.

I nodded, not trusting myself to speak; and hoisted her in my arms, and she felt like a china doll unhinged at all her joints. What had been flesh was cold and hard and hollow, utterly inhuman.

I followed my uncle up the slope, trying not to tangle what I bore in the sharp twigs and thorns of this wild wood; and he must have been ferociously angry where I could only mourn, because when we came to the wall there was no scrambling through gaps in fallen stonework. He marched up to the gates, and didn't even reach his hands towards them, didn't come close to touching.

This was a Macallan, a true Macallan in his wrath. There was a glare of ice-light in the silence, and the gates crumbled and fell to dust, while the rusted wire sang and snapped and fell in a tangle of glitter and flare to the muck beneath his feet.

He walked out onto the road, and I walked behind him as rich in envy as I was poor in everything else. I'd have traded anything, the brightest future in the world, for a touch of that talent now. For the chance to be angry as he was, to set the night on fire to light my sister her hasty road to hell.

* * *

His car was down the road a way, he said; he'd come across the fields by a route I didn't know, to avoid that hectic slide down through the wood.

Carol was right there in the gateway, waiting for us. Staring now, backing off with her hands a nervous flutter against my uncle's magic, *keep your distance, don't come close to me.* Allan noted her and as before found her of no importance, this time wasn't even polite enough to acknowledge her with word or gesture.

Having no words in my too-full throat and my arms too full of Hazel, all I could do was jerk my head, *this way,* and look back briefly to be sure that she was coming, trailing behind us in our thin procession.

Uncle Allan drove a Volvo, cautious man. Big and blue and heavy, it had a back seat wide enough to lay Hazel out neat and nice, though getting her in was a humiliating hassle. I wanted to kiss her for once, for maybe the first time in my life; but even in the dimness I couldn't bear to, knowing what my lips would be touching on her cheek. I was terrified of the way she might taste.

Allan went round to the driver's side, and looked at me across the roof.

"Get in, then," he said. "We'll go to my place. We need to talk. To the family also, but first I think to each other, and in private."

I was already moving to open the door, an obedient nephew again and at last, when Carol spoke in the darkness behind me.

Just my name, just "Ben?"

That was enough to hold me. The door swung open under my hand, the courtesy light was on; but I lifted my head to look, and found her fifteen metres away and holding station, shifting from foot to foot but not, definitely not coming any closer.

"Come with," I said, remembering that she had no other way of getting home. Thinking that was what she wanted, that she wouldn't presume but was only waiting an invitation. "You can sit on my lap, plenty of room . . ." Well, she wouldn't want to share the back seat with Hazel, would she? Even if either of us wanted her to; and there at least I could have spoken for my uncle as well as myself, I could have said no for both of us.

But Carol was shaking her head, shaking it hard, *you'll not get me in there with him. With her.* And, "Stay," she said.

"What?"

"Don't go with him. You don't need him, Ben. Last thing you need tonight, going back with him." *And with her*, unspoken but very much there, underlying everything she said.

If I was shaken, I think Uncle Allan was truly stunned. He wasn't used to contradiction, even from inside the family; from cattle, it was heresy. His head turned slowly, his eyes reassessed her. I was watching him, we both were, and I saw him rate her still at no account.

"Get in the car, Ben," he said, one last charitable gesture, pretending she hadn't spoken; though clearly she'd blown her chance of a lift.

"No," she said. "Please, Ben. For you own sake, you've got to think of yourself now . . ."

I thought she could usefully be doing the same thing, thinking of herself. She'd seen already what Allan could do, what he had done to the gates; and this wasn't putting him in any better a temper.

"Why," he said softly – surprising me, deigning to speak to her about this, even if the question was meant to be purely rhetorical, no answer required – "when his sister lies dead in my car, why should he not come with me? With us? He must. This is not a matter for you. Be still."

Be still, I echoed in my head, *and be glad you're still breathing.*

But no, Carol wasn't going to be faced down. She was scared –

and more than simply scared, perhaps, too smart not to know what she was doing here, what she was risking – but she caught her hands together to stop their fluttering, and went on regardless.

"It's a, it's a matter for Ben," she said. "He goes with you, he gets caught up in it all again. He won't get free again, you won't let him . . ."

"He never was free," Uncle Allan said, cold and blunt and truthful. "He is of our blood. That is not accessible to change. And his sister is dead."

"And he'll be dead too, if he comes back to you. The person he is, the person he's tried so hard to become – he shouldn't throw all that away. Not without thinking about it, at least, not without knowing what he's doing." And she turned to me then, and said, "It's your choice, Ben, it has to be. But for God's sake, no, for your *own* sake, just look at what you're doing . . ."

That was it, that was all she had the strength or the courage or the words to say. She fell silent then, only looking at me; and Allan looked at me also, and the burden of decision was all mine, and I didn't want it. I couldn't handle it, too heavy for me. I turned away from them both, from both their tense faces; and the movement brought Hazel into my sight where she lay lit inside the car, all the terrible damage hidden but still true, still there to be dealt with.

And then my feet did it for me, took the responsibility. It was simple enough, at the last. I didn't want to get into that car.

Only the latest and greatest betrayal of my sister, that was all it was. I'd been too late and too weak to save her, to answer her desperation; and now I couldn't bear even to sit in the same small space with her. Guilt and horror and disgust, all of them fierce in my body, twisting my gut, driving me off.

And so I stepped back from the car, and Uncle Allan took that as a rejection although it truly wasn't meant that way, I hadn't thought it out that far. Behind me I heard the car doors close, oh so quietly, and the engine start, and he drove slowly and carefully away from us, respectful of what he carried, and he left us standing in the road.

Not a long while before I heard the hushed sounds of her footsteps, of her breathing coming close. Not long, but long enough. It wasn't until she touched my arm that I realised how I was shaking.

She felt it too, I guess. Maybe felt the same shiver building inside herself also, tension released, adrenalin pumping into the system and finding nowhere to go. At any rate, she wrapped her arms around me and hugged me hard.

It was so welcome, so unexpectedly welcome. Just the touch of a warm and living body was good, to set against the touch-memory of Hazel; better was what underlay it, to have someone see the need in me and bring her own need to meet it.

Truly a long while, before I even thought to let go her trembling body and turn my mind and hers to the first and necessary question, where we should go from here. *Nowhere but down*, my private thought was; there was an emptiness in my head where my sister used to be, should still have been. A silence where the threat if not the actuality of her voice had always lurked, where I'd always had half an ear listening out.

But it was dark and it was cold, and we were both a long way from home; we could at least do something to get ourselves out of that.

"Got any money?" I asked, my voice rough in my throat, hard words jagging on soft flesh.

"What?"

"For a taxi. If we can find a phone."

"Oh. Yeah. Maybe. Hang on . . ."

She checked pockets quickly and came up with a purse, still

leaning into me so that I could feel the movement of her arms against my chest.

"Terrific."

She unzipped the purse, peered inside, shook her head.

Showed me: no notes, little cash.

"Sorry . . ."

"Well, no matter." I felt strange, disconnected, unravelled almost. My mind might be saying *taxi*, but my body didn't really care. "We can walk it. I can. You okay to walk?"

"Sure. Whatever." *Whatever you do*, her eyes told me watchfully, *I'm sticking with*. "But, Ben . . ."

"What?"

"There's the bike. You sister's, I suppose. I was looking at it, while I waited for you. Keys are in it, and I can drive it if you can't . . ."

Friends. Christ. What the hell would I do, what would I ever have done without my friends?

It hadn't gone away, that odd sense of detachment from the world. Gravity's grip was weaker suddenly; I had to watch my feet. They weren't a hundred per cent certain which way was down, or how far it was to ground.

But Carol held my hand, something better than physics to trust to. The needy don't let go, where they're truly needed. We didn't hurry, and we didn't talk; we just walked quietly back along the road, heads down, not to look into the dangerous future.

When we came to Hazel's bike, it was still ticking arhythmically. I laid my hand on the engine, and it was warm. Energy wasted in the combustion of gases, that was all, not Hazel's body's heat; nothing directly to do with Hazel.

Told myself that, loud in the privacy of my head, firm as I could be; and still stood a while not even stroking the metal, only with my fingertips touching, feeling for something that wasn't

142

there. Never would be there again, the *animus* that had driven this machine this far.

Almost I didn't want to mount it. *Lèse-majesté* it felt like, to displace Hazel so thoroughly and so soon, to sit in her seat of power.

Carol wouldn't laugh, probably would even think me morbid if I said so. I was learning this woman quickly, and here she'd let me draw the lines, she'd see it as my right to say what was proper and what was not. If I insisted, she'd walk with me all the way back to town. Hand in hand for comfort and probably she'd watch my dubious feet for me when my eyes couldn't manage any more, she'd make sure I stepped right and didn't stumble.

But, what the hell. Not what Hazel would have wanted, probably the opposite exactly, herself dead and my riding her bike; and hadn't I set myself up in opposition to my sister, shouldn't I seize the chance?

Should or shouldn't, that's what I did. In a rush now, in a hurry – as Brutus must have stabbed Caesar, surely, delaying and delaying and then going in there hard and fast and heedless – I threw my leg over the bike and sat astride, turned the key and pressed the button, and twisted the throttle and sent the engine's roar crashing into the night like something solid. Solid and alive and angry. This my inheritance and I claimed it now, echoed it more weakly. Felt none too solid and barely alive, and how I wanted, ach, how I yearned to be angry . . .

I could do it in seeming, at least: ride the riot and pretend that things were other than they were, that it echoed me, my fury made manifest. Silently in the noise, a jerk of my head gestured Carol onto the queen seat. When I felt her hands on my waist like a signal, *not letting go*, I kicked the stand up and we were away, movement's wind in our hair though the night had no wind of its own.

* * *

Hazel's bike was a Beemer, cool and raked and black as her bad heart, loud and strong as her soul, powerful like she'd always longed to be and never was. Sublimation, I guess, like everything in her life. Like her power over me. Lacking what she wanted, she took what she could, and why not? Nothing special in that, nothing different.

I turned deliberately the wrong way when we hit the dual carriageway, felt the question in Carol's hands and ignored it, hunched low and felt my way through unfamiliar gears until we were flying north, the road unreeling dizzily below us.

I wasn't going anywhere, only going for its own sake, only wanting to be gone. Travelling without hope, because that had to be better than the other thing, being hopelessly still.

That I could do this at all, that I could drive a bike tonight was something else I had to thank my closest cousins for. Mostly, whatever Hazel chose to take up I'd gone out of my way to avoid. But Jamie was all teenager with none of my hang-ups, he'd wanted the thrill of speed and noise, he'd wanted to be dark and hot and ultimately cool in leathers; and when Marty had offered to teach him I'd tagged along, not eager but invited, never good at saying no. We'd spent a Sunday afternoon in an abandoned quarry, wrecking the gears of an old Bristol; and we'd gone back to their house high as kites, with bruises and torn jeans and a new skill in our skinned and filthy hands. After that Jamie had taken up scrambling with a passion, and again he'd taken me with him as often as I was around. I'd been mechanic and mud-scraper much more than driver, not to be thought to be competing with my sister; but once learned, it wasn't a knack that went away. Long years since I'd touched any bike at all, and I could still find the old kick lurking somewhere in my bones, still lose myself in recklessness and rush.

Couldn't lose the night, not entirely. Couldn't drive out of my skin, and wasn't remotely tempted to drive altogether out of my life, to throw the bike in a screaming skid under the wheels of an oncoming juggernaut. Even if Carol hadn't been with me and clinging tight, that wouldn't have been an option. I'd seen Hazel cruelly dead tonight; however weak I felt, however useless, weak and useless was better than that.

Somewhere over the border – and I'd crossed more than one border that night, but this at least was physical and clear, territory well marked, explored and explicit –Carol drummed with both fists on my back, patient no longer. I turned my head, and she yelled above the engine's roar: "I need a piss, Ben! Can't we stop? Please?"

I nodded, suddenly feeling stiffness in my shoulders and a pressure in my own bladder also, and a pounding ache behind my eyes.

I could have pulled over on the hard shoulder there, we could have used the bushes; but I recognised this road now that I was looking to do that, wanting to know where we were. There was a service station, I remembered, just a couple of miles ahead. More comfort for Carol, a drink of water and with any luck some paracetamol for me . . .

I throttled back just a little, from crazy down to mere urgent, matching the swing of my mood. Unlocked from a near-trance I was coming down fast, only in a hurry to stop now; the lights of the service station rising ahead were nothing but relief.

I pulled up on the forecourt and Carol was instantly away, looking for the toilets before I'd even switched the engine off. I followed her more slowly, stretching and swinging my arms, grunting at the snag of muscles too long tensed.

Empty my bladder and fill the tank, two priorities; but first I fished in all my pockets, gleaning what coins I could find. My throat was achingly dry, but I didn't have enough for coffee and pills both; so I bought the pills, and washed three down with water from the tap in the gents'.

When I came out, Carol was waiting.

"Okay?" I asked her.

She nodded. "How are you?"

I shrugged. "Sorry about the hell-ride."

"No problem." She gave me a quick hug, gentle now, with the fever of horror drained into the night and the wind. "What now, what do you want to do?"

"Go back," I lied. It was the last thing I wanted to do, but, "I need to talk to Uncle Allan."

"Ben . . ."

"It'll be all right." Now, it would be all right. I'd established something by walking away from him, some ghost of independence, for which I thanked her with a silent, speaking arm around her shoulders.

Back at the bike, I rolled it over to the petrol pumps and unlocked the cap.

"Um, Ben . . ." Carol was looking worried, checking her purse again. "I can't help, I've got nothing left, hardly . . ."

I grinned at her wearily. "Then I guess your criminal career begins tonight. This morning," I corrected, noting the first faint tinges of light on the horizon. "I'm a Macallan, remember? We don't pay for mundane things like petrol, it's a family tradition . . ." And this was Hazel's bike, after all. It probably wouldn't recognise, would refuse to run on fuel honestly bought and paid for.

"Christ. Won't they send the police after us?"

"They might. Whether the police will catch us, that's something else." And nothing to worry about if they did. But it was a different world that Carol came from, hard to remember that sometimes; so I grinned at her again for reassurance, habits of childhood asserting themselves again. I'd had troubles and anxieties enough for any kid to cope with, but fretting about the law had never been a feature.

Tank full and bladders empty, "Hop on," I said, "let's go home."

Gunned out of there without even a glance towards the kiosk, where someone even now was probably reaching for the phone. *Don't waste your time, heart*, only I couldn't be bothered even to give them the message, even with just a flicker of my eyes.

Twenty minutes later, the police pulled us over.

As kids we always called it the Great South Road, at least when we were headed this way, back to town. *Roads run in both directions*, we used to tell our less-flexible elders, *why choose one and not the other?* And south was always downhill, it seemed to us, everything drained from Scotland. *Or England sucks*, we used to say, giggling. Whatever, there was always this impulse on the road that took us home, *hurry faster*, we felt it dragging at our wheels, drawing us on; and whatever they said, we knew the adults felt it also. Journeys back were always quicker.

Despite my intentions, my reluctance, my implied promise – *sorry about the hell-ride*, I'd said, and meant it – I felt that same urgency waiting again, lurking on this road as it always had. Not even a motorway, just a dual carriageway with bad sight-lines and a dreadful reputation, but it sang to me of speed, of rushing home under the paling sky, racing the dawn back to town.

So I was doing that regardless, crouched low again with a hard wind flattening my hair and the weight of Carol's head sheltering behind my shoulder. Her eyes closed, I guessed, only her tight grip anchoring her to me, to whatever reality I offered her this long, long night . . .

And then, like the final surreal joke, one last cast of a bent and weighted die by a malevolent god, there was another bike pulling slowly abreast of us. This one white as against our black, flaring with lights against our darkness; and just to complete the contrast, the bobby who bestrode it was decked out in all the gear we didn't have, helmet and gauntlets and luminous green bars on his jacket, *look at me!*

I did that, I looked at him; and one leather finger jabbed towards the hard shoulder. Jabbed, and jabbed again.

I could have ignored him, I suppose. He wasn't going to ride me down, or shunt me off the road. I could have driven straight and true, all the way back to town with him at my shoulder like an escort. But I thought that if he was stupid enough for this, he was stupid enough for anything: to call up reinforcements, perhaps, to bring the helicopter over and radio in for road-blocks up ahead.

It was generosity, nothing more, that pulled me over. Not to blight the man's career with such a great, such an insurmountable mistake.

God, the mistakes we make . . .

He was a heavy, leering man with a thick moustache; and oh, he was enjoying himself this early early morning. He took his time, doing everything in slow order: gauntlets off, helmet off, notebook in one hand, pen in the other. He gestured for us to stay where we were, on the bike, but I wasn't planning to move anyway. I'd kicked its stands down to save my having to hold it, but I liked the warmth and the weight of it beneath me, the sense of power contained, controlled. I collected illusions of power sometimes, gathered them to me, treasured and hoarded them against a certain need; and I needed this now. Weak and angry both I felt, dangerous and useless.

"Is this your own motorcycle? Sir?"

I looked him in the eye, and told him yes. Felt Carol stir behind me, but she didn't say anything.

"Uh-huh. Well, I'll check that in a minute, on the radio. Won't help you much, even if it's true. Stealing a tankful of petrol, doing a hundred without lights, without helmets . . . Got any insurance?"

"No."

"No." He made a note, then said, "Can I see your licence, please?"

"No."

"Left it at home, have we?"

"No. I don't have a licence."

"Ah." Another note, and, "Are you *sure* this is your own bike?"

I just shrugged and went on looking at him, waiting for the one questions I wanted, *what's your name?* I was looking forward to that.

It was Carol who spoilt things, wanting to make them easier. Trying to appeal to some supposed better nature in the man, she said, "Look, go easy will you? It's his sister's bike, and she's, she's dead, she's just died tonight . . ."

Carol made a noise, a vague and helpless noise, took her arms from my waist and was no doubt making a vague and helpless gesture also, *have a heart, I can't tell you that . . .* I didn't turn my head, to see it, just kept looking at the cop.

"Doesn't look like a girl's bike to me," he said, sucking at his moustache as he paced around us. "Dead or alive. Just sit still, son," as I twitched. "Tell you what I'll do, then, I'll call the number in, shall I, and we'll see what Swansea has to say?"

He walked back to his own bike, and fiddled with the radio there. I felt Carol's hands on my arm, heard her voice softly hissing, "*Talk* to him, for God's sake, Ben! You tell him, tell him who you are, he'll believe you . . ."

I shook my head, didn't take my eyes off the man. No giggle left in it now, but family pride still had a say. Held sway, even, stronger than I'd thought. I wasn't going to explain myself to a policeman, nor plead for clemency. Not tonight, not any night.

A minute of silence then, broken by the hiss-and-crackle of interference on his radio. *Busy old fool*, I thought, *unruly sun*, warming up the atmosphere, setting everything awry. Just peeking now over the horizon, we'd be full in the light of it in a minute or two; and how many dawns had I seen in my life, I wondered, and never any as grim as this, rising after a night of such desolation . . .

And then a voice, little more than modulated hiss-and-crackle, and I wasn't even trying to listen in; but the policeman was fascinated. He nodded, asked a question, listened again.

Eventually he came back to us, staring at me now with too much interest altogether.

"What Swansea says," he said, "is that the bike's not been registered with them at all."

What, had my sweet sister not filled in the paperwork? Goodness, what a shock.

"But there's a note," he went on, "on their computer. Belongs to a Macallan, they reckon. A girl, like you said, miss. A Hazel Macallan."

"That's right," Carol confirmed quickly, altogether too eager to please.

"Mmm. We know about the Macallans. Even up here, we know all about 'em. Really dead, is she?"

I heard Carol swallow against the confirmation of that news, felt her nod against my back. Heard her voice, thinned now with enormity, with what little memory she had, what she could have seen of my sister. "Yes," she said. "Yes, she really is . . ."

"Not the first, the way we've been hearing it."

"No . . ."

"No. Someone's doing our job for us," and oh, the gloating pleasure in his voice as he said that, the radiant approval. Knowing himself safe, this far from town and the sun coming up: even not knowing me, he knew enough not to worry. Not to check his tongue. "And you, son, you're nicked. Your family's writ don't run this far," *or not in daylight.* "That's if you've got any family left by now. Best thing to hit this coast in thirty years, the guy who's taking your kin to the cleaners."

And I stood up suddenly, with the image of my sister's ruined face in my eyes to blind me; and the sun's light fell across me as I rose. And I could feel nothing but heat in my fingers' ends, fire dancing to be free; and I could hear nothing but screaming as I freed that fire, as I lashed it and lashed it.

And over my sister's face now I could see the policeman's, laid with flame. I saw his mouth work, I saw his hands tear at his cheeks where my bright fire danced strictly in line, palely in the sun but leaving a dark path marked. I heard his cracked bellow and Carol's scream to underscore it; and I heard the hot sounds of his bike afire, and still didn't hear what I was listening for, my sister's voice to tell me I'd done enough.

TWELVE

LIGHT MUST FALL

There were chords in the air, though I could not follow their music. There were rhythms stranger than life – *all life is rhythm*, but not vice versa, Jacko – and colours I could see but never name. The sun laid threads on the breeze that my fingers found and plucked at. Afterwards, needing to label what I'd learnt, I thought it was like tripping: like times when I'd taken acid or mushrooms and seen the world through a different window, finding new patterns in what had only ever seemed chaotic.

At the time, though, it was only anger: all my life's anger right there in my hands to be hurled at the man who'd invoked it.

What brought me back, who brought me down was Carol. She snatched at me, seizing my arm and pulling it out of the weave of light, so that I lost grip on the net I was casting; and I turned on her in my fury, reaching to snare her also in a new web of fire. And saw the terror that was in her, branded on her face; and lost hold of the anger in that crucial moment, and let it all go, not to harm her.

Stood sobbing, staring, seeing her face blur beyond my fingers; and she was crying too, but against me rather than with me, everything she knew about me suddenly as disjointed as everything she knew about the world.

The air cracked now with questions that neither one of us was asking, or wanting to ask. I couldn't have told her in any case, what I'd done or how I'd done it; and sure as God made little green apples to be sour on your tongue and sour in your belly, I didn't want to ask how the policeman was.

Had to look in the end, though. Had to grind the heels of my hands into my eyes and lift my head and look, only to see what I knew already, all I was certain of.

That stupid, stupid man. Thought he could mock a Macallan, for God's sake, thought he was *safe?* Believed the rumours and figured it was okay to gloat in sunshine? If I'd been my sister maybe he'd have had longer to enjoy himself, but not long. Half a rotation, maybe; a little longer still if he was lucky with his timing, but only till the moon rose in darkness. And that would have been max. If she'd called a cousin, starshine would've been enough.

But bad cess to him, it was me he pulled over. Me he sneered at, with my fingers still clammy from the touch-memory of my sister's body; and me finding something in sunlight in answer, finding the family blood suddenly in me after all, though perversely twisted twelve hours out of true.

Me raging, a Macallan come unexpectedly into his true and terrible power; and him lying thrown onto his back, a fire-tossed destruct, a shell burned and broken and cast away. His bike was fallen and still flaming behind him, but that was only a smoke machine and a sound effect, only background, like the thin traffic that slowed and saw and hurried on away with no one stopping.

His arms outhurled, palms upward, I could see how his hands were scorched; but his sleeves weren't marked at all, nor his legs, nor the lower half of his jacket. Up towards the collar, though, closer to his face: there there were scorch-marks and stains, molten nylon with seared edges, *something's gone bang around here.*

And his helmet, his white helmet had black to border it now,

154

and again it was half charred, half molten in a frame around his face.

Only that his face wasn't there any more, or nothing you could call a face. First glance, that frame seemed empty; took a good close look really to see detail. Black in black: within the helmet's shadow his face, all his head was a seamed and blasted ball, flesh seared black and deeply trenched where the cords of my net had tightened.

Put plain, with the horror of it put aside, the facts remained: he was dead, and I was a murderer.

Join the club, my family ghosts, all my ancestors whispered inside my skull. *A little late, but nonetheless welcome*, they giggled as Carol moaned behind me, as I choked and turned away from the rancid smells of burning. *And so dramatically done*, they celebrated, *well done, lad, never seen it done better. And in daylight, too, that much we never managed, no, not at all, not a chance of it for us . . .*

Special, they were telling me I was. Different I'd always been; now suddenly I was special, and though I didn't believe in ghosts or ghostly voices, I still felt as though I'd been through a rite of passage, proved myself in a desperate court; and I needed desperately to talk to Uncle Allan.

Walked over to my sister's bike, touched it with pale fingers that still held a tremble in them, claimed it for my own. Never mind what records said: for the first time in my life I felt confident to take something from Hazel. Okay, she wasn't there to argue, but that only underlined the point. It had been hers and now it was mine, by right of survival.

Rights and duties ride pillion behind each other, take it in turns to drive. It was more than the bike I was claiming here, more than a possession I was taking on. And I knew it, and that was the choice I made. Swung my leg across the seat, settled myself, gripped good and hard and made my mouth work, called my passenger over. Said, "Carol, get on. We're out of here."

"Ben," she said, thin and sick, "you can't. You can't just drive away . . ."

"Would you rather stay here?" I demanded. *With him?* unspoken but very much there, as he was so very much there between us.

"We shouldn't leave him . . ."

"He's dead, Carol. Our staying isn't going to help that. It'll just make trouble, as soon as someone comes." More messages not needing to be voiced: *it could happen again* the loudest of them, *do you want it to happen again?*

And no, she didn't, because she didn't argue further; but she didn't come to me either. She only looked at me, directly across that little distance, and she said, "I don't want to ride with you."

"How, then?"

"I'll hitch it."

"No one's going to stop. Not for you, not after this." A burning bike and a dead policeman, and a girl trying to hitch away? No chance. "You'll just get picked up, and they'll screw you. You know they will." Whatever they thought and whatever she told them, she'd not be allowed to walk away from this. Could be a long, *long* time before Nicky saw his mum again. "Get on the *bike*, Carol . . ."

Her hands made shapes in the air, blank of any meaning, just little gestures of weakness and uncertainty; and at last she came warily over and got on the bike. Sat way back on the queen seat, putting her hands behind her for a hold and trying not to touch me at all with the least part of her clothing.

I felt briefly desolated. Powerful, dangerous, desolated. Not good, any one of the three.

Said nothing, nothing more to say; and started the engine,

kicked the bike off its stand, put it in gear and drove away from the climbing shadow of smoke.

Steady and careful now, too late, not to attract any more attention. I didn't ask what Carol wanted, I only took her straight to where she lived, a terrace in a village in the city's hinterland. Free of me she could maybe reclaim a little of her life, a little of her confidence in the world before she went to reclaim her son from his father.

She dismounted awkwardly, still trying not to touch; and stood looking around, breathing deep for a second or two before she could bear to look at me. And then it was only a glance, her eyes brushing across mine, any greater contact too much for her. She didn't speak, though she did try to sketch a nervous farewell with her hands.

I nodded, not to break that silence that was seemingly giving her some kind of shelter. Nodded and left her, and thought that was probably it. Another friendship dead on the altar of what I was, or what I was becoming. Goya had it wrong, I thought: it was only ever blood that begot true monsters. My begetting might have been a little delayed, but clearly blood would out in the end; and she'd been right there at the outing, and I thought she would never forgive me for that.

Hard enough to forgive myself, maybe that also would prove impossible. I had no right to expect it from her, neither did I.

I drove quietly through town, to Uncle Allan's house in the suburbs. Parked in his driveway and got off the bike, stretched in the cold sunlight and felt my traitor blood sing around my bones, soul's music too revealing to be borne; felt the unaccustomed tingle of power, and hated myself for smiling at its touch.

Allan and Jess didn't have money on Uncle James' scale, or if they did they didn't flash it about. Allan wouldn't be interested in extravagant cars and country houses, comfort was enough for him; Jess, I guessed, would think it ungenteel to be so ostentatious. Whatever, they lived in what was really a Victorian semi, albeit a big one: three floors of red brick, with gables and mullions and mansard dormers and all the fun that architects used to be allowed. It was an expensive street, where high walls and mature trees separated each family from its neighbours; but those neighbours were mostly surgeons or solicitors, successful but not exclusive. Nothing warned you here, nothing said that at the head of this short drive and behind that slightly weathered door lived the man who kept the town in his pocket, his to milk if ever he should choose to. Uncle James was the family milkman, but Allan could have taken that role to himself at any time. I used to think maybe that was one reason why Uncle James did wield his power so widely, simply because his quiet elder brother had so much more.

No grandeur inside the house either, unless there'd been a radical change since the last time I was here. Rare for my family, these two had had no children; but they still needed a large house, to demark the space between them.

Uncle Allan's Volvo was there in the drive; I felt a brief touch of gratitude – mingled with surprise – that there were no other cars, no family gathering yet convened. I couldn't stop myself glancing quickly through the back windscreen, to confirm what was surely obvious, that Hazel's body was gone from there. I didn't want to ask even myself where she might be lying now, though I would certainly have to ask Allan.

No weeds in the gravel, of course, just as there would be no tiles missing from the many angles of the roof and no smell of damp in the cellar. Aunt Jess liked to keep things nice. Wherever Hazel was now, I wouldn't find her here.

Three steps up into the porch, and I jerked hard on the old bell-pull, hearing a dim jangle inside that was instantly nostalgic and oddly comforting. I'd always found my reassurance here. Never called this early before, and I didn't expect Jess to be up yet; but even if he wasn't expecting me – and he surely couldn't be expecting the news I brought with me, the great change that had come upon me – I didn't think Allan would be sleeping.

Nor was he. He came to the door within a minute, greeted me just with a nod and a hand on my arm – and then checked, looking so startled that I couldn't keep a fleeting smile off my face.

"Ben . . .?"

"Yeah," I said. "Can we talk?"

"Of course. Come on through."

He led me into the hall, which was shared territory between the two of them, bland and characterless as a result. Long oak boards indifferently gleaming, nothing paranoid or obsessive; occasional rugs neither new nor worn, only ruggish; a dial phone on a table, not much else. Through open doors I could glimpse Aunt Jess's domain: the dining-room with its long table protected under a velvet cloth, silver candlesticks on the sideboard and dull prints on the walls; the sitting-room where I'd almost never ventured unless invited, where Jess held court among the smells of flowers and fresh polish.

Up the uncarpeted stairs, where I followed Allan now, other perfumes held sway. Learning has its own proper odour, particular to itself, compounded of papers and inks, dust and leather and age. There were traces of it on the landing, where a couple of bookcases narrowed the passage; but only pass through the door on your left into what was my uncle's favourite room, only close your eyes and you could have been in any old library or any don's study in England, entirely encompassed with words.

Open your eyes, and you couldn't have been anywhere else in the world. Only one man like my uncle and only one room like this, the only place fit to contain him.

* * *

A high room and not a bright room, for all that it faced south; the mullioned windows were tall but narrow, letting in only fingers of the sun. Books darkened it more: books everywhere, floor-to-ceiling shelves crammed tight and more books in piles on the desk and on the floor. Rare and valued volumes were more carefully treated, kept behind curtained glass where the slow-creeping sunlight couldn't fade their spines.

Books were only the leading edge of this room, though, only what came first to the eye. A locked oak door led through to Allan's laboratory, where he played with chemicals and fire, where he used to take Hazel and Jamie and me to show us wonders when we were kids; but his curiosity couldn't be contained so easily, nor his collector's soul. All the instruments of light had invaded his library.

Prisms and patterns in hand-stained glass hung in the windows, spilling motile colour across the room. Standing on every bare inch of shelf-space that they could salvage from the greedy books were telescopes and magnifying-glasses, other lenses that he'd ground himself; and on his desk, set up high on its own polished wooden case, was what I'd always loved best of all his treasures; gleaming tubes and cogs and curling arms of brass, an antique Victorian microscope.

What space was left in this busy room was taken by two old chairs, their leather soft and worn from many years of use. Allan gestured me to take one; I didn't sit so much as drop into its enfolding, body and mind both suddenly exhausted, wanting nothing more than this remembered comfort too long missed.

Allan looked at me for a moment, then went wordlessly behind me into a corner and came back with a bottle and two massive glasses. Just a splash of dark amber into each; he passed me one and I held it, looked at it blankly, needing his prompting before I thought to lift it to my mouth and sip.

Thirsty I should have been, and wasn't; but this had nothing to do with thirst. Cool and smooth and tingling in my mouth, it was fire in my throat, heat and life to my belly; and Allan was smugly smiling, watching me intently, his eyes measuring the potency of his prescription.

"Wow," I said ineffectually. "What is it?"

"Armagnac, you ignorant puppy. Cognac," being briefly didactic and enjoying that for its own sake, letting me see his pleasure, "is the wine-drinker's brandy; but this is the true drink, the brandy-drinker's brandy. Specifically, this is a Janneau, and it's, what, some seven years older than you are. Treat it with respect."

"Nah," I said, struggling to match him. "Let's get drunk, yeah?"

"Well, if you want to. If you need to. We can do that too."

"Oh, I do," I said, trying to raise up a young nephew's proper bravado. "I do want to," or I thought I did, or I wanted him to think so. What my body most wanted was a bed, anyone's bed, didn't have to be mine; and what my mind most wanted was to slip the last twenty-four hours into nothing, to come back to yesterday and have Hazel living again and myself a weak and powerless cypher, no killer me. Only neither one of those was on any reasonable agenda, so drinking just might be the next best option. Drinking and talking, and my uncle's old sweet wisdom to help make some kind of sense of this new world . . .

He passed me the bottle over, not a mean bone in his body, though I could as easily have got drunk on the cheapest spirit in the house; and while I poured myself an indecorous slug, he said, "I took your sister home, Ben."

For a second, I didn't know what he meant. "Home" had always been an elastic concept for me, and I'd long since snapped the elastic. Exiles can have no home, by definition; and what are the dead, if not exiled? I even had a crazy image of Allan like Holbein's Christ, *I am the Light of the World* and guiding Hazel's spirit the path to heaven. As if they'd let her in.

But I was forgetting, years of determined separation had loosened my grip on the family perspective; Allan's would be as tight as ever. Children belonged with their parents, that was fundamental, written in stone. The more so for Allan, I thought, because he had none of his own. He'd never been happy, those times I'd decamped to Uncle James' custody; better to have kept under my father's roof, he used to tell me, however difficult the relationship might be.

Hazel had been a shit all her life, but she'd always been a good shit, taking the family whip. Staying home. She'd never left my parents' house; and that would be where Uncle Allan had taken her this night. She'd be lying in state, and never mind the state of her: up in her own room with her own life around her, in the place that had always been most hers; and like any exile I could envy her that, I could yearn for a share in that poignancy.

And might yet regain it, called back to the fold, the strayed sheep returning . . .

"I'll take you to see her, in a little while," Allan said. "When the hour's decent."

I've seen her already, I thought. But he didn't mean quite what he was saying, of course. He meant that I needed to be seen there, decked in grief; and that I had to see my parents. And, bless him, that he would come to make it easier, to act as intermediary if necessary.

And maybe also it was a gentle suggestion, *don't get too drunk, Ben. As much as you need, but no more.* Unsteadiness would be understood, I supposed, and the smell of alcohol on me at close quarters – my twin, after all, and I'd found her – but reeling and vomiting, not.

I nodded, which would surely be enough for this subtle man;

and then, "Uncle? What's going on?" Sounding stupidly young even to myself, too young to be drinking. Young and frightened and whining for reassurance, and far too young to be a murderer.

Never old enough for that, though, by definition. Unless you're a Macallan born and bred and running true to form, of course, in which case empirical evidence suggests that sixteen is about right, though they usually want to get into it a lot earlier.

Unless you're me, of course, a Macallan born and bred and coming to the party hopelessly late and already wishing I'd stayed away . . .

Allan pursed his lips and ran a meditative finger around the rim of his glass, making the air shiver with the high sweet note of cut crystal.

"Two things, I think," he said at last, stilling himself as he spoke. "Two things, quite unconnected; though one may yet bring an unpleasant surprise to the man behind the other.

"First," he said, "the family is under attack. But you know that, and I can't tell you any more than you know already. I can't tell you who our enemy is. Your Uncle James is doing what he can to discover that, sniffing among the echelons of power, asking questions. Making himself very unpleasant, by all accounts; but he has a right to, and his methods are usually effective."

I nodded, suppressing a shiver. I'd seen Uncle James in his anger; spiteful and formidable both, an appalling combination. *Pity the poor cattle*, I thought. No fun, to be the object of James' interrogation.

But then, I wanted answers as badly as he must. If I were there, I thought, I wouldn't interfere. I had no self-righteousness left, no honour to support me in a protest.

"Second," Uncle Allan said, "is what has happened to you, since Hazel's death. I can't tell you about that, I wasn't there; but I do need to know. You have to tell me. In detail, please, everything you've done and felt and thought tonight . . ."

* * *

Took a long time, took the *longest* time: words were hard to handle and memories worse, and the Armagnac was very necessary and no pose at all, even if it only helped because I had persuaded myself that it would.

I sipped slowly, no bravado in it; and measured out my phrases, laid them against the truth I carried and saw how useless, how inadequate they were. Only that they were all I had to trade with, and if I wanted understanding – and I did, very much I did – then this was the only deal in town.

So I took it, I laid everything out for Uncle Allan as honestly as I could manage. Only the once did I try to elide the tale a little – "and the patrolman, he, he *died*, Uncle, I burned him and he died" – and I wasn't allowed even that much shelter.

"Died how, Ben lad? I need to know how."

Died horribly, died sick and cruel and all my own work, I'm a pavement artist and I screeved him, I drew his death on the road there . . .

I took a breath and a little more brandy, and somehow I found the proper words and I told him. As neatly, as accurately as I could.

"I laid a web, I guess. Like, like Hazel used to do, sort of; but she only ever had moonlight to work with, and I had the sun, somehow," which was what was so wrong with it all, the real McGuffin that we both needed to understand, "and that made it all so different . . ."

"Describe it," he said; so I did that too, as best I could.

He nodded, plucked at his lip a little, then said what I suppose he was inevitably going to say, what I should surely have expected. "Could you show me? If we go out into the garden, in the sunlight, could you do it again?"

Last thing, very last thing I wanted to do. But, "Yes," I said, remembering how my blood had stirred within me on the short walk from the bike to his front door. Whatever this was that I had, it hadn't left me. Nor, I thought, would it in the future. Once found, never lost again. "Yes, I'm sure I could. No question. But I don't, I don't want to kill anything . . ."

"No need," my uncle said, his smile saying more: that I hadn't changed so very much after all, that I still didn't have the true Macallan soul, and why the hell should I?

His hand strayed then, to touch a sheep's skull that had been on his desk for years now, that he used as a paperweight; and there was a message in that too, that I was obviously meant to read.

"Is that . . .?"

"Mmm," he said, nodding, smiling wider.

Hazel's sheep, that was: the one she'd webbed so long ago, the one we'd watched until it died. Its skull was traced with dark lines that I'd always thought he'd scored on it himself, for some arcane reason of his own. Not so, I realised now; that was the brand of Hazel's web. Not like mine, she hadn't woven it of flame, but it had still been vicious enough to leave its mark on bone.

"You weren't supposed to know about that," I told him; and he laughed aloud.

"I know a lot of things I'm not supposed to."

"Yeah, right." About his family, I thought he knew it all.

"Come on, sunshine. Let's go and see what you're made of. You can bring your glass, if you want to. Top it up first. Not to the brim, if you don't mind . . ."

Not slugs and snails was I made of, that was certain. Neither magic in moonlight, to be on a par with the rest of my blood. As ever, I was not what I was supposed to be.

He took me downstairs and out to the back, onto a broad lawn sheltered by trees and walls, where we couldn't be overlooked. On the way he picked up an old leather football from a scullery full of kipple, a lifetime's collection of stuff they had no use for but had never got around to throwing out; and even a ball could be potent in this house, could carry me further than I wanted to go. I remembered long summers of games we'd played out here on the grass, me always in goal because my sister put me there; and I remembered all the goals she'd blasted past me, all the many times I'd retrieved the ball from the borders while Aunt Jess frowned out at me from her window. Every damaged plant had been my own fault, for not doing better what I was there to do. And nothing new in that, I could never do anything right, for Jess or for my sister.

Today, though, today for Allan I could do it right, I could show him what he wanted to see. He rolled the ball across the grass, and said, "All right, Ben. Let's see that in the back of the net . . ."

"Puns I can live without," I muttered, dutifully scowling; but that was automatic, nothing at all. Already I could feel the heat in me, though the sun was still cool and low, barely making it down past the garden's high defences. For a moment I was confused and uncertain; power I had but no control, I didn't know what to do to use it. I'd been raving before on the road, it had all happened without thought.

But, Christ, I'd had lessons enough from Jamie and Marty and other cousins back when I was sprouting hair and hormones, back when no one could believe I couldn't do it. I dredged up those humiliating memories from where I'd buried them, deep in the back of my head; I must have been scowling ludicrously as I concentrated, as I reached to that place in my mind that had always been empty before . . .

And there it was, the prickle inside my skin and the surge, the stretch like an extra limb thrusting out where my eyes sent it; and my hands were stupidly pointing and waving like some hack witch in a bad *Macbeth*, but Allan would be used to that, everyone did it first time out.

Second time.

Didn't matter a damn, anyway, what I was looking like. Didn't even matter to me.

What mattered was the great blazing net of air and fire that scorched out ahead of me, branding his beautiful lawn with a brief neat chequerboard before thin flames caught dry grass and spread to smudge the pattern.

Didn't even matter that I missed the ball, though that made him laugh again.

"Never were any use at football, were you, lad?"

I grunted and dragged my net sideways, like an inept fisher-man cocking up an easy catch. The net engulfed the ball and seared its mark in the leather; quickly burned all the way through, and left a deflated rag of brown and reeking black.

I didn't know how to stop, either, no one had ever tried to teach me that, they'd had no occasion; but I blinked hard, unfocused my eyes and let my hands fall, and the mesh of light frayed and faded in the sun, and was gone.

Uncle Allan looked at the damage, and shook his head. "Well, I don't know what Jess is going to say about her lawn. And then there's the lad who comes in to do the mowing, he won't be happy either. He loves this bit of grass . . ."

Dry amusement, that's what he was aiming at, and he made it, more or less; but for once I could actually hear the effort it cost him to make his voice dance so lightly. And something rioted within me, as I realised that for the first time in my life, I'd actu-ally impressed – no, more, I'd startled and amazed my Uncle Allan.

Back inside, in the big kitchen now, chewing soft olive bread against the sour churning in my stomach, drinking black coffee against the brandy and the night:

"In many ways," Uncle Allan said, "this is what I've been looking and hoping for. What I've been working for, you might almost say. Certainly I encouraged the men of my generation to marry out. The older family was all against it, diluting the blood, they called it; but I thought the line needed strengthening. Too much inbreeding is always dangerous, we were becoming effete. Hybrids are more vigorous.

"James wouldn't listen to me. James knew what he wanted, for himself and for his children, and he wasn't prepared to take risks. But your father and I, we both found wives from outside the family. So did a couple of my cousins, those I could persuade against the traditionalists.

"Since then I've been watching, waiting, and I suppose measuring the children of your generation against each other; and up to now, all the evidence has said that the traditionalists had the right of it. Jess and I proved unable to have children at all; your parents managed only the one pregnancy, for all that your mother produced twins; and you both developed . . . unusually."

"A pair of freaks," I said, without heat. "That's how the family's always seen us. There was Hazel, a girl for God's sake and she had talent, however sickly thin it was; and here was I, I was the boy and I had nothing at all."

"Except that clearly we were wrong about you. Totally and bewilderingly wrong. I wanted to bring some strength back into the family blood, and I thought things might manifest themselves a little differently; but talent in *daylight* . . ." He shook his head, gazed at me across the table then picked up my own word and gave it back to me, dusted with a teasing respect. "A freak indeed, Benedict my boy. Something unique in this family. And such potent talent, too . . ."

"Oh, come on," I said, laughing, uncomfortable under his assessing eyes. "It was only a football, for crying out loud . . ."

"It was only the second time you've tried to use your talent; and that totally without training." And his manner, suddenly grave and not at all teasing, reminded me that the first time, a man had died. "You're a strength in this family now, Benedict; you must understand your own worth, or you could do yourself and us a great deal of harm."

"Yeah, right. Lethal weapon, me."

"Exactly."

And he meant it, and he was right; just now I was a loose cannon, charged and deadly. If in doubt, ask a policeman. But resolving that would have to come down to politics in the end – worse, it would be *family* politics – and I didn't want to think about it, then or preferably ever.

"But where did it come from, Uncle? All my life I've had nothing, and now suddenly this . . ." Ten years too late, my talent was in arriving. It was supposed to show with puberty and develop slowly, like chest-hair and acne and such. This was wicked, to give me a decade of zilch and then overnight to fill my cup to overflowing, to make me a heady threat even in my own headstrong and threatening clan.

"I can only give you a theory, Ben; but think on this, and see if it makes sense to you. It was all in your head, it seems to me. No, hear me out," as I made a move to protest that, to laugh it to scorn. "We're no more immune than anyone else to psychological pressures. If anything, we're possibly more vulnerable. Like any high achievers. It's hard to be top.

"Luckily, the Macallans have always been strong on confidence. I used to think it was in our genes, unless it's just a consequence of a long history of success. Whatever the cause, we believe in ourselves, very greatly; and we constantly confirm that belief, and underscore it, and reinforce it. It's a snake that feeds on itself.

"But it's also a snake that eats itself, by definition.

"You were unlucky, you were born second to a domineering twin who made sure that you stayed second. She never gave you any chance to believe in yourself, all through your childhood; so why should you ever believe you could inherit something that she could not? All right, the family history said you should, though we've never had twins before that I know of; and she said not, and it was always Hazel you believed. Even if you didn't talk about it directly, everything that you knew to be so said not, said she was queen and you were nowhere.

"And then, she hit puberty first, because girls do, by and large; and she manifested talent herself. Unheard of, but inarguable.

"No wonder, then, if you thought that she had yours. She'd spent a lifetime oppressing you; subconsciously, I think that you oppressed yourself also. That you felt nothing in the night light would only have confirmed what was already obvious, that you were a freak born without talent. I think you blocked out the truth, and it never had a chance to break free until last night, when Hazel died. She was the keystone in the dam, if dams have keystones; with her gone, the whole edifice crumbled.

"You lived in your sister's shadow all your life, Benedict. You know that. But say it the other way, and it all comes clear. I could still be wrong, of course; but this is what I think. I think that all your life thus far, your sister's simply been standing in your light.

"You were always the one with the significant talent; all she had was the leakage, that she probably picked up in the womb you shared. That's fascinating, it has a lot to tell us about the nature of talent, but it's not relevant now. What counts is that now, at last, the nonsense is over and you can see yourself, we can all see you for what you really are."

"So what am I?" I demanded. "Apart from a murderer, I mean?"

But he only shook his head, refusing comfort on this hardest of paths. "That remains to be seen. You've spent twenty-odd years having someone else tell you what you are; it's time you wrote your own description. Have a good look at yourself in the light, and then you tell me."

THIRTEEN

IN MY FATHER'S HOUSE

In my father's life were many mansions, but none of them was his.

My parents had bought their house back when Mum was pregnant and they'd never moved since, don't know why. Might have been my mother being very unwifely – at least for a Macallan wife – and putting her foot down. *I was born in the next street over, these are my roots; I like it here, all my friends are here and I don't want to leave.* Might just have been that Dad was no smarty, nothing like his brothers, never got a fair share of the family wealth.

Whatever, this was where they'd always lived with Hazel, where I'd lived when I was living with them. It was just an ordinary post-war semi among a dozen streets of semis, little garden at the front and a bigger one behind, and a one-car garage for Dad's car when he could be bothered to put it away, which wasn't often. Three bedrooms inside, woodchip and Anaglypta on the walls and Artex on the ceilings, everything about it dull and suburban and altogether a seriously strange place to find Macallans.

I drove there that day on the bike, my bike now, trailing Allan and Jess in the Volvo. What with exhaustion and too much of Allan's Armagnac, I was in no state to drive, and knew it; but I'd insisted anyway, almost tearfully, like a toddler with a new toy that he wouldn't let go. "Follow us then," Allan had said; and he led me slow and cautious, watching over me as he always had done, constant and reliable and careful of me in a way that my father never had been, even in those days when I depended on him for my care.

The street my parents lived on was lined with cars, although it was still early. The family was gathering again, as it had for Marty and no doubt for Tommy too. This time, though, I had a true place there and meant to claim it. Not by burning footballs out the back to prove my belonging – I'd asked Uncle Allan not to talk about that, and he hadn't even mentioned it to Jess, unless he was doing it now in the car – but by right of blood. Cousins were one thing, and I'd felt the loss of them far more than I'd wanted to; my own womb-sister was something else entirely, for all that I'd feared and even hated her for so much of our lives.

God help me, I wanted revenge. I wanted to see someone cracked and splintered, whoever it was had cracked and splintered her. Shattered mirrors of each other I wanted them, my sister and her assassin; and God help me, I could do it now.

Crowded with cars the street might be, but the family had always respected seniority; there was a space left in front of the house for Uncle Allan to park in. He drove by and stopped, his reversing light came on; and I nipped into the gap, quick, up onto the kerb and through the open gateway, past my father's beloved Cortina and onto the patchy oil-stained grass of the front lawn, bringing the bike home to where Hazel had always left it. Quietly killed the engine, no final wild revving the way she used to, not to spook the people inside by invoking her ghost too loudly; quietly got off and stood waiting for my uncle and aunt to join me. The door of the house was standing open, but I wasn't going in alone.

People, too many people: even the hallway and the stairs were crowded with the family's lesser lights, who couldn't claim a place any closer to my father's hearth. No big room here, to accommodate all my relatives in comfort. The air seethed with static, though I could bear it more easily now, it seemed, having found power of my own.

The pack pressed back, to allow my uncle passage; Jess and I went through in his wake. Past the telephone table where Hazel's black helmet was standing just where it always used to stand, it come home no less than she, and into the front room where the luminaries were gathered. Both my parents were there on the sofa, my father's bulk strangely shrunken as he sat in a room of people standing; my mother looked pale except for her reddened eyes, evidence of what might have been the only other tears shed for Hazel. Hers and my own, and only one of us had ever loved her. What I felt was a tearing at the heart of things, a sense of slippage, but not a loss of love.

Uncle James was there too, of course, standing portentously in front of the gas fire. He greeted Allan with a nod, as though he were host here, Jess with a dry kiss and myself with only a stare. I gazed back, neutral as I could manage, then turned my back on him and went to my mother.

She tried to smile, to let that speak for her in her grief, to say that I was welcome. Crouching down, I put a hand on her knee, my silence matching hers; and saw her eyes widen briefly, as though she felt something more in my touch. Probably she did: even in that crush of Macallans, even with the headache and sickness so much family had to be causing her – which, typically, none of them seemed to have remembered; grieving wife and mother, her place to be here at the heart of the gathering and never mind the damage it would do her, the damage that Jess was already escaping, slipping out of the room in search of some zone Macallan-free – she'd have known the touch of her own child, I guess. Would have noticed how it was changed.

She still didn't say anything, though. Just that moment of perception, and her own hand moving towards me and falling short. Wariness or weariness, one or the other, I couldn't say which and maybe neither could she.

Whatever, I patted her knee and stood up, went to stand behind her where Jamie was stationed already, his hands on the back of the sofa. Clenched hard, I saw, knuckles showing white.

People were talking in murmurs, all through the house; Allan and Jess were at it now, heads together with Uncle James. Only my parents weren't speaking, seemingly, or being spoken to.

Jamie cocked his head in greeting, then did what my mother couldn't manage or was frightened to try. Prised one hand off the sofa-back, transferred it to my shoulder.

Christ, his grip hurt. We used to do circuits at the gym together – with Marty again, the three of us, unless it was the two of them and me – way back when, and probably he still did. Me, I'd abandoned that when I abandoned my family and all its works.

I don't think he knew he was hurting. All his body was tense; his face was tight and white, sheened with sweat though the morning wasn't even warm yet. His eyes looked blind to the room, focused only on me.

"Have you seen her?" His voice was tight too, pitched high and hoarse.

I shook my head, remembering how he's been when Marty died, how angry. This was the same again. He was blazing, raging at what had been done to us. "Not here. Last night, I saw her."

That checked him, even in his fury. I saw him blink, saw him consider; and then, "How?"

"I found her, Jamie. She called me."

"I didn't know that." He understood, though. He was one of the few who'd been close enough to know how Hazel could lean on my mind.

"I was too late," I said, "too slow. Couldn't get there."

174

He grunted, and his hand slackened on my shoulder; his arm came round me in a hug that caught at my throat as much as my body. "Shit, Ben . . ."

"Yeah." Shit it had been, shit it was; but it had brought me up equal with Jamie now, at least in his eyes. I could read him, easy. He'd lost his big brother, I'd lost my twin. More, I'd had the chance to save her, maybe; that I'd failed didn't rub out the fact that I'd tried. He'd have expected my failure. He knew what I was.

What I had been, at least. What I was now, I hadn't really had the chance to find out even for myself; and Jamie wasn't my mother, however close we'd been once. He wasn't noticing anything different in me. No blame, the state he was in. But I thought I might tell him, later. He might again be one of the few.

Turned out this wasn't a meeting, in the sense that Uncle James had held a meeting after Marty's death. Perhaps the third death somehow didn't count for as much as the first; unless it was that my father's daughter didn't count for so much as my uncle's son. Whatever, there were no speeches, nor would have been any even if there were a room fit size to give them in. The family turn-out this morning was only to show solidarity, to murmur in cliques and to look for leadership: Uncle James held court by the fireplace, and I think everyone there came for a shake of the hand or a clap on the shoulder, a quiet word or two. Meanwhile Uncle Allan was mingling, drifting from room to room and again talking briefly with just about everybody. Promises and reassurance, I guessed at from both of them, undertakings and dark oaths of vengeance. Tonight, I thought, the streets would be very full of Macallans doing a detective job. Going in pairs and playing bad cop, bad cop, if I knew my family. Bullying was all they had to fall back on, they'd never bank on the efficacy of kindness. Nor of cash: Uncle James would never believe that you could buy true witness. *Fear keeps cattle honest*, he used to say, and he wouldn't have changed on that.

What had changed, what was very strange was to see fear on the faces of my family. It was suppressed, perhaps, they were ashamed and trying to hide it; but it was there, none the less. Not Jamie was frightened, only angry he; and not Allan either, I thought, though he would be cat-cautious till this was resolved, a man careful of his life and health. Uncle James, though, I thought Uncle James was a little frightened, beneath his bluster and his offended pride. On others it was more clearly to be seen: a nervous glitter to their movements, eyes shifting in search of a reassurance they couldn't find, a fidget in their fingers. Someone was biting his nails, someone else biting his lip. This was hard for them, an insidious and unknown enemy with power that was supposed to be private, for family use only; and they weren't coming through it too well. No experience, I supposed, they'd never learnt how to handle themselves in a crisis. Never expected to face one, being who they were.

They were facing one now, right enough: three cousins dead, murder stalking the streets of their own home town with their blood in its nostrils, and it could have been anyone next on the list. No way of telling, nothing to link Marty and Tommy and my sister to predict who might be written down to follow, unless it was simply what Hazel had pointed out herself yesterday morning, that they were none of them the brightest stars in our constellation of talent. Maybe our enemy in the shadows was following a basic strategy here, picking off the weakest first, just to reduce the numbers . . .

Watching, I felt suddenly disgusted, a surge of my old loathing for everything my family stood for. Gangsters and cowards, scared of the dark now because someone was doing to them what they'd spent so long doing to other people . . .

I turned away, and caught Jamie's eye in passing. Gave him a hint of a smile, a hint of a wink; if he'd read any of my thoughts on my face, I didn't want him appropriating them to himself. Jamie had always been a little different, a little better than the herd in my critical judgement, even at its most harsh; today he outshone them by factors of brilliance, a man prepared to be angry alone with me rather than fearful with them.

"I'll be back," I murmured. "I'm going upstairs."

He nodded, misunderstanding as I'd meant him to. Hazel would be laid out on display up there as Marty had been, *look what they've done to our girl*; but I didn't need to look. I wasn't going anywhere near her bedroom. I was more interested in my own.

Others had been up, and were coming down. I waited politely at the foot of the stairs, nodding quiet gratitude when they touched me in turn, in sympathy, and said what a dreadful thing it was. Then I squeezed my way up past the overflow of people standing on the steps for lack of anywhere else to stand, accepting the same from them and thinking it strange, so many of my family touching me and seemingly none of them noticing what their hands were coming into contact with, that tingle in my skin. Like Jamie, I supposed, they had excuse enough; or else simply no standards of comparison. So long since most of them had touched me or talked to me or wanted to be seen anywhere near me, they'd likely forgotten how dead and cold I used to feel, my blood unstirred by magic. Looking at me now they'd see only another Macallan lad, strayed perhaps but properly brought home by grief; and that's what their other senses would be feeling also, that ripple in the ether that marks out any Macallan lad. Small wonder if none of them remembered that I wasn't supposed to do that, that I had always been a eunuch among studs . . .

On the upstairs landing and blessedly alone at last, even unwatched once I got around the corner from the stairhead and the toilet door, I stopped, took a breath, ran both hands through my hair to hide their trembling – *not scared, huh, Benedict? Like fuck, lad. That's your past in there, and what could be scarier?* – and opened the door to my bedroom. What had been my bedroom.

I was half expecting, and I think half hoping, that the room would have been cleared: that everything that was mine would have been packed away or given away, the walls stripped and the cupboards emptied. At least then there would have been nothing to confront.

I should have known better. I did know better; it had only ever been half a hope, and not really an expectation. My father would have been squeezed, leant on from two directions at once, his two brothers; *he's gone, he's a traitor, throw it out* from Uncle James, and *no, keep it all; he's still your son, he'll come home in time* from Uncle Allan. Allan was senior, his words carried far the more weight; and I thought my mother also would have said no. Would have asserted herself, perhaps, even against James in his offended outrage, chin to chin and her frail arms blocking the door, *no pasaran!*

Strangest thing was to find my door closed. When I lived here bedroom doors never were, unless we were behind them. Even now, with the house full of people, the door to my parents' room stood a little ajar; and yes, so did my sister's. No secrets now or ever, no privacy for Hazel.

I turned the handle on my own door, closed but not locked, at least, not that; and then I was inside and closing it again behind me, and oh, this was a trap, it was a time machine. I was sixteen again and hurting, hurting all the time: hating myself, hating my life, hating everyone I was meant to love. Never had got past that here. Even at nineteen pushing twenty, I'd still been sixteen. Still hurting, still hating.

I'd taken little with me, when I left. A bag of books and tapes scooped almost at random from the shelves; a rucksack stuffed with clothes; nothing else but bad memories and a lifetime's burden of failure. All else that had been mine was here still, dusty but still fresh as tears, fresh as pain.

Posters on the walls: *camshafts and camiknickers*, my mother used to describe my taste in decoration. Sisterless, I'd have had motorbikes up there also; but sisterless I never was, and had never thought to be. So there were cars but no bikes, Bugattis and Porsches and no BMWs. Among the motors were the models, the actresses and the rock stars: some qualified by beauty, some by raunchiness or sheer sex appeal, embarrassingly many simply by the skimpiness of what they were wearing, those snipped from magazines as close to soft porn as I dared to go in a room that I couldn't lock behind me when I left. Anything I didn't want to share, I had to carry. *Everyone needs secrets*, my mother used to say, *but you don't need secret things. Keep your secrets in your head, not in your bedroom.*

I'd made promises and stuck to them, more or less; made only token efforts to conceal those things a mother shouldn't find. There were often cigarettes or cans of lager in the bottom of my wardrobe, barely hidden by an artfully-fallen jacket; quarter-bottles of vodka and the porn that Jamie passed on to me went classically under the mattress. I never could be sure if my mother snooped or not. If she did, she never challenged me with what she'd uncovered. My father snooped for sure, he made no secret of it; but he wasn't looking for smuggled contraband, all he wanted was clues to help him understand his wayward son. Alcohol and fags would have been reassurance to him: signs of a youth being properly misspent, my actions speaking – he would have hoped – more truly than my words.

What real secrets I was coming back to here weren't in the room at all, only in my memories, where my mother would have hoped to find them. Where I'd spent three years trying to bury them, and never was time more foolishly and uselessly wasted. One touch of eye or hand on the triggers that surrounded me now and out they came, toothed and eager, breaking through what thin crusts I'd coated over them . . .

My books: not as I'd left them, those that I'd left behind. Not tumbled across the carpet or tossed onto the bed. Nor put back the way they were before, in categories and alphabetical order; only shelved at random, as my mother must have picked them up. Even at random, though, and even with the curtains drawn against the light to make it hard to read titles, I knew them all by sight. And it seemed to me they spoke too loudly, of the boy I'd been back then. I'd left all my juvenilia, of course, the Enid Blytons and *The Wind in the Willows* and the Biggles books and *The Scarlet Pimpernel.* Most of the science fiction had been left also, dog-eared paperbacks bought second-hand and read late into the night, swapped with Jamie and read again when they came back to me. No fantasy, nor any horror: we'd never needed those.

And scattered through the fiction was the hard science, physics and genetics and biology, mostly stolen from school or from the library during a few cruel months as I struggled to become Uncle Allan in a hurry, to understand about my family's talent and my own clear lack of it. I'd made no headway, no surprise; and those had been the books I'd been most glad to leave behind me.

My tapes: again stacked neatly and not in any order, not as I'd ever left them. And the headphones on the shelf beside, with its cable neatly coiled as I never would have dreamt of coiling it; and these seemed like icons of my life or a shrine to the departed, and it was blasphemy almost for me to be back among them. Long hours, uncountable hours I'd spent with my eyes shut against the night and those headphones bonded to my ears, doing God only knew what long-term damage to my hearing but saving me surely in the then-and-there: blasting my mind with music, isolating me from my life whenever I couldn't bear it longer.

My photos: not the fantasies, not the cars or the sex-goddesses that had teased my adolescent hunger. These were snapshots, Blu-Tacked onto the wall in a tight little cluster just by the head of the single bed, where I could lie in my depression and see them ganging up on me, truly tormenting.

They were nothing really, only a diary in pictures, evidence of how I spent my days. It was pure masochism, that kept me taking my camera along; I knew what I was and what I did, I didn't need reminders. Except perhaps reminders that I could be happy: and I had some of those, photos of me with Jamie mostly, moments of brotherhood where I felt I really belonged. Out on the scrambling circuit, both of us grinning through filth, celebrating some triumph of his not now remembered; or candid-camera snaps at a party with the two of us out of our heads, pawing unknown girls and drinking from whatever bottle was handy, smoking tobacco and anything else that came around, looking pale and sweaty and bare seconds from throwing up. Which we usually were. That was the summer we were fifteen, we hadn't learnt to take it but still we couldn't get enough. My voice was deeper than Jamie's by then, we'd proved that on some piece of electronic wizardry we whipped up between us in his basement den; but his talent had shown itself that spring already, and I was still dead and flat and nothing. He had all his future to celebrate, I had bad feelings growing into almost-certainty, and good enough reason to spend the summer drunk. Marty helped, he was good to us all through those holidays, taking us to parties we wouldn't have got into without him – getting me into at least one bed I wouldn't have got into without him, starting me off on the trail that had led to Laura and my practising to be a virgin, not getting into her bed or anyone else's any more – and I had Marty on my wall there also, in his role as adoptive big brother and all-too-fallible hero.

My drawer: still stuck, still squealing when I dragged it open. My sister's bedroom had been remade every couple of years, to suit her changing tastes and quiet her demands; mine, not. I made no demands, and the room still had the units my father and I had put together from MFI when I was twelve. And nothing had fitted right even then, even before the years of teenage damage.

Drawer stuck, drawer squealed, and even that was barbed with my own particular, vicious variety of nostalgia; but inside the drawer was what I sought, another pile of photographs. Better pictures, these, but not for display, not for looking at. I'd inveigled Uncle Allan into buying me a good SLR and teaching me to use his darkroom – again the instruments of light: Allan approved of photography – and I'd spent a few months seemingly taking it and myself very seriously. Landscapes and portraits, mostly; and no one noticed, or no one appeared to notice how much licence this gave me to be on my own, either out tramping the moors or else locked in darkness with a prohibition on the door. If they did notice, they never commented. Not to me, at least. By then everyone was murmuring about me, I was well and truly cast in my role of family freak, and probably they were just as glad as I was to have me isolate myself so well.

Landscapes were landscapes, *oh look, here's another slab of countryside* and nothing more. Portraits, though, were something else. Portraits were people, and people mattered; specifically, my family mattered to me – even if that matter was dark, another kind of poison in the blood – and all the people I photographed were family. Back then, all the people I knew were family. The world divided, family and cattle; and how was it possible to form relationships with cattle? Not at all . . .

I'd left the camera behind, with so much else. It stood at a shelf's end, accumulating dust, even the lens not protected; and I didn't have a photograph of Laura, nor of any of my friends.

I twitched the curtains back to let some sun in, held my relatives in my hands in the light and leafed slowly through them. Black and white portraits of parents, uncles and aunts, cousins close and distant; three I took out and put separate. Sister Hazel, photographed astride her bike, in full gear: black boots, black leathers, black gauntlets and helmet, mirrored visor down to render her alien and utterly anonymous. Not, in truth, the way I saw her, only the way she wanted to be seen by the world. Possibly this was my most dishonest photograph ever, pandering to her self-image for my own protection; but it had served its purpose at the time, pleasing her in as much as anything I ever did could please her, and covering me against the inevitable penalties of truth. And it had been an interesting challenge technically, all that glossy black in harsh light. Uncle Allan was nice about that, I remembered: praised the skill, said nothing at all about the artistic choices. No fool, my uncle; or else dead giveaway, the work.

Cousin Tommy: I had a photograph of him in hard close-up, trying to let his face speak for him, as I had little enough to say myself. I barely knew him, except from rare family gatherings. I couldn't remember ever having five consecutive minutes of conversation with the guy, doubted if we could have found enough common ground to talk for five minutes together. So here he was, right in my face, every pock-mark and every bristle that he'd missed shaving that morning; and his eyes looked oddly pale and I wished, I really wished that I'd made one exception and taken him in colour, just to capture their faded denim blue like a memorial, just to say that at least one thing about him was unique.

Too late now, those eyes were gone. I set Tommy aside with Hazel, and looked for Marty.

And found him, striking and dramatic, me in my Richard Avedon mood and for once producing a picture that had gratified subject and photographer both. I'd taken him with his shirt off and his back to the camera, scowling over his shoulder, all muscle and threat and that great tattoo bulging and rippling on his back. Oh, I'd been proud of this, and found that I still was: even in monochrome you could see the dragon's glory, the sheen of its scales and the strength of it, clinging tight and digging in.

I'd give a print to Jamie, I thought, maybe; though not yet. Not till things were settled, and he could see more clearly.

And not this print. This one I laid beside the others, three blood kin linked now by more than blood or my photography.

I laid them on the bed, and sat in the window looking at them; and felt the heat of the sun through glass on the back of my neck and felt the prickle of power under my skin, the window no barrier to magic.

Because I knew I could now, I wanted suddenly to lay a web across those dead faces, to draw them together in a net of fire and send their images to ash. My fingers were already working, weaving threads of light, feeling the heat of them but no threat, no possibility of burning me.

Didn't do it, though. Opened my fingers instead, and let the threads fray. Too much of my sister: she was still making rules for me, it seemed, telling me what I could or couldn't do. Or put it another way, say that I was still making assumptions and taking my cues from her.

So no. No webs, no nets. And no hectic gestures, this time. I put both hands firmly in my pockets to be sure, looked at Tommy's photograph and maybe narrowed my eyes just a little.

A spot of discoloration, of blackness spreading out; a wisp of smoke, white and frail; and then a sudden flare of light, flame as pale as water, and the photograph curled and crisped and blackened and fell to crumbled ash and nothing.

And Marty followed Tommy, and Hazel Marty; and by then,

by Hazel there was no effort and I was sure no visible sign of effort. I simply looked, and my will needed no more than my eyes' natural focus. I was ruining the coverlet on the bed – the same that I'd slept under for years, candlewick of a colour utterly nondescript – but no matter for that, this was still my room and I'd done worse here with less excuse.

Hazel burned and crumpled, in a way that had no touch of Hazel to it; and I felt liberated at last, I felt limitless. I wanted to run, to soar, to play with fire while I learned just what I could do, how far I could go.

I didn't do that. I'd been too far already, back when something in me still looked to Hazel for its instruction.

Something else I wanted. I wanted to make a grand gesture to Hazel, a sign of final release. I hated the thought of her cramped in a wooden box and stuck in the earth, or else mechanically rolled into an oven and grilled. I wanted to see to her myself. I wanted to walk into her bedroom right now, draw back her curtains and take the sunlight in my hands, make a globe of fire and roll it all the length of her, set her ablaze from end to end and let her go from here, from home, from her own bed among her family . . .

Didn't do that, either. I couldn't burn my parents' house down, for God's sake. Not without asking.

So I didn't do anything much. Didn't so much as look in on my sister to say goodbye. Just walked down the stairs and out of the house: no fuss, no drama, no farewells. Onto the bike and away, with my eyes dry and my mind clear and none of my family on my back, though that state surely wouldn't last.

One thing I did do, though: I lifted Hazel's helmet from the table as I passed, as a *memento mori*. The bike had become my own now; the helmet remained hers, and I wanted it for that and that alone.

FOURTEEN

L'APRÈS-MIDI D'UN ANGLOPHONE

Alcohol or exhaustion or shock catching up with me, most likely all three: whatever the cause, my head had started pounding out of time with my footsteps as I walked down the stairs, and there was the first wire-thin, wire-sharp suggestion of a hot-needle exploratory op behind my right eye.

I drove back to the flat, still in no condition to be driving but I went slow and careful with the helmet on and there wasn't in any case that far to go. The student quarter was only just over the hill from where I'd grown up, very much same side of the city. I could have walked, except that I didn't want to have to come back later and the bike was fast becoming an icon: this was what I did now, this was who I had become. I was the Man Who Rode.

I was the man who rode into my flat on a rising tide of pain, head turned blistering bad; I was the man who found his flatmate's boyfriend busy in the kitchen for the second morning in a row.

This time Jonathan was wearing the scarlet silk boxers I'd given Jacko for Christmas last year. Otherwise, he was all gilded skin and promise. Another day, what with this long aching lag in my sex-life and him looking young and pretty and recently availed of, I could have fancied him myself, maybe; but not this morning. Not with my feet clumsy with weariness and my head skewered like a kebab and the dry sick feeling in my throat; nor with the way he skittered when he saw me, spilling coffee from the mugs he carried. I'd come in quiet, I guess, and he had the radio loud; but surprise wasn't enough to explain his suddenly-paling face and his nervous eyes.

Spot the difference, number thirty-seven: I didn't get off on frightening people. Still didn't, despite finding other family attributes in my blood after all. Whatever it was, that particular erotic charge so prevalent among my cousins, it had to be training rather than genes; and on me, clearly, the training hadn't taken. Too much used to victim status, I supposed, I just wasn't comfortable on the other side.

Jonathan swallowed visibly, steadied himself against the table and made a big effort to sound like yesterday, easy and untroubled. Didn't manage, quite, he'd given himself away too far; but I wanted to applaud him for trying.

"You're back. That's, that's good," when it patently wasn't, not for him. "You all right, then?"

I just shrugged, the only alternative to being a true drama queen and saying no, saying, *No, my sister's dead and my talent isn't, but a policeman is and I killed him . . .*

"What happened, do you want to talk about it?" The offer was kind, if standard practice for the people I lived among; but his voice went against his words, urging me to do the decent thing and decline. "We were worried, Jacko and me . . ."

"Thanks, Jon. I'm okay," doing the decent thing indeed, lying in my teeth. "I'm going to bed anyway, my head's murder. Catch you later, yeah?"

"Yeah. Sure. Good . . ." And he was out of there, still mumbling and slopping coffee as he sidled through the door.

I dug around for pills and found a tub of Co-Codamol, some good heavy-duty numbing power there; swallowed three with a pint of water and went stumblingly straight to bed, with my teeth foul and my skin feeling greasy even on the inside after a day and a night and half a day of wrack, filth under my fingernails and who gave a fuck? Not I.

Woke mid-afternoon, and didn't want to. I managed one moment of denial, *only a dream, that's all, only another bloody dream. Bobby's been in the shower all this time*, before the traitor sun found a way to finger through my curtains, strike off the wardrobe mirror and down onto my cheek, *hi there, remember me?* And my body reacted without my wanting it to, I felt my blood surging, soaking up strength and eagerness; and no, no dream then, and no denial permitted.

So then I wanted to sleep again. Too hot for a duvet, I slept under an empty cover in the summer; but I pulled that over my head to bar the sun, burrowed into pillows and went hunting after oblivion. And failed there too, couldn't find it anywhere I looked.

Besides, I needed a piss as a matter of extreme urgency. And my mouth was dry again and rough as bark, although my head was better. I rolled reluctantly out of bed and sought the bathroom, naked as I was; if the boys were in and in my way, they'd get a treat, that's all. Do Jonathan a power of good by reminding Jacko that we weren't all golden lads, some of us gotta be pale and frail to provide a necessary contrast . . .

The flat was empty, the dimple-glazed window into the back yard was open, the way Jacko always left it after he'd had a shit: "better to be burgled than stink," he used to say, shrugging at my protests. Steam in sunlight, then, the hissing of summer bathrooms; and I started the bath filling, yearning for the shower we didn't have. I wanted to batter the stiffness I felt in back and shoulders, I wanted to numb mind and body both with heat and pressure. Really I wanted a massage, someone with hard fingers to take me apart muscle by muscle, fibre by tense fibre; but lacking that, I wanted a long shower with the temperature cranked right up to scalding-point.

Lacking both, I was going to have to settle for a bath: a splash in six inches of hot water, or a wallow in a bathful of lukewarm. Luckily it was another hot day, and I could make a case for cool.

Hot or cold, it takes twenty minutes to fill that bath, so I looked for post – none – and wandered through to the kitchen still tempting fate, still naked. Made a cup of coffee, strong and milky; flicked on the radio we kept in the hall, where we could hear it anywhere if the volume was up. Turned the volume right up, and went back into the bathroom.

Big surprise, the immersion tank had drained itself already, and the hot tap was running cold. I got in anyway, just to sluice myself down while the water was still warm enough to cut through two days' sweat and terror; then I lay back, draped my feet over the rim not to have them in the full force of that cold flood, sipped coffee and felt chaotic currents swirl around me as the bath filled and the temperature dropped.

With the radio so loud, I could hear it even above the tap's guttering. I could hear when they went from music to news; and I could hear when, third item after the G7 summit – G8, I supposed they'd have to call it, now they'd let that toad Yeltsin join the gang – and the latest Bosnian breakdown, they reported on the policeman found burning with his burning bike. Passers-by had stopped, they said – *not while I was there, they didn't* – and done their best with fire extinguishers and car phones, but all of it too little and too late. Suspicious circumstances, they said, and the Borders police were investigating.

Not doing too much of that, I imagined. They'd make a show, for the press and the public; but they were close enough to home, one look at the body and they'd know more or less what happened. They'd know enough, *he met a Macallan*, and they'd know there was no response possible.

Here at home, it wouldn't even have made the news. An accident, nothing more: grieving relatives given a nice funeral out of petty cash, the coroner as complaisant as the cops and no investigation required. The police might have wondered a little *–wasn't it daylight? Thought we were supposed to be safe in daylight? –* and so trodden even more lightly for a while, but nothing more than that.

The neighbouring force didn't have their experience, and would generate a little more fuss; but it was all smoke, nothing more. That at least I didn't need to worry about.

Worries enough I did have. Cool water crept up my chest; I turned the tap off and subsided until only my face was above the surface, water tickling at the corners of my mouth. This was one advantage at least of a bath over a shower, at least in other bathrooms. When the mood and the place and the equipment were right, I could lie like this for hours – or at least until someone thumped on the door to shift me – with my eyes closed and my body almost floating, my mind almost detached. The closest I could come to an isolation tank, I guess. Like that, I'd learned to confront my problems – some of my problems, at least, the soluble or at least survivable: money, love, the easy stuff; anything that didn't include my family – in equilibrium of a sort, separated from the clawing panic that could grip me otherwise.

Today, though, all my problems were family and the water was too cold anyway. It always was too cold, in this flat. Not uncomfortable on a day like today, welcome even for the feel of it, like slithering between cold sheets in a solitary bed; call me pervy – others have – but I enjoy the twitch of that. I couldn't slip mind free of body, though, even a little distance while all my skin was alert, poised, teetering on the very edge of shiver. The water had to be warmer, I needed it neutral at least if not numbingly hot –

odd that heat was okay where cold was not, but that's life, or physics, or biology or whatever: rhythm, Jacko would say, no doubt – and that was impossible with our landlord's cheapo system, there'd be no hot water now for an hour or more.

So I lay with my eyes closed, trying to enjoy the coolth but wishing to be warmer none the less; and after a little, I was warmer. Or the water was. Currents of hot I could feel, stirring the surface and lapping against my skin.

So I opened my eyes to look, and saw the water burning.

Pale flames danced and leaped, and the water steamed to give them shape in the sunlight; and that's what it was. I thought, that's all it was. Sunlight falling through the open window and finding me – finding the tip of my nose, it must have been, nothing else available – and my mind vaguely wishing for the impossible, more warmth in the water; and this in consequence, this minor miracle. I rubbed my nose where it was tingling, wishing I'd noticed that earlier. Christ, I'd have to learn to be careful. *When the gods want to punish us*, I remembered, *they give us what we wish for.* On whatever scale you like.

I shook my head at the fire, and it went away. I stirred hot water into cold, and the temperature was perfect now, just blood or a little more, ideal to float away on. Only that there was no hope of floating, no hope of distance with my mind suddenly focused and watchful, weighing each thought against the chance of its happening.

God, I couldn't live like this, no one could. How did my relatives manage? *Badly*, was my immediate response and probably the right one. They came into talent as teenagers; and yes, there were always accidents or moments of simple adolescent malice. People got hurt. Rarely family, though, so who cared?

Me, I cared. I already owed the world one life I couldn't pay, and I had the hunger in me for another. Whatever magician it was decimating my kin, him I'd kill without a qualm. And after him, who else? If I got angry, or careless, or affronted . . . *Uncle Allan, how do I get rid of this?* Could I live a night life, migrate from pole to pole as the birds do, only backwards? Could I live and never see the sun?

And what virus had my family contracted, or what murky antibodies was the town using to defend itself at last, late but by no means little; how did this bad magic work? And how many world-shifting questions could a young man's life sustain, when answers seemed to be so sparse?

Almost a relief to have someone hammering on the front door, audible as a rhythm of disruption even above the radio. I surged out of the water and reached for a towel – and my hand passed through sunlight on its way to the rail, and I checked abruptly. Thought, *Why not?* and lit a cautious flame among my fingers.

Didn't feel a thing, didn't so much as smell a crisping hair; but my hand was dry in moments, and the flame danced lightly up my arm like a ring of fire, so long as I left my hand in the light.

When who knocked pounded a second percussion voluntary for fists, louder and longer, I was playing stuntman or comic superhero, standing swathed in flame and laughing at the tickle of it, anxious only not to set the bathroom alight.

I pulled away from the sun to kill the fire, grabbed a towel – checking to see if my fingers scorched it; they didn't – and headed towards the door, swathing for decency.

Opened it, and found Carol on the step.

Degrees of awkwardness, and she cheated; she ducked what was important, snatching with transparent relief at what didn't matter a damn.

"Oh, um, sorry – did I get you out of bed?"

"Bath, actually."

"You're bone dry . . ."

"Yeah." I gave her a grin, as best I could manage, and gestured with my head, both hands busy at my waist, checking the towel for incipient slippage. "Come on in. Give us a minute, I'll get some clothes on . . ."

"Look, I just, I wanted to say . . ." Her hands gestured at feelings she didn't have the words for, complications too great to speak about.

"Yeah," I said again. "Me, too. I'm glad you came. So come in, all right?"

She did, then. I closed the door firmly behind her, to be certain.

"In there," with a nod towards the living-room. "There's no one else around, so make yourself comfy. I'll be through in a sec."

Strong but soured as I was, this seemed like a gift to me, an unexpected chance to salvage something unequivocally positive from the churning chaos of this last day. Carol had been my rescuer last night; this morning she'd seen me for what I was –even before I'd seen it myself, in all truth – and she'd walked away. Now she'd come back, of her own choice. If I could only handle this right, if I could do a rescue act on my own account, then maybe I wasn't altogether lost; maybe I could still save some part of myself from the insidious embraces of family and power, suddenly a trap and a threat I could feel reaching for me, blistering new paths towards my heart.

I scrambled into clean clothes, not to carry anything with me of the night before, and went barefoot to find her, turning the radio off as I passed.

Kitchen people, some days we didn't use the living-room at all. No one had been in today, by the look if it: curtains still pulled, empty mugs on the carpet, ashtray a long way from empty and the smell of joints in the air. Carol had flicked the main light on and was standing in the centre of the room, revolving slowly, checking out the walls: her head cocking foolishly one way and then the other, to see the crooked posters straight. She knew I was watching, but she went on shuffling round and maybe even exaggerated the movements of her head until she'd done the three-sixty. Then, still not acknowledging me, she walked over to check out the music stacked in the corner.

"They're Jacko's," I said from the doorway. "Mostly." Mostly I'd left mine behind when I left home, subliminally bequeathing them to Jamie or anyone who wanted them, along with the rest of my life; and my tastes had changed since then, had moved to parallel Jacko's more or less, so that I didn't need to buy CDs or tapes of my own. Which was a blessing, because I couldn't have afforded them anyway.

"Uh-huh." She fingered out a CD and fiddled with the system for a minute, taking her time to work it out; I stayed where I was, showing her nothing.

Then music, briefly thunder-loud before she reeled it in to human dimensions; and her choice was a surprise, raw Springsteen off a bootleg, showing me something at least. Deliberate messages, I thought, if I could find energy and insight enough to interpret.

"Thought you were a folkie," I said, asking for clues.

"Did you?" Tight little smile over her shoulder, no clues there. She twitched and fussed with the cool array, playing sound engineer against crowd noise and the hiss of cheap equipment; and then she stood and turned and came towards me, saying, "Sometimes I'm a folkie. Sometimes not. Look, no accordion," with her empty arms spread wide. "Sometimes I have to be a mother, but look, no Nicky either. I did some quick negotiating, and he's staying with his dad for another night. Sometimes I don't carry baggage."

"So where does that leave you, then? If you're not being a folkie or a mother right now?"

"Leaves me being a friend, I guess. Sometimes I fuck that up, but it's like good music, or family: you can walk away for a bit, if you're lucky or you really really need to, but you can't stay away."

"In the end, you've got to come back for your baggage," I agreed, nodding wisely and entirely straight-faced.

And earning myself a fist in the ribs as she came into fisting distance, "I'm not bloody *joking*, right, Ben? This isn't a time for joking," and no, it wasn't at all a time for joking, so I didn't protest the punch; and Carol just kept on coming, closer than fighting-far now, right up to hugging. And she did that, she hugged me, all strong shoulders and tight arms and her face twisted with a fierce affection that changed as I watched, all the clue I needed. No surprise, then, when she said, "Hey, this is interesting. This is *strange*. You're all tingly . . ."

"Goes with the territory," I said lamely, standing tepid and confused in the tangle that she made about me. I felt like Laocoön struggling with his serpents. And remembered a little bleakly, a little miserably that Laocoön had lost; and lost the lot, not just petty things. Life and family and his reputation down eternity, all crushed into a bloody pulp for the lack of a little wisdom in juggling power against love . . .

Might have said that, might at least have mumbled something about Laocoön, thinking that she was too tied up around me to hit me again; I could place all her bones, all her major muscles, and not one of them was in place for retribution. But she was in charge here, she'd stolen what initiative the moment could hold. Her hands moved on my back, her fingers gripped my shoulders, she said, "Thought you were just out of the bath?"

"I am," I said, my turn to be bewildered by the news.

"You don't feel it. Baths are meant to relax you, yeah? You're tight as a wire, boy."

That didn't surprise me; nor had it her, for all she wanted to sound that way. Well, Christ, she wasn't stupid. She knew where I'd been and what I'd done today, or the major part of it. Water wasn't going to work that out of my system.

But she'd cheated earlier, I cheated now. I said, "Can't get it hot enough for that."

"Uh-huh." Her fingers dug a little, and even I could feel how my body resisted their digging; and then she grunted, slipped away from me, gave me a flat-handed push into the centre of the room. "Lie down, then."

"Unh?"

"Lie *down*, Ben. On the *carpet*. You can't go around strung up like that, it's not healthy. You'll do yourself some damage."

And she was right, and what she was offering – not, what she was *ordering* – was just what I'd been wanting before that curious and confusing bath. She might not be a Shiatsu wizard, but most of my friends could manipulate a tight muscle till it unkinked a little, and presumably she wouldn't be shoving me around this way if she didn't count among their number.

And it was a peace gesture too, I wasn't so blind that I couldn't see that. *I walked out on you, sure, but I'm back now and being useful, looking for ways to help . . .*

So I did what I was told, I lay belly-down on the worn carpet with my head nestled on my folded arms, eyes closed; and she knelt astride me, her arse cushioning itself with a friendly thud on mine as her hands reached and gripped my shoulders and her fingers started to work.

After a minute,

"Got any oil?" she said.

"There's some in the kitchen," I said dubiously. "Cheapo vegetable."

"Nothing else?"

"Well, I haven't. We could try the boudoir."

"Sorry?"

"Jacko's room," I said, lifting my head to grin at her. "He's so unqueeny, we all give him queeny presents at Christmas. Weird gunk from the Body Shop, you know the sort of stuff. He doesn't use 'em, they just stack up on his window-sill. If I go and look, there'll be something there. Coconut and avocado, maybe, something like that . . ."

"*I'll* look," she said positively. "You stay still, try to wind down a bit. And take the T-shirt off, I can't work through clothes."

Then she was gone from me, and I missed her already; but she wanted me to strip, and this was supposed to relax me?

Ah, what the hell. She'd seen me in a towel and nothing, ten minutes ago; and she wouldn't be the first to massage me skin on skin, only a film of oil between us. The first for a while, sure – ah, Laura and her white fingers, not for me! – but not the first.

I pushed myself up, hauled the T-shirt over my head and flopped down again, listening to the sounds of Carol snooping in Jacko's room. The suspicious silences I put down to her reading his Valentine cards, and why not? I'd done that too. If he didn't want people reading them, I figured, he shouldn't leave them on display in a room not locked.

And then she was back, and back on my case; back on my backside, indeed, a significant weight and warmth.

"That's better," she said, patting my bare ribs.

"Did you find something?"

"Mm-hmm. Not ideal, but it'll do."

"What is it?"

"Well, cocoa-butter, actually. Very good for stretch-marks when you're pregnant . . ."

Not useful information, that; but the stuff was good for rubbing into tensed shoulders also, or else Carol was just good at rubbing and never mind the lubricant. Feeling her thumbs press deep, yelping as her fingers suddenly plucked at tendons that

198

sang in my body like fiddle-strings, so tight they were, I realised or remembered suddenly just how tired I was despite those hours in bed. Body and mind both poisoned with exhaustion, with too much bad living; I should be sinking now, she should be pushing me way, way down and her strong hands holding me under . . .

"Christ," she grunted. "Did I say you were wired? Hot-wired, more like. Like a stolen car. Something riding you that doesn't belong . . ."

And then I guess she heard what she was saying, just about the same time that I did. I sniggered into my own armpit, couldn't help it; and she slapped me across the back of the head for being so obvious, and bounced on my back to underline it. And then we were both sober again, and God knows how far she could track my mind but I was all but engulfed in symbols. Something? Many things, more like. All riding me hard, as she was; and none of them belonged in my small and carefully-circumscribed world, as she herself did not.

After a mutual and mutually-respectful pause for thought and both of us making no offers for the other's, keeping our tarnished pennies to ourselves, I felt her slick hands once again on my skin and probing, coming back to what she knew. Or what she thought she knew, at least, what she could handle, though she knew for certain now what a task she'd taken on.

Fifteen, twenty minutes she must have worked my body over while I lay prone and passive beneath her, eyes closed and too weary now even to tell her that she wasn't really making any difference, she really wasn't getting through.

Fifteen or twenty minutes, where she took quick breathers but kept on coming back, kept on trying to break me down; and then she sighed, lifted her weight off me and said, "Roll over, then."

Rolling over, I opened my eyes, all ready to smile at her shrug of resignation, *sometimes a mouthful is just too big to chew on but thanks anyway, thanks for trying, Carol love* – and what I saw instead of a shrug were two small, pale breasts hanging loose above me where she'd pulled her sweatshirt off during one of those wee breaks, and what I did instead of smile was gape.

Carol it was who smiled, light and ironic; and Carol's hands that had been so hard and so ineffectual on the close-cranked muscles of my back were light and teasing now on my chest and arms, and my skin was tingling and prickling for reasons that had nothing at all to do with the excluded sunlight, and I couldn't believe what she was at.

"My thumbs are knackered," she said, and demonstrated her untruthfulness instantly, gripping my wrists and holding my arms down as I went to lift them in some awkward gesture of denial. "And don't lie to me, I wasn't getting anywhere near, was I? But if a bloke needs relaxing and massage won't do it, well, hell, there are better ways."

"Carol . . ."

"What? Flatmate likely to barge in on us?"

"No." I didn't know where Jacko was, but by this time – ten past six, the clock on the gas-fire said, which meant for sure that it was later than that but probably not yet seven – he was safe to be out for the evening, and Jonathan presumably with him.

"Well, then, what's your problem? Curtains are pulled, no one's going to be looking in at your humping butt."

"Listen, I don't . . ."

"I know you don't. This is one of your problems, Ben boy, we discovered that at Percy's last night. Long time ago, I know, but I don't forget confessions. I mean, talking of long times, how long is it since you got laid?"

I blinked up at her, Ernest Dowson on my mind. *I have been faithful to thee, Laura! in my fashion* – and my chosen fashion was a monk's habit and no young man's. Point of fact, I hadn't slept with a girl since before Laura; since before I left the family, even. I could never be sure that it wasn't my name bringing them to bed, rather than my arguable charms. That had started to matter when I was what, eighteen, or nineteen, somewhere around then . . .

"Precisely," Carol said, though I hadn't said a word. "If you have to work it out on your fingers, it's too long. And what I say is, if not bonking is part of the problem, then a good bonk must be part of the solution. By definition," with a tweaking little grin as she stole one of my own phrases; and then her fingernails closed and tweaked sharply on my left nipple, and I yelped and bucked a little beneath her.

"Just lie still, pet," she said, her hands working to ensure that I could not. Something turned over in my mind, a stray line trapped in teenage memory from a book that my cousins and I had passed between us, Sven Hassel or some war-porn lookalike I'd pinched off my father's solitary bookshelf. A wounded soldier sheltered in a barn; a woman tending to him, peeling away his clothes and then her own. I had a bad feeling that I'd read it with my mouth open; I knew to my shame that I'd giggled, we'd all giggled over and relished and treasured the line and used it inappropriately for months after.

When rape is inevitable, lie back and enjoy it.

Terrible, evil stuff, classic Macallanthink and very much what I hated, what I'd walked away from – but ah, what the fuck. There it was in my head, unlooked-for and inescapable; and here Carol was sitting astride my hips, sitting on my groin indeed and sparing one hand now to unflip the buckle of my belt, and she also was unlooked-for and inescapable, it seemed, and I was just too tired to fight.

Too tired to bonk, also, too shagged to shag: or so I'd have thought. But bodies are perverse and Carol was experienced, much different from the clumsy and ignorant girls I'd clumsily and ignorantly bedded as a teenager. And yes, I had four or five years'-worth of celibacy banked up behind me like a great weight of hidden water, dark and passive and still until something comes to crack the dam.

Images of Barnes Wallis and Carol as a bouncing bomb, the original blonde bombshell; and Christ help me I was giggling suddenly, near naked now and almost hysterical on the carpet there, almost losing it altogether.

"What's funny?" Carol demanded suspiciously, halfway through losing her own jeans.

"Nothing," I gasped, and tried to clench my teeth around the laugh and hold it; and succeeded only in snorting wetly through my nose.

"Oh, gross," she said, stretching for my discarded T-shirt and mopping it at me like a mother. I pushed it away and she thrust back hard, her turn to laugh at me now; and then I wasn't doing what I'd been told at all, not lying still, pet – *not lying back to enjoy it* – and we were wrestling, rolling and straining against each other and all else was slipping away, the world was only bodies after all and symbology could go wank, there were no figures in this carpet: only crumbs and dust . . .

And when the little death of orgasm – mine, at least: far be it from me to speak for her on that – had crumbled to its own little dust, we lay apart and my mouth was dry and bitter, and there was grit sticking to my skin. I looked for Carol, and found her looking at me; and as if my eyes gave her the cue, she said,

"Well. You needed that."

Maybe so, maybe I had. I felt as if the world had shifted on its axis, second or third time today; and maybe that was a good thing, maybe it would eventually come round to a point where it rolled more smoothly for me. Just now I found it hard to feel confident. Gratitude I thought perhaps I could manage; I shifted my shoulders against rough fibres, and yes, there was a tension gone from there. My bones sat more loosely within their sleeve of flesh, and that felt no longer ricked or twisted. Strange things, bodies, and hard to factor.

"Wouldn't want it, though, would you?" I said aloud, if only to see the puzzlement on her face.

"What wouldn't I want?"

"Gratitude."

"Nah. Got no use for it." She stirred, shifted onto her knees, then to her feet. "I could use your loo, though. Where is it?"

"Through the kitchen, and keep walking. When you bang your nose on the wall, you're standing in the bath."

Standard directions, they usually brought a smile; but not this time. Only a contemplative nod and she was gone, naked and easy.

Me, I just lay there, moving nothing that didn't have to move: not even chasing down the itches on my skin that yearned for scratching. Too indolent or too much overused, my aching flesh and the slow recovery of my heart; this was the time to do what I'd been told, to lie back and enjoy it.

Did that, then, and nothing else. Asked myself no questions, even, though I knew they only waited with the world, for me to roll over: *turn again, Macallan*, and there would be nothing but bad questions and worse responses, and I didn't want to be Lord Mayor of anything. Didn't have a cat, either. Refused to keep one, in the flat here. Bad country for cats . . .

And then Carol came back with something just a little different in her, carrying a question in her eyes. *Can't trust anyone*, I thought, grossly unfair.

"You weren't fibbing, were you? When you said I got you out of the bath . . ."

Oh, right. I hadn't pulled the plug out, in my hurry to answer the door; she'd walked in on a bathful of cold and scummy water.

Not nice, but I didn't see how it mattered.

"No, I wasn't kidding," I said. "But I don't get many visitors, so I got out to see. Don't worry about it." *Glad I did*, my naked, knackered body said in a whisper, that I hoped she could hear.

"Only you were *dry* when you came to the door, so I thought it was, you know, just a spur-of-the-moment thing to say . . ."

She thought I'd been having a wank, most like. I just shrugged, which felt silly lying down; and she said, "So how did you do that, how did you get dry so quick?"

Small thing, but it was worrying her, perceptive woman that she was, it obviously didn't fit with the universe she understood; and she'd seen me break the laws one time already today, so she was leaping to conclusions.

And dead right, too.

"You don't want to know," I tried, the classic dodge.

"Yes, I do," she said, managing to sound both doubtful and utterly certain at the same time. Neat trick.

So I rolled over and up, onto my feet and back into the world where all those questions waited, and this the first that would lead directly to all the others; and I took her hand for my own comfort as much as hers, and led her through to the kitchen where the late sun was still angling in over the back wall and through the window.

"Look," I said, and pale little flames as cute as I could make them danced in rank and file over the hairs of my arm, and didn't singe a one.

She shook her head slowly, more in wonder than rejection; then she glanced down at our linked hands and said, "You tingle more when you do that, did you know?"

"One of the perks," I said, winning a bubbling snort from her, and sweet revenge.

We dumped that old cold scummy giveaway water and ran a fresh bath, just deep enough still to be hot. Carol used it first, while I sat on the toilet and we talked; then she got out and I dried her, a trick I'd learned from Marty way back when. Not famous for his courtesies to girls, he did it because he liked to handle them, a dampening towel only an accessory and not much in the way. That they liked it too was a bonus, useful information that he'd passed on to Jamie and to me.

I'd brought her clothes through already, another small attention so that she didn't feel obliged to sit around naked as I had. I was just going to step into the bath myself when there was a second interruption, a second surprise knocking on the door.

This time I hesitated, and looked for Carol's permission before going to answer it.

Got that, with a twitchy smile and a jerk of the head, "Go on, it could be important."

Sounded important, certainly, another round of thumping as I hustled into jeans and T-shirt in the front room.

And it was important, by any measure. Could even be crucial, though I couldn't get my head around it.

When I answered the door, I found Laura there, fist raised to pound again; and Jamie stood behind her, hands on her waist like a message, very loud and very clear indeed.

FIFTEEN

FISSURES OF MEN

Me, I only stood and gaped. Laura moved, Laura did it all; seemed to be a day for that, for women claiming what they wanted from me, taking possession of selected aspects of my body.

She came one step forward and one step up, and we were pretty much eye to eye. Her dark beauty filled my world of sight, and that was all my world. I thought it tainted only by the muddy colours of her concern for me. Another day, an earlier day I'd have been so moved, to see her moved so much; today I felt all my skin fiery and my body suddenly awkward again, every muscle embarrassed and drawing back.

Or wanting to. No chance. Lovely Laura, not to be denied: she just kept on coming. From eye-to-eye she came too close to focus, and her arms wrapped hard around me and her face was in my neck as she hugged and rocked me.

Jamie must have told her, all the news that was fit to whisper. She hugged me for my sister, and also for my finding her; and she being Laura and me being me, because she knew I loved her, I thought she was hugging me also for my loss in love, for her going over to my cousin as completely as she had. Though she'd never been mine, she still had generosity enough to see the wounds of that in me. I thought.

And then she lifted her head and looked at me, her eyes squinnying a little and her nose atwitch. I looked away, looked past her at Jamie and then up in the air, looked anywhere but at her; I thought she could smell my guilt on me, all the sweat and secrets of the afternoon. But,

"White chocolate," she said.

"Unh?"

"That's what you smell of. White chocolate. What have you been *doing*, for God's sake?"

You don't want to know. Or I don't want you to . . .

"It's cocoa-butter," I said, snatching at feeble shadows of the truth, heaping guilt on guilt. "Carol gave me a back-rub . . ."

"Who's Carol?"

But then her eyes moved to look beyond me, to find their own answer. Carol was the woman standing in the passage behind me, barefoot and pink from hot water, rubbing damp tendrils of blonde hair with the towel Laura had given me last Christmas.

"Uh," I said, "do you two not know each other?"

I looked from one to the other; they both shook their heads, watching each other with what seemed a dangerous interest. Dangerous to me, at least.

"Carol, Laura. Uh, Laura's a medic, Carol's a musician . . . And that's Jamie, Carol, he's my cousin . . ."

They all nodded, said hullo. Very polite, very superficial. No one took much of a stab at smiling, but I guess it wasn't the time.

Then, "I left the water," Carol said, back working on her hair again.

"Oh. Oh, that's okay. Thanks, but I don't think I'll . . ." *I don't think I'll leave you two alone together.*

"Go on," Laura said quietly. "Go and have a bath, Ben. You don't want to go out smelling of chocolate."

"Are you going out?" Carol asked, eyebrows suddenly as high as her voice had gone.

"I don't know. I wasn't planning . . ."

"Yes, you were," from Laura. "It's Friday, remember? Jamie's birthday? We *fixed* this."

"Oh. Oh, yeah. But . . ."

"We want you to come, Ben," and that was Jamie putting his oar in at last and enjoying himself for sure, seeing me no doubt like old blind Phineus in *Jason and the Argonauts*, harried between two harpies. "You need a wake for Hazel, better than your family," *or the rest of it*, "can give you. And we need to talk, anyway. We do."

We did. And we should, and why not tonight? We could rage a little: get blasted for my sister, maybe build something from the rubble for ourselves.

"Okay," I said. "Right. Can you just give us ten minutes?" Laura was right, I didn't want to visit any of our usual haunts smelling like the Milky Bar Kid.

"We'll give you twenty," Laura said, smiling sweetly. And leading Jamie, leading Carol into the living-room; and again I was having dark fantasies that the reek of our bodies would still be hanging in the air there for her delicate nostrils to pick at. As they went, I could hear her asking: "So what do you play, Carol? What instrument, I mean . . . ?"

All my life a coward, I wasn't going to reform now. Not for this. I almost ran to the bathroom, with maybe as much as half an hour to hide in, if I really stretched it.

Carol's second-hand water was opaque and a little scummy, and cooling fast. If I'd stretched, I could have cupped the last of the sun in the palm of my hand, and worked my little magic once more; but I settled for chill and hard scrubbing. When I was sure I smelt of nothing but soap and myself, no exotic fragrance nor any earthly weakness, I thought again about hiding, and decided not. The old Benedict would have hidden, yes; but I was reborn, was I not? Remade, in a brighter image? Might as well act like it, try not to embarrass myself in everything I did.

Just about to stand in the water and cast about for a towel, I did the other thing instead, sank suddenly as low as I could to show face and knees and please God let the twice-dirtied water cover all else; because I hadn't bolted the bathroom door, of course, and it wasn't Carol who'd chosen to walk in on me.

"Come on, sit up," Laura said impatiently, perching herself on the edge of the bath and shoving the sleeves of her silk shirt up past her elbows.

"Why, what do you want?"

"I'll do your back for you." No *Would you like me to . . . ?* or anything so compromising. Just the fact, bald and undebatable.

"No, it's okay. I'm fine . . ."

"For God's sake, Ben. I want to, all right? Now sit up . . ."

And just to encourage me, she grabbed a handful of my wet hair and tugged at it. Not painfully hard, just hard enough to re-mind me that it could be painful.

I sat up, but, "You'll get water-spots on your shirt," I said.

"Shut up," she said, "and pass the soap."

So I did that; and again I had a woman's strong and slender fingers kneading at my naked flesh, second time in an afternoon after God knew how long without. And this time it was Laura whom I loved, whom I so hungered for; and I had no appetite for her now, nothing but embarrassment and shame. As though I had betrayed her, though she was never mine to betray.

She not mine but I hers, she knew that and perhaps she liked it, perhaps that's what this was about: that she was reclaiming what she thought she might otherwise lose, washing me clean of what Carol had put upon me.

Or perhaps not, because she wasn't aggressive now, and didn't seem possessive either. This could as likely be a message for Jamie, or for Jamie and Carol both: that Laura and I were two old friends who could be private and easy with each other, bodies not a problem. News to me, my body had always been a problem between me and Laura, but perhaps others weren't to know that. Or else I was meant to rise above it, now that so much had changed . . .

"Wow," she said thoughtfully, drumming her fingertips on my shoulders. "This is new, isn't it?"

"What?"

"You fizz. Like Jamie fizzes. You never used to . . ."

"It's in the blood," I said, and left her to work out why my blood should suddenly have woken up. She couldn't conceivably get it right, but I had no mind to explain. Let her build what theories she liked: contact with Jamie and the rest of the family, perhaps, or seriously-close contact with Carol, maybe she'd think bonking set it off . . .

"I asked Carol to come with us tonight," Laura said suddenly, working the lather up my neck and virtuously behind my ears, and showing how our minds tracked each other's.

"Oh. Did you?"

"Mm-hmm." And then she chuckled, put both hands on the top of my head and pressed down hard, submerging me without warning; and when I surged up again, coughing and spluttering and rubbing soapy water out of my eyes, she was gone.

So was the towel also gone from the rail, because Carol had taken that, of course; and the sun was gone now from the window, and I could either yell for help or else make a dash for my bedroom, wet and naked as I was.

I dashed, and the living-room door was wide open, and I didn't look through in my dashing but I heard all three of them laughing suddenly, and I thought that I could hate them all, I could definitely learn to do that . . .

* * *

Ten minutes later, damp-dried on a dirty towel out of the bin-bag I kept my washing in and dressed in the cleanest going-out clothes I could find, I went through to join them with a watchful smile faked on my face: showing my teeth, I guess you could call it. Ready to bite, if I needed to.

Carol was standing on one leg close by the living-room door, hands in pockets, shoulders and her other foot flat against the wall. Body language loud and clear, only that I couldn't understand it; but she gazed at me thoughtfully, unsmilingly, as I walked into the room, and then took a hand from her pocket to slap my rump as I passed. A message for me, a message for Laura? Christ knew.

Laura was sitting side-saddle on the floor, her legs getting acquainted with a carpet that Carol and I knew better; she was resting her back against the sofa and her head against the arm of the sofa. Jamie had spread himself all along that same sofa, looking lean and lazy and arrogant as shit, with his head propped on one hand and his other playing with Laura's hair. He also looked half cut already, as if his birthday celebrations had started early; but it wasn't all comfort and joy. Something more than gravity and the pressure of his head on his hand was twisting his face out of true. There were dark purple shadows under his eyes; and this room was full of messages, and it was all too much for me.

"Where are we going, then?" I demanded, falsely jovial.

"Somewhere we can talk," Jamie said.

"Yeah. Yeah, right . . ."

"And somewhere we can eat," from Laura, with a disapproving glance over her shoulder, *somewhere this stupid boy can get something other than alcohol into his system.*

"Suits me," I said. "I'm starving." And I heard a confirmatory grunt from Carol behind me, and only just bit down on a genuine smile. Come to think of it, though, I couldn't remember eating at all today, bar that olive bread at my uncle's; and I doubted she'd had much appetite either. No surprise if we were both suddenly ravenous, it was perfectly understandable . . .

"*Il Milano*, then," Laura said; and no question-mark on the end of that, she wasn't offering it for discussion.

Jamie wasted an eyebrow-quirk at the back of her disregarding head, then glanced over at me. "What's it like?"

I blinked, before recalling that Jamie might be my age but he lived very differently. I suppose I'd known intellectually that there were people in town for whom *il Milano* was not a gravitational centre, but it felt a little odd to discover that I knew one. "Food's good," I said, "prices are good, and we can stay all night if we want to."

"Fair enough. I'll give it a shot." He sounded unimpressed by what to me were major recommendations, and I thought probably he'd expect all three from any restaurant he chose to patronise. Nor would he be disappointed, at least anywhere that his face or name was known. Come to think of it, he probably didn't expect to pay at all . . .

And just as that thought meandered uncritically through my head, Laura tilted her own right back, trying to fix him with a steely if inverted gaze. "You're paying, by the way."

Her inflection was entirely neutral, so that I couldn't work out whether she meant *you're picking up the bill for all of us tonight* or *you're not getting this one for nothing, they're our friends.* Whichever, Jamie wasn't bothered; he just shrugged, and said, "Better be good, then, hadn't it?"

"Yeah, yeah. Tough guy."

He grinned and his hand slid over from her hair to her face, took her nose between two fingers and tweaked lightly. I looked away, to find Carol watching me with what seemed to be a purely scientific interest. Weighing and assessing, I thought she was;

and I wondered vaguely how I measured up. Personally, I thought I was coping pretty well.

Ten minutes later, out in the street and on our way at last, I did better still: walked up to where the two girls were strolling side by side ahead of me and Jamie, forced my way between them and took an arm of each.

Carol just smiled; Laura scowled.

"Bog off, Ben. We were talking."

"Too bad," I said, and kissed her cheek.

"What was that for?" she demanded.

I grinned. "A benediction. Obviously."

A groan from my left, from Carol; nothing so pacific from Laura. I was going to have to wear some protection for the rib area, if I went on inviting trouble: not slow with their fists, either of these two.

But Laura smiled, to sweeten the smart of it; and then she peeled away, dropped back a pace or two and linked up with Jamie. I tried not to look round, not to see where their hands had settled; but sideways spying into shop windows resolved that for me, far against my better judgement. His arm was round her neck, his hand hanging down at breast-caressing height. And guessing at what I couldn't see, calculating angles, I figured her own hand was most likely tucked neatly into the back pocket of his Calvin Kleins. *Between his wallet and his arse*, I thought bitterly; and then repented the thought a moment later, a moment too late. Money wasn't a factor here. Not that shallow, my Laura. *His Laura. And must've been his body, babe, if it wasn't his cash. Or his power, or his status, or his charisma or any of the other stuff he's got and you haven't . . .*

Vicious things sometimes, interior voices – but inaccurate sometimes also, or simply out of date. Late sun flashed off a window, bright into my eyes; I felt my blood spangle, and just for a moment I wanted to flash back. I wanted to see that window buckle and melt, just because I could. And I wanted Laura to see it too, to know what I could after all do; and I wanted to see what she would do thereafter. I didn't seriously think she'd instantly detach herself from Jamie's side and adhere instead to my own – but a guy can dream, can't he? I'd had a lot of practice, dreaming.

Wasn't room for her anyway right now, not if she wanted me solo. I had Carol there already, her body bumping against mine as we walked, reminding me of smoother frictions an hour or two since; and where that was heading I couldn't imagine, I had no space in my head to fit her into. Only a sense of awkward anticipation, of waiting to see what she would ask of me, as against what I could offer . . .

Jamie and Laura had come for me by taxi, they'd said; but the sky was clear and the breeze was warm, and there was no harm in walking. Town was only a stroll down the hill, in any case. Taxis home looked probable later; but thinking about that I could find a little private amusement even in watching the other two so tightly bonded, legging it along with us. I thought this was Laura's work: "No, you're not driving, Jamie, and nor am I. You'll want to get pissed, it's your birthday; and I'm not sipping orange juice all night. I don't care if the police ignore us, that's not the point. If you're with me you can drink or you can drive, but not both, it's not safe. And you drive like a zipped-up barracuda anyway, in that flash fuckmobile. We'll go by taxi . . ."

And Jamie seemingly had acquiesced, which must be something of a first for him, was pretty much of a first for the entire male Macallan line. Given the chance, Laura would probably try to reform the lot of them – the lot of us – and that thought tickled me up into a grin, almost into a giggle. The whole town had been resisting my family one way or another for generations, and losing all down the line. Call me a romantic, but me, I reckoned one slim girl, five foot seven and not twenty-two yet, I reckoned she could take us all on and win.

Except someone's doing that already, my mind skittering uncomfortably away from the thought, *someone out there's got a hat-trick already, and there's no reason to suppose that they've stopped, no sign at all that we're going to be able to stop them . . .*

Actually, it seemed like nothing in my life could be stopped just at the moment. Since the day I'd walked out on my family, I'd never felt quite so lacking in control. Great events were in train, world-shaking things were happening to me and around me, and I couldn't get a fingertip's-weight of my own will operating on any of them.

Which should have depressed me, I suppose, but right then it didn't. I only felt curiously footloose, freed from responsibility. I stepped deliberately sideways, from a dim red sunlight into shadow; the back of my neck stopped prickling – reluctantly, I thought – and now there really was nothing I could do to affect anything.

And my muscles twitched regardless, my blood bubbled lightly on its own account, no sunlight necessary. I tugged free of Carol's grip, kicked against the unyielding concrete and sprinted down the hill for the sheer hell of it, to feel wind in my hair and tense anxiety left however briefly behind me, with the calling voices of my friends. I ran hard and laughing, recklessly down the steep hill until the sun was lost behind it not to rise again tonight and the time of my strength was irrevocably over. I was sweating again and staggering before I got to the bottom, whooping and stumbling like I was mad or drunk, like I was both at once; but I ran until the ground was level beneath my feet, until I fetched up against a lamppost and just clung, needing that good help to hold myself upright now that movement couldn't do it any longer.

When they finally caught up with me – taking their time,

maybe even slowing a little to show how much they weren't hurrying – Carol looked at me quizzically and said, "Uh-huh. So what was that all about, then?"

"Not to go gently," I said, and left her to read what she liked into it.

Sharp left opposite the station, up a narrow alley that looked like it was leading nowhere, only drab backs to the glossy fronts on the street beyond; but the alley turned a corner and suddenly it was Little Italy, two or three pizzerias on each side and *il Milano* nothing like the biggest of them. Nor the trendiest nor the most popular, but only the best: a perfect combination.

We walked in as a group and got our usual table *pronto*, though other people were standing at the bar and waiting, with an obvious prior claim. Mario the *maître d'* might have done that in any case, because he loved us and wouldn't recognise the concept of formal queueing, not in his own restaurant; but the service was both sharper and much more polite than we were used to, and poor Gino looked positively scared as he handed menus around. His hands were trembling so much, three times his match went out before he managed to light a couple of candles for us; and him a good Catholic, so used to doing that. Or an observant Catholic, at least, even since we'd teased and tempted the goodness out of him.

He was praying now by the look of him, by the way his lips twitched as he eyes slid from the table to his hands to the floor and back to the table, our friend Gino trying not to look at any of us and very much not looking at Jamie.

What it was, I thought suddenly, no one here has ever made the connection before. Okay, I had the family features, maybe they might have wondered once or twice; but I'd not behaved Macallan, and I'd certainly not used the name. If I phoned up to book a table, I only ever gave my name as Ben.

Jamie they knew, though. It was important, for people with businesses in town to know Jamie. Important also that they should be properly afraid, *ab initio*; and here they were doing that, our wise friends, and I didn't like it at all and so far as I could see Jamie didn't even notice.

We should have gone somewhere else, I realised now, too late: anywhere else, not to risk what we'd had and were probably losing here. Even if this stupid, perilous visit didn't draw further Macallan attention to the place, the staff would never be easy with us again. How could they be, after we'd put them through this? There were no conceivable rewards for them here, nothing to justify the danger. I simply hadn't thought, that was all. Too focused on myself and Carol, on Jamie and Laura and on the night ahead, what needed saying and what avoiding, what ground I dare not tread on and what I must, I'd spared nothing for the side-effects of my being out with my cousin, taking him to my haunts and showing him my life. Which inherently meant letting my life see him, letting people who'd trusted me hitherto see him and me together.

Ah, *shit* . . .

Nothing to be done about it now. Not here, at least. When we went on after, I'd do my best to steer us somewhere we wouldn't normally have gone; although Laura might have something to say about that. Laura wasn't local, she wouldn't understand. She might know intellectually how my family ran the town, but she'd never really met it except the once at Morry's, when she'd met Aunt Bella in my sister's web. She'd probably be forgetting that as efficiently as she could manage, shovelling it into some dusty corner of her mind, turning hard away from it every time she felt herself straying in that direction. Certainly she wouldn't be connecting it with her new beau, this bright and intriguing young man at her elbow; and far from avoiding her normal friends in her normal world, she'd more likely want to seek them out to show him off a little.

So if we fought, we'd just have to fight. One of us would win, or the other would; there'd be more damage done, or there wouldn't. Most likely there would, one way or another. Wherever I went now, it seemed as though I brought damage.

Subsumed with guilt, I couldn't have concentrated on the menu. Luckily, here I didn't have to. I could order on auto: *gamberoni* in their shells and my usual sad pizza, the one that had my friends shaking their heads and muttering anxiously about my digestion and my mental health both, that I could do such a thing to my stomach.

Jamie was doing that now, indeed: staring extravagantly, manipulating his jaw back into position, saying, "Mussels, prawns, squid, tuna, anchovies, garlic and *what* was that?"

"Chilli," Laura told him cheerfully, apparently oblivious or immune to the atmosphere that had shaken me and taken me so very far from cheerful. "He always has the same. Seafood nut, Ben is, and he pays extra to have it stacked up high, or he does when someone else is paying; only then he gets them to do it so hot you can't taste any of it anyway. *And* he sprinkles parmesan all over, which is blasphemy with seafood. I tried a slice once, but never again. It's disgusting."

Actually it isn't, though it sounds like it. Like so much in my life, this had started as a gesture: looking for a way to eat out that would be a significant change from my diet at home and at the same time put no money of mine into my family's pocket – or at least as little as possible – I'd remembered that this was a coastal town that no longer had any fishing fleet at all. All the boats' owners had taken advantage of their inherent mobility, and moved to other ports where no one demanded a cut of their profits for protection. Since when I'd eaten as much fish as I could stomach or afford. Obviously someone had to bring it in, somewhere there was a wholesaler no doubt handing over just a little less than the maximum he could afford to lose – good accountants, my family, with an excellent nose for what the market could bear: no percentage for them in getting too greedy, putting people out of business – but at least I could salve my conscience a little. Fishermen were heroes on this coast, middlemen not.

So I burned my fingers peeling giant prawns, and drizzled garlic juices on my jeans, and remembered my paper napkin too late for more than an ineffectual dab; and after that came my fierce pizza mounded high, dribbling cheese and tomato and chunks of sea life barely dead; and I ate that with my fingers also, while Jamie watched me with all the fascination of an aristocrat meeting a peasant's manners for the first time. I ignored him. I'd seen him tear a roast chicken apart with his hands, when he was so stoned he could barely control what his hands were doing; but if he wanted to play the high sophisticate to impress his girl, who was I to tell her it was all fraud? Not mine to interfere, where I held no investment or interest . . .

But as we ate we talked, and that I couldn't ignore. That's what we were here for, after all. Birthday celebrations had slipped a long way down the list of tonight's priorities; it barely cost me a pang, that I hadn't remembered to find Jamie a present. Couldn't have bought him a good one anyway, had no idea what he was into these days – except Laura, of course, he was visibly and very much into her, his sweet Laura and not mine after all and never would be, never could be now – so let it go, better no present than the wrong one.

"Three dead," Jamie said, breaking a piece of good Italian bread and tearing it to fragments, rolling little balls of it unheeding. That was the refrain, that was where we were coming from and where we came back to time and again: three dead and everyone angry and afraid and no one doing anything because no one knew what to do, where to look for the blame.

"What does Uncle Allan say?"

"Uncle Allan says that if you burn a light in the darkness, you will attract insects; and some of those can sting. By definition, he says."

"That's no help."

"No," he said, "it isn't. He also says that it had to happen sometime, it's not reasonable to suppose we're the only family with talent; and this is a trial of strength, he says. Winner take all, he says."

"But we don't even know who they *are* . . ."

"No."

"Brilliant. So what about Uncle James?"

"Your Uncle James," his son said neutrally, "is filling the streets with family. Every bloke who'll listen, he's sending out on patrol; and you know what Dad's like. He just keeps yelling, until pretty much everyone listens."

"Except for you," Laura put in quietly, stroking his forearm where it lay on the table between them, *my hero*. Unless she was only doing it for the buzz, *my erotic hero*; but no, she wasn't that shallow. Was she?

"Except me. Right. In case you're interested," and he turned to me but his hand turned also, went palm-up to capture hers and hold it loose against its lack of struggle, "Dad doesn't see how I can possibly forget my responsibilities and go out for a birthday binge with cattle and a mental defective, while my family is under attack."

Oh, I was, I was very interested; but it was Carol beside me who spoke, who worked it out slowly on her fingers and said, "Presumably Ben's the mental defective, right, and Laura's the cattle? Given that he didn't know about me being here?"

"Uh-huh," from Laura, with a savage grin to salt it. "He's a right charmer, is Jamie's dad. You'll love him."

221

"I think I'll avoid him, thanks."

Laura's eyebrows gave a little twitch, *you'll be lucky*, aimed neatly between the pair of us, as if she were already leaping to conclusions that I was fairly certain would prove to be hopelessly misplaced; but then, what did I know? I was leaping myself here, in the dark and utterly without looking.

"What's the point of patrolling, anyway?" I demanded. "If you don't know what you're looking for?"

"Exactly," Laura said, backing up Jamie's shrug. " 'You men – strip-search that haystack, there's a needle in it somewhere.' 'Please, sir, what's a needle?' 'Damned if I know, but don't come back without it . . .' "

She was pretty good at voices, was Laura. Disregard the register, and her twit officer barked just like the Brigadier on reruns of *Doctor Who*.

Couldn't make us laugh tonight, though. Just smiles round the table, and the faintest hint of a chuckle squeezed out of Carol. Jamie tightened his lips, tightened his grip on her hand, and took us round the mulberry bush again.

"They've got to be somewhere in town, though. And if they can find us, why can't we find them?"

"Because you don't know what to look for, sweetheart," and this was her top-girl voice, slow and smart and patronising, like the little pats she was giving his hand now. "Everyone knows you lot, can't miss you with those great ugly hooters in the middle of your faces. Wouldn't call them noses myself, more like cow-catchers . . ."

"Cattle-catchers," he said, twitching his at her; though to be fair his nose didn't have the prominence of mine, that was traditional among my kin. Right shape, but significantly smaller; closer to young-man normal, really, even down to the kink where Marty had cracked it with a saucepan when they were kids. It was well within normal tolerance, at least. If you had a tolerant girl-friend.

222

Jamie, you bastard, she should have been mine . . .

All the evening was like that, us dropping with a desperate relief into mock-cheery banter, trying hard to play at young people out on the town whenever we allowed ourselves the opportunity, until some one of us would drag the talk heavily back to what mattered.

We were still doing it over late coffee and brandies, the restaurant all but empty around us and Gino laying tables for tomorrow, glancing our way every few seconds: not dropping hints like he might have done yesterday, nor showing any signs of coming over to chat and scrounge a cigarette, as he surely would have done yesterday; only checking, always checking that Jamie was content, he had everything he wanted and his friends likewise, no one was waiting for service.

Then the bell on the door jangled, as someone came in. I glanced round, we all did, glad of a moment's distraction; and I saw a man who was briefly a stranger, darkly dressed and dimly lit. He stood still, only his head moving as he scanned the room and the people in it, us; and I felt my arms prickle with chill at the threat of him, and was glad of the touch of Carol's hand suddenly on my leg, although that was only saying, *I'm scared too . . .*

Our own fault, partly. We'd been talking about unknown and threatening figures all night, we'd set ourselves up to be spooked by any combination of man and shadow. But it wasn't all fancy, there truly was something sinister, an air of danger about this man; and I knew it, I saw and understood it as soon as he stepped further into the light and came towards our table.

He was one of us, was what it was. Steven Macallan, blond and burly, another heavyweight cousin, pretty much of a thug: unexpected here and so I hadn't known him for a moment, had seen him instead as the cattle, as Carol and Laura and Gino and everyone in town must have seen him. Shadowed, dangerous, a constant threat and his close company a terror . . .

But Jamie raised his hand in greeting and so did I, just to give a message to the others: *no panic, look at his nose, he's got to be on our side with a proboscis like that.*

"Steve," Jamie said, going the second mile here, giving him a name for added reassurance. "You looking for me?"

"No. Just checking."

"Right."

Right enough. He'd be one of Uncle James' patrolmen, the town's new security force out pacing the streets all night. Looking into doorways, big noses sniffing for trouble. *And pray they don't find it*, I thought nervously, distrustful of the presumptions that underlay such patrolling. *I don't want to lose any more cousins . . .*

"Seen anything?" Jamie asked.

"Nah. No one has. We've got radios, see," and he tapped a neat walkie-talkie in a holster on his belt, "we keep in touch, but there's nothing happening. The whole place is dead as shit."

No surprise, with three Macallans dead and the rest on the warpath. If I were a normal citizen I'd be battening down my hatches, locking up my children and staying all night indoors and also as much of the day as I possibly could.

"Well, I guess that's good," Jamie said. "Be careful, though, Steve. Yeah?"

"Yeah, sure," Steve said casually, the wave of his hand a dead giveaway, sure guarantee of a young man who was not going to be careful. Who hadn't learned the lessons of these last days, who still thought himself immortal.

Oh, Christ, I thought. *And they're all going to be like him, all the young men, all my cousins . . .* Too many years of invulnerability, it was an attitude soaked into their bones; and of course they weren't going to learn from others' dying. Such men never had. It took their own to do it, too late by definition . . .

"What about you, then?" Steve asked, still addressing himself only to Jamie. Apparently I counted with the cattle. "You coming to join us, or what?"

"Later. Maybe," Jamie said, with a glance around the table that settled on Laura and said *no, I'm not.* "I'll see."

Steve grunted, obviously at one with Uncle James in this, that a cousin's duty as much as a son's lay in the street tonight, not in bedding a girl who wasn't even blood. Water off a duck's back, to Jamie; he didn't even look up, though I saw him smile and I saw his hand tighten very publicly on Laura's, all the protection she needed against the weight of Steve's glare.

After a second or two of difficult silence, Steve's radio crackled and a voice whispered his name through static. He stepped aside from us to answer it, having obviously labelled us all, even Jamie, equally unworthy to overhear; and then he glowered around at the apprehensive staff like Arnie, *I'll be back*, and he stalked out of the restaurant.

Soft breaths of relief, from Gino and Mario and the girls and me; but as the door crashed shut behind him, I said, "Something, something my sister said to me: whoever they are out there, they're picking off the weakest. People like Steve shouldn't be going around on their own, making targets of themselves . . ."

Jamie stared at me. "Steve's not weak. Nor was Marty," emphatically.

Not like he thought I meant, no: bruisers, the pair of them. But, "The ones with the crudest talents, then. Steve, he's got strength, okay; but he's got no finesse, you wouldn't back him in a fight with anyone smarter than he is . . ."

Which in all honesty didn't narrow the field too far. Jamie saw that, and nodded, and his eyes narrowed; and he pushed back his chair an inch or two, as if he had half a mind to leave right then, to go after Steve, not to let him be alone out there.

But if he had half a mind to do it, he had no more than that, because the other half was still hand-linked to Laura and not wanting to go anywhere; and then a moment later he had no mind at all, we none of us did.

Because a voice yelled, and the big plate window at the front of the restaurant shattered; and we were still sitting frozen, still trapped in the aftershock of that while Mario moaned and hid his face behind his hands and we could all see blood dribbling through his fingers, when the voice outside quit yelling and started to scream.

And that was Steve, just as if I'd made a target of him myself with my concern.

SIXTEEN

THE ELECTRIC HAEMOGLOBIN ACID TEST

It was Carol among us who moved first. That bit older, I guess that bit more used to crisis, she was up on her feet while the rest of us were still stricken. Her moving got us moving, but we could only follow her as she pushed her way between the tables and towards the door. She broke stride briefly when Mario came blundering from behind the bar, still seemingly blinded by blood and his big hands; but Laura said, "I'll see to him, Carol. I've done first aid, at least . . ."

And first aid won't do anyone any good out there, the footnote that we all heard, that none of us felt any need to voice.

"Good." Carol spared a second to grip Mario's shoulders, to guide him into Laura's arms. Lucky man. Twice lucky not to have to face, not to be able to see whatever might be outside. I'd seen its like three times now, and already I was shaking. "Call an ambulance too, yeah?"

"Only one?"

Laura glanced through the gaping hole that was the restaurant's front now, that let Steve's screaming in so loud; and her glance said, *Won't he need one too?*

It was me Carol looked at briefly, and our eyes shared a memory, Hazel far beyond the skills of any paramedic; but she shrugged, said, "Call half a dozen, if you like," and yanked open the street door with barely a visible hesitation, barely a confession, *I don't want to go out there* before she did, with Jamie and me behind her and someone else coming after me.

Looking back, I found Gino at my shoulder.

"Don't you want to stay with Mario?" I asked. I knew I did; and he surely looked like he wanted to stay with Mario, or preferably behind Mario, somewhere a long way behind. Down in the cellar, maybe, with the door locked and the lights on and all those bottles of courage to help him through till daylight. His eyes were enormous and all the flesh of his face was trembling; but he shook his head hard, almost managed to look insulted.

"Mario's cousin is the cook, he has nephews here too. They will stay with him. I want to help."

"Good enough. Come on, then."

I didn't see what help he could be; but the same went for me, very much so, and I was going. The other two had gone already, and though Carol was still in front, in truth only Jamie had any hope of helping.

Il Milano's wasn't the only window broken. All the length of the alley glittered with glass, in what light fell from the pizzerias on either side. There was little movement, though, no customers tumbling out to see what was going down; only the odd figure in a doorway standing as still as possible not to be noticed, craning to see from the shadows, squinting towards the sound of screaming.

It was darker than usual out there, darker than it ought to be; only the shattered shopfronts lit the alley. All the streetlamps had had their lights punched out, by the same force that had riven so much plate glass to splinters. The main street at the end was bright still, but of course we had our backs to that; we had to head the other way to where it was darker still, to where a keening song of terror thickened the air and twisted gravity higher, till we could hardly run against it.

We found Steve at the corner, at the furthest distance from the light; and he was a man of supplication when we reached him, down on his knees with his eyes tight shut to be sure not to see, and his hands held out palm-up into the air. His fingers curled around nothing, I thought.

I was wrong. Jamie, cruel Jamie made a globe of nightfire to shine its light around us; and then I saw how Steve's fingers curled around pain, as if he held a bowl of it cupped in his hands.

His flesh seethed and festered in that cold light; and Christ, no wonder he was wailing.

This wasn't like Tommy, when blood-leeches had writhed within his flesh. This wasn't like anything I'd ever seen before. All Steve's skin was blistering, and the blisters were starting to burst; and there was an acrid smoke wafting up, and a thin liquor dribbling off.

We stood and stared, and saw how his palms melted, how the flesh deliquesced and dripped away; and God I hated that, I hated that I knew the word for what was happening to him. There shouldn't even be a word, for something so appalling; it ought to be a nameless horror, even the possibility of it never foreshadowed in a dictionary. Certainly the word shouldn't come slipping like a gobbet of foul meat into my mind, just as I watched my cousin fester so fast.

"Steve," Jamie said, and his voice slurred in his wet mouth, words too slippery to get a grip on. I could have given him *deliquesce*, I could have given it up forever; only he wasn't interested in description, he wanted information. "Steve, did you see him?"

Slowly, dreadfully slowly Steve lifted his face towards us; and in the cold blue light I saw pale pustules rising on his cheeks and forehead, and no, that wasn't sweat running off his eyes. Nor tears either, I could see it steam.

Whether he could see us, God only knows; but he was hearing Jamie, at least, and there was enough strength or courage or humanity left in him, just enough to honour us with an answer.

He opened his mouth, and smoke rose around his teeth. Nothing by nightfire was the colour it ought to be, but his teeth were dark and pitted. His tongue I saw, a shrivelled thing weeping pus; he should not have been alive, nothing should be like that and live.

But he lived, he moved, he lifted one arm to point, although his finger would not do it; and although he was actually pointing at a wall, the message was clear. There were only two ways his killer could have gone, left or right, down the alley or up; and it was his left arm Steve was pointing with.

And his mouth hung open now, as though he had nothing left to close it with; and all the skin of his face was running as wet as his eyes, and I could see the shape of his bones too clearly and then the bones themselves, briefly white before they smoked and seared. And he was staring at us with sockets that were empty, and he had no voice to use in screaming; and Christ, it was such relief when Jamie ran off into the dark and I could follow.

Only to protect my cousin, of course: being pro-life, voting to go with my living rather than my dying cousin. Nothing I could possibly do for Steve, but I wouldn't have left him else. And Carol was with him anyway, Carol and Gino, he wouldn't have to die alone.

Except that, in the end, everyone dies alone; and if I couldn't do anything for Steve, I couldn't do anything actually to help Jamie either. No matter what he found down there before the alley's end, be it all the hordes of Hell or just one medical madman with a syringe emptied of acid, I would be equally useless. This was the darktime, their time, none of mine.

One thing certain, that there was someone – or something – down there. Jamie made another flare of cold fire and hurled it like a cricket ball into the dark, to show us whatever it could; and just before it guttered and died, too far for him to feed it, I did see what we were both looking for as we ran, what I most dreaded to see.

Only a suggestion, a hint, a shadow of movement in the night; and not all the hordes of Hell, no. But not a maniac medic either. Less than the one, surely, but infinitely more than the other: one man alone or one of an army, either way this was the man – or woman, I supposed, but all my training and all my understanding said not, said to expect a man – who had destroyed Steve. That at the least, and maybe more. Marty and Tommy and Hazel might be laid also to his account, but we had no way of telling. Yet. We might be facing a family of formidable talents for all we knew, they might be taking turns at us . . .

Whatever else they were taking, they were taking us. Knocking us over like skittles, they were.

Had been, at least. But they hadn't met Jamie before, presumably hadn't been expecting anyone other than Steve; and Jamie was a power in the land. If I had to come face to face with nemesis in a dark alley, there was only one guy I'd sooner have there with me – or preferably ahead of me, as Jamie was now – and that was Uncle Allan.

Jamie would do, though, in our uncle's absence. Jamie would definitely do.

Maybe that was how that fractional, that barely-glimpsed figure ahead of us felt also. Maybe he'd seen more than we had, maybe he'd recognised Jamie's face behind the nightfire or told his power and intent from the hurl of light. That, or else once a night was enough for him. Whatever, he had no stomach to stand and fight; Jamie's second bolt of fire, again made on the run and again thrown hard and flat, showed us nothing but the alley's walls and gates.

Hard to tell above the sounds we made ourselves, but I thought or felt that I could hear footsteps. Not sprinting, but running fast enough to reach the alley's mouth and slip away, perhaps, before we had better sight of what we chased.

Nothing I could do; but Jamie, yes. Jamie very much yes.

Jamie ripped the road up.

Way back when we'd been hopeful lads, when I'd still been waiting for the first glimmer of talent to show itself in my outgrowing and curious body, Jamie had had his already and was exercising it every chance he got. That was classic, everyone did it; just another angle on adolescent experimentation, to go with sex and drugs and all the rest. No problem, until the town had woken up one morning to find his mark left large in many places. Most notably in the main pedestrian concourse, an English 1980s stab at a Mediterranean piazza not much improved by having *JM* gouged out of it in trenches two feet deep, as if some lunatic had been playing graffiti with a JCB in the darkness.

We'd been high as kites during and after, convulsed by giggles; but Uncle James had been not at all amused. There were limits, even for family, and damaging the town's infrastructure apparently surpassed them. Jamie had had to promise not to repeat that particular trial of his impressive strength; but looking like any likely lad for a way around a promise he didn't want to keep, he'd come up with a real peach.

He'd taken me with him on a tour of the town's construction companies, and by the following night we'd had a list of half a dozen significant properties scheduled for demolition, and *carte blanche* to do with them as we chose. That last had gone without saying, actually, Jamie being who he was; but none the less he'd asked for and got permission in writing, to have some defence against his father's presumptive disapproval.

"One a night," he'd said. "Got to ration ourselves, yeah?"

So once a night for a short week – reminding ourselves

cacklingly that even God rested on the seventh day, and He was only *creating*, damn it, He was only putting things *up* – we'd stood together on a pavement in town or on waste ground somewhere in the outskirts and Jamie had torn things apart.

A couple of times we'd taken others with us, we'd gone as a gang and had a party in the rubble after; but most nights it had just been Jamie and me, and I'd watched him as much as I watched the buildings fall. We didn't often get to see talents in action, not for real, and I'd been fascinated to see how Jamie just stood there, hands in pockets and all his muscles easy, only the tight-lipped concentration on his face to belie his casual stance while his eyes had flickered from roof to wall to window, and destruction had followed wherever his eyes danced.

At first he'd just punched holes a metre wide in brickwork or slates or whatever, though concrete might take two or three blows to crumble; he'd worked like a crane-driver swinging an invisible wrecking-ball, and taken the buildings apart piecemeal. But all that practice had made him ambitious, and taught him tricks: he'd learned to drag as well as punch; he'd learned to lean against the whole of a wall at once; he'd learned to focus more narrowly, to snap a concrete beam with a single whipcrack touch of his mind. Above all, he'd learned to think. A couple of months later – and at the demolition company's request, and for a fee: they'd been well impressed by what he'd done that first fun week – I'd seen him level a multi-storey carpark that was in the way of some preferred development. It had taken him twenty minutes, and he'd made the whole structure collapse in on itself all at once, as if he'd brought it down with shaped explosive charges.

Around that time, some fuckheaded fool of an incomer had thought to challenge Uncle James over a financial deal; had reckoned he'd be safe, the way I heard it, if he only stayed indoors during the hours of darkness.

Not the first, of course, to come up with that particularly

unbright theory or a variation on it. If he'd been a local, or if he'd only done his research, he'd have found out what had happened to the others, and maybe he'd have shown a little sense. Or maybe not, stupidity on that level is probably genetic. Anyway, rather than just sending in Marty and a small army of tough young cousins to drag the moron out, which was always the traditional response, Uncle James had turned to his younger son instead.

I'd not been there that time, I hadn't been invited; but the way I'd heard it after, Jamie had just disassembled the house around the idiot's ears. Big house it was, expensive house, and he'd delicately taken it apart from roof-beams to basement without hurting a soul inside. The hurting had come after, I guess. Jamie had done what he'd been told, he'd picked and tweaked until there was nothing left but clouds of dust and rubble and holes in the ground, and the largest of those holes the erstwhile basement where the dickhead and his family cowered and screamed; and as the dust settled, Jamie had said, his father had sent Marty over from the car where they'd been waiting, and Jamie had just gone home. He'd done his bit, he'd said, enjoyed it, hadn't wanted to see what came next.

That was then, this was now; and I hadn't seen him work for years, but presumably he must have acquired even more finesse as he matured and hopefully grew out of that classic teenage obsession with raw power. As Jacko said so often, everything's rhythm, light and life and all; and rhythm is nothing but vibration and timing, and I thought probably Jamie could shake a building to the ground, if he chose. Set up a tremble, and watch it come down.

No such choice tonight. He didn't have the time or the patience to be clever. The road under our feet rippled and bucked and split open like turf before the plough, like it was being unzipped. We both staggered, and I slipped to my knees. Pushing myself up again with my hands, I felt sticky clods of tarmac shifting beneath my palms and I lurched off-balance again.

No one could run on this. We were as disabled as the man we were pursuing, and we still couldn't see him, though Jamie tried hurling his thunderbolts again to find him out. Only the suggestion of a figure scrabbling away, so low to the ground that he must have been crawling; we went on after him, but it felt hopeless. He was going to reach the street and good running-ground long before we did, he'd be well away before we could chase again . . .

So Jamie stopped suddenly, and looked up rather than squinting uselessly ahead. There was a telegraph pole right beside him, leaning at an angle British Telecom never intended; and suddenly the pole was aflame, cold and blue, and the flames were running out ahead of us along the telephone wires.

Nice, I thought, seeing that weird light dance from pole to pole. Not fiercely bright, still it was bright enough. Yes, there was a man there, only ten yards or so from the alley's end now; and yes, he was crawling. A pale flash of face as he turned his head, when the light reached him; then he levered himself to his feet and stumbled towards the yellow glow of streetlights, and again I thought we'd lost him.

There was a high wall running down one side of the alley, ending in a brick pillar topped with a great stone ball. Not looking at that, only watching the man scramble from one light towards another, only seeing him as a silhouetted shadow, none the less I saw when the pillar exploded.

Actually it imploded, at least from my perspective. There was suddenly a little fussiness in the air at the base of the pillar, just enough to jag my eye; I looked, and seemed to see the bricks sucked away from me into an impossible vacuum the other side of everywhere.

Actually Jamie had only gone crude again; gone back to basics and punched the lower course of brickwork into dust, the best he could manage at that distance and hope for the best; but even an experienced eye struggles to keep up sometimes in bad light, has to improvise occasionally.

Wherever the hell I thought its base had gone, I knew just where the pillar was going. It was toppling swift and sweet, straight at the head of the man we wanted . . .

Christ knows if I wanted it to hit or not, if I truly had the killing-fever on me. I didn't have time to wish, either way. The pillar fell, we saw how it was falling; the man looked up, and can have seen nothing but a new planet hurtling into his ken, hanging above him, filling his horizons. Anonymous to us he might have been, but that stone cannonball had his name on it.

What I'd forgotten or discounted, though, this was a talented guy. More talents than one, seemingly, he wasn't limited to killing my cousins.

It should have been impossible, but in the eyeflick that was all the time he had he must have seen and understood and acted, all three.

There was a flare of icelight, bright as magnesium; and again my eyes lied to me, they said he dissolved that stone into a little raincloud, that hung above his head for a moment and then showered him with water. Not so. It wasn't water, it was dust; I figured that out a second later, seeing how it swirled about him in the breeze, as the glare faded to an afterburn. But oh, it was clever, it was fast and frightening; and it meant he had Jamie's talent as well as his own, whatever that was. And whatever else it was, that wasn't fair.

Jamie's turn now to act in an eyeblink, in this last second that we could see our quarry. I looked to him, and saw him pale in the eerie light, tight and concentrated; and he made his decision as I watched.

It wasn't only buildings, not just bricks and stone and concrete. Jamie could punch flesh as easily, could pull and twist and destroy bodies with as little effort. We'd proved that on dawn rabbit-hunts, and once when a stupid Rottweiler on guard duty had tried to stop us sneaking into a building-site when we'd fancied some night-time climbing practice up the girders.

Jamie's choice, and he made it. He could have pulped that man, could have made nothing but a mess of blood and bone out of what was living, breathing bastard; but he stood and did nothing, and then the man was gone.

Too late, Jamie started after him again over that difficult ground. Maybe he was already regretting that quick decision not to change the habits of a lifetime, not to turn from dogs and rabbits to men; or else his killing heat had cooled but he still wanted to catch the man, as I did.

Jamie led, and I followed; and I caught up with him at the alley's end. He was breathing hard and turning, facing one way and then the other, seemingly as blind as Steve. All there was was the street and the station and the hill, the same hill we'd walked down earlier this evening. Little traffic and no pedestrians coming or going except on the far side of the wide road, under the station's massive portico; there also the only parked cars in sight, and a queue of taxis waiting.

"Over there," Jamie squeezed out, hoarsely between breaths. "He must be . . ." And he surged forward, and I could only just hold him at the kerb's edge, grappling with him as he tried to shove me away.

"Jamie, don't . . ."

"Get your hands the fuck off me . . . !"

He was glaring at me, spitting fury; and then he wasn't. Just inches from mine, I saw his eyes not move, but change focus. My hands stung and burned where they were touching his skin, and they wanted only to snatch themselves away; and that was only a side-effect of what he meant, only the static charge.

But I kept my grip, though it hurt me to do it. I kept his gaze, and I worked my mind and my tongue both, against the pain and the breathlessness that had me gasping. "Yes," I said, "you can do that. You're a talented lad. You can damage me enough to make me let go, though you'll have to work, because a prod won't do it; but that's out here under the stars, and it's only me. What are you going to do against him, Jamie, when he can turn your blood bad in your body? What are you going to do in there," jerking my head towards the great ironwork arch that covered the station over, "where there's no stars and no moon to light you, and you don't know how the fuck he does his little tricks? You're angry and you're scared," I knew because that's how I was and we'd always been close like that, only that Jamie felt things more, "but neither one of those makes you invulnerable."

He stared at me, every muscle in him tense and trembling and a sour sweat on his skin. I saw his tongue move behind his teeth, shaping words he never said, curses to go with the lightning-blast that might destroy me; and then he turned his head away. Slowly, slowly I felt the burning in him subside to a tingle, just the usual white noise you get around any Macallan. I loosened my grip finger by finger and took my hands away, still wary. He only stood still, though, staring towards the station but making no move now to cross.

So I worked my hands together, thumbs rubbing deep into palms and the pads of my fingers where they felt they'd been scalded in steam, all the nerves ascream though there was nothing to show for it, not a mark on my skin. And it wasn't only in my hands, every nerve in my body was jumping. All the years I'd been alive and among my relatives, only Hazel had ever, *ever* touched me with her talent; and that only because she was my sister, and because she could. It was the rule, the one rule that took precedence over every other rule at any time; cattle were legitimate targets, family not. You could choose like Jamie not to

hurt cattle either, but that was a separate matter. Those of us
who'd been touched by Hazel's web never let on to an adult,
rarely spoke about it even to each other. She was one of us so
we'd defended her, even I would defend her against the presum-
edly awesome anger and undoubtedly tremendous punishments
which that unforgivable offence would have brought down upon
her head.

And Jamie my cousin, my adoptive brother, once and I thought
again my friend –Jamie had been dangerously close to unloading
everything he had just then, and all of it aimed at me.

"You okay?" he asked dully, still not looking around.

No. "I'm fine," I said, fighting to keep my voice from trembling.

"Fucking hero," with no heat in the allegation, almost nothing
of my hot cousin. "Since when?"

I didn't know the answer to that. Since my sister died, and life
turned cheaper? Or since I cheapened life myself, to kill a cop?
Maybe only since this afternoon, since I found a little unexpected
value in myself. Or someone else found that value, rather, and
showed it to me. *Unless it was the buzz that drew Carol, just that
Macallan buzz working for me finally, eight or ten years late but
coming good at last . . .*

"We should go back," I said, and that was true; and my voice
was also telling truth quite independently, saying that I didn't
want to. Pleading, almost, for a reason not to. Some hero, me . . .

"Yeah." And now he did turn, now he looked me in the face,
searching for something though I didn't know what. Didn't know
if he found it, either, but he put his arm around my shoulder like
he needed me for balance, he was going to fall over without. And
of course I wasn't going to let him fall, so I slipped my arm round
his waist, and that's how we walked back into the dark and stumblingly, awkwardly up the ruined alley, like two brothers
inextricably linked.

* * *

Jamie's globe of light had gone, of course, extinguished by his absence; but Carol had stayed, Carol was kneeling in the road there with her shoulders bowed and her hands cupped over her mouth, which made every kind of sense except the big one. Quite why she'd stayed at all, I couldn't imagine; but having made that choice, of course she'd want to duck and cover as much as she could. I could still remember the stink of Tommy's dying, and even from here I was catching whiffs of Steve's, though we weren't half as close to him as she was. Not the same at all – Tommy's had been swamp waters and foul decay, Steve's was bad acid and burning chemicals, biting my throat and lungs – but equally awful to breathe. I was coughing already, and I could hear Jamie's wheezing at my side. He'd been asthmatic as a kid, though not for many years so far as I knew, not since they'd moved into the country.

I glanced at him, to see how bad he was; and saw instead that his hand was busy drawing light out of nothing, making another shining globe. He'd barely built it to a tennis ball, though, before Carol was snapping at him, waving a peremptory hand.

"Don't! Don't do that . . ."

"What?" It was probably just the shock of being challenged, but the nightfire flickered and died above his palm. "Why not?"

"He doesn't need it," she said; and that was sure enough, no arguments there.

But, "I do," Jamie said.

"No."

Actually, I agreed with her. The dark was light enough. Too well adjusted, my eyes were already showing me more of Steve's death than I really wanted to see or know.

My memory is at least as ill-regulated as most people's, maybe more so. It's both unreliable and unkind, letting me down when I need it, stirring me up when that's the last thing I need. It has a clear and recognisable system, though, there's method behind its meanness: I can remember very little of my childhood, when I was pretty happy on the whole, if utterly subservient to my sister; and I can remember almost every moment of my adolescence, when I was miserable at best pretty much all the time.

Blinking in the darkness there and wanting only to close my eyes altogether against what I was seeing, I remembered one time more than ten years earlier, when Hazel had been trying to bleach a pair of jeans. She'd left them in the bathroom, soaking in a dilute solution; and as an act of petty vengeance for some offence long since forgotten, I'd slipped in and emptied the bottle of Domestos into the sink to enrich the mixture.

And then I'd stood and watched, rapt with glee and terror both, as the denim unravelled itself before my eyes: as it frayed and rotted gently into nothing like some smart stop-motion video effect and nothing like real life at all.

Until Hazel came back and caught me standing there with the evidence in my hands and the wonder still on my face; and this was why the terror, of course, because then it was very much real life again, and for all my twelve-year-old innocence I knew one fact well, that real life *hurts* . . .

No Hazel to catch us this time, and my guilt was more abstruse, though I still felt guilty; but Steve's clothes, his T-shirt and jeans under an open leather jacket had dissolved into rags and slime and his riches had rolled onto the tarmac, coins and keys scattered about him like the rivets from Hazel's Levis falling to the bottom of the bathroom sink.

Rags and slime his flesh was too, my cousin Steve, and half his bones were showing. They were glistening wet in what light caught them, pale and dark in patches, and even some of them seemed to be crumbling; hair and skin had slithered off from the dome of his skull, and something claggy was oozing out of it. Revolted but still drawn, I bent to look closer and saw a tracery of dark lines against white bone, etched in, I thought, as if with a hot point.

Like a map, I thought, *all the pathways of pain marked out by its marching . . .*

Actually, my more rational side insisted, it was more like a map of the veins that feed the scalp; but rationality couldn't hold a candle to the crawling horror of that wet mess. Better to sing and soar a little, to give poetry its head against science; facts screw you down.

Screw you up, sometimes.

Jamie was with me there, I guess, with us both. He didn't after all make any light against Carol's veto. I could feel him trembling, unless it was my own trembling echoing back from his solidity; but I didn't think so.

He pulled away from me, though, which freed me to drop to my knees beside Carol, to put an arm around her and draw her up against my body, to offer her what thin comfort she could find there. Some at least, I guessed, from the way that she clung. She was gasping and choking on the acrid stench that rose from Steve's trickling flesh; she buried her face against my shirt, to use that as a substitute for the mask of her hands. Me, I hid my mouth in her hair, tasting salt sweat laid over sweet-scented shampoo.

Looking for something, anything to turn her mind away from what lay in the road, I mumbled, "What happened to Gino?"

"Who?"

"The waiter."

"Oh. I don't know. He went . . ."

Went where, I didn't ask; and then didn't need to, because he came back, true young hero that he was. I heard footsteps crunching through shards of glass, and looked up to see him coming nervously towards us with a tablecloth trailing from his hands.

Nice. I lifted my head for a second, just long enough to give him a nod of encouragement and croak, "Good thinking, Gino."

Actually it wasn't really, linen wouldn't last long against the strength of such corrosion, but as least he was trying. He smiled at me vaguely, advanced a little with the cloth held out before him like a screen – and then he checked, looking confused and uncertain.

I turned my eyes reluctantly, to see what was bothering him; and saw Jamie in the road, bending over Steve's body.

Saw him reach down and almost shouted, wanted to shout but only managed a grunt, half disgust and half warning, *don't touch that, don't dabble your fingers in corruption, it might do the same to you. It just might dabble in return* . . .

Too late. He reached and fumbled, gripped and straightened with something in his hand and a strange retching sound in his throat. Then he stumbled back, almost dropping whatever it was that he carried as he fumbled a handkerchief from his pocket. I watched him awkwardly trying to wipe both the object and his fingers where they'd touched it; then in the eerie silence of that alley I heard a crackling voice cut through what sounds there were, Carol's breathing and my own and Jamie's asthmatic wheezing.

More good thinking. He'd salvaged Steve's walkie-talkie, and it seemed like everyone was doing better than me just now. Nothing new there, then. Not so transformed after all, this life of mine; no miracles, at any rate. I was still a follower by nature.

Jamie touched a button uncertainly, and hiss replaced crackle. Working the words hard through his own wrack and the spoiled air, I heard him say, "Hullo? Who's there, who's out there?"

"Who's that?" came back, the voice thinned by electronics and disguised by static.

"Jamie, this is Jamie. Jamie Macallan."

"About bloody time. It's Lamartine, Jamie. Where are you?"

He looked at me, with a helpless shrug; I told him, and he relayed it. "Mason Chare. Apparently."

"I know it. Little back alley, right? Who are you with, then, Steve? That's Steve's patch . . ."

"Jesus, Marty," starting to crack now, "Steve . . . Get someone down here, will you? Steve's . . ."

"Steve's what?"

"He's dead."

"What? How?"

"I don't know, I don't *know* how. He was fine, and then . . . Just get someone to come, will you? And hurry . . . ?"

Not just someone, but a lot of cousins came. Lamartine himself, and Donny and Travers and half a dozen more. Too many for me, too many by far for Carol and for Laura, though she left Mario with his family in order to come and stand with her friends. I shepherded them back against a wall, as far as possible from all those fierce auras; then I read all the unspoken messages, all the contempt on the faces of my family – *what did Jamie think he was doing, for God's sake? Spending his time with cattle and the cattle-coloured, when we needed him . . .* – and I decided to stay with the girls myself, just to keep out of the family's way. My anger and distress were no less than theirs, possibly greater, but I was prepared to cede them the stage entirely, to avoid drawing any more of their attention. There was an advantage, I was think- ing suddenly, to being seen as weak: seen once and dismissed and never looked at again.

After the cousins, the uncle. James again, back in his big car but driving himself for once, nosing down the alley until his headlights painted us all too brightly in the night, gave us thick shadows and too little colour else. He left the lights burning as he got out, stood four-square in their beam looking down at what there was of Steve, then lifted his head and said, "Jamie."

"Here, Dad," and my cousin-brother stepped forward from the pack.

"You were with Steve when this happened?"

"Well, not exactly. In there," nodding towards *il Milano* with its shattered window. "He came in, had a word with us, went back out – and then he was screaming. I went after the guy who did it," he added: not looking for praise, only giving information, a soldier being debriefed. "Didn't get him though," and didn't say a word about the chance passed up, the road not taken.

"All right. Get in, we'll talk back at the house."

Obedient soldier or obedient son, Jamie moved towards the car; but then he stopped, looked around and found us, held a hand out and said, "Laura . . . ?"

When a hierarchy's working well, obedience runs all the way down. She didn't hesitate, ready to dance with dragons in exchange for the better comfort of his arms now and the promise of his bed later.

I saw Uncle James frowning in the light, and my less generous half wanted to hear the veto which all of me expected; but all he said was, "She was with you?"

"Yeah. Yeah, she was," though Jamie had avoided saying so earlier, a vaguely chivalrous gesture that he'd blown entirely now.

"Very well, then. And these, too?" as his eyes found us, Carol and me still backed up against the wall, Carol's two hands working hard on one of mine.

"Yes," said Jamie.

"No," said I. And when everyone stared, "I mean, no, we're not getting in the car. We've got nothing to tell you more than Jamie and Laura can," and I had my own agenda for the night, which didn't include spending it under Uncle James' roof.

This was the second avuncular invitation I'd turned down, in similar circumstances. Grown cocky, I guess, from my success in walking away from Uncle Allan last night, and encouraged by having Carol at my side now as then. There were enough bully-boy cousins here to throw me in bodily if Uncle James insisted, but I thought his dignity would rule that out as an option.

Too right, it did. He wouldn't even argue. He only looked at me consideringly, stepped out of the car's fierce beams into the night's shadows, and broke the first and only commandment a Macallan ever recognised as right.

He used his talent on me.

SEVENTEEN

SOUNDS OF BREAKING GLASS

Parents apart, the only thing my two uncles had in common was their talent. It often goes that way, that brothers develop the same skills, though in different proportion.

My uncles were manipulators, both. Mostly these days neither one exhibited their talent much; they had other ways to achieve their ends, they manipulated with money or terror or political guile. I'd once seen Allan pull a punter's strings, and never James. Family wisdom had it that Allan's was far the finer control: that if he chose he could have a punter pick up a pen and sign their name to something, and the signature would be incontestably their own, although it was no will or intent of theirs that had managed their fingers as they wrote. Legend said that finesse like that was far beyond Uncle James; but legend said that Uncle James had been threatened once, by a carload of thugs up from London. Out to extend their overlord's hegemony and believing nothing of the rumours, they'd followed Uncle James' car across one of the high bridges; and halfway over the thug driving had suddenly wrenched at the wheel and stamped on the accelerator, so that they'd careered up onto the pavement, ploughed through pedestrians (there'd been a baby, legend said, crushed in his buggy, and his teenage mother left legless) and slammed head-on into a stanchion.

Those inside that could still move, legend said, had dragged themselves one by one from the twisted wreck of their car, staggered or crawled to the railing, hauled themselves over and plummeted down to the tidal suck of the river.

And Uncle James had all this time been sitting quietly in his car, twenty metres further down the bridge and watching it all happen, making it all happen, legend said, without so much as turning his head to look. He did it with mirrors.

That was the legend of James' talent, and I'd always thought it stretched, as legends are. But now I felt it, now I learned the truth and something more also, something of the life of the untalented in this town. How it feels to be cattle on a Macallan ranch. There had always been Hazel giving me hints, giving me clues and little nudges; but this was different, this was emphatic, a lesson writ in flame inside my body, burned deep into the bone.

Uncle James' will closed over me like intentional water, surrounding and engulfing and then forcing in through inadequate barriers of skin. It gripped me as a hand grips a glove, from the inside out. Nothing was mine except my thoughts, and briefly I wasn't certain even of those.

I guess I must have looked strange, but only slightly. A little stiff, a little jerky in movement, nothing more than that. The light was bad, stark black and white and mostly black; and no one was close enough to see my eyes, beyond maybe a panic flash as they rolled in my skull. Even those were outwith my own control, but Uncle James wasn't bothering to take charge there. Not for lack of ability, I reckoned, only lack of interest. Right then I profoundly believed every rumour I'd ever heard about his preponderance of talent – and Christ, Allan was supposed to be *better* than this?

My aimless eyes jerked and slithered: faces and walls, the

pavement, the car, spinning at bad angles like a hectic movie montage. I was caged, I was floating. I could touch nothing, couldn't get a grip; nor would the world grip me.

A skilled puppeteer, my uncle walked me to the car, opened the door for me himself and folded me in. Only a few seconds it took, before he stepped back and released me; but already I was frantic, I was desperate, I was soul cruelly exiled from body and I thought not very much more of it would madden me forever.

When he left me, when the cloak of his desire slipped from my shoulders, I felt utterly disorientated inside my own skin. Sweating and soul-sick, I lifted shaking hands towards my eyes only to see myself to do that, to know that I had control again of hands and eyes both; and then I toppled more than leant sideways, a sour urgency rising in my throat and only one clear thought in my head, *don't spew in Uncle James' limo, don't do anything ever again to upset Uncle James* . . .

I got my head out of the open door of the car just in time; a thin vomit burned my mouth and spattered on the pavement. The acrid stink of it in my nose was like smelling-salts, almost, it sharpened my reeling mind and gave me focus. My eyes watered and my nose was running, there was foul dribble on my chin; I reached up instinctively with the back of my hand but someone intercepted, gripping my wrist to still it. Thin fingers, female fingers: I could see legs also, carefully straddling the pool of my vomit. Looking up, thinking *Carol*, I found Laura instead.

Her face said she was shocked and frightened and curious, all three; scientist and medic as she was, the greatest of those would be curiosity, I thought. But not yet, because she was friend also. Even from her side of the great divide, what lay between us was strong enough to overcome the rest. For a while, for a little while . . .

"There's a box of Kleenex on the back," she said, nothing more than that; but then she put one hand on my shoulder for balance, stretched past me into the car and came up with treasure, a fat handful of tissues.

And shook her head when I reached to take them, and quickly and efficiently did the work herself instead, mopping my sweat-slick brow and my eyes and my mouth against my mumbled protests. What was left of the wad after she pressed into my hand, and said, "Here. I'm not blowing your nose for you. But what happened, Ben?" The curiosity was rising like oil through water, pushing to the surface regardless. "You look dreadful; and the way you just caved in like that, it's not like you, stubborn as shit you are . . ."

Either Jamie hadn't told her about his father's talent or she just hadn't made the connection, seeing it at work for the first time. But I only shook my head, seeing no reason to help Jamie out here, wondering what else he hadn't told her.

Behind her, Uncle James said, "Get into the car, please. We don't have time to waste."

Laura bit her lip, glanced at me briefly and read my surrender in my face. She climbed in over my legs and sat down beside me, squeezing my knee as she settled; after a second the door opened on the other side and Carol got in. She seemed confused, unhappy with the arrangements; but this was no time to start swapping around.

Jamie sat in the front, although he could have joined us three without squeezing, the car was wide enough. It felt like a class division, real Macallans only in the first rank of seats. He did his best to bridge that, sitting awkwardly sideways and peering Chad-like at us over the headrest, even reaching between the seats to fumble for Laura's hand before she shook her head at him, *don't be ridiculous*; those were gestures, though, gestures at best. This was Uncle James' car, Uncle James' world we were sat in, and that meant them and us with barriers between too wide to breach. Even Jamie couldn't punch those walls down; and he knew it, and he wasn't really trying.

His father was still out in the street, talking to Lamartine. I could see them through the windscreen, and the harsh-lit white shape in the road that was Steve cloaked with Gino's tablecloth. Dark patches were spreading already through the linen, doing more than stain.

A few abrupt words, a jab of his hand towards that tablecloth, and Uncle James came back to the car. Got in, sat down, twisted like a mirror-image of his son to see back for reversing, and Laura said, "Could we have this window open, please? Ben's side?"

He just stared at her.

I heard Jamie suck a warning breath and I guess both of us were sending her telepathic messages, *be careful, for God's sake, you don't know what he's like when he gets mad*; but, "Ben needs air," she said calmly, seeming totally unfazed. Only her fingers on my leg said that was a lie, twitching nervously at the wrinkles in my jeans.

"Don't want him throwing up again," Jamie murmured. Uncle James' finger stabbed on a button, the window wound itself quietly down beside me, and pity me because I caught the look that Laura gave my cousin then, her own sweet sending.

I love you, that look was saying; and I turned my head away into the flow of dark air, dark thoughts as the car shot backwards up the alley, crunching broken glass with no respect for its tyres.

Uncle James drove us quickly out of town, and none of us spoke again before he'd pulled up with a scatter of gravel in front of his big house. I'd kept my face in the wind all the way, slowly recovering my body, testing my possession of it: clenching fists and toes, flexing muscles, reclaiming what should never have been lost. I wanted yet another bath, deeper and hotter; I wanted to wash the taint of my uncle from my flesh inside and out, but I wasn't Laura, and I knew I wouldn't dare to ask.

Probably I wasn't the only one glad of the breeze in the back there. It couldn't have been easy for either Laura or Carol to be cooped up in a car, even a car so large, with three Macallans setting their nerves to shiver. Too much else on their minds, I thought, for either my cousin or my uncle to have noticed the change in me, but I had to be adding to the girls' inevitable discomfort. Guilt again: for the first time I was irredeemably part of the problem, and no solution in sight.

As soon as the car was still I had the door open and was out of there, stamping and stretching, still feeling weak and uncertain. Carol was no slower, on the other side. One glimpse of her across the limo's roof and my own face twisted in sympathy with hers; she looked close to chundering in her turn, and I hated myself and all my blood. And hated my uncle for dragging her along, and myself again and more for having been the catalyst that drew her into this.

"Just breathe deep," I told her quietly. "It passes."

She nodded, *thanks* or maybe *thanks, but I worked that out for myself already*, and then she doubled over, propping her arms against bent knees for balance. I was around the back of the limo without pause for thought, but when I got there she lifted her head to greet me with a half-hearted grin.

"Thought you were going to throw up," I muttered, oddly embarrassed.

"Not me. I never throw up. Felt dizzy standing, that's all. But what is it, damn it? What does that? It's fun, sort of, with one of you. With you," making me look around quickly, see if anyone was listening; but Laura was only just getting out on the other side with Jamie helping, and Uncle James was already halfway to the door, expecting us to follow. There were lights burning all through the house; no sleep for anyone tonight. "But Laura says it's always like this when there's a bunch of you together. You make us poor mortals feel awful . . ."

252

"We're mortal," I said, and winced to hear myself say it, so soon after Steve had proved it. From the expression on her face, she didn't need reminding either. "Uncle Allan says it's psychic resonance, we've each got our own and they sort of clash when we're together. Like music, yeah? A lot of instruments, all tuned differently. Sets up bad harmonics. If it's any comfort, we're not exactly immune. It can get difficult, if there's too many of us."

"There are loads too many of you," she said flatly. "And no, that's no comfort at all."

But she straightened slowly, and slipped her arm through mine; and we went into the house tracking my cousin and my love, and Laura was leaning on Jamie as much as Carol leant on me.

No sign of Uncle James in the hall, but the door to the big room was standing open, and there was the murmur of voices inside. Long displaced here, in what had once been my second home, I was glad to be going in behind Jamie; he even held Laura up briefly at the door, looking back to be sure of me, so that we could all make our entrance together.

Uncle James was standing down at the end, by the big fire-place, striking a pose as ever. Uncle Allan was there too, quietly in an armchair picking at his fingernails, striking no poses at all. And my father was there, giving me a nod of greeting and a frown for the company I kept; there were others there, just about all the senior men of the family; and surprisingly Father Hamish was there also, and I couldn't work that out at all. This was family business, surely. I couldn't see the need for a priest.

Uncle James beckoned us impatiently forward, and we stood in a little group in the centre of that watchful circle, holding close together, feeling like witnesses at a star chamber.

"Very well then," Uncle James, said, talking directly to Jamie. "Tell us everything: everything you saw, everything you heard. If he leaves anything out," scanning the rest of us with a single flick of his eyes, "you tell us."

"Everything you thought," Uncle Allan put in mildly from his chair. "That, too. Impressions. Even if they don't seem relevant."

Jamie did his best, I guess we all did, though it didn't seem to satisfy.

It was a hard audience we had to play to and they made no concessions. Even Allen was rough with his questioning, trying to squeeze out of us more than we'd consciously absorbed. And they wanted to know precisely how Steve had died, exactly what we'd seen and what he'd done, what had been done to him; and though Jamie and I could start it off, at the last that came down to Carol because of course we hadn't been there, we'd been away chasing a man with more than his fair share of talent.

Spotting him, chasing him, and in Jamie's case at least blasting away at him – and then that moment, that instant of decision when he could have played splatterpunk with the man's body and had chosen not to.

They were good, our interrogators. I don't think either one of us had intended to tell them that, but they learned it anyway. Which made it my turn to rescue Jamie suddenly from his father's cold and malignant anger, as Jamie had rescued Laura in the car; so I said, "Come on, it's no use shouting at him. He made his choice, and it's over now, we can't go back and do it different. But I'll tell you what's interesting."

"What, then? Apart from my son being afraid of his responsibilities?"

Jamie shifted at my side; Laura grabbed his wrist, I talked loud and urgent over the top of his hissing protest.

"What's really interesting is that the other guy didn't do anything either. It should've been a classic shoot-out, only neither one of them fired . . ."

"Too far away," Uncle James said dismissively.

"We don't know that, and we certainly can't assume it. We don't know how he does it, what he does; but it wasn't too far for Jamie, and whatever else, this guy's strong. He's got a lot of talent. We can't afford to make assumptions, and I think that one's wrong anyway."

"What, then?" Uncle Allan butted in, and at least he sounded interested in my opinion. "You've obviously got a theory, Ben. What is it?"

"Light," I said. "I think he lost his light. Otherwise he would have splattered Jamie, and me too; Christ, why not? That's obviously his goal in life, to kill Macallans. Only he'd just been playing slam-dunk with a stone basketball, and the dust of that was all around him, we could see it like a cloud; and I think it worked like a cloud, like ten-tenths cover. I think he didn't zap us because he couldn't, he was cut off from the source."

"So?" Uncle James demanded impatiently. "Is this leading anywhere?"

"Yes," from Uncle Allan. He was way ahead of me, I could see; but he was a gentleman above all, he left it to me to finish.

"It means they – or he, or whatever – work the same way, the same way you do," and God help me, I'd almost said "we". "Which means with the same limitations, pretty much. This guy seems to have two talents at once, he can blast things like Jamie as well as doing that blood trick, whatever it is; but apart from that, it means we know what we're up against, at least. Nobody knows about talent, better than you. And it means the playing-field is pretty much level; or else it tilts your way, because there are more of you." *Even if he is picking you off one by one, while we still don't have a clue who he is . . .*

Uncle Allan was nodding approvingly. Uncle James simply snorted. "If you're right. Seems to me you're making assumptions yourself, all down the line . . ."

He was right, of course, I couldn't dispute that; only that it made better sense to assume that whoever we were facing obeyed the same laws that we did, until it was proved otherwise. *Another close shave for Occam*, I thought, and shut up.

Eventually they let us alone and talked among themselves. Didn't dismiss us, though, kept us around for supplementary questions; and didn't offer us a chair or anything so civil. In the end the girls just sat down on the carpet there, looking totally beat. Jamie squatted behind Laura, wrapped his arms and legs around her, drew her head back against his chest; I blinked, looked the other way, couldn't do likewise for Carol however much she might have appreciated it. Whatever she was or might be to me, I couldn't just use her as a Laura-substitute. Not fair, not honest; and if I wasn't honest, I wasn't anything.

So I compromised, I stood with my legs together for Carol to use as a back-rest if she chose, which she did. Which anchored me, upright and alone; I couldn't whisper to her as the other two were whispering to each other, so instead I listened in to what our elders and – certainly in their own opinion – betters were saying.

Turned out that Father Hamish was there as a consultant. As a parish priest, he was far more in touch with the town, with the mood of the community, than any Macallan could be. Apart from myself, perhaps, because I at least tried to live in the community. A student's life is always fairly artificial, though, too much insulated to be true; and doubly so in this town, where the university was just about the only institution my family left alone.

"No," Hamish said in response to the obvious, the only real question. "There's no sign of any opposition to you, that I've seen. No rival, I should say. Opposition in the other sense, of course, you're pretty much detested," and he was the only non-relative who could get away with such straight talking, and that only because he had God very much on his side, he had my family charmed, "but you know that. Nothing new there. There's no sense of things shifting, or the balance of power being disturbed. Rumours about the deaths, that's inevitable; but they think it's internal, if anything, some kind of power-struggle between you. There'll be no revolution."

Uncle James snorted. "Of course there'll be no revolution. It's not the cattle I'm concerned with, unless they prove to be harbouring this mob, in which case there will be retribution."

"Mob?" Uncle Allan queried.

"Mob, gang – family, if you like. Does it matter?"

"The kids only saw one man."

"Even so. There must be others," stated with absolute assurance, absolute pomposity. Uncle James couldn't possibly admit that a single man could throw the Macallans into such turmoil. Me, I thought he was absolutely wrong; and I also thought that such certainty was dangerous. And, of course, I said not a word.

It was Jamie's mother who rescued us at the last, my long-suffering Aunt Lucy. Some species of distant cousin she was, totally cowed by her bully of a husband and not of course invited to join the men's debate, though she'd lost a son to the enemy; but for once, for the first time I could remember, she asserted herself now. Her territory, I guess, looking after the kids. Never mind that we were all of us adult by now, and more adult than we'd been a couple of weeks before. She knocked lightly on the door, came in just a few hovering, nervous steps, and said,

"If you don't need the children any more, James, I've made beds up for them. It's too late to send them home now . . ."

Uncle James grunted, and waved a dismissive hand. Carol reached an arm up to me, came lightly to her feet as I lifted; Jamie and Laura took a second longer to disentangle themselves but still weren't far behind us, equally glad I guess to be allowed to leave.

"I've put you in your old room, Benedict," Lucy said as she led us upstairs, her voice as pale as ever, pale as her face and her sad life. "Your friend – I'm sorry, but I don't know your name?"

"Carol."

"Carol. How do you do? You're in the guest room, along here," turning left on the first landing. I went along with her, of course, to see her comfortable; and smiled privately, thinking that even if Carol had been a well-known and long-established girlfriend my decorous aunt would still have done this, still have given her a room to herself on another floor from me. Propriety was all Lucy had to keep a grip on, all she'd ever had in all the time I'd known her. Nice manners and tea at four o'clock, dinner at eight and the house always pristine, her wild and rowdy sons always a problem and a grief to her. She'd have preferred daughters, most likely, except that she was Macallan stock and married to a Macallan, and the male line was the only one that counted.

Thinking that, I thought that she hadn't said anything about a bed for Laura; and I glanced back, just in time to see the other two heading on up the next flight of stairs, hand in hand and heads together. My problem, my grief; his mother wouldn't challenge Jamie. And my room was right next door to his . . .

Keep it quiet, guys. Though it wouldn't matter, actually. They could romp all night or be as silent as cats curled together in a basket, I still wouldn't be sleeping this night.

One door stood open, waiting; and Carol at least could sleep tonight. I'd never tell her that the last time I'd been in this room, so had Marty. And on the same bed, yet. Queen-sized and comfortable, the bed, as I remembered it; though it had been pushed back to the wall now, it wasn't so much the focus of the room, a dais for a death.

Lucy left us alone to say goodnight, as she would have thought proper; but I thought she'd still be hanging around outside, waiting to see me out of there.

"Are you going to be okay?" I murmured.

Carol nodded uncertainly, looking around her at the blandness of the room, seeing towels and a toothbrush laid out on the dressing-table and seeing nothing of what I saw in my mind's eye, cold body and thick black scabs. "Sure. Why not. It's a bit like a B & B, but I'll be fine."

"All right, then. But listen, if you need me, I'm just upstairs in the attics. First door on the right, that'll be me."

She nodded again. Then, practically, "Where's the bathroom?"

I had to stop and think, for that one; this had been the grown-ups' floor, no part of my territory. But I worked it out on my fingers. "Other side of the corridor, two doors down. Come on, I'll show you."

"No need, I'll find it. How about you, Ben, will you be all right?"

"No problem," I said, finding myself dishonest after all. "This place is a second home to me."

She grunted, and I didn't know what that meant; but then she hugged me, kissed my cheek and said, "Goodnight, then," so I simply said goodnight and left.

Came out, pulling the door to behind me; and said goodnight to the hovering aunt, and climbed uncarpeted stairs into what had been lads' land, absolutely my territory for all that I'd really only ever been a guest, the attics of the house.

Up there the walls were only wooden partitions, and my bed – the same old bed where I'd slept or sweated out so many teenage nights and mornings, with the same squeaky springs and the same dip in the mattress, renewing old aches in my spine and heart both – was right up against the wall that divided me from Jamie; but bless them, they didn't make a sound to disturb me. Jamie, I reasoned, must have held out for a new bed.

But whether they slept or were tactful, silent lovers, it made no difference. I Tiresias had foresuffered all, enacted on this same divan or bed; and no, I didn't sleep.

In the false light before dawn I broke, finally and irrevocably. I padded softly down the stairs again, barefoot and barechested, camp as they come in just my jeans; and I made my way along the dim corridor to the guest room, edged the door open and slipped inside.

Carol was a hunched ball under the covers, and the room smelled heavy with sleep. She stirred as I watched her, turned over and opened her eyes, tousled and frowning.

"It's only me," I whispered. "Sorry . . ."

"Ben." Her voice was only a croak, but she managed a smile regardless. "Hi."

"Can I come in? Just for a bit?"

"Sure. Welcome. Long as you like, fool."

She twitched the duvet back and slid over, to make room. I shucked off my jeans and slid into the warmth and softness, the comfort that she offered; and there I could sleep after all, nestled in against her and if not Laura, she surely was a substitute for something.

It wasn't till I woke, to bright sunlight and an empty bed, that I thought again of Marty in this room, or of Steve and the night just gone.

Carol had left the curtains open, so that the sun fell directly onto my face, tingling sharp and fresh like aftershave. I stretched into it, like a cat stretching into its skin again after sleep; the duvet fell away, and oh, this was my time and no question who was in possession of my body now. Before I knew it I'd walked all the way forward into light and was standing naked by the high window, wrapped in radiance brighter than any body was ever lit by sun.

Caught myself at it and frowned, shook it out of my head and turned away; felt the tingle still on my back and stepped deliberately out of the fall of light. I'd get used to it, sure; but at the moment magic was nothing but distraction, and I really wanted to think.

So I scuttled upstairs in my jeans again, meeting no one on the way, hoping everyone but Carol would assume I was simply sleeping in. Desperately hoping no one had looked in on me already, or tried to . . .

When we were teenagers, the attics had been made over almost into a private flat for us, our own distinct domain. Privilege without responsibility, this was, we didn't even have to keep it clean. There was Marty's room, and Jamie's, and my own; there was a phone on the landing, on a separate line; there was a wee little kitchen corner with a fridge and a Baby Belling cooker and a sink, a cupboard for tins and a couple of shelves stacked with old saucepans and cracked plates; and there was a bathroom with a shower and a deep old Victorian tub, where I'd first discovered the pleasures of long immersion and slow contemplation.

No one around up here either – or no one in Jamie's room, at least; I didn't try Marty's – so I could take all the time I wanted, run the bath hot and deep, relearn the habit of luxury . . .

But I'd long outgrown my life here, and dressing myself in old and ill-fitting clothes wouldn't make me young again. I had a shower instead, scalding water hammering on my neck and shoulders, beating out residual tensions from the long night. Then I raided my cousin's room for clean clothes – ignoring what was scattered across the carpet, Jamie's rig from last night and Laura's also, both of them cruelly intermixed –and went downstairs.

The big kitchen at least showed signs of recent occupation, though it was empty now. There were wisps of steam coming from the kettle, smells of bacon and burnt toast, plates heaped in a sink, a bottle of milk left out and wet mug-rings on the long deal table. Aunt Lucy's maid must be busy somewhere else in the house, and Lucy herself gone off to a coffee-morning or whatever. She would never have tolerated such a mess being left unsorted.

I went in search of company, and was drawn again by the open door to the big room, the sounds of talking inside. I was just a step or two away when I heard my own name mentioned, in Laura's clear warm voice; and shame on me, I stood still and breathed quiet and listened in.

"The trouble with Ben," she was saying, "is he builds these dreams, and then makes out that they're real. Makes out to himself, as much as to the rest of us. That's the problem, really, is that he believes them absolutely; and they give him such a bent picture of the world."

"Like how?" Jamie, of course. He sounded dead interested, like this was a whole new perspective on someone he'd grown up with. "What sort of dreams?"

"Well, there's this group of us at college, for a start. We're friends, and sometimes we do things together. Three, four times a term we'll all go out. But talk to Ben and you'd think we were inseparable, blood brothers or whatever. And that's just not true. I've got a theory about it, mind."

"Sure you've got a theory," Jamie said, chuckling. "You've always got theories, you." And then he yelped, and there were a couple of seconds of scuffle-noises before they settled down again. "So what's your big theory on this one, then?"

"It's just, what it is, I reckon after he walked out on you lot, he needed to find himself a new family. Some sort of emotional security, yeah? And he met us, we were all freshers and we had some fun together, and we got appointed. So he's created this whole thing in his head about how close we are, and how important to each other; and it worries me. It's not safe, him building so much on an assumption that's fundamentally false."

Rick and Angie, Dermot and Vanessa, Colin and Laura and me; my clan, yes, my substitute family if she liked. Fundamental, and nothing false. So all right, I'd barely seen any of them except her since Marty died; but Christ, that was fair enough, wasn't it? This was crisis time. And we'd all get together again when it was over, when things were normal again if they ever could be normal after this. Of course we would, we were bonded; and none stronger than Laura and me, I couldn't believe that she didn't see what I saw . . .

"And then there's me," she said more softly, sighing. Into his shoulder, at a guess; it was harder now for me to overhear, I really had to work at it.

And did, and heard:

"What about you?"

"You must have noticed. He thinks he's in love with me."

Thinks? *Thinks?* Jesus, if she'd sat in my head at all, any time these last two years . . .

"It's the same again, only bigger. He was so insecure when he cut himself loose, I'd say he desperately needed something to hang on to, to give himself some kind of value in his own eyes; and he fixed on me. I mean, I love the guy, I do; but not like that, it's hopeless."

"You'd better not," Jamie said, trying to lighten the mood a little; and yelped again. Meeting Laura's fist, I imagined.

"Shut up, this is serious. I've told him and told him, but oh, he's stubborn. Won't look at other girls, gets mad jealous if I show any interest in a boy. Come on, you *must* have noticed, he's been dead difficult with you."

"Ben and me is difficult anyway," Jamie said slowly, accepting the inevitable, that he couldn't tease her out of this confessional. "And just now, with everything else that's happening – well, no, I hadn't really noticed. First time, maybe, when I met you; I could see he didn't like that. But I thought that was just because of who I was. And what about Carol, then: I mean, those two, I thought . . ."

"Yeah. I don't know about Carol. I think, maybe something could happen there; but . . ."

I was just thinking that I didn't know about Carol either, and that I was glad Laura didn't know about what had happened already, when a cool hand closed over the back of my neck and I startled around to find Carol right there, eyeing me curiously.

"What are you up to, then?" she demanded, keeping her voice cautious.

"Eavesdropping," I admitted, just as quiet. "Did you know I suffer from terminal self-deception?"

"Yes," she said. "You're a bloke."

And smiled, and slipped her arm round my waist and towed me through the door with her, so that I lost my chance to learn any more about the way Laura saw me in the world.

They were curled up together in one of the big armchairs, Laura and Jamie, right by the door there; and Laura smiled a greeting at me, pushed a hand through her hair, said, "Hi. Thought you were going to snooze all day."

I just shook my head, I couldn't talk to her. I was muddled, mostly, but how I felt was angry. The sun was blazing in through all the windows; I pulled away from Carol and walked over to where it lay bright on a clear stretch of carpet. Sank down into it, tilted my head back and closed my eyes to its fierce touch, closed my ears and my mind to the company and centred in on my confusion.

It felt like coming home. I'd done a lot of this here, feeling totally adrift, feeling all my securities snatched away from me. Feeling hollowed, meaningless, no part of the life of this or any house . . .

If they spoke to me, I didn't register. I was sinking badly, losing it altogether, when the sound of a car door slamming finally penetrated my misery. I opened my eyes and saw Uncle James out there, crunching over the gravel.

A minute later, he came in to talk to us. To orate, rather. He took up his favourite position by the fireplace, and said, "Now, listen, all of you. Benedict, your Uncle Allan agrees with you, that whoever it is we're facing here most likely draws on the same sources that we do, and largely to the same effect. He left very early this morning, to see whether he can come to any further conclusions about the nature of their talent, or who they are." His voice said he thought that was improbable. "Jamie, I want you with me today. If they operate as we do, they are powerless by day; but we are not. We have an organisation in this town, and we should be able to find them. We *must* be able to find them," and his voice promised desperate retribution to anyone who hindered the search. "You others," he said, "you may stay here for the day," and once more his voice was saying more than his words, saying that we were insignificant to him and tolerated only for his son's sake, to assure his son's obedience: our presumed safety the price he bought it with.

"No," I said flatly.

For a second he didn't seem to understand at all. Then, "No?" he repeated. "In what sense, no?"

Jamie was making urgent faces at me, I could just make them out in the corner of my vision; but I looked straight at Uncle James and said, "I want to come with you."

Useless to my friends, apparently I was; deluded, even, lacking those meaningful relationships that I'd been so sure of, that I'd built my new life upon. I couldn't spend all day with Laura, knowing now how she thought of me; didn't want to spend a minute more than necessary with her, and what a change was there.

"For what purpose?" Uncle James enquired, while his eloquent voice added a subtext, *what use are you to me?*

And I remembered Steve's death last night, and how he had screamed when he felt his blood turn bad in his body, how he had lashed out blindly with his talent and shattered every window in the alley; and I turned my face to the sun and slowly and deliberately punched out every one of the many windows in that big room, and never moved once from where I sat on the carpet.

EIGHTEEN

MORE BRICKS THAN KICKS

Of them all, only Carol took it with anything approaching cool; and she looked anxious, as if she thought I should have kept my secrets better.

Laura was frightened, which was sour Pyrrhic victory for me: *don't know me so bloody well after all, do you, girl?* But however bitter my feelings, it was more bitter still to see her so, dark eyes wide in a pale face and her hands white-knuckled on Jamie's arm, and to know that I had caused that. I'd dreamed of her wide-eyed and clinging tight, but not for this and surely not to him.

Jamie himself was looking gobsmacked, with a bit of a stretch to his own hazel eyes; but his mouth was stretching also, coming up into a wide grin – as a young man ought to grin, perhaps seeing his brother come unexpectedly good.

Uncle James, though – Uncle James was so shocked it would have been comic, only that I didn't feel in the least little bit like laughing.

His head turned between me and the windows and back to me again, and it was his turn to say no: "No," he said, "that's not possible."

"Tell that to your glazier," I suggested, pushing myself now to my feet, to meet him eye to eye.

Only he wouldn't do that; his eyes were shifting still, all around the room and the long lawns and gardens outside, as a fresh breeze wound its way into the room through the jagged ruins of his glass.

"It's a trick," he said, "that's all, just a cheap and stupid trick. You've got someone out there with an air-rifle, shooting out the windows . . ."

"Try again, uncle," I said, regretting almost that I couldn't raise a laugh, his response was so contemptible. It did tickle the back of my mind for a moment, to wonder quite why he was trying so hard to deny this; but that was just Uncle James and the world he lived in, where things were so or not so and not subject to debate. Talent was starlit and always had been, therefore what he'd just seen demonstrated was a lie. Some manner of illusion, it had to be, if he could only figure it out . . .

"All the glass fell outwards, Dad," Jamie pointed out, still cradling Laura in the chair. She was still and silent, accusation in her eyes as she watched me. I gazed back at her, just as accusatory and let her figure that out if she could.

Seeing Uncle James baffled and snorting and perhaps a little afraid himself, heavy with anger and still fighting to reject what was manifest, I changed my mind. Did I really want to spend all the day and likely the night following with this man, in this mood? Did I hell.

So I turned away from him and from the sun both, and from the spoiled beauty of that long-remembered room; and I said to Carol, "I'm getting out of here. Want to come?"

At first I didn't understand why she looked to Laura; but of course, if Jamie went with his father and Carol came with me, that left Laura alone. Alone with my aunt and the household staff, at least, and anyone else who came along through the day, be they friend or family or foe. Or any combination thereof.

Laura hesitated, took silent counsel with Jamie – and then

slithered herself awkwardly out of his entanglement and onto her feet, and said, "Can we both?"

A little *tic* in my mind, a spasm of meanness that wanted to say no, wanted to say, *No, you chose him, you take what comes with him; which means his family, which means being left with the women while the men go out to play.*

"Sure," I said, shrugging. "If someone's got the bus fare." Alone I might have walked it, to work some of the muddle and temper out of my head and leave it in the road; but it was five miles or so along the river, and the mood wasn't right for a quiet amble. I wanted to storm, and I couldn't drag the girls along for that.

"Take one of the cars," Jamie said instantly. "Take the jeep."

"You sure?"

"Yeah, go on. I won't be using it." And then, just as a reminder, maybe, wanting to stake out his territory a little more clearly in view of what she'd told him, "Leave it with Laura, yeah?"

I nodded, jerked my head at the girls, *follow when ready*, left my cousin and my uncle without further ceremony. Didn't look back, to see if Jamie claimed a final kiss before parting. At least he didn't come with, to wave goodbye.

Jamie's jeep had been his delight when he was seventeen; I was glad he still had it, and kept it on the road. The keys were hanging where they had always hung, just by the back door in the kitchen. I twitched them down and went on out, with the girls quietly at my back, murmuring between themselves.

They were quiet also on the drive into town, sitting together in the back. I watched them in the mirror, each hanging onto the roll-bars with one hand. I thought probably their other hands were tightly linked, down out of my sight. Warm sun, wind in our hair and all day ahead of us: ach, we should have had the world at our feet. We should have been laughing and yelling and whooping at the sky, not trapped in these terrible tangles, grief and fear and confusion conspiring to bind our tongues and our spirits.

The hurt of it killed the anger in me, but I still couldn't talk to Laura. I drove straight to her flat, parked neatly in front of her door and climbed out, pressed the keys into her hand before she'd even set a foot on the ground; and she didn't speak either, and her fingers seemed to flinch away from mine as if she were frightened even of my touch now. Maybe she was, maybe she understood that Macallan tingle better now. She was sure to have a theory, at any rate, to explain why my skin was suddenly as electric as Jamie's, though far less welcome to her.

The hell with it, the hell with her and her theories both; I turned and walked off, finding my anger again as quickly as I'd lost it in that pang of wishing for our ravaged innocence. I could have my walk now, it was a long stretch from her flat to my own; and if I walked streets rather than river paths, so what? This was where I belonged, and I could be just as alone here, among the crowds. Ask Laura, she'd probably say I'd always been alone, even when I thought I was with twin souls, the friends of my heart . . .

Steaming up the hill, I heard running footsteps behind me. Didn't turn to look, because actually I didn't care just then, neither one was welcome. Still, no surprise when it was Carol who grabbed my arm and hauled me to a stop, breathing hard. What did surprise me, she seemed pretty much as angry as I was.

"Ben, what the *fuck* is the matter with you?"

Me, I was breathing just as hard, though I hadn't had the sprint to set me off. I yanked my arm free, so violently that her feet stuttered for balance on the pavement; and I said, "Do you want me to enumerate?"

Good word, enumerate. It blocked her, just for a moment; and that gave me the time to look back, to see Laura disappear behind her front door and slam it behind her. The sound of it came up the hill to chase us. Another time, that might have hurt the most; but today I just hoped she'd be sensible, she'd shove the bolts over and put the chain on and camp inside all day and all night and well into tomorrow. The streets would not be safe, I thought, for anyone tonight.

Carol must have done some quick enumerating of her own, because all she said was, "No. Don't bother. You want to sulk, you go ahead and sulk."

Sulk? God, was every woman in my life going to misunderstand me so wilfully? I headed off up the road again, so that Carol's next suggestion came from a pace or two behind.

"And when you've done that, d'you want to tell me how you did that trick with your uncle's windows? That was impressive, that was."

I almost stopped again, for that. I did check, just long enough for her to catch me up and tuck her arm through mine. From the weight she put on it, I understood that this was not exactly a friendly gesture, more a sort of anchor to hold me to an answer.

Actually, the only thing I wanted to tell her was to go home and leave me alone; and there was a sneaky way I had to do that. It was dirty, but a gift none the less, and I grabbed it. "Haven't you got a son you should be looking after?"

"Yes," she said, and the savagery in her voice said that she too knew what a low blow that was. "I have to pick him up from his dad's sometime this morning; but I can get a bus from your end of town. All right?"

I shrugged a reluctant acceptance, and then offered an olive branch of sorts, as I remembered that I had wheels of my own now. "I'll run you over, if you like. On the bike."

"Okay. Great. Now. Windows? I don't know much about it, but I thought you lot only got one dip each in the basket of tricks."

And you got fire, the unspoken addition there. Memories of a man's face, burning; those I didn't need.

"And slow down a bit," she added. "Please? I feel like a toddler, running to keep up with Daddy."

I sighed and made an effort to walk more slowly, a harder effort to explain.

"Traditionally, that's right. One talent each. Except that we can, no, *they* can all make nightfire, that's like the base that everything else springs from. Sort of like athletes, they specialise in jumping or throwing or whatever, but they can all run, right? So I guess I can make, what, dayfire, I suppose you have to call it; and it seems like I can punch windows out, too."

"How did you know?"

"Dunno. Just felt that I could, and I wanted to." *I wanted to smash something, and Uncle James' face wouldn't have been politic.* "But don't ask how I did it, okay?"

"Why not?"

"Couldn't tell you, is why not. It's magic. Literally. You want a theory," *you want to be like Laura*, "talk to Jacko sometime. He'll tell you all about how rhythm holds the universe together, on the molecular level; and that's what it comes down to in the end, one way or another. It has to. Our blood dances to a different drummer, is all, and his beat is the stronger. We can change the rhythm in things, and that's what makes them break apart."

What else I had on my mind, what I didn't want to say until I'd played a little in private, was that I was a sport by definition. I was a freak, using sunlight; and if the bog-standard, the absolute rule about nightlight didn't apply to me, maybe the other rules didn't apply either. I remembered that man from last night, who could break stone balls with a glance but who could also turn blood bad in Macallan bodies. That was two tricks, it seemed to me; and if he could double his luck, then maybe I could too . . .

* * *

We walked on, and I walked at least some of my temper off, so that we were fairly amicable partners by the time we came back to my flat. Carol even stroked her hand up and down my arm, chuckling a little at the tingle. "You now, a girl could get used to this. It's very sexy. Other men are going to seem kind of flat, I think."

I didn't tell her, but a man could get used to it, too: to having that effect on women. My cousins took it for granted, by and large took their women for granted also; and Jamie had better not, had better never do that, or he'd have me to answer to. In daylight, naturally . . .

"Time for a coffee?" I asked, ripping more foliage off the olive-tree. "I want one anyway, I'm parched."

"Yes, of course. You should, you didn't have any breakfast, did you?"

Didn't have anything, last night or this morning; and I was curiously glad of that, not to have taken any refreshment in my uncle's house. Call it a fine line, but in my code there's a distinction between bed and breakfast. Accepting shelter under someone's roof costs them nothing, so that beyond a measure of thanks nothing is what you owe. Taking their hospitality also, eating and drinking makes a transient into a guest irreparably, would have made one of me last night; and guests have obligations, and not breaking windows seemed pretty much the least of them.

Inside the flat, there was no sign of Jacko or Jonathan except that the place was unwontedly clean; one or other of them had had a binge. Nothing to say where they were and when – or whether – they'd be back; but I did find a couple of notes pushed through the door. One was from my tutor at college, asking why I'd missed a crucial seminar and where was that overdue essay, and hadn't I better get in touch with him pronto if I wanted to survive this term? The other was from our telephonically-unchallenged neighbour upstairs, relaying a message from the manager at Medicall, who assigned the drivers' shifts: did I realise I'd missed a shift last night without even calling in with an excuse, and was I aware that that was a capital offence, and that I should consider myself lucky simply to be sacked?

"Ouch," said Carol, listening in to that. "What was the note?"

"Same thing, really, only from college. It's just threats; they'll let me back if I grovel."

If I grovelled. Things were changing so fast around me, all my realities had been snatched up like a hand of cards and shuffled and redealt: it was hard to see myself going quietly back into that loose and fragile life of mine, where the chief worry was money enough to get me through another term of books and alcohol, the two luxuries so crucial to a student.

We had a coffee, and she kept asking questions I couldn't answer; and even when she wasn't doing that I was asking questions of myself, and couldn't answer those either. It wasn't the best hour I'd spent with her, out of the last twenty-four. Not the worst either, but it was hardly likely to be that. Too much competition there, it didn't stand a chance.

Eventually she glanced at the clock, and made a rueful face. I nodded.

"Come on, then."

"Hang on, Ben. What are you going to do? I'm not sure it's a smart idea, leaving you on your own. I can always ask Richard to keep Nicky for one more night, he wouldn't mind. It's just horse-trading, I can pay him back later . . ."

"No," I said, "really. It's what I want, to be alone for a bit."

"Mm, I figured that. But why?"

"I want to try a few things," I said, as offhand as I could manage it. "Test myself a little, figure some stuff out. And then I'm going over to see Uncle Allan, and I'm sorry, I can't take you with me. Wouldn't if I could, I don't like you so much involved with my family, it's not safe to make them notice you; but I couldn't anyway. Allan's too private, he wouldn't talk to me if you were there."

"Unh. Well, all right then. As long as you're not just fobbing me off?"

"Not a fob. Promise."

She still didn't look convinced, but, "Look, do me a favour then. Keep in touch, yeah? Phone me. A couple of times today, and tonight. Just check in, so that I know what's what."

"You mean like heroes in the movies never do?"

"That's exactly what I mean, yes. Don't be a hero."

"Promise," I said lightly, said again; and probably I meant it as little as any hero ever meant a promise to a civilian non-combatant in time of war. I meant to walk on some dangerous water, with only the hope of miracles to keep me up; catch me phoning in to confess.

She accepted it, though, or seemed to; and she rode pillion behind me on the bike, wind in our hair again but no dreams now, no space for dreaming in my busy head.

She kissed me briefly when I dropped her off. Then she clipped me over the back of the head where I sat astride the bike, and said, "Wear a helmet, fool. And don't forget to phone me."

I nodded, put the bike into gear and roared away, suddenly urgent: not stopping even to say hi to Nicky, which I would have written down as criminal any other day. There are duties owed to children, and making time to observe the civilities is definitely one of them. As is not breaking promises.

Luckily, that doesn't apply to adults. They're not burdened with a child's trust; they can make their own assessment of your reliability, and if they misjudge you, that's just tough.

Too bad, Carol. Don't wait up.

* * *

That promise might have been a lie, but not what else I'd said to her. I did want to find Uncle Allan that day, to try to learn where his mind was leading; and first, yes, I wanted to try a few things. Test myself a bit; and test also the sunlight that was beating down on my bare head now, to see just what strength it was ready to lend me, what talent I did have.

So I drove not home, and not yet to Allan's house: but down to the river and the land laid waste, where the Duke survived in the midst of nothing, standing above destruction like a lord of misrule. Like Jamie all those years ago, I wanted to pit myself against bricks and concrete; and like Jamie's first night out, I didn't intend to ask permission first.

Didn't need to down here, even if I'd been in the mood. Any damage I managed would be doing a favour to the town. This was one of several sites bought up by an incoming company that didn't understand the system. They'd taken over acres of derelict housing to redevelop, and got halfway through the demolition before they learned how much it was going to cost them to operate here. They'd pulled out then, with the taste of fear strong in their mouths and a major loss to explain to their shareholders; and the result was what I faced now.

Behind broken and graffiti-covered hoardings, there were mounds of rubble where as a child I'd known long rows of terraced houses. Not all the buildings had been flattened; some were only roofless shells still lined in places with peeling strips of wallpaper, different patterns all that remained sometimes to map the different rooms, where interior walls and floors had fallen. Joists hung at crazy angles, many charred by fires the local kids had set.

There was a long-abandoned petrol station here too, the pumps and workings salvaged but a glassless kiosk still standing under a canopy supported on concrete pillars.

I parked the bike by the pub and set off up the crumbling road. No problem of access; I walked in through a gap in the hoardings, and scrambled over heaps of broken brick till I came to where a lone wall stood proud among the wreckage. Again no glass in the neat square holes that were its windows, but that didn't matter. I knew about glass already. I was here to learn about other things.

I didn't see them, but if there were any kids on the loose down there that day – and there must surely have been some – they would certainly have seen me. And seen also what I was doing, making magic in broad daylight under a generous sun.

I learned quicker than Jamie had, or else I was more mature or simply more in need of knowing urgently what I could and couldn't achieve.

After a couple of hours' hot work, there was nothing left of that wall, nor any others in my line of sight.

At first I was crude, as Jamie had been. It was like breaking windows, just a mental punch cracking into brickwork; I swear I even flinched the first couple of times. Foolish, but my fists were bunching at my sides, and I expected to feel my knuckles splinter.

It was brick that splintered. I stood ten metres from the wall and hurled my invisible thunderbolts, and sent great blocks of it crashing to the ground. The early ones flickered with flame as they broke away and landed black and smoking, before I learned to control the dayfire.

Then I tried what I shouldn't even have been thinking of, according to family lore: I tried a different talent. I reached out for loosened bricks left awkwardly balanced at the margins of where I'd struck, and raised them delicately up. The first time or two they slipped from my imaginary fingers and fell, but I had unmistakably had a grip; a little more practice and I was juggling, I was making bricks dance in the air before I brought them down to build new and shaky walls on the rubble, like a child playing with wooden blocks.

Elated but somehow not surprised, I changed again. I lifted a solitary brick, and squeezed it. And watched it crumble to dust before my eyes and swirl to nothing in the wind, and couldn't hold in a triumphant yell. Briefly it seemed as if there was nothing I couldn't do; I felt more than powerful, I felt omnipotent. Yes, and vengeful.

Until a stray cloud drifted across the sun, and the tingle left my skin and I was abruptly weak and helpless, reminded that I had only reflected power. No sun myself, I was only a moon in daylight, dependent on another source to shine; and all the long hours of night lay too soon ahead . . .

When the sun came back, I walked down a little further, to that big petrol station. Whichever company had owned it, they'd taken their decals off, leaving the frame oddly naked; but it was still solid otherwise. The development company hadn't reached this far with its machines and manpower.

I stood under the canopy, where the sunlight just warmed the back of my neck, and I squeezed the kiosk as I had squeezed the brick. I watched its walls fold in on themselves, listened to them crack and saw them craze and collapse.

Then I turned my eyes upward, to the canopy.

It might have been twenty metres long and ten deep, standing foursquare above the pits where the pumps had stood. Not heavy, I thought, only wood and plastic with metal girders to keep its shape; but oh, it was big. Maybe too big for me, or too well-rooted, but I had to know.

Call it a push, call it a lift; doesn't matter, I guess. I reached underneath and thrust upward; and again I heard the sounds of internal breaking, and dust and filth showered down as it trembled and stayed anchored on its fat concrete pillars.

I scowled, took a breath and tried again.

Those watching kids, if there were any, would only have seen a man standing still and doing nothing. If they'd been close enough perhaps they'd have seen me sweat, perhaps they'd have giggled when they saw the weird faces that I pulled, but they'd never have known how hard I was working there, how brutally I was straining.

The structure shook visibly, a lot more shit came cascading down; and at last, with a great tearing sound and splinters flying, the whole canopy broke free in one piece and went spinning end over end like a sheet of cardboard in the wind.

It hit the ground some fifty metres away, and fell apart. I dropped to a crouch, dizzy with success and wonder, gaping at what I'd done. Sheared metal rods stuck up from the pillars, bent into crazy shapes by the force of that breaking; sunlight washed all the concrete forecourt, where it couldn't have come since the canopy was first erected.

Took me five minutes before I could stand on trembling legs and totter away to find the bike again. My T-shirt was sodden on my back, even my jeans felt damp, and I only wanted my bed with no one else in it, just my own bed in bright sunlight and space enough to stretch out and groan a little and then sleep and sleep.

And couldn't afford even to lie down for twenty minutes, didn't have the time to spare. Gone noon already, my ally the sun slipping down the sky on its way to leaving me. Clouds were building, also; that first stray had been a herald.

Wind in my hair once more, only this time my hair was sticky with dust and sweat and my scalp chilled in the flow of air. Does Superman catch cold? I wondered. And what would happen to me if I sneezed in sunlight? And to those around me? Jet-propelled Macallan, first man to fly; and all his friends – no, sorry, his few and uncommitted acquaintances, and thank you Laura for reminding me of that – caught in the backblast while he soared. Blown to smithereens, and who would miss them . . . ?

Well, actually, I would. Regardless of how they felt themselves: I'd miss their company, and I'd miss more the comfort of their being constantly in the back of my head and the background of my life, an ever-present help in trouble . . .

Which was, I supposed, what Laura was talking about. Didn't want to think about that. Again, didn't have the time.

Drove to Uncle Allan's house, vaulted off the bike and actually ran to the door, as if a second's difference were worth any amount of ache and weariness in my legs. I yanked on the bell-pull, once and twice and again, and danced my fingers slowly across the brickwork in the porch while I waited for an answer. Thinking, *Let the sun get a little lower, let it shine in here, I could pick you apart with my bare hands. That's if I could be bothered to use my hands at all . . .*

At last slow footsteps coming and going, louder every time they came: someone walking down the hall towards me, treading alternately on boards and rugs. I prayed for Allan, but never believed it; and sure enough, Aunt Jess opened the door.

"Benedict." Ah, she looked sour, did my aunt: the martinet with the heart of gold, only that someone had stolen away her heart, and that recently so that she still felt the pain of its stealing. Looking at her, thinking of her and Aunt Lucy and my mother, all the other aunts and female cousins – and I was leaving Hazel out of this but probably you could stick her in the same pot with the rest of them, for a little added spice without really changing the dish at all – it occurred to me that maybe it was as well for Laura that she wouldn't be marrying me, though bad bad news that she was so hot for Jamie. Macallan womenfolk didn't seem to survive the status very well. Especially those that weren't blood, the poor deluded fools who married in . . .

"What can I do for you?" my aunt asked, as if she were some vague acquaintance and not a loving aunt at all.

"I need to see Uncle Allan, it's dead important . . ." Almost dancing on the doorstep with impatience, *let me in, let me run up the stairs and find him* . . .

"I'm sorry, Benedict, he's not here."

That stopped me, that stumped me, that was the worst news imaginable. "Not . . . ? Oh, *shit!* Um, sorry, Aunt Jess. Can you tell me where he is?" He should have been here, surely that was what Uncle James had said? But tracking back in my head, I realised that I'd misunderstood, and maybe wilfully so. All that had actually been said was that Allan was on an intellectual quest for answers; I'd simply assumed that meant he'd be coming here, home to his books and instruments. That was the best solution for me, the easiest way to find him, so I'd voted for it and conveniently forgotten that the world was subject neither to my dictatorship nor to my curious notions of democracy, where one vote could carry the day so long as it was my own.

Her face expressed her distaste, but she told me. "He said he needed to study the remains from last night's activity."

'The remains' meant Steve, of course, if there was anything left of him. "Uh, do you know where . . . ?"

"The mortuary, I should imagine. Unless they took him to his home."

No, they wouldn't have done that. Not this time. The mortuary got the decision, except that I didn't know where the mortuary was. All those years of living here, and I didn't know where the dead went; nor would most of my friends, I realised, ripping through a mental list of people I could ask. Christ, I might have to come down to a policeman . . .

"Okay, thanks, Aunt Jess." No good asking her at any rate. "Can I just nip up to his study to leave him a message?"

"I will tell him that you called, Benedict," her acid voice saying also, *Woman I may be, and not in my prime form now, but you can trust me that far, boy.*

"Yeah, but it's a little more complicated than that . . ."

"Oh, very well, then." She pulled the door more widely open and stepped aside; and I did run up the stairs, even though I knew now that he wasn't there to greet me.

Never been in his study alone before, never been trusted enough; and quite right too. There was too much here to play with, too much to touch and most of it fragile or dangerous or both.

My hands strayed aimlessly, reaching for everything, touching nothing until at last I picked up that sheep's skull from his desk. Hazel had killed it, he had saved it; it was knowledge, I supposed, or evidence at least. And his favourite kind at that. All its secrets were family.

I ran my finger over the dark lines of the web that marked it, felt how they were scored into the bone, and remembered Steve last night. How his skull too had borne its marks after his hair and skin had sloughed away: though that was more intricate than this, no simple web. And then my reluctant mind reminded me that there was another body still that must bear a similar brand, unless his family had chosen to finish what I'd started, and had burned what was left of my policeman.

Sick at heart, I dropped the skull back on Allan's desk. My questing hands moved on, seeking comfort; they settled on what I'd always loved the best, the cool smooth tubes of his old brass microscope . . .

Ah, shit. I had no time for this, for reaching back to childhood in search of a dream of better times. I jerked myself away, and quickly did what I'd come up here for; I left my uncle a message he couldn't miss, to say that I'd been here in search of him.

Then I picked up his phone and dialled, still moving fast, before my nerve could fail me.

One ring, two rings and she answered.

"Hullo?"

"Laura, it's Ben." And quickly on, in case she still wasn't talking to me. "Where's the mortuary?"

"What?"

"The town mortuary. Where is it?" If anyone knew, she must. She was a medic, after all.

"At the hospital, of course. What do you need to know that for?"

"Sorry. I'm in a rush. I'll explain later. Thanks . . ."

And I hung up on her. First time for everything, I guess.

Down the stairs again, to where my aunt still waited for me in the hall. I put my hands on her stiff shoulders and kissed her cheek, managed a faint smile at her startlement and said goodbye.

Out of the house and onto the bike and away I raced, down into town under a sky that was suddenly and unfairly clotting up, threatening rain.

The hospital sprawled over many acres, and I didn't know my way anywhere, except to Casualty and the private rooms. Took me ten minutes to find the mortuary, and the porter I ran into at the door – literally ran into, spinning round a corner to collide with the poor bastard, almost knocking us both to the floor – said that no, not Allan Macallan nor any other living visitor was there. Nor had been there, since he came on duty.

Which left me stranded, desperate and clueless, no chance of finding my uncle now.

NINETEEN

DESPERATELY SEEKING SAFETY

Desperate times drive you to desperate measures. Me, I was frantic enough to drive around town spotting this year's Volvos. There were dozens of them, and they were all dark blue, or seemed so; and of course I didn't know Allan's registration number, or anything useful like that.

Volvos on the move were easy to discount, just one glance at the driver and forget it, that wasn't Allan.

Parked cars took more work. Each one I came across I pulled alongside and peered in, trying to spot clues. A child seat in the back meant the wrong car, for sure. So did a jacket in an ugly dog's-tooth check, hanging from a hook behind the door. Aunt Jess bought Allan's clothes for him, and she would never have been guilty of that.

A copy of *Cosmo* on the passenger seat and a mess of peppermints and used tissues on the dashboard: wrong car.

Another car, another magazine; this time I had to bump the bike up onto the pavement and squint. *The International Journal of Alternative and Complementary Medicines* – not likely, but possible. Uncle Allan pursued knowledge as a dog rabbits, and the more arcane the better. On the dash, though, was a fat thriller, and there was a Krooklok on the wheel.

Case thrown out of court, on two counts.

Allan used to pay Jamie and me to clean his car for him, every Sunday until he caught us with our heads under the bonnet, fiddling with the leads, trying to hotwire the beast. These days he'd have some other young hopefuls on the payroll; dirty cars could be discounted.

There were still a few, however, that were neutral inside and out, telling me nothing, saying neither *yea* nor *nay*. But Volvo owners are careful souls; a foot stretched out from bike to bumper, a little pressure applied, and it was safe money that an ululating alarm would bite through my bootsole and thrill up my tibia, fouling the air for a couple of hundred metres in all directions but down.

As soon as it did, I was away and looking for the next. Volvo owners might be careful souls in general, and my Uncle Allan one in particular; but not in this. I doubted if he'd ever set an alarm in his life, he wouldn't see the point . . .

But alarmed or otherwise, if he was anywhere in town I couldn't find him, neither the man nor his wheels. Allan travelled far more than most Macallans, in pursuit of his researches. Some stray idea might have taken him fifty or a hundred miles away, distances undreamed of in the narrow philosophies of my less far-seeking family. Coincidence can't be forced, and it was only ever coincidence would have produced his car for me, just when I wanted him the most.

So I abandoned the search, reluctant despite its futility. At least it had given me something to do, it had kept me moving. Movement promised progress, its natural illusion; and the constant supply of cars of the right age, right make, right colour had dangled hope before me, vividly carotene, keeping me frantic but just the right side of despair. I could think of nothing more productive. Without Allan, I thought, I was lost, we were all lost.

Without Allan, I had nothing to do but hide in the oncoming night. The sky was darkening already, tinting towards Volvo-blue to the east. I felt my time slipping from me, the day all run to waste. As the world turned, we turned with it; wannabe hunter turned to hunted, definitely and unquestionably hunted, and I was desperate suddenly for cover.

Couldn't hang out at home, couldn't do what I so hoped Laura and Carol were doing, barring their doors and pulling their curtains and burrowing deep beneath their duvets. Walls and doors were no defence for me, this Englishman's home was no kind of castle. If I'd not been a target before, I sure was now; and anyone looking for me would of course look there first, in case I hadn't twigged it yet.

I wouldn't even have thought of going home, except that I didn't live alone, and anyone found at the flat would be in as much peril as me. Questions would be asked, and answers sought by any cruel or unusual means available. So I spun the bike around and raced the failing light away from the centre of town, up the long hill with all the speed I could squeeze from the throttle and thank God for my sister's machismo, this powerful machine a needful substitute for her inherent weakness.

When I reached the flat I found lights burning, music playing and Jacko fooling around in the kitchen with Jonathan. To be specific, I found Jon at the back end of a fit of giggles, sagging against the wall and trying weakly to buckle his belt and tuck his T-shirt in while Jacko bent unconvincingly over a steaming pot on the stove.

Took both of them a second to remember that things had changed, that they were frightened of me now. Then Jon sobered abruptly, one last gasp for air and even his smile died. He straightened up, sorted his clothes out with quick movements, looked to Jacko for guidance.

"Ben, hi. Er, have you got time to eat?" Jacko offered with a gesture towards the busy cooker, while his voice pleaded for me to say no.

"No," I said, ever the cooperative flatmate. "And neither have you."

"Unh?"

"I'm sorry, you've got to get out of here. Can you go to Jon's place?"

A mute shake of the head from Jonathan said not.

"Well, friends, then. Take a couple of sleeping-bags, you can borrow mine, and go crash on someone's floor tonight."

"Ben, what the hell for?"

"It's getting dark out there. Dark is dangerous, right? Remember? Somebody's after me; and they'll take you too if they find you here, just in case you can lead them to me."

Jacko looked at me, looked at Jon; said, "Get your jacket, hon. We're gone."

I turned the gas off under their abandoned dinner and followed them out into the narrow hallway, where Jacko was ignoring my suggestion of sleeping-bags and organising the evacuation of his instruments instead.

"If you can manage the bodhrán and the flute, Jon, I've got the rest."

"Jacko, man!" I said, almost laughing, almost. "For Christ's sake . . ."

He just looked at me and said, "Can you guarantee, absolutely *guarantee* that if I leave these behind, nothing at all is going to happen to them?"

I started to say yes, of course I could, it was me that was the target here, not a one-man ceilidh band; and stopped before the first word was halfway up my throat. Thought about major talent confronted by a locked door that no one was going to answer, and did the other thing instead, said no.

Said, "No, I suppose I can't."

"Right." And then, just a little belatedly, all his priorities exposed, he said, "What about you, what are you doing? Are you going to be okay?"

"I don't know," I admitted.

"You could, uh," Jon started, hesitated, waited for Jacko's support and then carried on regardless, "you could come with us. We're going over to a mate's, I don't suppose anyone'd look for you there . . ."

Too scared to want me along, he was too warm-hearted not to make the offer. I found a real smile for him, along with the shake of the head that he was looking for. "No. Thanks, I mean really thanks, but no. I don't know what he's got, the guy who's after me. Wherever I hole up, he might still be able to sniff me out." I couldn't bring that down on my friends.

"What, then?" Jacko demanded, working the door open with his elbow, his arms full of latent music. "Got any plans?"

"Not really. Maybe I'll just get on the bike and drive, get right out of town . . ."

"Good. Sounds good. Luck, Ben . . ."

"Thanks." I was going to need it, whatever I did. "Now go. Go on, scoot."

And they did that, they scooted. They all but ran up the road to the bus-stop, encumbered as they were; I locked the door, realised I'd left all the lights on and decided against all policy to leave them, a misleading beacon in the twilight.

Back on the bike again; much more of this and I'd be getting saddle-sores.

Which would either be the last or the least of my worries, depending.

What I'd said about driving all night had only been spur-of-the-moment, Jacko's payback for showing concern; at the time I hadn't meant it. Wasn't such a bad idea, though. Driving in circles all night would only attract attention, but there was a whole nother country out there beyond the city limits, and it was user-friendly to me in a way that my own home town was not tonight, pretty much a magic-free zone . . .

As a self-rescue plan, that sounded pretty good to me. Though it did of course depend on the one assumption, that I could make it to the city limits unassailed.

I thought I could. I was sure I could. The odds were stacked high in my favour. Big place, and me very small within it; and so far as I knew only one man out there to oppose me. And him equally small on the physical plane, though his talent might be enormous . . .

The quickest way out was straight on up the hill and along the river to the west; but if he was thinking ahead of me here, if he was covering any route at all – listening out for what was becoming my sound-signature, perhaps, my leitmotif, the throaty roar of the BMW working hard, just as my sister used to work it – then that's where he'd be, on that road with his fingers sparking fire and death in his eyes.

Smart money said to find another way to leave. Cross one of the bridges and head south, perhaps, and just pray that he didn't happen to be there on that particular bridge as I crossed. Or go north on the Great South Road, or the quieter coastal route: wherever he chose to watch if he was watching, he surely wouldn't be watching that. Least likely road of all, that was.

So maybe he'd be watching that road, on the Agatha Christie principle. I couldn't know, all I could do was guess and guess again, ultimately toss a mental coin and hope.

Probably I should have dumped the bike in a back alley somewhere and gone for a bus or a train, or hijacked some nonentity's undistinguished car. But my paranoia-quotient was running high tonight, I could see a shadowy figure stepping into the road or onto the tracks, I could hear the squeal of brakes and taste doom like terror in my mouth; and I'd be trapped that way, taken in a metal box and risking other people's lives as I gave my own away. Better to die on the bike if I had to do that thing at all, better to be brought down with speed and noise and my eyes on the dark horizon, bidding for freedom; better by far to die alone than in company.

Better still not to die at all, of course. One feeling persisted, though, that if I didn't die I was going to have to kill instead. Me personally, and deliberately so. Not enough to be on the killing side, lined up for once with my family; it was on my shoulders to finish it myself, if I could survive through to daylight.

Jamie had had his chance, and hadn't used it; and if my hot-tempered cousin couldn't kill coldly, then what chance did I have? With all my mixed motives and confusions, and above and in front of everything the memory of that traffic cop dancing his death before me, I didn't, I couldn't possibly trust myself where I had trusted Jamie and seen him fail.

Which was another excellent reason to get out of town: not to know that I was letting my family down again, condemning God alone knew how many more of them to a terrible death, slow and agonising and – oh, Christ forgive me but the word was there in my head and what can you do? – bloodcurdling.

Maybe I should just keep on going, once I'd passed the city limits. Not come back even in daylight, to prowl the territories of my latest betrayal and learn just how much it had cost, in blood and other things . . .

Running away has always been one of my strengths. I'm good at spotting opportunities for escape, good at seizing them and particularly good at riding the scorn and the self-contempt that come after. No macho illusions to be shattered, I guess.

This time, though, I wasn't confident even of getting the chance, let alone surviving the fallout. Whichever way I picked, I was sure he'd outguess me and be waiting. I juggled and shuffled ifs and maybes in my mind until I was dizzy with possibilities.

In the end, though, I performed a decisive mental twist that I instantly labelled a reverse Occam, dumped all the complicated scenarios I'd been building in my head and seized instead on the nearest, the simplest, the quickest way out of town. Blaze of glory time: if he was there, primed and ready to pick me off, he'd have a moving target to aim at. A *fast*-moving target.

"Die young," I told myself with a fake cheeriness, saying it aloud to fool myself the better, "leave a beautiful corpse . . ."

In the interests of which I got off the bike, fished my keys out and went back inside the flat after all. Not to turn the lights off, only to fetch my sister's crash helmet and seat it securely on my head. Not that that would protect my delicate features from the inward assaults of the blood-curdling stunt; but the speed I meant to drive at, any more normal manifestation of talent could simply throw me off the bike one way or another, and I'd sooner not leave my face in shreds on the tarmac. Not nice for my mother when they came to lay me out.

Besides, I fancied the anonymity, the implicit threat of a full-face helmet with a darkened visor. I had nothing to back the threat up with, this time of night, but everyone knew that anyway. It was all image, and self-image; and what better time to bolster your self-image than the night you tread the primrose path to dalliance with death?

So. Helmet on, visor down and no matter that the dark tint robbed the streetlights of half their usefulness. There was no traffic around in any case, the cattle were all cooped up and I could see well enough to drive on empty roads.

Up the hill and over the top at speed: there before me was the yellow ribbon of light that marked the highway, falling down to the bridge over the bypass where all the rest of the country seemed to pass us by and then on and on and out of my sight, and I had fuel enough to race all the length of the ribbon to the opposite coast if I chose to . . .

There were lights moving north and south, there was traffic aplenty on the bypass. My own was always the road less travelled, and tonight the citizenry was well advised to stay withindoors; but even with that as a given, there should surely have been a few trucks coming and going, what trade my family sanctioned. In fact there was none. Mine was the only light moving, as far as my eyes could see.

That was strange, disconcerting, but not for long. The rate I was going, nothing could last long. The nervous tension in my body, that already had my fingers trembling right through to the bone where they were clenched around the handgrips, resolved itself into panic as soon as my squinting eyes could distinguish light from light on the road ahead.

There were the orange sodium lights that drew the line of the road on into the night; but just this side of the bridge, delineating the town's border, there was a line of ice-blue light that flickered coldly. That was nightfire, that explained incontrovertibly why the road was deserted but for me; and I did think I'd been outguessed, I thought my enemy waited for me at the roadside, confident enough to show me that he was there.

I braked with a scream that I hoped was only tyres on tarmac, though it resonated within the confines of the helmet so that I thought some part of it at least had come from my own throat. The bike skidded, and more than anything I wanted to turn that skid into a spin, to let momentum carry me over onto the other carriageway facing the other way. If he was here, he couldn't be elsewhere; the bridges would be clear, the Great South Road would be safe, I could find another way out of town and be free and gone before he caught up with me . . .

I didn't do that, though. I controlled the skid without thinking, brought the bike to a halt and only sat there, one foot on the road and the beam of my headlight spearing down towards the road-block, announcing me to any watching eyes.

Nothing moved. I tilted the visor back to see better, and saw how the tarmac itself was burning in a neat, tight line, straight across the road from one kerb to the other. Whoever had laid that fire was feeding it richly; nightfire was a thin light normally, re-flecting its source, but this was throwing flares three or four metres high, a fierce warning and an absolute prohibition.

Shielding my eyes against the dazzle of it, I could make out the high boxy shadow of an off-road vehicle, some Japanese Landrover-substitute, pulled appropriately off the road. Figures also, standing on either kerb; two on one side, at least one on the other. I couldn't see their faces, but their number was enough. If I was sure of anything, I was sure I had only one man to face.

I rolled the bike slowly forward – and had to stop to lift the visor and spit suddenly, as sour saliva flooded my mouth. Sure I might be, but I'd been wrong before, about things I was certain of. And Christ, I was scared now; I could hear the beat of my blood in my ears, and not only my mouth was flooding. My mind spilled over with memories of the dead, and how their blood had turned bad in their bodies. Blisters or boiling sludge, crystal or acid, it all came down to blood; and *any moment now*, my own traitor thoughts were whispering, *any moment, just keep getting closer, make them a gift of your own blood to play with. Why not? It'll show the family, at least, show the world that you belong* . . .

I spat again, wiped my mouth with the back of my hand, tipped the visor down and went on forward.

A little nearer, and if I couldn't see faces I could at least see that they had faces, those shadows on the borders of the road. White their faces were, and turned to me: squinting into my light as I into theirs. Powerful headlamps, Beemers have. One stepped further back onto the grass verge, trying to avoid the cone of my fierce light; the nightfire flickered and paled, seemed to die a little before it fed again.

Nearer still, and I was better off than they. They'd not be seeing anything but dark – dark helmet, visor down; dark jacket and dark jeans – and that only if they could see anything of me at all behind the light. Me, I saw them and I knew them, and my terror slowly ebbed.

Cousins, of course. Minor cousins, these, and three of them together because only that way could they hope to meet or match a major talent: a Jamie, say, if Jamie were provoked. *Or a Benedict*, my unabashed ego put in, breaking through in a rush as though I had nothing more to be frightened of all night, *if the sun were shining on him* . . .

Reminding myself that even minor cousins could tear me apart in darkness if they had a mind to do it – or if they were spooked enough not to look closely, not to see that I was family: and maybe the helmet wasn't such a smart idea after all – I brought the bike to a halt still some little distance off. Killed the engine, but left the lights alive. Couldn't hold all three of them in the beam at once, but two I had, and those I was holding on to.

I dismounted, looking at the tension in the two that I could see and feeling my shoulder blades itch with knowledge of the one that I couldn't; and decided reluctantly that discretion at this point was far the better part of image-building.

So I lifted the helmet off, ran a hand through my hair and walked deliberately into the light, calling ahead as I went.

"Hullo, is that Conor?"

A moment's more silence, and then an explosive breath and, "Jesus fucking *Christ*, it's only bloody Benedict!"

Mutters of relief and resentment, and I didn't need to hear the words, I knew the sentiments too well already. Only Benedict, untrustworthy but harmless. Just a sport, a freak of nature, had no talent so he ran away and the family was well rid of him, no use for hangers-on . . .

"What the hell are you doing here, Benedict?"

"Came to see. What's going on?"

He ignored that, squinting past me. "Is that your bike?"

"Yes," I said flatly.

"Only I thought, just for a moment there, I thought . . ."

You thought I was my sister, right? Till you remembered that she was dead. And then you didn't know what to think, was this a ghost come to visit or an enemy or what? Couldn't be cattle, no cattle would be so foolish as to stray so close . . .

"Well, it's me," I said, momentarily generous, hauling him out of a hole. "So what's with the roadblock?"

"Big stuff going down," he said, vague and full of import; though in fact all he was telling me was *I don't know, I just follow orders, me.* "Cousin James asked us himself. Seal off the town, he said, don't let anyone in or out. That includes you," he added, frowning. "Must do. You shouldn't be out anyway, it's not safe for you . . ." *Go home and hide with the cattle*, he was saying now; and no, he really didn't know a thing, did he? Just a good soldier, doing what he was told. If I'd been Jamie, or Lamartine, or any cousin but me, he'd have let me through; me being me, no chance. The family name was a passport, sure, but not by itself enough. Talent was the key, and this door wasn't going to open without it; and obviously there'd been no leaks dripped down to Cousin Conor, Uncle James hadn't let slip a word about his windows. No surprise there. He'd probably told his glazier it was a sonic boom.

He might be a pompous bastard, but James was nothing else if not efficient. If he'd closed this road, he'd have closed them all; God knew there were cousins enough, through all the cadet branches of the family. If I went down to the river and drove along the footpath, there's be someone even there to stop me, I'd lay money on it.

There must still be ways to escape; even Uncle James couldn't isolate a town this large in a single night. I could climb fences, scramble through hedges, surf the trains if they were running. If not I could steal a boat or play chicken with the bypass traffic. I could certainly get out, if I tried hard enough.

If nobody caught me trying.

But I'd be lucky, more than lucky if I found a way to take the bike with me; and I didn't want to leave it. Apart from the convenience and the simple speed, the sweet get-me-out-out-of-here spirit of the thing, it was turning into a talisman for me. Riding it, I was Hazel's representative on earth and the instrument of her revenge; I carried her letters-of-marque, I was privileged and potent. I didn't want to lose that, even temporarily. Knowing what I had to do, not knowing if I could ever bring myself to do it, I needed all the help I could get, and help from my hard sister was more valuable than most.

"Go on," Conor said, roughly authoritative. "Get yourself home, and leave family business to those of us with the strength to handle it."

Oh, that was cocky, from him; but I let it pass. Not much else I could do, in all honesty. I even managed a humiliating nod of submission as I turned and went back to the bike. Uncle James' punctured dignity might yet work to my advantage; it's always useful to be underestimated.

No speed in me now. I didn't know what to do; driving laps of the town would simply be asking for trouble. I thought again about seeking shelter with friends, and again I rejected it. I just couldn't tell how much talent there was ranged against me; for all I knew my enemy could have a witch-finder's nose, sensitive enough to sniff me out wherever I holed up.

Fe fi fo fum, I smell the blood of a Macallan man. Poor poetry, but a poorer prognosis for me if it were possible and true.

I drove slowly, indecisively back to the brow of the hill, and pulled up in the middle of the empty road. All the town lay spread out below me, shimmering with light and all of it useless to me – or so I assumed, thinking regretfully that it was too bad there was no way to store sunlight and carry it around in my pockets like ammunition for a later date in the dark.

But then again I saw nightfire where I wasn't expecting it; and this no roadblock, no. This was a beacon and a rallying-cry, blazing bright against the pollution of a whole city's neon and sodium glare. Not one man's work, surely. Even the strongest of my family couldn't light up the town alone.

What it was, was the tip of the spire on St Dominic's, Father Hamish's own church. There was an ancient iron weathercock up there, the gift of an eighteenth-century relative of mine, who held the whole parish in his gift; it was shaped like a phoenix, and that bird was in the fire right enough tonight, though I didn't think it was going to rise in the morning.

It burned incandescent, like a brand in the night, like a summoning; and I couldn't see for the fierce shine of it, but the metal that made it must be writhing and collapsing in the chill of the fire, undoing itself as it burned.

I'd have been worried for the spire, for the church itself, except that nothing that acted to Hamish's loss was going to worry me. And besides, if the clan were gathering, they'd see the building safe. Enough to make such a nightfire, there must be enough also to control it.

And that many of my blood, all in the one place – there'd be enough there to see me safe also. Protection in numbers; it was isolation that was dangerous. Each of my cousins who'd been attacked, had been attacked alone.

So down the hill I went, and for the first time in years I went to church.

Cars again, once more so many cars, crowded onto the hardstanding in front of the church and lining the street beyond the fence, both sides: their numbers alone spoke of crisis, and never mind the sheen on their blank windows as the glass reflected the nightfire glare from the steeple above.

Being on a bike was good, even a big bike. I could wind my way between the skew-parked cars, bump sacrilegiously over the turf that sheltered so many ex-Macallans and other citizens of this town that there wasn't room for more, hadn't even been room for Marty or for Hazel, and finally hoick it onto its stand close to Jamie's jeep likewise heretically parked on bone-containing grass. Nearby a small side door stood open in the high wall of the church, letting a cool creamy light and the hiss of muted voices slither out.

One of the cars I'd wangled the Beemer past had been a big Volvo. Couldn't truthfully tell the colour in the weird light back there, but there wasn't really any question in my mind. *Where were you when I wanted you?* I growled silently, casting a last look back at its smug solidity before I walked unhesitatingly in through the old iron-studded door, down a short corridor and so into the church proper, where I was swamped once more with memory.

Too many Sundays, all the bloody Sundays of my childhood I'd been brought to this dim temple to sit through Mass. Right at the front they set us kids, with our parents in the pew behind to clip our ears if we fidgeted or whispered. Which of course we did, religiously. Sharp pains and boredom were my abiding recollections, coupled with the height and chill and sheet weight of stone arching above me.

Wouldn't be bored tonight, though pain was not at all impossible and perhaps very high on the agenda.

It was still heavy and cold in there, despite so many people. Vaulting ambition had raised this church too high, spread it too wide. It was cathedral-sized, and all my family couldn't have come close to filling it, even if half the tough young cousins weren't out manning Uncle James' roadblocks.

It still smelled of smoking candles and incense and dusty velvet, of polish and flowers and overbearingly of stone; and it still swallowed the sharpness of sound, muffled voices to a whisper and wove them together into a background hiss of interference, nothing more.

I walked in, and that familiar hiss faded slowly. One by one they saw me, and stopped talking; and that was the helmet and leathers once more, some of them surely were taking me for Hazel come again to prove true all their hopes of resurrection. More would simply be startled by a dark unknown, disturbed by anonymity in this place where every face was known.

I enjoyed that moment, lingered a little in the cool pleasure of it before I lifted the helmet off and let them see me.

A collective sigh, and the many whispers started up again: *only Benedict, for God's sake, and what's he doing here walking in on us like that, what does he think he's playing at?*

Wasn't often I'd had all my family talking about me at once. I could almost have enjoyed that also, except for the occasion and the cold feeling in my bones that was actually nothing at all to do with the ambient temperature at church.

I held the helmet under my arm, and looked around. Saw that most, maybe all of the men had brought their womenfolk along; there was enough simple space here that even so many clashing auras wouldn't sicken the stomach of anyone accustomed to being with Macallans.

Some of the faces in the nearer pews nodded to me when I glanced their way; one or two even managed a smile. Others just looked disgruntled, or looked away.

Hamish was standing by the altar in full vestments, talking to Uncle James. He'd turned his broad back to me, all the acknowledgement I was going to get from him.

But I wasn't here for Uncle James, nor for my mother, whom I spotted now over by one of the fat stone pillars that supported the wagon-vaulted roof. She waved nervously; I lifted a hand in response, but that was auto-pilot. My eyes and my mind had moved on already.

Moved on, and found the man I was watching for coming towards me up the nearest aisle.

"Benedict. I'm surprised to see you here . . ."

"Hullo, Uncle Allan," I said. "You've been avoiding me."

"Well," he said quietly, calmly, "wouldn't you have done the same, in the circumstances? Or no, obviously you wouldn't, because here you are," touching my arm to be certain of it, assuring himself that I was no fetch in this place of mystery. "But perhaps you should have done, mm?"

"Perhaps I should," I agreed, just as quietly. "Might have been more sensible. But then I never did have much sense, when it came to my favourite uncle. I never could stay away from you."

"Ah, Ben. I got your message," so he must have been home, though probably not until sunset or later, my cautious uncle. Must have gone home, talked to Jess, walked or trotted or maybe even run upstairs to find what I'd left for him; and I wondered whether it had hurt him as much as it had hurt me, the splintered, mangled wreck that I'd made of that sleek and shining beauty, his old and precious microscope. "What are we going to do with you, eh?"

"Something pretty disgusting, I imagine."

He laughed shortly, and his hand closed more firmly on my

arm, no casual touch this time. "Let's go outside, shall we? Where we can talk without being interrupted?"

"No," I said, "let's not." It was dark out there, dark and clear, all the rainclouds of the afternoon perversely blown away again. I'd sooner stay in here where no starlight could penetrate, where even the moon was only ever the dimmest of globes distorted by old stained glass and no use to anyone.

"Ben, lad," and he maybe said something more then, he most likely did, but I wasn't listening any more. Even at the cost of my life, I was suddenly and appallingly distracted.

Because my father came in, my own Christless father came to church tugging Carol by the wrist, and she was sweating and fearful at his side when she should have been a mile away from here and safely under a duvet behind locked doors; and there was a swallowed cry from a pew at the back and suddenly footsteps rushing forward, and that was *Laura*, for God's sake, and what the fuck was going on?

TWENTY

BLINDED BY THE LIGHT

I wasn't the only one distracted. Uncle Allan also was watching the girls, his attention crucially wrenched away from me; which gave me the chance to wrench my arm from his grasp and run.

Not far, only over to the doorway, where my father stood smugly posing with his captive and sneering at Laura as if she were nothing more, just a couple of heifers herded in for butchery or sacrifice or God alone knew what. But again I wasn't the only one, and I didn't get there first though I was closer.

Jamie must have been sitting with Laura way up at the back, or else standing with her round behind a pillar somewhere nice and private. Now he came hurtling down faster than either reason or respect would suggest to a nicely-brought-up ex-altar boy in his parish church and surrounded by his family.

No doubts about him, but a dispassionate observer might have found some amusement in laying bets, whether I was running to Laura or to Carol. Lord knows, I was far from certain myself, though not by any means dispassionate. It didn't matter, though, it wasn't a choice I had to make. We arrived in order, Laura and then Jamie and then me; Laura hugged Carol close, Jamie didn't so much hug them both as brake himself against their bodies, and they were all three so wrapped up in each other by the time I arrived, there was neither space nor need for me.

So I turned on my father instead, fear and frustration both driving me as I snarled, "You get your hands off her!" as I chopped down hard at where his hand was still locked like a cuff around Carol's wrist.

"Mind your temper, son," my father said mockingly, snatching his fingers back with rare sweet timing so that the edge of my palm sliced only through empty air and I was left looking and feeling stupid. I glanced to the side, where my cousin and my friends had their heads tightly together, and there was still no room for me; and I gave a shrug of surrender, and just said, "What's she doing here, anyway? Where the hell did you find her?"

"Language, boy. You're in church, remember." He was well into father-mode here, and loving it. "I found her at your place, actually. I was looking for you. You weren't there but she was, hammering on the door like nobody's business; so I thought I'd bring her along. Thought she might tell us where you were. If we asked nicely."

All the hair on my body prickled at his soft smile then, and it was nothing to do with my standing so close. If I hadn't seen the flare of nightfire on the spire and the opportunity to hide right up front, to take shelter in the open – well, I'd seen my family asking questions, once or twice. Like any self-respecting inquisitors, they never believed a claim of ignorance.

"What did you want me for?" I muttered.

"Ask your uncle," my complaisant father said, and I nodded slowly. If I'd not chosen to come here, not Laura nor Jamie nor anyone could have saved Carol from interrogation; and as she couldn't have told them where to find me, and as that would have been unacceptable to them, they would have gone on asking until she wasn't able to give any answer at all . . .

Me, I didn't need to ask my uncle anything; not even what the concomitant threat was, when he sauntered over to join us under the eyes of the interested congregation.

Slipping his arm once more under my elbow, he murmured, "Would you like to change your mind, Ben? About that walk in the air?"

And his eyes danced and smiled, and slid briefly over to the huddle of humanity that held the people I cared most for in the world.

Straight trade-off, me or them; and after he'd taken them he'd probably get me anyway. So many people here and his tongue so silver, and they so used to listening: he could lay the bodies out in rows and they'd still believe that he did it for the best, they'd still hold me ready for his killing.

I nodded jerkily, and was proud of myself for the way my voice didn't noticeably shake, and neither did my body except my elbow to shake him off. "In a minute," I said. "Just let me, let me talk to them, okay?"

"Of course," he said, all confidence and ease, not a worry in the world. And quite right too. What was I going to do, suddenly start shouting accusations to the crowd? This man, this wise and talented man, head of the clan, yet – this is the guy who's been killing your children, your cousins, your brothers and my sister? With some unrecognised talent never before recorded in all our family's long and talented history, and for some unrecognisable motive that a day's scrambled thinking hasn't come near to identifying for me?

And of course all that from me, whom hardly any there would recognise as anything more than a freak child from the weakest branch of the family tree? I'd be laughed out of church, and Allan knew it.

Luckily, so did I. I went to join my friends, and never said a word out of place.

What I wanted most just then was a share of that huddle, but it broke apart at my arrival, each of them stepping back a little, loosening the linkage so that we all stood in a circle rather than a hug. Still close, though, and still closed off from everyone else there, still private. No point to the brief bitter twist in my gut; I tried to ignore it, but there was an edge of anger in me as I reached to touch them all individually, as I fired the one question that applied to them all but came out aimed at Carol.

"Why?" I demanded, just the one word containing all my grief and sorrow, *why aren't you safe at home where I left you, where you ought to be?*

"You didn't phone," she said, matching my anger with her own. "You promised, and I was waiting for it, and just bloody nothing all day. So what was I supposed to do? I couldn't phone you, you aren't on the bloody phone, and I was worried about you . . ."

You were supposed to stay home, stay safe . . . But I just shrugged, helpless to change what had happened already; and I looked at Laura, and at least she had the grace or the understanding to sound a little defensive. She said, "Same here. Of course we were worried. Christ, you don't recognise family when it's right under your nose, do you? Jamie came for the jeep, and even he didn't know what you were up to; so I made him bring me too. I thought at least there might be some news if I came down here . . ."

I glared at Jamie, wanting to scream at him for being so stupid; and he said, "What's the big deal, Ben? We're all here, we can look after them. Safety in numbers," cruelly echoing my own hope, now in ruins. "Nothing's going to happen," he added confidently.

Wrong, I thought, *so wrong . . .* But I said nothing more, only praying in this place of prayer that I'd have the courage and the wit to play the hand well now, so that nothing happened to anyone except me. That was all I had left, and it was little enough, in all conscience. Particularly as none of my family was big on con-science, and Uncle Allan seemingly less than any . . .

I glanced across and saw him watching me, waiting by the door with all the patience of the utterly certain. I gestured to him, *I'm coming*, and saw his nod; and then I turned back to make what would surely be my last farewells. And oh, the drama of it was heavy on me, and I couldn't let them see it, for their own safety couldn't let them guess.

But if I couldn't be selfish now, I never could; and I could forgive myself one last indulgent weakness, after a lifetime of being nothing but weak. So I went around that circle, went from one to the next; and fuck them if they didn't want to be hugged, hugs were what they were getting.

Carol first: I held her tightly, kissed her when she frowned up at me and whispered "Thanks" into her hair. Let her work out later, thanks for what.

Then to Laura. I went gentle with her, not to be presumptuous of her body; just my arms loose around her shoulders and a touch of my lips to her cheek, far too little for all that had been between us but as much as I dared afford.

Jamie I hugged like a cousin, like a brother; but I startled him too with a kiss, just so's he shouldn't feel left out, and I muttered, "Look after her, okay?" against his stubble. And stepped back and punched him lightly under the ribs, all male bonding and no import, *nothing going on here, honest*; and I turned my back on them all and walked over to Uncle Allan and out of the church with him at my back, quiet and deadly.

I am just going outside, and may be some time, I thought, and had to swallow a hysterical giggle. Me, I'd always had my own theory about that – on a diet of pony and no fresh veg, the guy must've been constipated; I reckoned he just crawled out for a shit and froze in mid-straining, and Scott was far too Brit and stiff-upper-lippy to record anything so bathetic in his diary, and hence all the heroic assumptions – but maybe I was ready to change my mind just then. Here I was, after all, self-confessed coward and failure, recognised expert at running away; and I was doing much the same thing that the Oates story alleged, going gentle into that bad, bad night for the sake of my friends.

It had never been so hard simply to balance, let alone move: to keep upright against all the weight of air above me, to force my legs not to falter. But I could feel too many eyes watching me, too many questioning thoughts and uncertainties; so I walked out and never looked behind me, not for one last glimpse of those I loved.

Right outside the door the bike would be waiting, still hot, keys in the ignition even; I was showing signs of acquiring some truly Macallan habits, just a little too late to make myself truly one of the family. What I wanted to do, I wanted to run for it: to sprint out and vault astride that great black beast and twist the key in a single motion, press the starter, jerk the throttle and kick the stand up and be away, roaring into the night in a great escape while Allan was still static and stunned in the corridor, only running after me too late, far too late to touch me now . . .

And of course I didn't try any of that, because Allan was only a moment behind me and he'd only need to come out through the door while I was still bumping over grass or weaving through the clot of cars beyond, and so much for great escapes. Besides, there would be retribution to be paid by others, all implicit in a single shift of his eyes towards my friends; and that threat was enough to hold me, whatever chances I had to get away.

Though he must have known that, he still flicked off the light in the corridor, to give him access to starlight a half-second earlier if I should choose to run. A cautious man, my uncle.

So down the dark corridor, and out into the cold-lit night; and yes, there was the bike, close enough to touch. I patted the seat, felt the warmth in it, wondered which of us would cool first.

Just past the bike was Jamie's jeep, likewise warm and ready in this place of cold and abandoned bones. Some vandal had tidied all the gravestones away, years back; they lined the graveyard wall now, nice and neat, but the bodies were still allegedly undisturbed. *Wake up, you idle buggers*, I wanted to shout, *come up here and see murder done. You'll like that, it'll be just like old times for most of you . . .*

Out here, where there was nothing but nightfire – which didn't – to interfere with the sky's light, Uncle Allan didn't need a grip on my elbow to be sure of me. Actually he needed nothing more than the grip he had already, on my inconvenient conscience; but he took another anyway, belt-and-braces time.

Chill, subtle cords laid themselves under my skin and around my skull, and briefly it was my turn to think that Hazel was back for a visit, *just dropping by, bro, make sure you don't forget me.* No danger of that, nor any danger of forgetting this, once felt before; and I'd felt this often when I was younger. This was Hazel in a temper, in a mood, doing what was utterly forbidden. This was Hazel's web from the inside, looking out: a mesh that gripped so lightly it hardly hindered a muscle in its movement, except that the constant whisper of its presence was a constant reminder also that it could be pulled taut at any moment. A netted fish I was, and fit to be reeled in . . .

And Hazel was dead already, dead before me and not doing this. I turned my head against the faintest resistance, and said, "So what happens now, Uncle Allan? You going to curdle my blood for me?"

He smiled. "No," he said, "I'm not going to curdle your blood for you. Just keep walking. Down the path a little way, I think," and the web twitched to hustle me along the cinder path that was circumjacent to the church. We were walking widdershins, but I thought I wouldn't tell him that. Maybe the bad luck would come down in my favour, given that I had no choice here.

"You're not supposed to be able to do this," I said softly, and heard him laugh in response.

"No," he agreed. "But then, it's hardly alone in that category, is it? I learned this from your sister, though she never knew I was taking lessons. It's one of the great follies of this family," sounding vehement suddenly, teasing no more, "that they're all so embedded in the tradition, no one ever tries to look beyond it. You wait for your talent to develop, and then that's it. Everyone knows you only get one, so everyone accepts it. No one questions why it should be so, or whether it even is so.

"In point of fact," he said, "it isn't. I've been experimenting for twenty years, and I can imitate most of our blessed relatives now, and probably outclass the bulk of them in their own talents."

I was sure of it. "I've seen you," I said.

"Last night," he acceded, totally unfazed. "That wretched stone bauble . . ."

"No, before that. When Hazel died, when you appeared so conveniently after I'd found her body. You did the same trick that night, when I was carrying her out of the garden; you blasted the gates into nothing, to make it easier for me. Took me a while to realise it, but you shouldn't have been able to do that either."

"Ah," he said, after a brief pause. "Yes, I should have thought of that; but you'd startled me, turning up so quickly. I'd forgotten you had that primitive telepathic link with your twin. Pity you two didn't get on better; that might have been interesting to study, further than I did. But if you'd got on better, of course, the dynamics between you would have been different, and the telepathy might not have worked at all. I always had the impression it was more a case of Hazel shouting at you, rather than a genuine dialogue, yes? That's far enough," added unhurriedly as we approached the transept. There was a little puddle of shadow in the angle it made with the nave, where the light from above was blocked off; the path ran through that darkness, and Allan was being more than cautious, it seemed to me, he was being positively paranoid.

"Just step out onto the grass now," he said, and the web nudged me even though I'd had no thought of disobeying. "A dozen paces, say. Yes, that's about it, that's excellent."

"For what?" I demanded, losing just a little control at last: fussiness without purpose, this seemed to me, and I could live without it.

Die without it.

For answer, Allan glanced up. I followed his gaze, up the wall of the church and on up to where the spire stabbed into the sky almost directly above us now, with that flaring phoenix atop it; it was relief to my eyes and my neck both to look lower again, at Uncle Allan as I began to understand.

"I think we need an accident," he said. "Don't you? Anything else would be just a little suspicious, perhaps. Accident is better anyway, people prefer it. It lets your friends mourn more freely."

Then he turned away from me and whistled, and half a dozen men stirred and rose from a corner of the churchyard.

"Thank you, lads," Allan called. "You can put the fire out now. Everyone's here, who's coming." Then to me, with a smiling glance, "And one or two surprises also, mm, Benedict? You really were foolish, you know."

"I hadn't expected hostages," I said, trying not to sound heated about it.

"Not your friends, perhaps – but your mother?"

"Hadn't expected her, either."

"No? Well, it is contrary to practice, I suppose, having the womenfolk. But I thought someone would find you sometime tonight and bring you in, if you hadn't already come of your own ignorance; so I wanted her here. As a lever."

"Yeah." Would it have worked, would a threat against my

mother have been enough? Probably, yes. Not necessary now, though. Didn't matter. Allan had a stronger lever far, and I was in his net before ever he webbed me. Now I was watching the men make their way into the church as the nightfire died on the steeple, leaving us in the dark, nothing but stars and a late-rising sliver of moon to light my way to damnation.

"That is one knackered bird," he said cheerfully, his eyes in the skies still. I flicked my gaze briefly upward, it was irresistible; and saw the phoenix only a mess of twisted metal now, still glowing faintly against the night.

"No surprise," my uncle said, "if that snaps off now, and falls. Just another family tragedy, if it happens to fall on you. Nothing I could do to stop it, everyone knows my talent doesn't lie in that direction."

"Any particular reason, then?" I enquired, trying to sound genuinely curious when actually all I wanted was another minute, another thirty seconds of being alive if I could scrounge that much. God knows why, I wasn't feeling so hot just then, but even the terror clutch of a web seemed a little better than nothing at all, which was the alternative on offer.

"Reason?"

"Why you're doing this. Killing us off. Or is it just because you can?"

"Well. There is a satisfaction, in extending my range of talent. I admit that. Scientific exploration. Like you kids with that sheep, I'm intrigued by my own abilities. But yes, of course I have another reason."

He paused, and I saw him smile at me; and the smile said, *Just as you have a reason for asking. I know you, Ben, I understand you intimately.* And then he said, "I don't think we need to go into that, though. Do we? Why delay the inevitable? I'm not being cruel, but it's not exactly going to be useful information for you, and I'd sooner just get on with things. The family will be waiting for me; and the longer we're out here, the more they're going to wonder what we were doing . . ."

And he glanced up at the raddled phoenix, and so did I, again couldn't resist it.

Dimly I saw the soft-shining thing topple from its perch, and start to slide down the steep slated roof of the spire; and he'd worked out the trajectories fairly well, I thought, he wouldn't have to help it much. Just a twitch when it hit the gutter, perhaps, and goodbye, Benedict . . .

The web tightened then, held me rigid in a way that even Hazel never had. It hurt, more than anything had ever hurt me all my life; I wanted to scream, I needed to scream and couldn't shift my jaw or my throat enough to do that, couldn't breathe or even focus my eyes now to see my death come down.

Except that there was light suddenly, a blaze of white light engulfing me and an engine racing, and above that another voice screaming for me, screaming my name; and the web was gone as my uncle lost it in the light, and the pain was gone too. And I wasn't thinking to move, I wasn't thinking at all, but it had only been the web that held me upright and with that gone I collapsed, my legs gave way and I fell sideways and the brutalised metal bird came crashing down to earth so close to me that I felt the fierce chill of it as it thudded into the grass just by my head.

The engine revved and roared, came louder, closer; and there was that voice again, yelling at me.

"Ben, get up, for God's sake . . .!"

And I knew the voice and the note of the engine both: Carol and the bike, Carol *on* the bike.

Carol in appalling danger, because Uncle Allan had legs and a brain, and shock wouldn't hold him in the bike's light more than a second or two. As soon as he was out of the beam, Carol was dead; and then me too, a moment later . . .

I pushed myself up onto hands and knees, and then onto my feet, though every muscle I had was shaking; and I dashed my arm across my wet eyes and blinked into the light, saw the bright eye of the bike coming at me across the grass.

And thought, *That won't do it, girl, you'll drive right past him and he'll be in the dark again, and that's us fucked, the pair of us together . . .*

But I didn't have time or breath enough to tell her, even if she could have heard me shouting; and I couldn't even see Allan now, blinded as I was, had no idea where he'd got to.

Rescued and doomed regardless, both at once. Life loves irony. I tried to signal Carol with a wave, to say *Not me, don't think about me, just keep the light on him*; but if she saw she didn't understand. She was there instead, right by me on the bike, and I didn't have the strength even to run from her, to hope – vain hope – that he would let her go and just come after me.

It was all I could do to swing a leg across the bulk of the bike behind her, to slump onto the queen seat and grab at her slim body for support, to stop me toppling right over and off the other side.

"Hang on!" she called, her voice high and tight as the bike carried us away.

She wanted to get us around the great bulk of the transept, I guessed, and out of his line of sight; and there'd never be time to do that. Once more I couldn't help looking round, expecting only to see my uncle's shadow dark and deadly behind us; and yes, there he was, but far too clearly for my dizzy mind to comprehend.

He was a silhouette trapped in light, stranded and alone; they were twin beams that had caught him now, twin points of brightness jouncing right at him and he was helpless in their glare. Gone *tharn*, perhaps, with the double shock of all this. I was kind of tharny myself, truth to tell; took me too long to click that it was

314

the jeep that had him now, that Carol wasn't saving me alone.

Longer still to click that the jeep wasn't just doing a holding action, keeping Uncle Allan in its light, keeping his talent quelled until we'd made it away from there.

Didn't click altogether till I saw those headlights one on either side of Allan's shadow and coming hard now, and him trying to dive aside too late, far too late . . .

Not possible, with the roar of the bike beneath me and the roar of the jeep behind me, but I still swear that I heard it, the abrupt thudding sound and then the softer, wetter noises as the jeep's tyres ploughed over my uncle's body.

And then we were round the transept, and the massive church was a line of dark, fast eclipsing what I could see; and for a little we were alone then, Carol and me, until we were washed with light again as the jeep came round after us.

How much Carol had seen or guessed – or heard – I couldn't tell; but she wasn't trying to escape any more, she'd slowed right down, so that the jeep could draw up alongside.

And that was the last terrible shock of a terrible evening, because I looked across and all I could see was that I still hadn't got it right, still hadn't got my head around it.

Jamie, I'd thought at the instant of contact. *Jamie's cottoned on, and he's done tonight what he couldn't do last night. Stranger is one thing, uncle is something else; and that's been the trigger, he's taken revenge for Marty . . .*

Wrong again, Ben boy. Not Jamie, not at all.

Jamie was sitting over on the passenger side, hanging on tight, his face tense and dreadful.

Laura was driving the jeep.

TWENTY-ONE

LOOK HOMEWARD, UNCLE

There was a police car parked outside the main doors to the hospital, brightly white in sunlight.

That wouldn't have worried me, only that because I noticed it I noticed also the car parked beside it, a chunky 4 x 4. That I recognised. I'd seen it around town a few times this last year, and seen it again last night, at the roadblock where I'd been turned back. Looked like Cousin Conor was on guard duty again, the police permitted a presence only as a sop to the collective civic ego.

What the limits of Conor's duties might be, I wasn't certain; but best to avoid him, whatever. I didn't want to get into an argument this morning, let alone a fight.

So I didn't go in, I went around.

Laura had had to shunt a Merc aside before she could get off the grass last night. She'd picked up a couple more dents to the jeep's off wing and some long scratches on the paintwork, done rather more damage to the Merc.

No trouble weaving a bike through the gaps that blocked a car; Carol and I had been down on the road already, waiting for them. I'd been watching the side door of the church, and only as the jeep came down to join us had the first curiosity been shown from inside: shadows in the doorway followed by the people who made them, first looking and then tentatively stepping out, their voices distantly calling.

Carol had driven away, hurrying no longer, only wanting to keep that sensible distance. Laura had followed, and we Macallans had been nothing but passengers in the girls' hands, which had felt as strange as anything that had happened all night.

As the church had a cinder path, so the hospital had a flagstone path that tracked all around the irregular outline of its main building.

After last night, my superstitious soul couldn't decide which way to walk. Widdershins had brought both doom and rescue; was that ill luck or the other thing? Or did it just turn your fate around, so that only if you went in badly could you come out well?

I dithered shamefully, disgracefully and in the end went deasil, simply because that was the shorter route to where I wanted to be.

Compromise, it's all compromise between faith and pragmatism.

Rhythm, Jacko would say. Oscillations.

Carol had driven a while, five or ten minutes, without reference to me or to those who followed us. Once I'd looked back, seen the jeep, seen nothing else behind; then I'd stopped worrying. We'd got Jamie with us anyway, if the family did come after. He could play hostage or hero, depending.

Then Carol had pulled into the kerb. Laura had drawn up beside us, looking a question; Carol had said, "I want to go home. Can Jamie get us through that?"

Her hand had lifted to point, and I'd seen another road-bridge up ahead, and another roadblock just this side of it. Here they'd

set a minibus across the carriageway, that burned with a pale
light. Carol lived in a village that grew closer every year, but still
had a couple of miles' separation from the town; she must have
been lucky – or the other thing – with her bus in that night, just
getting through before the road was closed.

We'd all looked at Jamie; he'd nodded. "If it hasn't been set
there to stop us," he'd said, his voice harsh and strained, ready to
snap.

"I don't think so," Laura had said. "They wouldn't have had
the time, even if they knew where we were going."

"Well. Let's see, then," though he'd sounded far from ready.

The jeep had taken the lead, slowly down the hill to the burning bus. Figures had moved out in front of it, one raising his hand
to halt us; but I'd seen the hand falter in its determination and
then drop quickly down to his side again, as he'd recognised the
jeep.

I'd recognised him also. Cousin Marlon, fat and forty, this
probably the most responsibility he'd ever been given in his life.

"Jamie, hullo, lad. What are you up to, then, sentry-go?"

A shake of the head, and no matter how tight-wound he was,
Jamie's brain had still been briskly functional. "Dad says you
might as well pack up, nobody's moving tonight. Clear this off
the road," with a casual wave, "and go home, okay?"

"Okay, terrific. Thanks, Jamie." Marlon had almost saluted,
before he'd turned to his shadowy companions with expansive
gestures and hoarse commands.

We hadn't waited for them to haul the bus out of the way.
Jamie had yelled at Marlon to kill the flames, and then Laura had
just bumped two wheels of the jeep up onto the kerb and edged
past with us trailing. I'd seen Laura hunch her shoulder up to
shield her face a little, as she passed; when it was our turn the ice-
burn of it had stretched my skin dry and tight in a moment, while
the stink had caught like barbs at my throat and lungs.

But then we'd been through, we'd been free and clear and Laura had already been accelerating away down the road, so that we'd had to race to overtake, to lead them to Carol's.

It wasn't the thrill of speed, I'd thought, or the wind in her face that had had Carol whooping suddenly into the sky; it was only the knowledge that we were driving into another country now, a brave new world with only two Macallans in it.

The private rooms in the hospital were all on a single side-ward, branching off the main corridor. I knew them well from a couple of stays in my childhood, once when I'd had my appendix out and again when I'd broken my leg, trying to follow my sister and our cousins on a climb up the side of a quarry. I'd slipped and fallen, and what I remembered most – better even than the pain of it, or Marty bending over me to ask about the pain, more curious than concerned – was the sound of my sister's mocking laughter, coming down to me from high above.

It was a stray thought that struck me now, that all my family's talents were destructive. Not one of them had any gift of healing.

Shaking that out of my head – too harsh a judgement on myself, that was, with the sun on my back and all my skin alive to it, blood singing – I turned my mind back to hospital, to private rooms; and particularly to the rooms on the south side of the corridor, with their french windows wide enough to wheel a bed outside on sunny days. Always those rooms my family had, my mind remembered. Not only my own stays, but paying duty visits also to sick cousins, always the bright rooms and the wide windows . . .

Carol had had to hire in a local teenager to babysit her son, while she came to town to rescue me. We'd found Tina doing what was classic, snuggling up on the sofa with a boyfriend, a can of lager between them and the telly on. Nice thing was, she'd been utterly unembarrassed about it, though they'd both been rendered mono-syllabic by the influx of so many of us where they'd only been expecting Carol. The only smiles had come when Carol had discovered she'd got no money to pay Tina, and she'd had to touch each of us in turn, coming round to Jamie at the last.

We'd hustled the kids out after that, not hard to do. What had been hardest was the minute after the door had closed behind them, when we'd all been facing each other in the living-room: staring from face to face, seeing our own tense exhaustion mirrored in one another, monosyllabic ourselves now, confronted seemingly by something too big to talk about.

Carol had made coffee, and dug half a bottle of cheap brandy out of a cupboard to fortify it; and then we'd had to talk, or I had. Jamie had demanded that. It was the girls, he'd said, who sensed something wrong with my big farewell scene that I'd thought I was handling so cleverly; they insisted on quietly following us out, me and Allan. Carol's idea apparently to go for the vehicles, to flood the churchyard with light when Allan sent the other witnesses inside. And then the weathercock came down, he'd said, and the girls at least were certain. Carol certain enough that I needed saving, not to think of her own safety as she came roaring in on her charger; and Laura certain enough of Allan's villainy that she gave no heed to consequences, she only used what she had against him, the strength of metal and speed and a blinding, disabling light.

But Jamie had been all the opposites of certain, he'd been all confusion and doubt; and he'd made me tell them everything I knew, all the hints and clues that built together into a case against Allan and then what Allan himself had said, his irresistible confession.

What I still hadn't been able to tell them was why, because Allan had drawn back from telling me, content to let me die not knowing.

* * *

Needing to know, I came to the long single-storey stretch where french windows looked out on what was almost a private garden for the private patients. Some of the windows stood open, and long lacy white curtains billowed gently in the breeze.

I walked slowly along the line of windows, looking in. There were nurses busy in some rooms, visitors in others; those I barely glanced into. Sleeping patients I gave more attention to, stopping sometimes to look closely, to be certain before moving on.

I found Uncle Allan finally where I should have known to find him, in the last and largest, the best room on the ward, right at the end where he could have windows in two walls and all the privacy he wanted.

He was alone, as I'd hoped to find him, though I was sure there would be guards in the corridor beyond the closed door, police and family both. Peering through the half-drawn curtains I could see that his eyes were shut, but he was lying propped up on pillows: only dozing, then, most likely.

The french windows were locked, and there was no handle on the outside, but that was not a problem. I laid the flat of my hand against a single small pane beside the lock, and sunlight fell on my fingers' tips; and oh, it was easy now, I felt so strong. The glass warmed and folded beneath my touch, turned so plastic I could squeeze it in my fist and tug it out. Then I reached in through the vacant space, turned the key and pushed the window open.

There'd been no sound except the single metallic scrape of the lock unlatching. Perhaps it was that which roused him, or else the change in air as I brought the breeze in with me; but my uncle opened his eyes, looked directly at me – and smiled.

Said, "Hullo, Benedict. I thought perhaps you'd come."

After I'd told them everything I could, Jamie had hovered, had paced the small space of Carol's living-room, had finally asked to use the phone.

Had dialled a number and waited while we all pretended not to listen, while we listened hard; had finally said, "Dad, it's Jamie."

A pause, then: "No, sorry, I won't tell you that. What about you, where are you? ... Oh. The hospital, right," passing the information on to us without letting his father know there was anyone else tuned in. "How is he, then? ... Uh-huh. Yeah ... No, look, he's your brother, but he's my uncle, right? That's just as ... Well, I'll tell you why. If you'll stop shouting, I'll tell you ..."

And he'd done that, neatly and accurately, his mind still sharp though his face was still pale and there was still a tremble in his fingers; he'd told his father everything I'd said and everything we'd done except the last thing, where we'd come for shelter.

No way to tell, he'd said to us afterwards, how Uncle James had taken the news, or what he'd do about it. But Jamie had dropped onto the floor in a collapse so sudden it was almost frightening; he'd slumped back against Laura's legs where she was sitting on the sofa, he'd tilted his head against her knee and closed his eyes while her fingers played soothingly in his hair, and he'd looked five years younger all in a moment. Infinitely relieved, I guess, with the burden of responsibility rolled off his shoulders and onto his father's. *Nothing more for me to do*, his body had been saying, *I've put it out of my hands now.*

The relief for me had come a few minutes later, when Carol had told Laura to take him up to bed.

"You two can have my room," she'd said. "I'll sleep in with Nicky, he's got a spare bunk in there for when one of his little friends stays over. It's embarrassing, but I fit it."

"What about Ben?" Laura had asked.

"Sleeping-bag in here. Lots of cushions, he'll be fine."

After the other two had gone up, while Carol was bustling around in mother-mode to organise my bedding, I'd suggested diffidently, "You don't have to squash in with Nicky, you know.

You could stay down here with me. It's a warm night, we could unzip the sleeping-bag and just nest together . . ."

But she'd shaken her head, firm and decisive. "Not tonight, Ben. Laura needs company, you could see, that's why I've given them the double bed; but I need to be alone. And with my son, I need that too. To remember what's important. All right?"

"Sure," I'd said. "Fine," I'd said. "Good night, then," I'd said.

"You wouldn't have liked it anyway," she'd told me, ruffling my hair, still playing mother. "Tonight, maybe, but not tomorrow. Nicky gets up early, and he's *horrible* if he finds men in my bed. He's going to be bad enough with strangers in the house, me camped out with you down here would be unthinkably awful. Sleep well; and if you can't, I've left the brandy out in the kitchen, okay?"

And she'd kissed me on the forehead and left me, and I had neither slept nor drunk myself to sleep, but only stared at the little patch of sky I could see through the window from where I lay while it changed from black to white, though all my thoughts were grey.

Only a thin smile my uncle gave me, in a face turned unexpectedly thin and sallow; and his voice was thin also, weak in a man who had never seemed weak. He looked dreadfully ill. I didn't need the drip into his arm or the electrodes taped to his chest or the bedclothes raised on frames to keep their weight off his legs to tell me that he'd been more than hurt last night. Damaged beyond repair, was how he looked.

But then I'd seen the damage done, and the only surprise was that he'd survived it at all. A tough breed, we Macallans: hard on others and hard in ourselves.

"Hullo, Uncle." I walked over to sit on a chair beside the bed, and it was no surprise that he wasn't yelling, he wasn't calling his undoubted guards in to repel boarders. I'd never expected him to.

A logical man, my uncle, logical above all; and a man of words and arguments, he'd want to talk.

Besides, he knew what I was capable of, and he knew what likely mood I'd be in when I came, if I came. I could toast his guards if I chose to, if they made trouble for me.

"Well, Ben. This isn't good, you know," and he didn't only mean his state of health, though his faint gesture took in all the machinery he was attached to, signifiers of all that damage.

"No," I said. *It's fucking awful* was what I wanted to say, what I hoped he'd hear from me regardless; but Aunt Jess had trained me not to swear in front of senior family, and it's hard to break the habits of a lifetime.

For a minute neither of us said anything more, we only looked at each other; then, "Worst thing about hospital visits," he said, "those long silences where you can't think of anything to talk about. What shall we talk about, Ben?"

"Let's pick up where we left off last night," I said, grabbing with relief at the same light, easy, superficial tone, as if it really didn't matter a damn. "You were going to tell me why."

"Was I?" He sounded momentarily doubtful, just a teasing little reminder that actually he'd chosen not to do that, to kill me in my ignorance; but, "All right, then. It's a cull, I suppose is the best way to say it. A necessary weeding out."

"They were *family* . . ." I said, the reality breaking through for a moment. *They were my twin, my cousins – your niece, your nephew, your blood also, every one of them your blood . . .*

"Exactly."

Walls of containment weren't doing their job any more. I stared at him, and even to my own ears sounded like a child in despair, hurt beyond bearing, as I said, "I thought you loved us . . . ?"

"Ben, Ben." He shook his head a little, smiled a little, just exactly like an adult with his taller perspective on a child's griefs.

"It's the body that matters, not the cells. Not the individuals. Yes, I have loved you – but that doesn't matter either. You can't preserve a weakened or corrupted bloodline, simply for sentiment. The family deserves better of us."

Fuck the family, I wanted to say. Would have done, perhaps, only that I'd said it so often before and with so much less cause, it was devalued past recovery.

Besides, Allan wasn't giving me the time to interrupt.

"The family *expects* better," he said. "There's historical precedent for it. If you look back at the records, all our history is a tale of feuds and schisms, one branch warring with another – and the weaker always lost. By definition. It's survival of the fittest, you see? The family corpus doing its own pruning, thinning out the inferior stock.

"And we need it again now, we need it so badly. Our ancestors were so much the better men. We've grown stunted, Ben, we're losing our magnificence; and losing it so fast, on a historical scale, it's frightening.

"I'd hoped that marrying out would bring some mongrel virility to the line, but that was an experiment that largely failed. Except with you, of course. You're aberrant, obviously, but it's a fascinating aberration. And potentially fruitful. I'd love to know if you're just a sport, or if your talent will breed true.

"For that reason, I didn't mean to harm you. Not until you got too close to me. I was sure of Jamie – even if he'd recognised me, I could have squared him with what I was doing – but you're too volatile, and you've lived outside the family ethos for too long. You're also very powerful, I think, and we can never have a trial of strength. Except at twilight, perhaps, or dawn: but even then one would be waxing and the other waning, it wouldn't be a true test."

I was barely listening to him then, rather thinking about Jamie, and whether Uncle Allan could really have talked him around.

Maybe he could have, even despite Marty, though I hated myself for conceding the possibility.

But, "So you killed Hazel because she was a half-breed freak," I said. "Is that right?"

"More or less. She couldn't be allowed to breed, Ben. The bloodline is fragile at the moment; it needs purifying, not further dilution."

"Uh-huh." Wasn't going to think about that right now. *Wasn't going to think about it.* "What about the others, then: Marty and Tommy, and Steve? How did you *pick* them, for God's sake?"

He sighed at my vehemence. "Tommy again had too much outside blood in him," *ah, those giveaway blue eyes, shoulda worn contact lenses, Tom,* "but there's more than one corruption in the line. They were all of them weak, to start with; rough, certainly, but their talents were very crude. I didn't hold out much hope for their children, or their children's children.

"But more than that, they were too much your Uncle James' men. Seeing talent only as a means to an end, a way to grab more for themselves; and that's what will destroy this family, as much as an encroaching dissipation. Marty and Hazel already had their own private little business running, milking extra on their own account, did you know? And doing it badly, greedily, as you'd expect from those two. Misuse and miscegenation, those are the forces at work against us now. Either one of them could prove fatal, and working together they're deadly. And of course they work from the inside, necessarily, so no hope of attracting allies, I had to work alone."

And then he sighed again, and his face twitched with pain as he settled against his pillows. "I've done a little," he said, "but only a little, and there's such a job needs doing. I've barely scratched the surface. But I don't suppose I'll be allowed to go much further, will I?"

"No," I said, "I don't suppose you will."

"James came to see me earlier. Stood at the foot of the bed, scowled at me, went away again. You must have told him, did you? He can't have worked it out for himself, he hasn't got the agility."

"Jamie told him." I only said that in my cousin's defence, hoping to make Allan think he couldn't have recruited Jamie after all; because if Allan was thinking so, I might manage it myself.

But Allan only smiled, and said, "Ah. Yes. After the fact, of course he would."

Oh, he was a manipulative bastard, was Allan. Even then he knew exactly what he was doing to me. It wasn't cruelty, nothing malignant; he was still trying to remake me a little, to have me see the world a little closer to the way he saw it, even if all he could influence now was my perspective on a cousin I loved.

We were both silent again, for a little; then Allan said, "There'll be a doctor coming soon. They check on me every hour or so."

"Yeah. Right. Thanks."

I stood up, and walked back into the path of sunlight where it was falling through the open window. It was the dazzle of that which had me rubbing at my eyes, nothing more.

"Goodbye, Ben," my uncle said softly, at my back.

"See you."

Came to the window, didn't want to look around at all; but some things you have to do if you can, so I gripped the frame for strength and turned my head, and saw how he was resting his cheek on his pillow as he smiled a farewell, and saw how sick he really was though he'd worked hard to disguise it, saw his own mortality deep-printed in his flesh, and –

Reader, I martyred him.

TWENTY-TWO

GOODBYE TO ALL THAT

Doesn't matter now many questions you ask, how many are answered. There are always more come burning, bubbling into your head like bad blood, keep you awake, keep you jumpy and unsettled in your life.

Plus ça change, right?

So, questions. Carol was a question in her own right, but she answered herself obliquely. Already had, really: *I need to be alone. And with my son, I need that too. To remember what's important. All right?*

Sure, fine. Thanks, Carol. As long as we've got that straight . . .

Ach, I could sicken myself sometimes. Morbid self-pity a speciality.

Jamie, what would Jamie do? Jamie, I thought, would stick close to his dad for a while yet. For a wee bit. The comfort of what's familiar, he'd fall back on that. Only I thought he'd find it not so familiar now, he'd find it changed and his father also; and Laura, I thought, would change him if they stayed together.

If. That was another question, that was a big one. What hope for those two now —and what did I hope for there, and was it the same thing at all, at all?

Actually, what I hoped for most was to stop thinking about it, and that was a different question also, that was *when?* and that at least I could do something about, in an indirect way.

The full question was longer, it was *Things have changed unbearably; when will they change again?* and it carried its own answer along with it, at least for me.

When you make them change, I told myself. *Unless you just want to wait, and let it happen by erosion?*

And no, I didn't just want to wait.

Packed a rucksack, packed the panniers on the bike; took me half an hour and I was off, I was out of there.

Call it running away, why not? My speciality. Or call it moving on, it doesn't matter. Either way, I maintained my reputation; I did what no Macallan lad before me had ever truly managed. I hit the road, crossed the scarred tarmac that demarked the city limits, headed for the wide blue yonder carrying nothing much in my pockets and nothing I wanted in my mind.

Finally and at last, I left home.